THE 13: STAND

BOOK TWO

ROBBIE CHEUVRONT AND ERIK REED

WITH SHAWN ALLEN

BARBOUR
PUBLISHING

© 2013 by Robbie Cheuvront, Erik Reed, and Shawn Allen

Print ISBN 978-1-62029-959-3

eBook Editions:
Adobe Digital Edition (.epub) 978-1-62416-507-8
Kindle and MobiPocket Edition (.prc) 978-1-62416-506-1

Cover design: Jason Gabbert Design

For more information about the authors, please access the following Internet address: http://www.thejourneytn.org/

Published by Barbour Publishing, Inc., P.O. Box 719, Uhrichsville, Ohio 44683, www.barbourbooks.com

Our mission is to publish and distribute inspirational products offering exceptional value and biblical encouragement to the masses.

Member of the
Evangelical Christian
Publishers Association

Printed in the United States of America.

THE CLOCK ON THE WALL TICKED DOWN THE SECONDS AS HE STARED INTO THE CAMERA.

This was it. In a matter of minutes, his life would change. Everyone's life would change.

He rehearsed his lines, though he knew them by heart. There would be no teleprompter. There would be no script. There would only be him. And the camera, of course. And the person who would receive this message.

A small television sat off to the side, monitoring the feed. He could see his image staring back at him. He watched as the second hand ticked off the final seconds. *Tick. Tick.* And then it was time.

The red light above the lens flicked on. With the remote in his hand, he zoomed in and watched the monitor. This was it. No turning back.

He closed his eyes for a moment and took a deep breath and let it out again. His heart was pounding through his chest. He opened his eyes and set his jaw firm. And then he began.

"Good evening, Mr. President. I am the Prophet. And I have been commanded to give you a message."

Praise for *The 13: Fall*,
named one of Library Journal's Best Christian Fiction Books of 2012

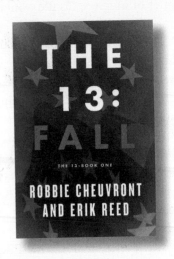

The nation is in serious trouble, politically, financially, and spiritually. Will America be able to pull itself together and set itself on the right path? You'll be spellbound from the first page. The authors have joined forces to produce a real winner that you will surely enjoy. Don't miss this one!

—Viki Ferrell, FreshFiction.com

The characters are well developed, the plot is superb, and the action is continuous. I highly recommend this novel as it portrays a very possible future for the United States. This is the first in a series, and the book leaves you waiting for the next installment!

—Joan Nienhuis, Book Reviews from an Avid Reader blog
(bookwomanjoan.blogspot.com)

To all who still believe in "One Nation Under God."

"It is impossible to rightly govern a nation without God and the Bible."

—George Washington

"And if a house is divided against itself, that house will not be able to stand."

—Jesus Christ, The Gospel of Mark 3:25

PROLOGUE

The room was just like any other space: adequately furnished, old hardwood floors that had scuff marks on them from all the years of tables and chairs being scooted across their surface, and a few unassuming paintings hanging slightly crooked on each wall, in order to give the room a more. . .homey feel. An antique desk stood against one wall with an Aresline Xten chair—the world's most expensive office chair. Opposite the desk stood two others—for guests—which could have been bought from Walmart. The old man didn't know. Nor did he care. His second wife had bought them. He would never think of sitting his old frame down in anything but the Aresline. The Shed, as it was called, was the perfect place for this meeting. And for one reason, one that only those who had been there were aware of: its location. The old man checked once more to make sure he had everything he needed and then went back up the stairs to the main house.

The house sat just off Durant Road, a few miles out of downtown; an old, fully restored Civil War farmhouse sitting back, nestled in the tall pines. Unless someone knew exactly where it was, they would probably just miss the little, narrow dirt road that led the three-quarters of a mile back through the wooded area leading to the house. The old man had bought the house twenty-five years earlier, for his third wife. She had thought it cute, and a good place for her daughter to stay while finishing nursing school. He hadn't cared much for the house itself, but the grounds behind it were perfect for the project he had been planning. And though the project was going to cost close to a quarter of a billion dollars, he didn't care. He had the money. Old money. The kind that came at the expense of hundreds of thousands of unsuspecting human beings. Tobacco.

The old man had since divorced his third wife. And his fourth. His current wife, number five, was never around, either. She had extended family all over the country. And she liked being gone and visiting them more than staying home with him, which he was fine with. After six years with her, the relationship had pretty much run its course. He would've divorced her a year ago, if she were ever around. But after four already, he just didn't have the energy to spend on it. She didn't care what he did anyway, and so he just let it be. So, now, the house was used for visiting friends and family. But for the most part, it remained empty. And that was a good thing. Because it allowed the old man to conduct his more sketchy business away from inquiring minds. Because behind the house, stood the Shed. Buried fifty meters below the surface was a room constructed of three-foot-thick, steel-reinforced concrete walls. And though this room, by itself, was impressive, it was only the northern wing of an eighteen-hundred-square-foot, state-of-the-art survival shelter, stocked with provisions for up to ten people to live for as long as five years, complete with its own water and air filtration system. All constructed and designed by himself, Gavin Pemberton III.

Pemberton—or the old man, as he was called by his friends—had offered the Shed for tonight's meeting. An offer that was readily accepted by all parties involved. *One can't be too careful these days,* he thought. No one ever knew whether or not the Chinese were going to come over the mountains at any second, or if that imbecile Walker was going to negotiate more land over to those communists. Sure, Walker had promised that he was going to see to it that they did everything they could to ensure the United States' return to greatness. The only problem was, the idiot was trying to change everything great about what was left of the country.

As he kicked back and forth in the old wooden rocking chair on the wraparound porch, Pemberton saw the headlights from the cars bounce off the trees, swinging back and forth as the small dirt road curved and twisted. Moments later, two vehicles—an older model pickup truck and a new SUV—stopped in front of the old yellow farmhouse. Pemberton waited for the two men to exit their vehicles and then, without a word, stood up and motioned for them to follow him around the side of the house to the backyard.

A small, dilapidated structure sat at the edge of the yard, leaning against the back row of thirty-foot-tall pine trees. The Shed. No one would ever guess this old shed was the entrance to one of the most secure facilities on earth. Pemberton held a hand up to halt everyone outside the door and silently stepped inside and found the hidden keypad behind the workbench. He punched in the numbers and stepped back outside. He motioned for the others to follow him.

As Pemberton moved over to allow the others in, he reached out and pulled one of the others back. "Wanna watch where you're steppin' there, hoss." With almost surprising swiftness, the concrete slab on the floor had released a *phst!* and began to rapidly move to the side, revealing a set of stairs that led down into the dark earth.

Pemberton began to descend the stairs. "Better shake a leg, fellas," he called over his shoulder. "This thing's gonna reset itself in a minute."

The guests followed him down the dark stairwell.

Once inside the room, Pemberton gestured for his guests to take a seat. He, of course, took the Aresline. Once everyone was seated, he began.

"Good to see you, Judge. Thanks for coming, Governor."

Both men nodded.

"Milton said this was urgent. That it was something that needed my direct attention," the governor said.

Pemberton looked at the other man. "You tell him anything, Milton?"

"Nothing specific. But I think we all know why we're here."

"Do we?" It was the governor.

Pemberton pursed his lips and folded one of his long skinny arms up under the other one, resting his finger in the cleft of his chin. "Lemme ask you something, Joe. When you were a little boy, when you thought about what you wanted to be when you grew up, what was it?"

The governor thought about it for a moment. "I wanted to be a fireman."

"So then why aren't you a fireman?"

The governor shifted in his seat. "Well, I guess because. . .well. . . Look, I just wanted to help people, really."

"And that's why you ran for governor," Pemberton said.

"Yes."

Pemberton leaned forward. "And that's why I got you elected. Because I saw something great in you. It's why I spent the kind of money I did on you, boy. Because I knew you couldn't be shaken. That you'd do whatever you needed to do, in order to maintain the greatness of this state."

"Thank you, Gavin. I appreciate your kind words."

"And I know that you ain't gonna kowtow to any special interest groups," Pemberton continued. "It's your beliefs on God is what's got me fired up!"

"I don't understand," the governor said. "You know my position on that. I'm an atheist."

"Exactly!"

"Perhaps I can shed some light here," the judge said.

Pemberton swept his arm out in a gesture, giving the judge the floor.

"Joe, it's been over four months since the Chinese attacked. We all know how close this country came to almost losing everything. If it weren't for sheer dumb luck and an exceptional operative named Jon Keene, we'd all be wearing red and pledging allegiance to the People's Republic of China.

"Gavin and I have been talking for a while now. President Walker is adamant about his decision to stand still at this time and exhibit no aggression toward the Chinese." He pursed his lips and shook his head. "That's ludicrous, in our minds. Once our boys got back here on our shores with the help of the Royal Navy, we should have gone full throttle back at them. We should have pushed them right back through those border towns they crossed and right into the Pacific Ocean." He jabbed a finger through the air. "Not just stop and negotiate new borders. What kind of president does that?"

"A coward! That's who!" Pemberton snapped.

The governor nodded. It was no secret he had objections to the way President Walker had handled the crisis. He had called him misguided and accused him of playing upon the fears of people who ignorantly placed their hope in something that didn't exist by giving credence to the man who called himself the Prophet.

"Listen, Joe," the judge continued, "they may call this part of the country the Bible Belt, but I'm here to tell you that there are a lot of people who couldn't give a care about changing the kinds of things Walker is talking about changing. The man's gone mad! People down here don't want that kind of change. We liked our country just fine the way it was before Walker and Grant let it get sold out right out from under their noses."

"So what do you want me to do about it?" the governor said.

"We want you to be our president," Pemberton said.

The governor laughed a throaty, short laugh.

"We're serious," the judge said.

"And how do you plan on making that happen?" the governor said, still chuckling.

The judge stood up from his chair and went to the wet bar. He poured himself two fingers of Pemberton's thirty-year-old scotch. He glanced over to the other two to see if they, too, wanted one. They both nodded and the judge poured the round.

Sitting back down, he continued, "I've been on the North Carolina Supreme Court for eighteen years now. I've seen a lot come and go. I've seen laws that should have never been remain laws. And I've seen laws that were rock solid get thrown out like yesterday's table scraps.

"I say that to say this: in 1869, the United States Supreme Court ruled that a state did *not* have the right to secede from the union. But here's the thing. It was against the law for us to secede from England when we wanted our freedom. They said it was against the law when the South tried to secede from the North. But the bottom line is this: our own Declaration of Independence lays out the grounds for when the people of this country should rise up and defend what they know to be right."

He pulled out a small piece of paper and unfolded it. Retrieving his reading glasses from his pocket, he smoothed the page and began to read aloud.

"When, in the course of human events, it becomes necessary for one people to dissolve the political bands which have connected them with another, and to assume among the powers of the earth, the separate and equal station to which the laws of nature and of nature's God entitle them, a decent respect to the opinions of mankind requires that they should declare the causes which impel them to the separation."

The governor cleared his throat and tried to say something, but only a squeak came out. He coughed and pounded himself in the chest. "I'm sorry, I guess that scotch went down the wrong pipe. Milton, Gavin, I've known you two for a long time. You both are like a second set of granddads to me. But gentlemen, what you are suggesting is treason."

Pemberton shot out of his chair. "Treason? Treason! I'll tell you what's treason. Letting the gal-dern Chinese set off ten suitcase nukes on our West Coast is treason! Sitting back and watching them come unimpeded across our border was treason! President Walker ain't fit to run a shoe store, let alone this country. And I *won't* sit by idly and watch them ruin everything my family and I have worked for almost three hundred years to achieve."

"Calm down, Gavin," the judge said.

Pemberton drained his glass and slammed it back down on the desk before taking his seat again.

"Joe, what Gavin is saying is, there are those of us who have already been moving toward a solution. This thing has come together quick, I must say. But in the end, it was inevitable. We can't sit back and let some wacko religious zealots manipulate this country into changing what we are. We have to act now."

The governor twirled his finger around his glass. He took a big swallow, stood up, got himself a refill, and sat back down. "So this isn't just some fly-by-night fancy that you two have cooked up?"

Pemberton leaned forward onto the desk. "Son, I've got no less than two hundred of the top business minds in these southern states ready to pour resources into whatever we need to make this happen. Milton has been in meetings with justices from every state supreme court from Virginia to Georgia. We don't like Walker's idea of running this country. What's left of it. We need to take it back. We need to kick these Chinese back to where they came from. And we don't need some crackpot calling himself a prophet dictating government policy. We're doing this. And we want you at the helm."

"Why me?"

"Because," the judge said, "you already have executive experience and people love you. And like you said. You don't even believe in God. Why would you base your country's future on what some kook says, 'God says. . .'?"

The governor finished his second drink and grabbed the other two men's glasses. He poured them all another round and sat back down. "You realize what you're asking. Right?"

The old man and the judge nodded.

"I mean, this is going to cause a lot of waves."

They nodded again.

"I'm serious, gentlemen. I mean this could cause an all-out second civil war. Are you prepared for that?"

Pemberton raised his glass. "Son, we're not just prepared for it." He slowly tipped it back and took a sip. "We're counting on it!"

American Hospital, Dubai

She could hear them. They would come and go, in and out of the room. She knew they were talking about her, but she couldn't make out anything they said. It was like she was underwater. She could hear the voices, but they all sounded muffled and distorted.

Over the last few days, she had tried to open her eyes. To let them know she was there. But they just wouldn't open. And it hurt. It hurt to breathe. Not long ago, she thought she had moved a finger, but she couldn't tell. It was like she was trapped inside a padded room, with someone squeezing her eyes shut. She tried to fight against it, but nothing happened.

This last time they came around, though, was different. The voices weren't muffled. She was able to understand them. At first she was excited. *Finally!* But still, she couldn't move. Couldn't speak. But she could hear them.

The first voice she was able to make out was a woman's. Arabic. It took a few minutes for her to will her brain to translate. But finally, she had made her mind shift gears. She only grabbed sporadic words at first, but then after a few minutes of trying to concentrate, her brain was translating.

". . . Charts are the same. I don't understand. How can she be showing improvement, but not responding?" the woman was saying.

I'm here! she screamed—inside her head. *Can't you see that?*

The woman, whoever she was, had left again. She was alone.

She started to get angry at herself. She had no idea what was going on. Why was she here? Why couldn't she open her eyes? She felt the rage building up inside her. Someone was coming again. Footsteps. Several sets.

"We cannot keep her on support much longer," a voice said. "She's using up valuable resources. We don't even know who she is."

A new voice: "Yes, but the sheer fact that she has survived this is extraordinary! If she comes out, we need to study her. Ask her what she remembers."

"Well," the first voice said again, "Director Hassan will not permit us to keep her on like this. He has instructed that we stop life support. I'm sorry. We cannot continue this."

The second voice again: "Are you mad? This woman is a medical miracle! There is absolutely no reason whatsoever that she should even be alive right now. Tell Rashid I will take full responsibility for her."

"I'm sorry, Dr. Naser," the first voice said. "I have my orders. You can take it up with the director yourself."

"Wait!" It was the second voice. "Let me have a few minutes alone with her."

"For what?"

"To. . .say good-bye. Make my peace with it."

She felt her heart rate increasing. What was happening? The one man had said something about life support? What did he mean? She didn't need life support. She was here! She was alive! She just couldn't communicate that.

She felt a warm, soft hand touch her arm. She recognized the touch. It was as if she had experienced it before. Suddenly, a wave of blurry memories came at her. This man, the one who was touching her, had been here before. Many times, actually. She was remembering. She could recall hearing his voice several times recently. As she came out of the blackness. He was there. He had talked to her. Often. And now he was arguing with someone else about something. . .life support. What did that mean?

Suddenly, she realized what was happening. *Oh, my goodness! I'm in a hospital. I'm unconscious. They think I'm dead. Am I in a coma? What if they disconnect the life support? Can I breathe on my own?*

She began to panic. She hadn't come through everything in her life just to end up dying at the hands of a stupid hospital administrator. She focused harder than any time in her entire life. She had to let them know she was in here. She couldn't let them just throw her away.

She felt the man's hand slide down her arm and grasp her hand. She cleared her mind. She relaxed and felt the rise and fall of her breathing. She placed every conscious thought she had on her fingers. And then she told herself, *Squeeze!* Nothing. She did it again. *Squeeze!* She tried to empty her thoughts and just focus on her fingers.

The man had been talking to her. Saying good-bye. She could hear, and sense, that the man was upset. She needed to do this. *Squeeze! NOW! SQUEEZE!*

Suddenly, the man stopped talking and jerked his hand away.

"Hello? Di–did you just. . . ," the man stammered. "Did you just squeeze my finger? Hello? Are you in there? Please! Please, wake up."

Slowly, she felt the control coming back to her. She could tell, now, that she was moving her fingers.

"Ha-ha! You did! Director Hassan! Come quickly."

She was moving her hand freely now. And she could hear the gathering of several people around her.

"She squeezed my hand, Rashid."

"Dr. Naser, we really don't have time for these antics."

Antics! Was this guy kidding? It took everything she had to make her hands move. Who was this guy? And who put him in charge? And why couldn't she open her eyes? How did she get here? What was going on?

14

"I told you, Rashid," her advocate said. "I told you she wasn't a lost cause! She's alive!"

She really didn't know what was going on. But one thing was for sure. She wasn't about to sit here and have two Arabic men arguing over whether or not she was dead. She had made her fingers move; the rest was sure to follow. She tried to focus again. It was still all black. *That's okay. I've been in worse places,* she said to herself.

She tried to concentrate with everything she had. *Open your eyes. . . . Open your eyes. . . . OPEN YOUR EYES!*

She felt her lids flutter. They felt so heavy. *Do it!* she screamed at herself.

At first, it felt like she was looking directly into the sun. The light was so bright it was painful. She blinked a few times and tried to bring everything into focus. After a few seconds, she began to make out shapes. People. Lots of them. At least ten. Slowly, little by little, the shapes took form and she saw faces. Doctors and nurses. But how did she get here? And why was she even here in the first place?

And then it all started to flood back. The car. The wreck. She had tried to fight back. But it was bad. Real bad. She remembered. . .she remembered. . .that she had died.

"Hello." It was the voice called Naser. She recognized it.

She tilted her head to face the voice. A young, attractive man was kneeling beside her. He had a white lab coat on with a stethoscope hanging around his neck.

"I'm Doctor Farid Naser. I have been taking care of you."

She tried to sit up a little. But her head started swimming instantly.

"No, no, no. . .lie still," Naser instructed. "Everything is going to be okay. Can you talk?"

She tried to open her mouth and speak, but only a guttural, dry sound came out.

"Here," Naser said, tilting a small cup of water to her lips.

She sipped at first. But after a few seconds, her throat opened up and she began to drink the water in gulps.

"Easy," Naser said, smiling. "You've been away for quite a while."

She drank the cup dry and licked her lips. She felt like a plant that had been dying in the dry desert heat that had finally been watered. She took a deep breath and said, "More."

Naser reached over to the small table sitting beside her and filled the cup from a pitcher there. She drank two more cups before nodding she was finished.

Naser sat back and looked to the others who were standing by. "See? I told you!"

An older man, the one Naser had spoken to, stepped forward. "Hello, miss. I'm Doctor Hassan, chief of medical operations and director here at American Hospital, Dubai. Can you tell me. . .do you remember anything? Do you know how you got here? Can you remember your name?"

She thought for a moment. She still couldn't remember everything. It was all sketchy. But one thing was for sure. She didn't need to tell these people a lot.

"Can you remember anything at all?" It was Naser. "Your name? Anything?"

She could. Slowly, it was all coming back to her. She wasn't going to offer anything important. But she figured she could at least tell them a name.

"My name's Alex. Alex Smith."

PART 1: REBIRTH

CHAPTER 1

Megan Taylor rubbed her eyes and tried to focus. Her breath was coming in rapid, short gasps. Sweat poured from her forehead. Her skin felt clammy and cold—just like it did every time she had the dream. Which lately had been every night. Sometimes two or three times a night. She tried to calm herself and stay her breathing. But the tears started. Just like they always did.

The dream was always the same—she had found Keene in the prison camp. She didn't know how she got there, or where it was. But she was there. Outside the barbed-wire perimeter. And she could see Keene, standing in the middle of the courtyard. And Chin was there—standing in front of Keene, holding a gun to his head. From there, everything always happened in slow motion. She would reach for her gun, but it would get caught in her holster. Then Chin would turn around and look at her. Keene would yell to her. "*Shoot him!*"

But she couldn't get the gun out. Then Chin would turn back to Keene, laughing, and squeeze the trigger. The gun would go off in his hand like a cannon. And Keene's lifeless body would slump to the ground.

She'd been having the dream now for almost a month. Ever since President Walker and Director Jennings had made the call to let him go.

"We can't spend valuable resources, any longer, trying to find him," Walker had said.

The decision had come down the morning after Walker's address to the nation—in which he had announced the cease-fire agreement only a few weeks after China's attack.

Jennings had argued vehemently with the president about Keene. But in the end, Jennings had conceded the president was right. The country was in a fragile, vulnerable condition right now. They needed to focus on

19

how to move forward. And with Walker refusing to launch a counterattack on American soil, General Chin had agreed to negotiate new borders.

And why not? They had what they came for. The United States had been sitting on one of the greatest oil reserves in the world. And still, with Congress refusing to drill, coupled with the fact that China had become the leader in world oil consumption over the last fifteen years, the Chinese could not afford to let such a great resource go unused. Add that to the fact that the United States had borrowed almost seventy-three cents of every dollar they spent from China and it was only a matter of time before something like this happened.

The Prophet had tried to warn them. Hadn't he? He told them God wanted them to change. He said America had gotten so far away from what it once was that God was displeased and was going to give the nation over to someone else.

Now, here they were, a nation—if you could still call it that—occupied mostly by China, trying to figure out how to move forward. The Prophet was still nowhere to be found. And the government had abandoned Jon Keene.

She kicked the covers away from her and swung her legs over the side of the bed. She took a couple of deep breaths and forced herself out of bed. She checked the clock on the dresser and let out a long, exasperated sigh. It was going to be another long day.

Halfway to the bathroom she heard the buzzing of the sat-phone on the bedside table. She thought about just letting it go. But then she rationalized, *Who in the world would call at four thirty in the morning?*

"This is Taylor."

"You up?" It was Director Jennings.

"I am now."

"Get in here. I just heard from Jon."

CHAPTER 2

Milton Hayes closed the door to his office inside the North Carolina State Supreme Courthouse. He had always, even before the invasion, been the first person in the building. Five thirty every morning for more than twenty years.

After taking off his robe and hanging it on the wire hanger beside the door, he sat down at his desk, picking at the stack of briefs that had been there for a few weeks now—though he had no idea why he was even bothering. Since the invasion by the Chinese, the entire country's judicial system was a complete and total mess. But the president had demanded that state and local governments get back to "business as usual," as he had put it. As if nothing had happened. *What an imbecile,* he thought. Did the man not see that the entire country was still walking on pins and needles, waiting to see what was coming next?

But America was resilient, if nothing else. It was now almost five months since the attack, and the country was showing the beginning signs of pulling together. Domestic crime was almost nonexistent. The economy was showing marks of stability. Americans—*being gullible once again,* he thought—were buying into this notion that the Chinese had what they came for and weren't going to continue to push forward. As if, magically, everything was just going to go back to the way it was.

Still, companies were trying to restructure. People were returning to their jobs. Banks were scrambling to work with other international banking systems to get the money flow back on track. It was still a huge mess. And it was probably going to take several months—perhaps even years—to get back to some sense of normalcy. But regardless of how long it took, when everything settled, the Chinese were now going to be the world's foremost superpower. And that didn't sit well with North Carolina

21

Supreme Court Chief Justice Milton Hayes.

He pushed the stack of papers aside and reached for the clunky office phone. *Funny,* he thought. A typical American conversation used to be, *What would we do without our cell phones?* Well, now they knew. Cell phone communications had been completely destroyed with the attacks. The Chinese had targeted cell towers all over the Midwest, as they entered the country. Cell companies were working tirelessly, trying to reroute communications so that the infrastructure would bypass the destroyed towers and utilize only those in the east that were working. "*It's a technical nightmare,*" a spokesperson for one of the main carriers had said. They hoped they could have things somewhat normal—provided there were no further aggressions from the Chinese—in the next six months. Until then, back from the brink of extinction, Ma Bell was back at the top of her class. Landlines were being reinstated and used again. Since most of the technology had consisted of large fiber-optic lines that were buried beneath ground, it had been relatively easy to get them back up and running. *Funny,* Hayes thought, *my granddad was right. There is beauty in simplicity.*

He picked up the receiver and punched the numbers. There was some buzzing then a series of clicks—though they were working, the landlines still had some issues. Finally, he heard the ringing on the other end.

"Yeah?"

"Gavin, it's me. Everything set?"

"Yep."

"You want to drive?" Hayes asked. "Or do you want me to have my driver take us?"

"No sense in bringing someone who doesn't need to be there. I'll drive. Where you gonna be?"

"I'm at the courthouse now. We're supposed to hear a couple cases today, but I doubt counsel will even show up. They haven't all week."

"It ain't gonna get any better, Milton. Not until something changes."

"Yeah." Hayes sighed into the phone.

"People are scared, man. They still don't know if we're coming or going. That degenerate in the White House is laying down, man! He's nothing but a yellow-belly."

"Well, then, we had better be convincing, huh?"

"Don't you worry about me. What I'm offering is pretty convincing. You just make sure you can sell it from a legal and judicial standpoint."

Hayes bit the tips of his fingernails. What he and Gavin Pemberton were doing could get them killed. But he couldn't stand by and watch his country just lie down and die. He wouldn't. "I can sell it."

"Good. Then I'll see you in an hour."

CHAPTER 3

New Chinese Territory

Keene was cold. Freezing, actually. He opened his eyes and took in the scene around him. Dark room. He was in a bed, and there was something sticking out of his wrist. An IV. He traced the small tube with his eyes from his arm to the drip-bag hanging on the metal frame beside the bed. He was here alone. But where was here?

The last thing he remembered was sitting on the floor of his cell. They had finally broken him.

After he and his team had taken out the nuclear device that was meant for Washington, he had followed General Chin to a remote farmhouse somewhere just across the Canadian border. But he had been careless. Chin got the drop on him. He had been knocked out and taken to a prison camp.

Outside of being in a prison camp, he hadn't known where he was. But at least he knew that he and his men had stopped the invasion. That was enough for him, then. Past that, the only thing he could remember was that they came for him. Regularly. For weeks on end. They would beat him until he was almost unconscious. Then they would send a medical staff in to tend to him, until he was well enough to be beaten again.

He had been brought to his wits' end—the once hard-core, black ops operative, turned CIA agent. He had been reduced to a broken shell of the man he once was. He remembered wanting to just die. And he had asked God to let him die.

It was coming back to him now. He had been sitting on the floor, leaning against the cold steel slab that was his bed. He couldn't take it anymore. He had been replaying all the conversations he had had with Boz and all that stuff about God that Boz had been trying to get him to listen to. At the time, he hadn't cared. It was all just ridiculous to him. He hadn't wanted anything to do with God.

But something changed. Lying there in that cell, after weeks upon weeks of getting beaten, he realized how alone he was. And he realized that he had been that way long before the prison camp. Suddenly, all the things Boz had been saying started to make sense. And just when he thought he had been broken beyond all measure, he felt himself break in a new way, when Boz's seemingly childish statement came rushing back to him.

"Jon, Jesus Christ loves you."

He had finally let go and cried out to God. It was like some huge weight had lifted. For the first time in his life, he felt as though he had peace. Even though he was broken and beaten nearly to death, he had peace. He had no misconceptions of getting out of there. And he hadn't asked God to do that. Rather, he had come to grips with the fact that he would most certainly die in that cell. But the idea that there was a God who loved him and cared for him gave him the strength he needed to just let go and die. So that's what he had asked for.

God, please, just let me die.

He was ready. He had closed his eyes and drifted off. But it never happened.

Now, as his eyes adjusted to the darkness in this room, he realized he was somewhere different. This definitely wasn't the prison camp. The room looked more like a dirtbag motel room. There was a bureau at the foot of the bed with a small television sitting on top. A small round table with a couple of fold-up chairs sat beside the bed. To the left was a little alcove with a sink and a small mirror with a single low-watt bulb hanging from the ceiling.

He tried to lift his head to look around but immediately put it back down, as he felt the pounding race down the back of his skull through his shoulder and into his back. His teeth were chattering now. He was so cold.

He lifted his hand to feel his face and noticed that he was soaking with sweat. But how was that possible? He was cold. How could he be sweating?

Forget how bad he hurt. He had to find out what was going on. Where was he? How did he get out of the prison camp?

He took a few deep breaths and pushed himself up on his elbows. He lifted his head and waited as the pain coursed through his body. There was a time when he had been trained to take the pain and use it. To master it. To let it turn into anger that would fuel him when he had no strength. He had no need for the anger anymore, but he needed the energy for sure. He waited as the pain ticked through his muscles. He focused his mind and felt his body begin to come alive. But just as he swung his legs over the side of the bed and sat up, the door to the room opened. Blinding white light from the outside rushed in at him. He lifted his arm to shield his face and saw the outline of a figure in front of him.

"Mr. Keene, you're awake!"

Suddenly, everything came back to him. He had asked God to let him die. And he had passed out. But then they came for him again—or at least that's what he had thought. He remembered starting to cry, thinking that even though he'd cried out to God, maybe God hadn't heard him. That he was too far gone. That somehow God had turned His back on him, as he had turned his back on God for so many years. But it wasn't them. It was someone else who had come for him.

He had barely been conscious. He was in so much pain. But then he had heard the voice. It was a nice voice. One that wasn't yelling or laughing at him. And he remembered now that he had recognized the man. But from where? Who was he?

And then he remembered.

"Mr. Keene, please lie back down. You're not completely well. Your fever seems to have broken. That's good," the man said as he came into the room and closed the door.

The man grabbed him by the shoulders and pushed him back down on the bed. He looked up and tried to focus on the man's face. It was him. It was the same man that had come for him in the prison.

He laid his head back down on the pillow and realized how hard he was breathing. What little energy he might have had, he had just expelled completely trying to sit up.

"There," the man said, placing the pillow behind his head. "Just lie there for now."

The man sat back down in the chair beside the bed.

"Mr. Keene, I don't know how much you remember. But I—"

"I remember."

The man nodded. "You had been looking for me for a while, before you were captured. Do you remember what I told you before? That when the time was right, God would send me to you?"

Keene remembered.

"My name is Quinn Harrington, Mr. Keene. I am the Prophet."

CHAPTER 4

Even with the chaos of the last few months and the fact that more than half the nation was operating like a third-world country, traffic on the Beltway at 5:30 a.m. was none the wiser. Already, cars were nearly bumper to bumper as men and women tried to traverse the labyrinth into downtown.

"It's like they've already forgotten," Megan said to no one. But with President Walker touting the line, *We must move forward,* it seemed the American people were eager to try.

As she made her way off the ramp and into downtown, she looked off to the side at one of the thousands of tent cities that had been erected, housing a few thousand of the several million displaced citizens from the other side of the Appalachian Mountains who had braved the journey to safety. As far as the East Coast stretched, makeshift communities like this one had been erected throughout what was left of the country. Still, millions of others were either too scared to try or had just given in to the Chinese government's new way of life—because for many of them, not much had changed. They still went to work. They still sent their kids to school. But instead of working for an American company or learning American history, workers and students now adopted the Chinese ways of business and education. Many still protested, but many more were just too lazy to do anything about it. As long as no one was trying to kill them and they could still live more or less like they had before, they were willing to settle.

Pulling up to the security gate, Megan badged the waiting marine. He made the required walk around her car then motioned for her to continue. She knew the marine recognized her. They had played out the same scene for a month now. But she was still irked at the flippancy with which the man casually waved her through. She had said something to Jennings at least twice now.

"Does he not remember what just happened?"

"I'll remind him," Jennings had said.

Maybe I should remind him! she thought, passing through the gate.

Inside, she was greeted and led to the waiting room where Jennings was already finishing off a pot of coffee. His second of the morning, if she had to guess.

"Can I get you a cup?" he asked.

"No thanks. Just makes me jittery anymore."

"Suit yourself." Jennings put the pot back on the burner. He tore open a new pack of grounds, dumped them in the filter, and hit the button. Within seconds the gurgle of the percolator began.

Though she was bursting at the seams to find out about Jon, she knew—after working with him for five months now—Jennings had his routine. The man was unshakeable. Kicking in the door, demanding information at this hour wasn't going to generate any kind of favorable response. She sat down and waited for her boss to fill her in.

Jennings pulled a chair up beside her and sat down. "Before you start railing me for details, let me tell you what I know. You can ask questions when I'm done."

She nodded, her heart rate beginning to increase.

"Last night—or this morning, however you want to look at it—I got a call. But it wasn't Jon."

"I thought you said—"

"And I thought you were going to let me finish."

She bit her lip and folded her arms across her chest.

"It was Quinn," Jennings continued.

"The Prophet?"

"Yes. He has Jon."

"Where?"

"I'll get to that in a minute. The Prophet—Quinn—said that when he found him, Jon was barely alive. Now, I don't know how he found him, or how they got out of there, but he assures me they're safe. For now."

"What about Jon?" She couldn't help herself.

"He says Jon has been beaten severely and probably has a few dislocated bones and joints. But he's alive. Quinn has him in a motel in the Chinese territory. He wouldn't say where, in case someone, somehow was able to listen in. But he says he's taking care of it."

"What does that mean, he's taking care of it?"

"It means what it means, Taylor. Jon's alive. And he's in bad shape right now. But Quinn says. . ." He sighed and gave his shoulders a shrug. "Quinn says that by the time we get there, Jon will be fine."

Megan was about to lose her mind. "What do you mean, by the time we get there?"

Jennings shoved his chair back and stood up. Frustration lined his face. "Taylor, I'm as new to this as you are. I have no idea what that means. I guess it means Jon is gonna miraculously be healed, like some Lazarus, or something."

"Lazarus was dead and raised. Not healed."

"Whatever! All I know is that Quinn said not to worry. Jon is fine. They're fine. And we can come get Jon in a couple days. Maybe sooner."

"What are we doing to help them in the meantime?"

Jennings gave another frustrated sigh. "Nothing."

"What do you mean—"

Jennings pointed his finger at her like an angry father. "Taylor, if you say, 'What do you mean' one more time. . . Quinn says we're to do nothing. That Jon is going to get better and then we can come get him."

Megan pursed her lips and shook her head.

"But right now, we need to check some things out."

Megan leaned forward on her chair. As much as the vagueness irritated her, the FBI agent in her was intrigued. "Check what out?"

"Quinn didn't say exactly. But he did say that the Chinese are not our biggest problem right now."

"I don't understand," she said. "I think they're exactly our problem!"

"Yeah, well, Quinn says they're not. And that we should not concern ourselves with them right now."

"And who *should* we concern ourselves with?"

"Us."

Megan stood up now and began pacing back and forth. "I don't even know what that means! *Us!* What are you talking about?"

"Seems we've got another skunk in our backyard."

Megan immediately felt her stomach weaken. After the debacle of Marianne Levy selling out the country the way she had, the mere thought of another turncoat undermining the integrity—or what was left of it—of the country was sickening to her. "Who? Not President Walker?"

"No. Quinn was adamant that it's no one we're aware of. And he says it has nothing to do with the Chinese this time. Just that something's festering within our new borders that will cripple this country worse than it already is."

"And let me guess." She set her jaw tight. "He's not saying who."

"And that about brings you up to speed, Taylor. Now I suggest you get Boz in here so we can start trying to figure out what the heck is going on and how we're going to stop it."

She reached for her sat-phone and her jacket. "I've got to go by my office and get a few things. I'll call Boz on the way."

CHAPTER 5

Boz Hamilton sat on the porch of his old farmhouse and looked out at the rolling field in front of him. The house was said to be more than a hundred and fifty years old, but no one knew for sure. He only cared that it was out of the way, peaceful, and gave anyone who sat on its front porch at 6:15 in the morning a spectacular the view of the sunrise. That, and the unseasonably warm weather, made it an almost-perfect morning.

Boz closed his Bible, having spent the last forty minutes studying the book of Acts—chapter 20, verses 13 through 38. His personal devotion time had been in the letters of the apostle Peter the last few weeks, what with the invasion. Peter's letter to the church always comforted him whenever he was facing any kind of trial or persecution in his life. And if the last few months didn't qualify as that, nothing did. But this morning, something had caused him to flip elsewhere in the scriptures. He figured it was God's Holy Spirit directing him there. And for what reason he had no idea. But it definitely troubled him. He might not have been the most intuitive person on the face of the earth, but the fact that he'd definitely felt God's urging to study this particular portion of His Word caused his pulse to quicken and his anxiety level to bump up a couple of notches.

He stood up from the old wooden rocker and knelt down on the dry, cracked boards that made up the wraparound porch. With the warm rays of the ascending sun cascading on his neck, he bowed his head and began to pray.

Thirty minutes later, he rose and went inside the house. He could already smell the sharp scent of bacon as it drifted along the fall breeze being carried throughout the house via the open windows. He found Eli Craig standing over the stove with a ridiculous apron tied around his waist and an even more ridiculous chef's hat sitting atop his head.

"G'mawnin, Uncle Boz," the Brit said in his best Virginia drawl. "You want some fried pig?"

Eli Craig was perhaps England's best operative, sort of a *real* James Bond. He had served in His Majesty's Navy, where he'd risen to the rank of admiral in a very short period of time, before being hand selected to serve in England's most clandestine intelligence service, MI-5, following in his father's legendary footsteps. If his father had put the Craig name on the map concerning spy work, Eli put it on the globe. He was a world-class operative, with King William's own personal endorsement.

Eli had been a teenager when he met Boz for the first time. He and his mother had been kidnapped, the target of a wealthy Saudi because of the elder Craig's involvement in bringing down the Saudi's family patriarch, a man who dealt heroin and illegal arms. Boz Hamilton and his team had been sent into a volatile, unstable region to retrieve the Craig family, which they'd done without setting off even the slightest alarm; they had gone in and out as if they'd been ghosts. And a friendship—no, a family bond—had been born between Boz and Eli.

Boz became like an uncle to Eli, visiting regularly, sending him birthday gifts and even getting his boss to get the president to recommend Eli to the prime minister for acceptance into the Royal Naval Academy. From there, Eli made his own way, but he always looked to Boz for advice and guidance. Especially in matters of faith.

Boz figured it was the very reason why Eli had risked his entire career a few months earlier, when Eli literally led a mutiny against Prime Minister Bungard and made off with almost the entire Royal Navy, coming to the aid of the United States in its most dire hour. *Had it not been for Eli and his actions, who knows where we would be today,* Boz thought.

"I'm always down for some fried pig," Boz said. "But not from a guy wearing that. You look ridiculous!"

"Hey, I'm not the one who bought this getup. I just happen to make it look really good!"

"And make sure my omelet is fluffy," Boz continued. "I don't want any of that dried-up rubbery stuff."

"Don't let the hat and apron fool you," Eli joked. "You'll be lucky if they aren't burnt!"

Boz moved over to the stove and pushed Eli out of the way. "Listen here, son. If there's one thing you should've learned from me, it's never screw with a man's eggs."

They both laughed, and Eli turned to get some plates while Boz finished off the omelets.

"So I talked to Bungard last night," Eli said.

"Yeah? What's he saying?"

"Not much. The man knows how to hold a grudge. He won't admit it, but he's still sore that I stole his navy. Not sure why, though. I mean, they made him a national hero."

"But only because you gave him all the credit."

"That's what I said!"

"And?"

"And he quickly changed subjects. He wants me back, though. Said we have some things to work out."

"You're leaving soon, then?"

"Well, not before we eat these overcooked eggs."

Boz chuckled and sat down with Eli at the table. They bowed their heads and Eli gave thanks. They were five minutes into the meal when Boz's sat-phone chirped.

"Hey Boz, it's Megan."

"Hey, kiddo. What's up?" Boz could already sense the nervousness in her voice.

"Jennings heard from Jon."

There was silence on the line for a few second before Boz found his voice. "You mean—"

"He's okay. But it's complicated."

"Complicated how?"

Megan relayed the conversation she had had with Jennings about Quinn and Jon. Boz felt a huge wave of relief sweep over him. He had been praying diligently that God would somehow bring Jon back to them. His mind was trailing off in thought when Megan's words brought him back.

"Jennings says we have another problem."

"What?"

"I don't know the details, but you need to get in here. Jennings wants to talk with us and we have to figure out what Quinn is talking about. Quinn says it could cripple the nation even worse than it already is."

Boz was taken back to his time on the porch earlier. He'd learned a long time ago not to question God's leading; there was a reason God had led him to that passage of scripture. Now it was all becoming clearer. He still didn't know exactly what it meant for them, but given the content of the scripture, he knew it wasn't good. "Wolves, Megan," he said.

"I'm sorry, what?" Megan said, obviously confused.

"We have wolves in our midst," Boz said. "I'll be there as soon as I can." He punched the button and set the sat-phone down on the table.

"That doesn't sound good," Eli said, mouth full.

"Call Bungard back," Boz said. "I may need you to extend your holiday."

CHAPTER 6

Alex opened her eyes for the second time in twenty-four hours. Fighting to wake up out of the coma was the most exhausting thing she had ever been through. She had only been able to remain awake for a little more than thirty minutes before exhaustion set in and took her back down into the deep recesses of her consciousness.

She dreamed, but nothing like before. These dreams were a little more elusive. Harder to grasp. And sketchy, unlike the terribly real state she had been in before. Everything then seemed to just be one very real, dark, and twisted nightmare. This was more pleasant.

She opened her eyes and found the same man sitting beside her. What was his name again? Oh, yeah, she remembered. Farid Naser or something.

"How are you?" he said in his thick accent.

"Better," she said. "May I have a drink of water?"

Naser sat forward in his chair and reached for the pitcher of water on the bedside table. He filled the little Dixie cup halfway and tilted it to her lips.

She drank slowly at first. But after the first few sips, she opened her mouth and let the water spill down her throat. It felt good. Life giving.

"Can you talk?" Naser asked.

She nodded her head as she swallowed the remaining gulp in her mouth. "Yeah. I can talk."

Naser shifted nervously in his seat. He lifted his hands and his mouth started to move, but nothing came out. Finally, he chirped a few breaths of laughter. "I mean—y–you. . . ," he stammered.

"What?" she asked, concerned.

"I mean, you were dead!" Naser said, half laughing again. "Dead! No one, and I mean no one, ever thought you and I would be having this conversation right now."

"I remember dying. What happened? How did I—how did all of this. . ." She waved a hand around.

"I shouldn't say dead. Not dead. Unconscious. Very near death, but not dead."

"Obviously," she said sarcastically.

"No, I don't just mean *not dead*." He was sitting on the edge of his chair again. Talking faster, like a five-year-old telling what he got for Christmas. "Your body must have gone into some kind of *safe* mode. You know, like a computer's hard drive? Your pulse had slowed down so much that your body wasn't even pumping the blood out of the wounds. They had already started to coagulate." He stood up now, waving his hands around. "Your heartbeat was so slow that if I hadn't had my hand on your carotid artery when it finally pulsed, I might have pronounced you dead. And when I felt it—when I started CPR. . ." He ran a hand through his hair and laughed again. "It was like someone hit the power button on you. All of a sudden, your heart rate picked back up, your body started convulsing, your wounds started bleeding again. . . ."

Alex knew exactly what the man was talking about. She had spent nearly a year in a Tibetan monastery where she had studied meditation. During that time, she had learned to control her heart rate and her breathing to that which was just above what was necessary to remain alive. There was only one problem with the technique: unless someone else triggered you back, it could be very difficult to do yourself. Only the great masters whom she had studied under had learned to do it at will and without any assistance. *And it was utterly impossible when you've been shot and thrown from a speeding car,* she thought to herself. And at the time, she didn't even realize that that was what her body was doing. She just thought she was dying.

"Lucky for me, huh?"

Naser blew out a big breath and sat back down. "Miracle, I'd say."

"How long have I been like this? Unconscious, I mean."

"Almost five months. No one believed that you would ever return to a conscious state."

"You did."

Naser lifted his head to meet her eyes. She saw the longing in them. It was an effect she had on many men. This one, however, looked a little different. She met his gaze and felt a tinge of something. She didn't know what, but it was there.

Naser shifted his eyes away and said in a whisper, "Yes."

"So what now?"

"Now, we run tests. Now that you're awake and have recovered from your wounds. . ." His words drifted off. Lingering. Waiting for her to perhaps fill in the blanks.

That wasn't going to happen. She needed to get out of this place as quickly as she could. But she had no idea how her body was going to respond to anything physical. For all she knew, she had been on her back for the last couple of months and her muscles had atrophied to the point that she wouldn't even be able to walk.

"Listen, Dr. . . . ?"

"Naser."

"Dr. Naser. Yes, I remember." She smiled at him. "I appreciate all you've done for me. But I've been lying in this bed for quite a while, yes?"

He nodded.

"I think I would like to get up. Is that possible?"

Naser moved closer to the bed. He pulled the blanket down from her legs and pointed. Little electrodes were attached from her hips to the balls of her feet. Clear tubing connected them with what looked like streaking blue light passing back and forth between the little pads.

"What are those?" She was somewhat scared of what the answer would be.

"Those"—Naser smiled—"are the newest thing in electro-light muscular therapy. Two years ago a physical therapist from North Korea developed these. You could say it's been like you ran two miles every day since you've been here."

Naser reached for her hand. He gently removed the few tubes and wires that remained attached to her and helped her stand up beside the bed. Immediately she felt the blood course through her veins. She tentatively let go of the bed rail and straightened up. She still didn't know what to expect yet. But as she stood there, shifting her weight from foot to foot, she knew that Naser had been right. She felt as though she had just woken up from a good night's sleep. She looked at the young doctor and his smiling face.

"See!" he said. "I told you! It's like you never got hurt."

She *was* amazed, she had to admit. "That's incredible! I feel great." She slowly walked around in a circle beside the bed. She could feel the blood begin to pump even more now. It felt good.

"Dr. Naser, can you tell me something?" she said, tracing a finger along his shoulder and down his bicep.

"Yes." He swallowed. Perhaps a little too hard.

"Are there any residual. . .effects? From my injuries?"

Naser wiped the bead of sweat that had formed on his forehead. "None that I can think of—"

"Good!"

"—but there could possibly be some psychological reactions." He reached out and grabbed her gently by the arm. "Perhaps you should sit back down now. I think that is probably enough for today."

"Doc, I feel like a million bucks. I think I'd like to take a walk. Like down the hall. Wanna come?"

Naser looked nervous. She guessed he'd been assigned to keep her confined to this room. There were too many questions still to be answered. A woman with an American passport—fake, but American, nonetheless—full of gunshot wounds and injuries consistent with a major car accident doesn't just show up in a Dubai hospital every day. The police were probably already on their way. She couldn't be here when they arrived. She thought for a moment.

She had known from the first moment she laid eyes on him that Naser had feelings for her. He told her he'd sat beside her bed, two, sometimes three times a day and talked to her. *It's like some bad American love story*, she thought. All she would have to do would be to bat her eyes and give him that sheepish smile and it would be all over. He'd be eating out of the palm of her hand.

"Farid. . . ," she said softly.

The use of his first name was all it took. The man was hers. He smiled a big, toothy smile.

"Please can we go for a walk? I promise, just down the hall and back."

Naser walked over to the blinds on the window of the room. He used his forefinger and thumb to spread apart the little plastic strips and looked out and down the hall.

"Just down the hall? And then right back?" He repeated her request.

"Then right back. I promise."

"Okay," he said. "But if anyone stops us and asks a question, you let me do the talking. Got it?"

She made a crisscross over her heart. "Promise."

Naser opened the door to the room and led her out. The hall was relatively empty. She had no idea what floor they were on, or where in the hospital they were. But she'd been in enough situations like this to know how to improvise.

As they passed the nurses' station, she took note of the small tray of surgical equipment sitting there. She caught the syringe sitting on the tray out of the corner of her eye. She had no idea what it contained, but she palmed it anyway. She continued to follow Naser down the hall as she stole a glance at the vial label. She recognized the name on the vial. A highly potent sedative. This would incapacitate Naser for at least two hours, if she emptied the plunger. Although she should probably just kill him.

Naser turned to make sure she was still behind him. He smiled at her. It was a warm smile and it made her feel. . .well, she didn't know what. No one had ever really smiled at her like that before. Sure, guys would flash her a grin all the time, but no one had ever looked at her like Naser looked at her. Almost like he put her on a pedestal.

Again she thought she should just kill him. She didn't need the complications.

As they got near the end of the hall, Naser began to slow. "This is the end of the line for you, Alex."

She knew he meant it harmlessly. But those words brought her back to the reality of who she was. When she had had her run-in with that FBI agent, Taylor, she was in the middle of an assignment for General Chin, after assassinating the president of the United States. She hadn't had the chance to make contact with Chin and let him know that, one, the new target, Marianne Levy, had been eliminated. And two, she had his money. And now she'd learned it had been a couple of months that she had been unconscious and hadn't made contact with Chin. She needed to get out of here. Now. She was suddenly surprised that Chin hadn't already sent someone after her.

She felt the syringe behind her back. Her thumb was on the plunger and ready. She started to pull her arm out from behind but stopped. Naser was looking at her like that again. She didn't know what was going on with her, but for some reason, she didn't want to just knock him out and take off. Or kill him.

"Farid, let me ask you something."

"Anything." He shrugged his shoulders.

"Do you like your job?" She watched the quizzical look on his face. "I mean, do you come in here every day and say to yourself, 'Man, I'm so glad I'm a doctor who works here'?"

Naser seemed to think about that for a moment. "You know. . .I actually don't. I started out thinking I wanted to be a doctor. But then a year into my residency, I realized I hate everything about the medical field. Especially my boss."

Behind her back, she placed the plastic tip back onto the needle of the syringe. "Do you want to get out of here?"

"Tell me why you're in my hospital with gunshot wounds. And tell me about the car accident. What happened?"

Everything in her screamed to just distract him and then snap his neck and get out of there. But she didn't. Instead, she took a deep breath and let it out again. She couldn't believe what she was about to do. "Come with me and I'll tell you everything."

Naser looked at her. And then to the elevator a few feet away. Then back to her. Finally, he reached out and pushed the DOWN button. The doors opened up, revealing the empty elevator car. He flashed her that smile again and said, "Let's go."

CHAPTER 7

Raleigh, North Carolina

Pemberton picked him up in front of the courthouse exactly one hour after they had ended their call. Hayes waved at the giant pickup truck rounding the corner and jumped in as Pemberton slowed down only enough to let him in. Hayes hadn't even gotten his seat belt fastened before the old man hit the gas again.

"How long you think it'll take us to get there?" Hayes asked.

"You got somewhere else to be?" Pemberton narrowed his eyes.

Hayes had known Pemberton for over thirty years. His old friend could be many things. Subtle was not one of them. "I just finished my third cup of coffee. I'm going to have to go to the bathroom soon."

Pemberton mumbled a few curse words under his breath.

Hayes shifted in the seat and looked at his watch.

" 'Bout two hours," Pemberton finally said. "Think you can make it that long?" His tone wasn't one of genuine concern.

"I think so."

Pemberton made a face and pulled over at the next gas station to let Hayes empty his bladder.

They spent the rest of the drive mostly silent. Not an awkward silence. More the kind of silence that two people who've spent so much time together can endure, neither one feeling like they need to manufacture conversation.

Besides, the tension was already thick. The man they were heading to meet was not someone you just casually dropped in on. He was a man of great renown. A hero to many people, as the former secretary of the navy; a partisan, backstabbing politician to others. Either way, what the two of them had planned couldn't be accomplished without him. If they were going to make this happen, they needed the man.

Pemberton edged the giant truck through the wrought-iron gate of the estate's drive. Suddenly, he stepped on the brake and came to a stop.

"What are you doing?" Hayes asked.

Again, Pemberton looked at him with those narrow, beady eyes. "There's no going back from this. You good?"

Hayes took a deep breath and let it out. "Drive."

Pemberton pulled the gear lever again and stepped on the gas.

When they got to the end of the long drive, their man was outside waiting for them. Pemberton put the gearshift in PARK and shut the engine off. Both he and Hayes got out and stood by the truck.

"Well, don't just stand there," their host snapped. "I ain't got all day."

Pemberton huffed. "Jake, as old as you are, you could be right."

Former secretary of the navy Jake Irving laughed a huge belly laugh. "Well, then, let's go, before I keel over and die!" Pemberton followed him around the side of the house and into an old barn with Hayes in tow.

Inside, a small table with three chairs sat in the middle of a dirt floor. Long leaves of tobacco hung from wooden beams all around. One of the new John Deere hybrid tractors sat off to one side. Several bales of hay sat along the other wall. Some antique shears and scythes hung on some rusty nails above the hay bales.

"I suppose you're going to tell me you still use those." Pemberton pointed to the antiques.

Irving dismissed the snide remark. "You want to talk about farming? Or did you come here for something important?" He motioned for his guests to sit.

"Did Gavin tell you why we're here?" Hayes asked.

Irving looked at Pemberton. "Nope. Just said it was important." He folded his arms across his chest. "But I got a pretty good idea, if it's coming from you two."

"You ought to," Pemberton shot back. "That idiot Walker is ruining what's left of this country."

"Calm down, Gavin," Hayes said. "I'm sure Jake has his own opinions about our *fair* president."

"That I do," Irving admitted.

The three men sat there in silence for more than a minute. Finally, Irving spoke. "So what do you want to do about it?"

Hayes looked at Pemberton and gave him a look that said, *I'll handle this.* Pemberton just nodded and leaned back in his chair.

"Jake, Gavin and I have been. . .building some relationships." Irving didn't say anything, so he continued, "These relationships are of an interesting nature."

"How so?" Irving asked.

Hayes shifted his position and opened his mouth to talk again.

"Oh, for goodness' sake, Milton!" Pemberton sat up in his chair. "Jake, this president is rolling over for the Chinese. He's got the whole country convinced that this *Prophet* is real, and that the whole reason the Chinese came in the first place is because *God* tried to warn us and we didn't listen. And he's not about to try and take our country back. He's just gonna let sleeping dogs lie. Now I don't know about you, but me, Milton, and a lot of other people aren't ready to just lie down."

Irving unfolded his arms. "So I ask you again. What do you want to do about it?"

"We want to overthrow President Walker." It was Hayes.

Irving recrossed his arms and began tapping his chin with his index finger. "Let me get this straight. You two want to start a coup d'état in the middle of the most chaotic crisis in our nation's history."

Both men nodded.

"And you need me for. . .what?"

"Jake. . ." Milton sat forward in his chair. "We have already set this thing in motion. Half the Senate and House—what's left of them—are on our side. Even if they won't admit it. The people of this country are divided. Half just want everything to be okay going forward. The other half is furious that we're sitting by, not doing anything to take our country back.

"Now, we could go through the process of trying to have him impeached. But you and I both know that'll take too long—I'm talking congressional hearings and the like. As if anyone would even care to go through that right now. Our government can't handle that. This needs to be done quickly and with force."

Irving set his jaw. "And you want me to get the Joint Chiefs on your side."

"We've already got Matthews, Smith, and Campbell," Pemberton jumped in. "The problem is we need Sykes."

"And you think because I'm the former secretary of the navy, I can get my successor to side with you."

"Right now, he and he alone is in control of our military," Pemberton said. "This thing is going to go sideways quick. Walker isn't much of a president. But if push comes to shove, he *will* instruct Sykes to use any means necessary to squash any kind of uprising from within."

Irving pursed his lips. "And if Sykes is on your side. . ."

"*Our side,*" Hayes corrected. "You know this is the right thing to do, Jake."

"You can't just remove a sitting president, Milton," Irving said condescendingly. "We don't do that in this country!"

"This *country* isn't *this* country, anymore!" Pemberton slammed his fist down on the little table. "It stopped being *this country* the day Walker went on TV and made that speech. Something's got to be done!"

Irving pushed back from the table and stood up. Pemberton was afraid they were losing him. "Jake, we need—"

Irving put his hand out to stop him. "Just—hold on. I need to think." He stuffed his hands in his pockets and started walking around the room.

Hayes looked nervously to Pemberton. If Irving said no, they weren't done, but it wouldn't be easy. Pemberton gave him a reassuring nod. Finally, Irving stopped and leaned forward, placing his hands on the table in front of them.

"You're going to need someone the people love to replace him."

Pemberton could see the grin on Hayes's face out of the corner of his eye. Irving was in!

"We already have him," Pemberton said.

"Who?" Irving asked.

Pemberton reached inside his coat pocket and pulled out a cigar. He bit the tip off and lit it. He took a long, slow pull and then blew the smoke out in short wisps. "Your son-in-law."

CHAPTER 8

Megan saw Boz and Eli round the corner to Jennings's office as she was kicking the vending machine in the hall. It was the third time this week it had stolen her money and refused to give up its goods. She gave it one final, hard, front kick and watched the teetering power bar slip out of the metal spiral and fall to the bottom of the machine. She retrieved her prize and hurried down the hall to meet her friends.

"Did you kill it?" Eli asked as she took a seat next to him.

"I'm going to shoot the glass next time and just reach in and take one. That stupid thing owes me like a month's worth of stuff." She ripped the top of the wrapper off and took a big bite.

"If you two are done," Jennings said dryly.

Everyone sat up straight and gave the CIA director their attention.

"This morning I got a call from the Prophet. He has Jon." Jennings held up his hands to stop Boz and Eli from the same barrage of questions Megan had already hit him with. "Let me finish and then you can ask questions."

Boz and Eli nodded and Jennings continued, uninterrupted. When he was finished, he leaned back against his desk and shrugged his shoulders.

"That's it. Now you know what I know."

"So we're supposed to do. . .what?" Boz asked.

"I've put a few calls out this morning, trying to see if anyone has heard anything."

"And?" It was Boz.

"And it seems that there are some people who aren't exactly happy with how President Walker is handling our situation right now."

"There's a lot of people not happy with that," Boz said.

"Yes, but apparently whoever this is, is willing to do something about it."

"What does that mean?" Eli asked.

"I don't know yet," Jennings said. "I only started digging a couple hours ago. After Quinn called. But I can tell you this. It's not coming from Washington. I got a guy—Peterson— lives down in Newport News. He's a former Company guy. Says he heard some things coming out of Raleigh."

"What kind of things?" Megan jumped in.

"Don't know yet. Says he's going to get back to me in a little while. But I can tell you this. Peterson may be retired, but he never left." Then to Boz and Eli, "Know what I mean?"

Megan looked on, agitated, as Boz and Eli both nodded. "No. I don't know what you mean," she said. "Please, fill me in."

Boz shifted in his seat to face her. "Megan, the FBI and CIA are a lot alike in many aspects of their operations. But there is one difference. When an FBI agent retires, or leaves, he usually just. . .leaves. Puts it behind him. I mean, I know guys who still hang on to that fed mentality, but most of the time, they let the job go. A CIA guy never stops being a spy."

This time Jennings and Eli nodded.

"And more often than not," Boz continued, "it gets him into trouble."

"Or killed," Eli added.

"Well, lucky for us," Jennings said, pushing off his desk, "Peterson hasn't gotten himself killed. But that could change if he starts asking questions down there and someone doesn't like it."

"Well, you said you guys don't ever stop being spies," Megan said. "What's the big deal?"

"Peterson's seventy-six years old." Jennings said. A worried look creased his brow. "And he's a good man. I don't want to see anything happen to him. He's served this country well." He walked back around to his side of the desk and sat down and pointed at Megan. "And that's why you are leaving in the next five minutes to go see him."

"So that's it?" She stood up. "We're just going to put all of our eggs in Peterson's basket? You said you made *calls*. Plural. We're not going to wait to see what else comes back?"

Jennings leaned back in his chair and put his hands behind his head. "Megan, I made three calls. Two of the guys I called, I woke up. They said they'd poke around, but hadn't heard anything. When I called Peterson, he was on his way out the door. To Raleigh. Said he was *just about to call me*." He twirled his finger in the air, noting his disbelief.

"And that means he'd already heard something." She nodded.

"Like I said. Retired. Not gone."

"What about them?" She pointed to Boz and Eli.

Jennings turned his attention to Eli. "You staying or going?"

Eli curled his lip. "Well, I was sort of looking forward to going back and getting into it with Bungard, but. . ." He waved a hand in the air. "I really like Uncle Boz's chef hat. I just don't think I'm ready to part with it so soon."

"Good. Then you're with her." Then to Boz, "And you're going to go get Jon."

Megan immediately felt her heart sink. She had wanted to be the one to go get Jon. Her feelings for him had grown more each day he had been gone. She laughed to herself. She remembered when they had met how she could hardly stand him. And now she was jealous that Jennings was sending Boz to get him.

She had to admit, though, it was the right move. Boz was a former operative. She was an FBI agent. A computer specialist, at that. She knew she didn't have the skills to operate in a theater like the one Jon was in. If anyone was going to get him, Boz was the right guy. Raleigh was still American soil. And that meant it was her territory. She narrowed her eyes and looked at her new partner. "I appreciate everything you've done, Eli. And I'm glad to have you along. But. . ."

"Hey, I'm just along for the ride." He held up his palms.

Megan nodded.

"Unless someone starts something," he finally said. "And then I'm going to finish it."

Megan shook her head and grabbed the door. "Do they just upload you guys with the same generic program at spy school?"

Eli stood to follow and smiled at Boz and Jennings. "No, milady. I'm afraid we're uploaded with that from birth!"

"Just let me do the talking when we see Peterson," she said.

CHAPTER 9

Farid Naser was hyperventilating. He sat down on the couch that was provided in the private lounge area and placed his head between his knees.

Breathe, you idiot! In from the nose. . .out through the mouth. Just breathe.

It hadn't really hit him what he'd done until they'd stepped off the plane a few minutes ago and he'd set foot on Moroccan soil. He'd left. All of it. Just threw his lab coat in the trash on the way out the door and got on a plane to Africa. A private plane. Completely bypassing customs. With a complete stranger. *Who does that?*

But she wasn't a stranger. At least not in his mind. He'd spent weeks by her side. Watching her. Listening to her breathe. Imagining who she was. Where she came from. What her story was. . . Imagining a life with her. And then she woke up.

Still—it all happened so fast—he was here. In Morocco. She hadn't explained much yet. She was even more secretive about how she got the plane to get out of there in the first place. She hadn't said more than a few sentences on the flight. She was tired, she explained. Everything was still groggy, she had said. She slept. For almost the entire flight.

Now, here he was. Sitting in the Salon Convives de Marque lounge. Alone.

"Stay here," she had said. "The lounge has anything you need. I'll be gone less than an hour. When I get back, we'll need to leave again."

"Where to? And where are you going?"

"You'll see. And I can't tell you. But I will."

"You'll see!" he muttered to himself again, now sitting here trying to catch his breath.

He checked his watch. She'd been gone for only fifteen minutes now. He lifted his head and looked around. A small bar sat to one side

48

of the room and some food trays at the other. He decided he could use a sandwich. And a drink. He moved across the room and fixed himself both.

He sat back down on the couch and had been eating for only a few minutes when the door to the lounge opened. He checked his watch again. Thirty minutes had passed. But she was back. She smiled and came to him.

"Okay. We're ready. Let's go."

"I thought you said an hour. Where to? What's going on?"

"I said *less than* an hour. And I told you. You'll see."

He sat there. Still.

She reached for his hand. "Farid, we need to go. I'll explain on the way."

He wiped his mouth with the napkin and took her hand, leaving the sandwich. He picked up the glass of bourbon and drank it down in two long gulps. But when she pulled at his arm for him to stand, he pulled his hand back.

"Alex, listen." He ran his fingers through his hair. "I just completely walked away from my life. Why, I don't know. Other than, I just want to be with you. But I can't just follow you around like a puppy, not knowing anything about what's going on or where we're going."

He stood up and grabbed her by her arm. "I'm not stupid. Nor am I naive. I don't pretend to think that you're someone who happened into my hospital by virtue of some weird accident. I've imagined a thousand times the reason you ended up on my floor. And though I may not know the answer, I know it involves something that could get you into a lot of trouble. And now probably me, too. But I'm here. I'm here because. . ." He let go of her and held his arms out to his side.

"Farid—"

"No, listen. I'm here because I want to be. Because you're here. And I knew you couldn't stay in Dubai. And I didn't want to never see you again."

"Farid—"

"Please, let me finish." He took her hand again. "You don't have to tell me everything right now. But I do need you to tell me."

She blew out a long sigh. "I will. I'll tell you everything. As soon as we get on the plane."

"Okay." That was going to have to be good enough for now, he conceded. But she was going to have to answer at least one thing. "Where are we going?"

"We're going to Boston."

CHAPTER 10

Washington, DC

Boz let Eli and Megan leave Jennings's office and waited a few more seconds until he spoke. "What aren't you telling me, Kevin?"

Jennings looked at him straight faced. "You know everything I know."

"But. . ."

"No but. I'm just worried."

"About Jon?"

"About the whole thing, Boz. We've been sitting around here for weeks on our heels. The Chinese have stopped taking potshots at us. The country—what's left of it—is starting to get back to some semblance of normalcy—if you can call it that. And Walker is actually doing a decent job of managing this crisis."

"And then Quinn makes contact and says it's all about to fire back up again."

"Exactly! It's no secret that there are those around here who aren't happy with the fact that we're not advancing back on the Chinese. It was only a matter of time before something like this would come up."

"Kevin, you and I both know this is what we're supposed to be doing. If God wanted us to take back our country right now, He would have made that perfectly clear. Instead, He has chosen to humble us. We need to be happy that He has spared us at all."

"I agree. But that doesn't stop the fact that we're now looking for another Marianne Levy."

"Listen, if someone really is organizing something, he's not going to be able to keep it quiet. News like that is going to travel fast and gain support. Let's just wait to hear back from Megan and Eli. Then we'll figure it out."

Jennings got up, walked around his desk, and closed the door. Boz could see there was something else Jennings wanted to tell him. But the man was holding back for some reason.

"What is it?"

"Boz, are you sure? About what you said? About God making it perfectly clear?"

"What? That we are supposed to just move on from here, and not advance back on the Chinese?"

"Yeah."

"Why? C'mon, Jennings. What aren't you telling me?"

Jennings sat down in the chair next to Boz. "Listen, can I talk to you in like a. . .pastor-type. . .or whatever it's called—"

"You mean, like pastoral counseling?"

"Yeah. That."

"I would be honored."

"Boz, I've been going to church off and on my whole life. I mean, I guess I always believed, but. . .you know. . .I—"

"You never really walked the walk."

"Yeah, that's it."

"Okay. Well, let me ask you a question. Where's your heart? I mean now."

"I think it's where it's supposed to be. I mean, I want to do whatever God wants from me. I never really cared about that before. But recently, I've found myself questioning every decision I make. Asking myself, *Is that really what God wants?*"

Boz laughed out loud and shook his head. "Kevin, you're fine." He stood up and reached for the door. "You holler at me when Quinn calls back and tells us where Jon is. We need to get our boy back."

"President Grant woke up this morning."

Boz stopped cold. He took his hand off the handle and came back to his chair. "Calvin is awake?"

Jennings stared straight ahead, like he was a million miles away. Finally, he folded his hands in his lap and nodded. "Sit back down, Boz."

Boz's heart sank. He and President Grant had been close friends for years. Like brothers. Boz had even baptized Grant's children. When the Russian woman had shot Calvin before the invasion, Boz thought he'd lost his friend. But Calvin was strong. He'd managed to survive, albeit in a coma. The doctors had said they had no idea whether he would ever wake up. Or if he did, whether or not there would be any residual effects or permanent damage. Boz sat back down and prepared himself for the worst. "How is he?"

"They don't know yet. He only woke up for a few minutes."

"What about the coma?"

"They say he's responsive. But they're keeping him sedated until they can run tests. They want him out of the coma, but need him unconscious to do their evaluation for brain damage and any lasting effects."

"When will they know?"

"They haven't said. But the initial conversation with him leads them to believe that Calvin seemed to have full control over his thoughts. I mean he was confused about what had happened. But he remembered everything once they told him. He seemed to be fully functional. I mean brainwise."

Boz let out the breath he hadn't realized he'd been holding. "That's incredible! That's great news."

"Yes, it is. But it brings up another problem."

"What are you talking about? What problem?"

"Boz, technically, Calvin is still the president of the United States. If he wakes up and is fully capable of continuing in his office, what are we going to tell Walker?"

Boz stood up from his chair. "We'll cross that bridge when we come to it." He moved past Jennings again and grabbed the door.

Jennings nodded. "Right. You've got a bag to pack. And if I had to guess, you haven't had to pack *that* bag for a long time. You better go get it ready."

Boz knew exactly what Jennings was talking about. He was about to go dark. He was going to cross over into Chinese territory and bring back one of their own. And that meant that the only resources he would have would be the ones he could carry with him.

"You call me, Jennings. The moment you hear anything. And I mean about Jon or Calvin."

He pulled the door closed behind him and headed for home. Not a single morning, afternoon, or evening had passed since Calvin had been shot that Boz hadn't spent time on his knees, praying for God to heal his friend. As he walked down the hall, a single tear slid down his cheek. He lifted his head to the sky.

"Thank You, Lord."

CHAPTER 11

Chinese Territory

Mr. Keene, wake up. . . . Mr. Keene. . . It's me, Quinn. . . . *Jon!*"

Jon Keene felt his eyelids flutter. A voice. Someone calling his name in a hurried whisper.

"Jon Keene. . .wake up! I need you to wake up!"

He felt the blood stir in his head. Everything was still foggy. Where was he? He needed to open his eyes. *C'mon Keene, get ahold of yourself. You need to wake up. . .something's not right.*

He forced his eyes open. Someone was standing over him. A hand. . . coming at him. . .reaching for his throat. . .

Immediately the adrenaline kicked in. His fight-or-flight response was engaged. He reached up and grabbed the man's wrist and used the man's weight to carry him off to the side. He sat up, still holding on to the man, and reached for the first thing he saw. A small wrought-iron lamp in the stand beside him. He grabbed hold of it and brought it up to swing.

Suddenly, the other man had reversed his position and caused him to lose his own balance. In only a second, the man was back on top of him. Keene struggled to fight him off, but he was still weak. The other man quickly overpowered him and had him subdued. But he wasn't hurting him. The man had one hand holding him down by his chest, and the other clamped tightly over his mouth. The look in his eyes told Keene that he wasn't trying to hurt him. Rather, he was trying to keep him still and quiet. After a few seconds, Keene recognized the man. Suddenly everything came back. The prison, the escape, the hotel room. . .coming in and out of consciousness to see the Prophet—Quinn Harrington—taking care of him. But now something was wrong. And Keene understood. He nodded.

Slowly the man lifted his hand off Keene's mouth and put it to his own. *Shh.*

Slowly, Quinn walked over to the window, tiptoeing as quietly as he could. He leaned against the glass and ever so slightly pulled the corner of the drape back an inch. Keene watched as Quinn stayed glued to what was happening outside. Finally, Quinn gently placed the corner of the drape back into place and turned back to Keene.

"Armed Chinese guard," he whispered. "First time I've seen them here."

"Where?" Keene whispered back.

"Here. At the hotel. It's been quiet since I brought you here. Haven't seen any Chinese soldiers at all. But I guess I should've expected it sooner or later."

"Why? Did God tell you they would come?"

"Mr. Keene, I know you and I haven't seen eye to eye on everything. I know you think that I'm some kind of nut—"

Keene waved him off. "No, I'm serious. I'm not bustin' your chops. Did God tell you they would come?"

Quinn looked at him with a questioning stare.

"A lot's happened since you and I last spoke, Quinn."

"Yes, I guess it has."

"When you came for me in the prison. . .you said God had heard my prayer."

"I did. . .but—"

"Let's just say He and I had a come-to-Jesus meeting. Literally! I think you and I play for the same team now."

Keene watched a smile crease Quinn's face.

"Guess He didn't tell you that, huh?"

"He might have mentioned it," Quinn said. "I just wasn't sure how you were going to react to me. . .now that you're. . .you know."

"Right. Well, then we better get to it. How do we get out of here?"

"Mr. Keene—"

"Jon. Please call me Jon. I hate Mr. Keene."

"Okay, then. Jon." Quinn walked back over to the window and pulled the drapes back an inch. "Looks like they're gone." He let the drapes fall back into place again. "But I'm not sure you're ready to move. You were pretty beat up and sick."

"Well, Quinn, I'd say you missed your calling in life to be a nurse, or a doctor, but that would pretty much be a demotion on your part, huh? I feel great. I'm starving! But great."

And he did. He actually felt alive for the first time since getting captured by General Chin and his men. Still a little weak, but other than that, great. The bruising from the beatings could still be seen on his arms and legs, but the effects of them had passed. He felt like he'd just woken up from a twelve-hour night of sleep and had a hot shower.

Quinn made a face and said, "Yeah, doesn't surprise me."

Keene didn't understand. "I'm sorry?"

"Nothing. Never mind. I guess we need to get you ready to move out."

"Move out? Move out where?"

"Home."

Instantly Keene was angry. "What do you mean? I'm not going anywhere, except after Chin."

"No"—Quinn poked him in his chest—"you're going wait here for Boz. He's going to take you back across the border. That's what He wants." Quinn pointed a finger in the air.

"I might be new at this whole *Christian* thing, but there's no way I'm going back across that border without Chin's head on a stick. Got it?" He poked Quinn back.

"Jon, you need to listen to—"

"*Quinn,* you need to listen to me! Do you know the hell that man put me—our country—through? Huh? Do you? He's responsible for everything!"

Quinn backed away and nodded. "Beloved, never avenge yourselves, but leave it to the wrath of God, for it is written, 'Vengeance is mine, I will repay, says the Lord.'"

Suddenly, something like a sharp pain shot through Keene's heart. It made him slump and he had to sit back down.

"That's Romans 12:19," Quinn said. He pulled one of the chairs out from under the small table against the wall and dragged it over to where Keene was sitting on the bed. "Jon, you need to understand. God is responsible for this. For everything. Yes, Chin, because of his sinful, wicked heart, was used to perpetrate this act on our country. But make no mistake. God has brought this judgment. And though He used Chin's wickedness to bring this about, Chin acted because God decreed it. He will exact His justice upon Chin, whether it's in this life or the next. But know this. Right now, until God says otherwise, Chin is no longer your concern."

They sat in silence for a few seconds. Finally Quinn reached over to the bedside table and poured Keene a glass of water. "Here."

Keene took it and drank.

"That sharp pain you felt just a second ago. . .that was the truth of God's Word cutting you to your soul, Jon."

Keene lifted his head. "How did you know—"

Quinn clucked his tongue and rolled his eyes.

"Oh, yeah. Right." Keene set the water back down and rubbed his hands over his face. "Is He going to do that to me every time?"

Quinn bobbed his head back and forth for a second, as if contemplating. "No, I don't think so. That was just to get your attention. The problem you now have is God has decided to let our country remain."

"Great! So what's the prob—"

"Remain. . .as it is now," Quinn interrupted him. "If we are to return to the nation we once were, we are going to have to change a lot of things. And I'm just going to be honest with you, Jon. You and I may never see that in our lifetimes. When Israel was dealt judgment in the Old Testament, sometimes it would be hundreds of years before God would restore them."

Keene felt the air go out of him.

"In the meantime, you and the others are needed to set that course in motion. And that's why you can't stay here."

"I don't understand."

"You will. He will begin to reveal certain things to you. Others, I'll have to inform you."

Keene slapped a hand on his leg. "Why? Why can't He just tell—" He looked up into the sky. "Why can't You just tell me?"

" 'For my thoughts are not your thoughts, neither are your ways my ways, declares the Lord,' " Quinn said. "Isaiah 55:8."

Keene pinched the bridge of his nose, thankful there wasn't another sharp pain. "Okay, then. So what?"

"A new threat has risen from within our borders. One greater than even Marianne Levy and Chin. You need to stop it."

Keene looked at him stone faced. "Seriously? 'A new threat has risen. . . .' Who talks like that? Are you going to do that every time you—"

"Are you going to play games? Or do you want to listen?"

"I'm sorry. I guess I need to work on my personality a little."

Quinn just stared at him for a few seconds. Then, "Yes, you do. Sorry for snapping at you like that."

Keene nodded.

"All right, then. As I was saying. . .China is the last of our worries right now. If God is going to allow us to be restored—at some point in the future—we're going to have to still be a nation."

"What's that supposed to mean?"

"It means that something is happening over there right now that could tear the very fabric of the United States apart. And it's up to you to stop it."

"How? I mean, what am I supposed to do? What's going on? Did He say?"

"No. Just that you can't allow it to happen."

"What about Boz, Megan, and the others?"

"They, too, are involved. But they need you. You're the one who will stop it."

"How?"

"Don't know. But *you* will."

Keene stood up from the bed and started pacing back and forth. None of this made sense. The Chinese were the ones who invaded their country. Why weren't they the biggest threat? "I have no idea what you're saying. I don't understand."

"I'm saying"—Quinn stood to match his stare—"that you need to get home and find out what's going on. And when you do, you need to stop it."

Keene looked down and noticed for the first time that he was wearing some sort of hospital gown, with only his boxer shorts on underneath. He swept the room with his eyes and saw his clothes piled up on the small table against the wall. He walked over and grabbed the pile. He undid the gown, let it fall, and pulled his shirt down over his head.

To Quinn he said, "Then I suggest we get moving."

CHAPTER 12

Raleigh, North Carolina

Pemberton spit the tip of his fourth Louixs for the day over the banister of his front porch. The wind outside was whipping back and forth, which made lighting the cigar difficult. It was starting to look like maybe this unseasonably warm weather had run its course. He hoped not. With this weather, he had been able to get almost an entire second crop out of his tobacco production. He cupped his hand and flipped the lid of his old lighter. A collector's edition, hand-engraved Zippo. He took a long pull as the flame disappeared into the belly of the rich tobacco. Even after twenty years of his favorite cigar, he still smiled at that first drag.

The jangling from the old landline phone forced him to get up from his rocking chair and go back inside. He had been expecting any one of three calls today. He figured this was one of them. He grabbed the handle and answered the same way he had since he could remember.

"It's your dime."

"Gavin, this is Joe."

"Yeah?"

There was silence on the line for a few seconds. Finally the governor spoke.

"I just had a very interesting phone call."

"Yeah? By who?"

"I think you know."

"Joe, I'm many things. A mind reader isn't one of them."

"I'm talking about my father-in-law."

"Interesting."

"*Interesting!* Have you lost your mind? Do you know what could've happened if he'd said no?"

"Didn't have a choice. This doesn't happen without him."

58

"And you didn't think that I needed to know that?"

"Not yet."

"Not yet! You've got to be kidding me! This whole thing. . . I'm the one going to be sticking my neck out front on this. I don't appreciate being blindsided by my own father-in-law telling me something that you should've already told me."

Pemberton grabbed the cradle of the phone and stretched the cord outside, back out onto the porch. He flicked the ash of the Louixs over the rail and blew on the tip to stoke the ember. He could tell the governor was waiting for a response, as the other end of the line had gone quiet. He took another long drag from the expensive cigar, swished the smoke around the inside of his mouth, and slowly blew it out again. Finally, he cleared his throat.

"Milton and I didn't tell you because we didn't want you running to him before we had a chance to talk to him. You might be the face of this little shindig, but Irving's the backbone. He needed to hear it from me. Not you. Because I'm running this show. Not you."

That seemed to quiet him for a second. Pemberton knew the governor was a great man of the people, but he was not, nor had he ever been, a great strategist. He was the face that everyone liked and followed. But his ideas had never been his own. The political machine that had driven him into the governorship of the state was, and always had been, Pemberton. And the governor knew it.

"Listen, I didn't mean to jump all over you. It's just that—"

"Forget it," Pemberton said. He let the line stay quiet for a few more seconds just for emphasis. He needed the governor to know his place. When he was sure he'd made his point, he continued, "Cancel whatever plans you have for tomorrow night. You and I are going to meet up with Milton and Irving at the Shed. Seven thirty. Don't be late."

"Can't do it. I'm supposed to have dinner with Senators Buchannan and Gilmore. Now that we've got all these refugees—I guess that's what you'd call them—from across the mountain living here, we've got to figure out how to get them housed—especially before this weather turns—and their kids back into school. Just another stupid mandate from President Walker."

"Cancel it. Seven thirty. The Shed."

Pemberton placed the receiver back in the cradle and took another long drag from the Louixs.

CHAPTER 13

Boz sat on the edge of the bed looking at the rucksack he'd prepared, going over each and every detail, making sure he didn't forget something. Forgetting something that needed to be in *this* bag could be the difference between life and death. For him and Jon. And he wasn't about to make a mistake like that. He unzipped the bag, dumped its contents out on the bed, and started again. Just to make double sure.

When he was satisfied that he was as prepared as he needed to be, he walked downstairs and set the bag by the front door. He then moved past the living room and into the kitchen. He wasn't terribly hungry, but the old soldier in him reminded him of the military's rule number one: *always eat and sleep when you can*. You never knew when you would have the chance to do either again.

He took the sandwich and chips into his office, set them down, and grabbed his Bible, remembering Boz Hamilton's rule number one: *always feed on the Word of God every chance you get*. You never knew when you would have the chance to again. He thumbed through the old, worn-out leather-bound pages until he came to one of his favorite passages. He said a quick prayer and grabbed the sandwich and began to read.

He'd just finished the last few chips and all of 1 Peter when the sat-phone on his desk rang. He swallowed down his last mouthful and clicked the button on the phone.

"This is Boz."

"Hello, Mr. Hamilton."

"I've been waiting for your call, Quinn. I'm ready to go. Just say when and where." Then, "How is he?"

"Remarkably well. Which is good, because you two have another long road ahead of you."

"I'll take care of him."

"Yes, I know you will."

An awkward silence hung in the air for a moment, as if the Prophet wanted to say more but couldn't.

"Is everything okay?" Boz felt that sinking feeling in his gut.

"Everything is fine. You'll need to leave now to make it where we are by dark. You'll need to move fast once you're here. You'll only have a few hours before daylight to get back across the mountains." Then, "Are you armed?"

Boz was slightly taken aback. "Yes, of course." Immediately, he sensed the Prophet was going to tell him God had directed that he go in there with just his bare hands. A slight panic coursed through his veins. *Okay, God,* he thought. *If that's how You want it. . .*

"Good. You cannot allow yourselves to get captured again. At any cost. Do you understand, Mr. Hamilton?"

"Roger that," Boz answered, allowing himself to slip back into the black ops persona. "What's your location?"

"Just outside of Nashville. A small row of motel rooms. There's a road here called Murfreesboro Road. Runs directly out from the city. About two and a half miles south is where you'll find us. Pinkish stucco building sitting back from the south end of the road. Lots of unsavory characters out and about. Shouldn't be too hard to find."

"What's the room number?"

"Twelve. All the way in the back."

"Okay, so I guess I'll see you sometime around dark, then."

"Just Jon, Mr. Hamilton."

"I'm sorry?"

"Just Jon. I'm afraid the two of you will be journeying without me. But don't worry. If I'm needed, He'll send me to you."

Boz was immediately disheartened. He had thought about sitting down and having conversations with Quinn about the whole Prophet thing. He was so intrigued and in awe of how God had used Quinn. Boz just wanted to pick his brain. See how it all worked.

Boz sighed. "Okay, then. I guess we'll just wait to see if we hear from you again."

"Good-bye, Mr. Hamilton."

"Good-bye. Oh, and Quinn?"

"Yes?"

"It's Boz."

"So it is. Good-bye, Boz."

As soon as the line went dead, Boz punched in a new number. Jennings answered on the second ring.

"Quinn just called. I'm on."

"Then go get our boy."

"I'm walking out the door as we speak."

CHAPTER 14

Raleigh, North Carolina

Megan opened the door to the small café and walked inside, Eli right behind her. The café was where Jennings said they would find Peterson.

They'd spent the three-hour drive mostly in silence. Eli was asleep, thirty minutes in. But that was good. Megan didn't feel much like talking anyway. Her mind was racing, thinking about Boz and Jon. How was Boz going to get across the border undetected? Was Jon really okay? What if they got caught trying to get back? And then there was this new threat. What was going on? And who was doing it? Lots of questions. No answers.

Eli woke up about an hour out of Raleigh. They spent the rest of the drive with Eli looking at a map, and Megan following his directions. They found the café easily enough. Now they just had to find Peterson.

The place was a normal coffee shop, a bacon-and-eggs kind of place. Not a lot of patrons, but the ones there, Megan could tell, were probably regulars. Jennings had given them a description of Peterson, but it wouldn't have mattered. The man stuck out like a sore thumb, with his sport coat, khaki pants, and loafers, sitting among a bunch of old men wearing overalls, blue jeans, and ball caps.

"I thought you guys said once a spy, always a spy," Megan muttered over her shoulder.

Eli rolled his eyes. "Yeah, well. . ."

They walked over and sat down at Peterson's table. Peterson, who had not even glanced at them as they walked in, looked up from his newspaper.

"I saw you two from the parking lot. Not very subtle, don't you think?"

"Really?" It was Megan. "And you with your suit coat and loafers? Yeah, you blend right in."

Peterson smiled and turned to Eli. "I like her."

Eli rolled his eyes again.

"Listen," Megan started in a whisper, "you need to leave here with us. We can go somewhere we can talk."

Peterson sighed. "Jennings thinks I'm going to get myself hurt. Doesn't he?"

"Or killed," Eli said.

"Bah!" Peterson waved him off. "I'm seventy-six years old. Who cares!"

"Okay, let's go." Megan stood up and grabbed Peterson by the arm.

"Where are we going?"

"Somewhere where you're not going to draw attention." She looked around the room and noticed that some of the patrons were looking at them. "Like you're doing now."

Peterson reluctantly stood and allowed her to lead him out the door. They got in the car and pulled away from the diner.

"What was all that about?"

"Look, Mr. Peterson, I know you're just trying to help. But whatever it is you're looking for down here is something that's probably going to turn out really bad." She jerked a thumb over her shoulder to Eli. "Jennings sent me and him to find out what it is. Now, if you've got information that will help us out, you need to tell us. But going around asking questions on your own is just plain stupid."

Peterson waved a hand in the air. "Ah, you're probably right. But I'm not about to sit by and wait for something else to happen around here. Bad enough we already lost most of our country."

Megan figured she wasn't going to win any arguments with the old man. So instead, she decided to try a different tactic. "Mr. Peterson, no one expects anyone to just sit by. We've all been affected by this. You were a valuable asset to the Company. Jennings said that if anyone could find out what was going on, you were the guy."

That brought a smile to the old man's face.

"So if you've heard anything or have a lead on anything, we need to know. Let's face it. You might still have the heart, but you don't have the physical ability. Let *us* traipse around and poke our noses into dark corners."

Peterson looked at her with a confused look. "Can I ask you a question?"

Megan shrugged. "Sure. Go ahead."

"Who *are* you?"

She started laughing and realized that she and Eli hadn't even introduced themselves earlier. They had just shuffled the old man into the car and sped off. She stuck her hand out across the seat.

"I'm Megan Taylor." She shook his hand and pointed again over her shoulder into the backseat. "That's Eli Craig."

Peterson shifted in his seat to look at Eli. "Craig? Hmm. . .Craig. . . yeah, I knew a Craig. Englishman. Good man. What was his name. . . ?"

"Mackenzie," Eli said.

"Yeah, that's it! Mackenzie. Everyone called him Mac."

"My father," Eli admitted.

"Hmph. . .well, good to know you, son." Peterson nodded to Eli. Then to Megan, "Don't know any Taylors."

Megan smiled and pulled the car off the road into an old abandoned junkyard. She and Eli had found this place on their way to the diner and had picked it specifically for talking with Peterson. She put the lever in PARK and shut off the key.

"Okay, now that everyone knows everyone, let's talk. What do you know?"

Peterson shifted again in his seat so that he was facing both of them. "About a week ago, I got a call. Got an old friend used to be heavily involved in the political goings-on in Raleigh. He calls me and asks if I know about a guy named Gavin Pemberton. Well, I tell him I've never heard of him, but that doesn't mean anything, and I ask why. He tells me that this guy, Pemberton, is a mean ol' son of a. . .well, you know. Says Pemberton has his fingers in everything down here. Comes from old money. Tobacco. Family's been in the business for over two hundred years. Anyway, says Pemberton likes to stick his nose in places it doesn't belong."

"Like where?" Megan asked.

"Like everywhere." Peterson laughed. "Including politics. Seems this guy has been single-handedly responsible for the last four gubernatorial wins in the state."

"How's that?" Eli asked.

"Money, son. Money! Heck, everyone knows—well, you might not, being a Brit and all, but you,"—he pointed to Megan—"you know how that game works. Whoever has the most money runs the show."

Megan shrugged. "Mr. Peterson, people have been saying that for years, but you just can't say—"

"Then you're naive, young lady!" Peterson's demeanor changed suddenly. His eyes narrowed and his lip drew tight. "Listen, I may be old, but I'm not senile. I've been around this ball of mud and doing this job longer than both of you. So don't patronize me."

Megan pushed back in her seat. Peterson's sudden change caught her off guard. "I wasn't trying to—"

"Never mind," Peterson cut her off. "I didn't mean to bark at you like that. Sorry. But that doesn't change the fact that politics is politics. Money talks, young lady. And I'm telling you, this Pemberton is bad news. I asked around a little and nobody, and I mean nobody, will talk about him."

Megan looked over her shoulder at Eli. "So what do you think?"

"I think Mr. Peterson, here, isn't being completely forthcoming."

"Yeah."

Peterson lowered his eyes.

"Mr. Peterson. . ."

"Oh, all right!" He shifted in his seat again and folded his arms over his chest. "I might've heard about a judge that Pemberton is close with. If someone knows anything about what Pemberton's up to, he'd know."

"Name?" Megan said impatiently.

"Milton Hayes."

"Where can I find him?" Megan asked.

"Well, I'm told he comes in that diner, which I was sitting in before you so rudely removed me, every morning and afternoon for coffee."

Megan looked over the seat. "Eli?"

"I think it would behoove us to find this Judge Hayes and see what he knows."

She bit her bottom lip and narrowed her eyes. "My thoughts exactly."

"What about me?" It was Peterson.

Megan turned the key and pulled the shift lever. "We'll drop you back off at your car. And then you can drive yourself back to Newport News. How's that?"

Peterson turned back around in his seat, facing the front. "Guess I don't have much choice."

Megan didn't even look at him. "Nope. And that comes directly from Jennings."

CHAPTER 15

Boston, Massachusetts

Alex Smith gathered her things and made her way off the G-5, Farid Naser following behind. There was a car waiting for them at the bottom of the stairs. They threw their bags in the trunk and got inside.

Alex had told Farid not to say anything once they landed; they should just be completely silent. If there needed to be any talking, she would handle it. The driver got back inside after closing the trunk and, keeping his head facing forward, reached his hand over the headrest.

"I was told you would have an address for me?"

Alex placed a folded piece of paper inside the driver's hand. The driver took it and pulled away from the tarmac. No more words were exchanged.

The drive was spent in complete silence. Just like most of the plane ride. Alex was able to divert Farid's questions, promising to disclose everything once they landed and arrived at their final destination, a little house just outside of the city in a town called Middleton.

Traffic was mostly light. They were able to make the twenty-mile drive in just under forty-five minutes. However, the driver was not taking them to the house. Rather, he dropped them off in North Reading, by the high school, where Alex had a cab scheduled to pick them up. Alex waited until the driver of the sedan was out of sight before taking Farid's hand and walking across the street and down the block to the cab. The cab was waiting as they arrived. A short drive later, the cab dropped them off six blocks away from their final destination. They walked the rest of the way, still in silence. When she closed the door behind them, Farid immediately started in.

"Well, that was interesting. I don't know that I've ever been in the company of another individual and not had any form of conversation whatsoever, for so long."

His tone was filled with contempt. She understood, though. She had been nothing but vague with him for the last twelve hours. And he had been patient. But now they were here. And she had promised to tell him everything.

She had a problem, though. For whatever reason, she really liked this guy. Maybe it was because he was responsible for saving her life. Or maybe it was just because she hadn't had any kind of real relationship in. . .well, she couldn't remember, and she felt a connection to him. Whatever the reason, she wanted to tell him. Everything. She was just afraid that after doing so, he would revolt at the truth. And then she would have to kill him.

"Let's sit down, Farid."

"You own this place?"

She nodded as she moved to the sofa. "This and a few others."

Farid looked around the room. "Quaint."

"Well, it's not what I would call home. . . ." She patted the cushion beside her, gesturing for him to join her. "More of a vacation place."

Farid sat down. "You said you were going to tell me—"

"Everything," she finished for him. "Yes. I'm going to."

And she did. Everything. Everything from the day Joseph had come for her at the girls' home, to the events that had led her to his hospital. Farid hadn't moved the entire time. Not even a facial expression.

"You can breathe now," she quipped as she finished. She hadn't been able to get a read on him the entire time.

Farid blinked a few times and leaned back in his seat. He ran his hands through his hair and then sat back up. "Okay. . . Okay. Not quite what I expected, but okay."

For the first time in a long time, Alex felt her heart sink. What was she thinking? Like she was just going to tell him everything about herself and he would just be all right with it? Talk about amateur. She was an idiot! And now she was going to have to kill him. And that made her truly sorry. She had hoped, however stupid it might be. . .

"Alex. . ."

She picked her head up to look at him. He had a weird grin on his face.

"So. . .what you're saying is. . .you blew the President Grant job."

Not what she was expecting.

"No." She looked back at him with a hesitant glance. "I put a round right in the back of his head," she said. "I didn't blow anything. Last I heard, he's in a coma."

Farid raised his eyebrows and clicked his tongue playfully. "Okay. If you say so."

Definitely not what she expected.

"Oh yeah, and what would you know about it, Mr. I-fix-people-for-a-living?"

Farid's look changed to a somber one. "I've killed before."

Alex prided herself on many things. Not revealing being caught completely off guard was one of them. In her line of work, that could get you killed. But her face must have betrayed her. Because of all the things she had expected to hear from Farid. . .that was like number nine million on the list.

"Twice, actually."

"What!"

"When I was a young boy my family had no money. My father died when I was five. The man who owned our building liked to take advantage of my mother. I watched this go on for many years. When I turned seventeen, I bought a gun and followed him home one evening. I knocked on his door. When he answered, I put two bullets in his forehead."

Alex reached for his hand. "You did what you had to do."

"That's what I told myself."

"But you said twice."

"Yes. After I shot the man, his wife came running out of the bedroom. I shot her, too."

Alex felt a tingle start to spread up her spine. "And how did that make you feel?"

Farid sighed. "At first, I was repulsed by it. I was petrified that I would get caught. I spent the next six months looking over my shoulder, wondering when they would come for me. But they never did. And so I decided to become a doctor. To help save lives. I guess it was kind of my own self-imposed penance."

"But you weren't repulsed by it. Were you, Farid?"

He quickly averted his eyes but then came back to meet her stare. "No. I was. At first." He swallowed hard. "But then I realized it was the first and only time in my life that I ever felt alive. Like I had the power over life and death. And I. . .I. . ."

"You liked it. Didn't you?"

Farid just stared at her for what seemed like an hour. Finally he sighed and said, "Yes. Yes, I did."

Alex's heart was racing. She didn't know what she was feeling, but she knew it was something she'd never felt before. She grabbed Farid by the back of the neck and pulled him to her. Their lips met.

When she pulled away, he reached for her hand. "So why are we here?"

"I've been offered another job."

"What job?"

Normally, those details were only discussed between her and the client. But Farid was different. *This* was different. She wanted to tell him.

"When I left you in the airport in Morocco, I went to check an answering service that I keep. There was a message on there from someone. Someone I've never heard of. But he'd heard of me. Long story short, he was about to contract another hitter because I hadn't responded. I told him I had been indisposed. He said if I could get here in the next day or so, I could have the contract."

"Who is he?"

"Told you. Don't know yet." She stood up, grabbed her bag from the floor, and walked into the bedroom. Farid followed.

"What's the job?"

"Don't know. He'll give me details when I meet with him."

She tossed the bag on top of the bed, unzipped it, and began to unpack. "Right now, I've got to get packed and head out. You can stay here—don't worry, it's safe. Or you can come with me. But either way, I need to leave within the hour."

"Within the hour? We just got here."

"And he wants to meet tonight."

Farid didn't hesitate. "Yes, I'll come with you."

"Good. We can stop on the way out of town and do some shopping for you. But when we get there, I'll need to meet with him alone. I can drop you at a café or something for a little while. It should only take a half hour or so. I'll come pick you up afterward and then I'll take you around to see the city."

"Where?"

"Raleigh, North Carolina."

CHAPTER 16

Nashville, Chinese Territory

It was dark when Keene woke up. His head was fuzzy and he couldn't remember why he was lying here. The last thing he remembered was talking with Quinn and having decided that they needed to get out of here. The United States was in trouble again. Next thing he knew, he was opening his eyes here, to find himself alone and still in this dank, crummy hotel room. And Quinn was gone.

Remembering there had been Chinese guards outside the last time he had woken up, he didn't immediately reach for the light. He blinked his eyes a few times, trying to get used to the level of darkness surrounding him. When he was sure he had his wits about him, he quietly got out of the bed and walked slowly over to the window. He pulled back the curtain and looked around outside.

The way the room was situated, within the block of rooms, gave him a good view of the street in front of him and the main road that ran in front of the hotel. The occasional car passed by, and down the street, he could see some people milling around what looked to be an old convenience store. But for the most part, the place seemed quiet and left alone.

Satisfied it was all clear, he turned on the small light on the side table. A handwritten note lay beside the lamp.

Jon, I'm sorry, but I couldn't let you leave. And just for the record, I didn't knock you out. That was Him. I just put you in the bed afterward. Anyway, you need to know Boz is on his way. He should be there sometime after dark, barring on any unforeseen circumstances. You CANNOT leave until he gets there. It is imperative that you both make it back safely. And you're going to need each other to do that. Trust me.

*Here's what you need to know for now: God has spared our
country and given us another opportunity to turn to Him as a
nation. And He desires greatly that we should do this. However,
there are those within our own borders who stand as enemies of God.
They would have us turn our backs on the mercy that has spared
us and given us this chance. They would trust their own abilities
and knowledge. And unopposed, they are a dangerous threat to the
survival of our nation, as well as the rest of the world. You must stop
them. If you don't, the opportunity for repentance will have passed.
And our nation will be lost forever.*

May He be with you,
Quinn

"Seriously!"

Keene crumpled the paper into a ball and threw it across the room.

"Seriously!" he said again. "God, are You kidding me? I'm barely a
believer myself. I royally screwed up the last time You tried to warn us.
And You want *me* to try and stop something else now? Seriously? This is
ridiculous, You know that?" He looked up at the sky and wagged his finger.
"See, Boz told me about this. . .how You tell one of us to do something,
and then expect us to just blindly trust that it'll all work out. I mean,
really. How am I supposed to stop something, when I have no idea what
I'm trying to stop! Please, God, please—just tell me. Just tell me who it
is, where they are, and I'll go, right now. I mean, You talk to Quinn. Why
can't You talk to me? If I'm the one You're sending out to stop this junk. . ."

He sat down on the bed and strained to hear something. Anything.
But the only sound that came was from the buzzing of the light from the
little side table.

"You're not going to say anything to me, are You?" He looked up at
the ceiling for a few seconds. "Yeah, didn't think so." He lay back on the
bed and rubbed his forehead.

He had been lying there for a few minutes when he heard it. Someone
was outside. Quickly, he sat up in the bed and killed the light. He moved
swiftly across the room and loosed his belt from his trousers. He wrapped
one end around his left hand and held the other end with his right like a
garrote. He stepped quietly across the room, so that he would be behind
the door when it opened. He steadied his breathing and waited.

The dead bolt began to turn slowly. Someone was picking the lock.

Another ten seconds and the knob on the door slowly began to turn. Keene hoped it was Boz, but he wasn't about to just holler through the door. If it was the Chinese, he wanted to be able to surprise them. Probably the same reason Boz—if it was him—wasn't announcing himself on the other side of the door.

The door slowly swung open. Keene saw the reflection of light from the streetlight outside as it shimmered off the barrel of the Kimber 1911 .45 semiautomatic pistol that appeared in the crack as the door began to open. Keene recognized the pistol and thought about having some fun. But he didn't want to draw any unnecessary attention, either.

He readied himself—just in case he was mistaken—and whispered, "Boz, it's me."

The barrel of the gun lowered and the door pushed the rest of the way open. Boz stepped inside and swept the room with the Kimber. "You alone? Everything okay?"

Keene stepped forward and closed the door. "I'm good." He crossed the room to his friend and embraced him in a huge bear hug. "It's good to see you."

Boz was squeezing him back. "You, too, Jon. You, too."

After a few seconds, the two stepped back from each other. Keene quickly grabbed the backpack he had started packing earlier. "This is all I have. Let's blow this Popsicle stand."

"My thoughts exactly," Boz said.

Keene eyed the blued barrel of the Kimber Boz held. "You got one of those for me?"

"Sorry, bud." Boz held the .45 up and waggled it. "This guy's mine. But I brought you his little brother." He reached inside his waistband and produced an M&P subcompact 9mm. He tossed it to Keene.

Keene ejected the magazine to see if it was full. He pulled back the slide and noted that the chamber was loaded. He replaced the magazine, stuck the pistol into his own waistband. "Okay, then. Let's go."

Boz put his hand on Keene's chest to stop him from walking out the door. "You follow me. I've already sussed this place out. There's a little Quick Mart about two hundred yards down the road. Couple Chinese guards hanging out there. But they shouldn't be any problem. Long as we stay clear of them."

"What's our transport back?"

"There's a main road about a mile up called Briley Parkway. I got a car

73

stashed up there. But we need to be careful. Chinese got checkpoints and roadblocks set up about every twenty miles out. We'll try to stick close to the interstate, but we may have to bail onto secondary roads."

Keene let out a long breath and nodded. "Man, I don't care if we have to see every square inch of this state, if it means getting back across that mountain range into US territory."

"Roger that," Boz said. "We might just have to." He checked his own weapon again. "Let's roll."

While both men had been trained how to exit a hostile environment quietly and undetected, they agreed the best course of action, in this case, would be to act casually. Like they were supposed to be there. They would deal with the what-if when and if it became necessary. There was a lot of open space that needed to be covered before getting back to the car. Dodging in and out of bushes or behind parked cars might draw even more attention.

The two set out on foot, Boz in front, Keene following a couple of paces behind, as the shoulder of the road was narrow. Even though the time of night was late, there were others milling about. This portion of Murfreesboro Road was home to all kinds of transients, junkies, prostitutes, and the like. A couple of guys walking down the side of the road was nothing out of the ordinary.

Less than a half a mile ahead, a small two-lane offshoot led away from the main road, looping up and over the main road, forming a sort of overpass. Boz stuck his arm behind his back and thumbed to Keene that they were headed that way. They had no sooner changed directions and started up the ramp when headlights from a large truck appeared from behind the cluster of trees that waited at the other end of the overpass. Boz tilted his head slightly and called over his shoulder in a hushed whisper.

"Chinese patrol. Just keep your head down and keep moving."

"Roger that."

The truck came around the bend and started down the incline of the ramp where Boz and Keene now were. The truck slowed down momentarily as it approached the two but then passed without stopping. Keene felt a small relief as he heard the driver let off the brake and the truck continued to roll down the small hill. His relief was short lived, though.

Everything in him wanted to look back over his shoulder as he heard the air brake on the military truck engage, but he knew that if he looked back over his shoulder, no matter what the reason for the truck stopping, it would take notice and become suspicious. For all he knew, the truck was stopping because the driver dropped something, or whatever other stupid reason a truck would stop in the middle of the road.

He noticed that Boz, too, had realized the truck was coming to a stop behind them. Boz had increased his pace significantly and was now almost at a slow jog. The unspoken act was communicated to Keene loud and clear. Time to move. Keene picked up his pace as the two of them rounded the top of the ramp of the offshoot road.

The sound of the gearshift being ground into REVERSE echoed up the ramp to Keene's ears. He and Boz were about fifty yards ahead of the truck, but the overpass was a good hundred and fifty yards long. The only escape was over the edge to a fifty-foot drop back onto Murfreesboro Road. Not an option. The tree line at the other end of the overpass led into a residential area. If they could make it there before the truck reached them, they could disappear into the neighborhoods around. The third option was to let the truck reach them and see what they wanted. There was chance, albeit a small one, that the Chinese soldier who was driving was just lost and needed to ask for directions. Or perhaps he was looking to score some dope and thought Keene and Boz looked like the kind of guys who could help him out.

The whining of the transmission of the truck was now screeching up the ramp. The truck was going to be on them in less than fifteen seconds. Keene caught up to Boz and was walking side by side now.

"We can't make it to the tree line before he gets up here," Keene said.

"Nope." Boz continued his pace.

"And if we run, that dude's going to get on the radio and call it in."

"Yep."

"So what do you want to do?"

"Just keep walking and let's see what happens. And keep your head down. They know what you look like. But not me. Just stay behind."

"Roger that." Keene stepped back in behind his friend and kept pace.

He had just fallen back in line when he felt the big truck rolling up behind them. The rear of the truck came into view and continued backing up until it was in front of him and Boz. The driver turned the wheel and the truck moved sideways so that it was sitting in both lanes and blocking their path. Both he and Boz stopped, standing in the wash of the headlights.

The driver's-side door opened up, and the shadow of a figure leaned out.

"Who are you two? And what are you doing out here at this time of night? It's after curfew."

"Who, us?" Boz looked around, as if the guard had been talking to someone else.

"Yes, you," the guard snapped.

Boz chuckled and waved him off. "Man, look around. There's a ton of people out after curfew. We're just a couple of Joes trying to get somewhere warm, man. It's cold out here."

Keene noted that the driver now had leveled his arm across the open door. Though it was dark, he could make out the shape of the barrel of the pistol that was now pointed at them.

"Whoa, dude!" Boz said in his best stoner voice. "What's with all the aggression, man? We ain't done nothing wrong. Just trying to get somewhere warm, man. I got a girl lives up the road here. That's where we're headed."

"Show me your papers." The guard waved them over with the barrel of his gun.

Boz turned to move in front of Keene. As he did, he mouthed, *Quietly.*

Keene nodded and understood. Boz would take the lead by moving around the front of the truck and toward the guard. Keene would follow behind. As they got closer, Boz would pick up his pace, so as to somewhat startle the guard. When that happened Keene would make his move.

Boz did just as Keene knew he would. As he rounded the hood of the truck, he pulled out his wallet from his back pocket. He started talking to the guard as if nothing was wrong, waving the wallet and mocking a protest over being stopped. As he did, Keene came in behind him and moved out and around his friend. By the time Boz had reached the door of the truck, Keene had overtaken him and had slipped off to the side unnoticed by the guard, who was focused on the commotion Boz was making. Keene rounded the door of the truck and in a split second was on top of the guard. He reached up and cupped his hand over the guard's mouth while placing his knee in the middle of the guard's back. With one quick snap, he pulled the guard's neck back and thrust his knee into the man's back. The guard immediately went limp and fell out of the truck into Keene's arms.

It all seemed so easy and perfect. Until he looked up to see Boz crashing forward into the door. A second later, he saw the butt end of the SKS-56 the second guard was holding, which had just knocked Boz over the back of the head. The second guard must have come around from the back of the truck. All of his instincts began to kick in and he was about to lunge for the guard when he heard the clank of the metal from the slide of a third guard's SKS-56 behind him.

The next thing he felt was the cold steel of the barrel of the rifle against the nape of his neck.

CHAPTER 17

It was just a couple of hours after dark when Megan and Eli finished eating back at the diner where they had found Peterson. After dropping Peterson off, they had come back to the diner to wait to see if the man Peterson had been waiting for would show up. After a couple of hours of sipping coffee and no Hayes, they decided to put a call in to Jennings to see if he could find anything out about Hayes or the other man, Pemberton. Jennings had called back an hour later and told them all he knew. Which wasn't much.

Pemberton, he had said, was a very secretive man. And good at it. The agency had never had any kind of run-in with him. He never gotten so much as even a speeding ticket that they knew of. But that didn't mean that no one had ever heard of him, either. Just as Peterson had said, Pemberton had a reputation for being in the middle of lots of goings-on. The problem was, no one could actually tell you what that meant. Hayes, on the other hand, was a little more accessible.

Milton Hayes, Jennings informed them, was a North Carolina Supreme Court Justice. Known for his socially liberal agenda, he was a fierce lawyer who had come up through the ranks as a defense attorney, getting acquitted some of North Carolina's most dubious characters. It hadn't taken long for Hayes to find himself on the bench of the Circuit Court of Appeals. Only after a year and a half on the bench, a vacancy had opened on the state's supreme court, where he was quickly confirmed as the new chief justice by the state Senate. Although it seemed out of character, Hayes had a propensity for being a friend to big business, something most liberal justices weren't. And that, Jennings had said, made him interesting.

When Hayes failed to show up at the diner, Megan and Eli decided to just go ahead and eat. They had Hayes's home address and figured by the time they had finished eating, Hayes would be at home. If Chief Justice Hayes wasn't going to come to them, they would go to Chief Justice Hayes.

More importantly—at least for Megan—was the fact that Boz should have already gotten to Keene by now. At least a hundred different scenarios were playing out in her imagination. Some—the ones she was praying for—were good. Others—the ones she expected to actually be taking place right now—not so good. She let her fork fall to the plate and sighed.

"Don't worry, Megan. Uncle Boz will be just fine."

"Yeah, I know. It's just hard to convince myself." Then, "And where's this Hayes guy? Thought Peterson said he comes in here, like, three times a day."

Eli looked around the room. "Dunno. Maybe today he had something else to do."

Megan picked her fork up again and pointed it at him. "And *that* is exactly what worries me."

"I hear you."

Megan noticed that Eli had finished his food and was just sitting there waiting on her. She had actually finished before he had but then ordered a piece of pie for dessert. She took one last bite of the sweet flaky crust and pushed away from the table. "Come on. Let's get out of here. I'd say he's probably home by now."

They left the diner and pulled out onto the road. Eli flipped the dome light on above them and opened the map again.

"Know where you're going?" he asked her.

"Isn't that why you're looking at the map?"

Eli pulled the paper down under his chin so that he could see her. "Oh, don't worry, *I* know where we're going."

"Then why are you asking me?"

"Well, I just figured since you pulled out going the wrong way, you knew a shortcut or something."

Megan frowned at him, flicked the map back at his face, and pulled a U-turn in the road.

Eli laughed and said, "That's better! Now, just go that way until you see East Chatham Street. Our friend lives down the way a bit in a neighborhood called Cary."

"Should that mean something to me?" she asked.

"Just that, from what Jennings said, it's a rather affluent little place. Apparently Mr. Hayes does quite well for himself."

"He was a scumbag defense attorney. Of course he did well for himself."

Megan didn't realize how much of an understatement that was until they turned on Hayes's street. The homes lining the road looked more like small compounds than simple residences.

"Holy cow!" She let out a low whistle.

"Yeah."

She eased the car along the road, watching the numbers of the addresses until they came to the one they wanted. Before coming to the drive she pulled over to the side of the road. Alongside them, a security wall at least seven feet tall ran the entire length of the property.

"See that?" She pointed just a short way into the drive.

"Yeah. Not surprising."

They both looked ahead to what appeared to be a guard shack. A light emanated from the single window facing the drive.

"Well, you think we should go in announced? Or you want to hop the wall?"

"I thought you FBI types liked to make a big scene."

"Yeah." She twisted her mouth side to side. "I'm not exactly like most FBI agents."

"So over the wall, then?"

She undid her seat belt and reached up to flip the switch on the dome light so it would stay off when she opened the door. Eli quickly followed her out of the vehicle.

They walked back away from the drive and followed the wall around to the back of the property.

"Here, give me a boost." Megan jumped to grab the top of the wall.

Eli grabbed her by the legs and pushed her up until she could get her forearms over the top of the wall.

"See anything?"

"Nah, just a big backyard with a gazebo and a killer water feature. This guy's like Mr. HGTV or something."

"I *meant*. . .see anything like *people*. You know. . .like security."

"Oh. No, nothing like that. Couple lights on in the north wing. Looks like an office or something from here."

"Okay, then. I'll boost you the rest of the way up. Straddle the wall then, and when I jump, grab my arm and pull me up."

Eli pushed her the rest of the way up and then took a couple of steps run-up to the wall. Megan grabbed his forearm and pulled him up onto the wall with her.

"All right," she said when they were both up. "Let's go. We'll just look around the outside for a few minutes and then go knock on the back door."

"Look around? What are you expecting to find? Blueprints to an evil scheme or something?"

"Funny, smart aleck." She swung her legs over to the inside of the wall. "I don't know. Just get a lay of the land. Never know when we might have to take cover or make a quick exit."

"Good point."

They both dropped down from the wall and started looking around. The grounds were well kept. The lawn had been manicured perfectly. The shrubbery lining the house was uniform throughout. A covered patio, complete with furniture and an outdoor grill station, stood directly off a set of ornate french doors, which appeared to lead inside to the kitchen. The patio stepped off into an Olympic-sized infinity pool, with a stone-faced hot tub on one end.

"Man, this guy is living large," Eli said.

"Like I said, scumbag defense attorney," Megan said.

"Well, I've seen enough. How about we go introduce ourselves?"

"Yeah. Let's go."

Megan reached behind her and undid the safety strap from her holster. *Can never be too careful these days,* she thought. Walking through the covered patio, she stepped up to the double french doors and rapped her knuckles on the glass.

The house was quiet inside. She knocked again, a little louder this time. Still nothing.

"Surely, if someone were in there, they heard that," Eli said.

"You'd think." She drew her arm back again to pound a little harder. Eli reached out and grabbed her midswing.

"I've got a better idea."

A year ago, she would've protested vehemently. But after what she'd been through in these last few months, she knew what Eli meant to do was probably the right move. However, they had a small problem sitting before their eyes. Eli waved her aside. She stepped back to let him work.

"This," he said, pointing to a little black box mounted to the side of the door frame, "is a Millennium CX-3. Perhaps the best home security technology on the planet. Developed by—"

"The Chinese. Yeah, I know."

"Most experts will tell you it's completely impossible to bypass."

"That's what I hear."

"Yeah, well, most experts are wrong." He popped his eyebrows at her with a sly grin. He pulled a tiny screwdriver from a little pouch he had taken from his pocket. He made quick work of the four screws holding the cover in place, removed the cover, and handed it to her.

Inside the box, a series of small chips and processors stood, mounted against a motherboard. Each one looked like its own little supercomputer hard drive.

"See, no wires." Eli pointed to the chips. "That's why they say it's impossible to bypass." He pulled another tool from his pouch. "But this guy right here"—he showed it to her—"doesn't believe in impossible."

The tool looked like a typical writing pen. But instead of a ballpoint ink dispenser, a little red LED protruded from the end.

He then reached behind his back and retrieved his iPhone. "And it even comes with its own app. I might not be able to make calls on it, but the pen will connect directly to the hard drive of the phone. The phone acts as a sort of laptop and just runs the program."

Megan was impressed. She was considered one of, if not the best, hackers in the world. It was the very reason she was employed at the FBI. And yet, not even she had heard of this technology. "Does it work?"

Eli stopped short and turned to her. "Dunno. Never used it before. It's a prototype."

"What do you mean, you've never used it before?"

"I'm a spy. Not a thief. I've never used it before. Never needed to."

"But you just happen to have it. Just in case."

"Right. Something like that." He nodded and turned back to his work.

Megan ran a hand through her hair and let out a long, slow breath. "So how do we know if it works?"

Eli looked back up at her and placed his hand on the door handle. "We're about to find out."

Megan drew her Glock, just in case. The last thing she needed was for some alarm to start going off and the guard from around front to come running around the house looking to shoot first and ask questions later. She watched as Eli slowly pushed the lever down and waited.

Click.

Nothing. The door swung inward without a sound.

Eli looked back to her and shot her a mischievous grin.

"Doesn't mean there isn't a silent alarm," she said.

"No, it doesn't."

"So how do we know if that's the case?"

"I'd say, in about twenty seconds, if there is one, we're going to meet that nice young man we saw sitting in that guard shack out front."

Megan drew a breath in and nodded. They both stood motionless for over a minute.

Nothing.

"Right. Well, then." Eli swept his arm over the threshold. "After you."

Knowing Hayes could return home any moment, they made quick work of the house. Eli took the upstairs, while Megan stayed down. She quickly rifled through drawers in the living-room end tables. Nothing. A baker's rack caught her eye, back in the kitchen. It had some mail scattered on the countertop and several drawers underneath. She quickly went through those. Again, nothing.

She moved through the rest of the rooms downstairs with no luck. The entire house seemed to be void of life. She wondered how anyone even lived there. It was completely sterile, as if it were a museum or something. She wondered if Eli was having any luck, or just more of the same.

Finally she came to what she assumed was Hayes's office. A large room with twelve-foot ceilings, lined with built-in bookshelves. Some of the books she recognized from her time at Quantico. The floors were dark bamboo. Beautifully tailored drapes hung from floor to ceiling, lining the windows. A deep, leather reading chair sat at one end of the room, complete with end table, lamp, and footstool. At the other, Hayes's desk. Megan didn't know anything much about antiques. But if she had to guess, this one was pretty old. It looked like something from the private study of a European king.

She was about to start going through everything when Eli returned.

"Find anything up there?"

"Just typical stuff. Clothing, toiletries. You know. How 'bout you?"

"Same. Besides, I don't even know what I'm looking for. This house doesn't even seem like it's lived in." She pointed to the desk. "That thing there is the first sign of life I've seen on this floor." The desk had several papers strewn about the top of it. There was a drinking glass, half filled with a brownish-amber liquid. An ashtray sat beside it with some tobacco residue stuck to its bottom. And next to that, a beautifully carved pipe, resting on a little wooden stand.

"Well, he might be a scumbag, but he definitely has good taste." Eli stepped over to the pipe, picked it up, and ran it under his nose. He drew in a long, slow inhale. "Mmm. . .and that isn't cheap tobacco, either."

"What are you talking about?"

Eli held the pipe up for her to get a better look at. "This, Megan, is a Bo Nordh."

She looked at him blankly.

"What do you drive?"

Megan was genuinely confused. "What?"

"Your personal vehicle. Do you drive a Porsche or a Mercedes? A Land Rover?"

Megan just laughed.

"Right. Well let's just say, then, this pipe probably cost more than your car."

"That's ridiculous!"

"It's only ridiculous if you don't have the money to spend on it in the first place."

The voice was a new one. And it came from behind them. Both she and Eli immediately whirled around, guns pointed, only to come face-to-face with a shadow, standing halfway down the hall, with his arm extended toward them. Slowly, he inched his way closer, until the light from the office glinted off the barrel of the easily recognizable revolver—ironically enough called *The Judge*—pointed at them. The nose of the gun swept back and forth at the two of them, as its owner, Judge Milton Hayes, came into view.

"Who are you? And what are you doing in my house?"

CHAPTER 18

Pemberton checked his watch. His guest should be arriving any minute. He chose this place specifically for its quaint, sophisticated—and ridiculously expensive—menu, complete with privacy, yet *very* public. To the casual observer—or any of the staff who knew him as a regular patron—it would appear that the old man had done it again. Just another date with a young lady—not his wife—who found his Southern charm irresistible.

His server came by and topped off his water. He lifted the other half-empty glass on the table and wagged it back and forth, to let her know he wanted another bourbon. She politely nodded and said, "Yes, Mr. Pemberton. I'll have that right out."

As she left, another young lady appeared. The hostess. Following behind her was a tall blond woman with a strong jawline. She had ice-blue eyes—eyes that said, *I'd just as soon kill you as look at you.* Her gait was upright and sophisticated—he hated women that walked slouched over, as if they were carrying a backpack or something. She was attractive, for sure. But not so much that every guy in the place strained his neck to see her pass by—though he figured that was intentional. With a different set of clothes, hair done differently, and the right amount of makeup, she could probably stand out among a line of supermodels.

The hostess pulled a seat out for the woman and gestured for her to sit. "May I get you something to drink while you wait for your server, ma'am?"

"Water is fine. Thank you."

The hostess left again. Pemberton waited till she was out of earshot.

"You're seven minutes early."

"Punctuality is kind of a thing for me," she said.

Pemberton smiled. "I like that. Good business."

85

She nodded.

"I, on the other hand, like to make people wait," he said. "Let's them know who's in charge."

"My last boss was that way, too."

"Sounds like my kind of guy. What happened to him?" He reached for his glass.

"Her. And I killed her."

Pemberton's eyebrows shot up. He coughed as the swig of bourbon he'd just taken somehow managed to go down the wrong hole. He glanced around to see if anyone had noticed. Nothing. Good. He was quickly reminded why he liked this place. Little tables tucked into nooks and pockets. Not too much interaction with the other guests. Quaint. Private. "Works for me." He set the glass back down. "Guess she had it coming?"

A thin smile crossed her lips. "Mr. . . ."

"Carlson."

"Mr. Carlson, I don't make much of small talk. Especially with someone I don't know."

"Well, now you know me."

Again the thin smile. "I don't think so. For instance, just now, you didn't even tell me your real name."

Pemberton sat up in his chair and was about to speak.

"But. . ." She cut him off. "That's fine. I don't put much stock into names. Mr. Carlson, Mr. Moroney, Mr. Johnson. . .whatever. A name is a name, is a name. What *is* important is that I've seen your face."

At the mention of that, Pemberton felt the blood drain from his. And that unnerved him. Because he didn't get unnerved for anyone. But this woman was different. There was something very unsettling about her. *Probably the fact that she's a world-famous assassin, Gavin,* he told himself.

"Don't worry, Mr. Carlson. I have no intention of killing you. At least not now. And until you give me a reason to. Killing employers is bad for business. I prefer repeat customers."

"Pemberton."

"Excuse me?"

"Pemberton. That's my name." He decided she was right. Names were irrelevant at this point. If she ever decided to kill him, it probably wouldn't matter what name he gave her.

She stuck her hand across the table. "Nice to meet you, Mr. Pemberton. I'm Alex. Alex Smith."

The server came with his bourbon. She pulled a small tablet from her apron and asked if they'd like to order. Pemberton ordered a filet, medium rare, with the parmesan sautéed asparagus and creamed spinach. He pointed to Alex.

"I'm fine, thank you. I won't be staying for dinner."

Again the server nodded and left them alone.

"Not staying? This is one of the finest restaurants in all of Raleigh."

"Thank you, but I have other things that need my attention."

Pemberton shrugged. "Suit yourself." Then, "Let's get to it."

"That would be agreeable."

"I need you to take care of something for me."

He watched as she slowly took a sip of her water. She let the glass dangle next to her cheek and leaned in closer. "Mr. Pemberton, as I said before, I have other things to do tonight. So I'm going to save you and me the runaround and skip right to it. I have a rule. You could say it's kind of like my *thing*. I enjoy it. Some may find it superfluous, but nevertheless, it's my rule."

Pemberton leaned in, in anticipation.

"You are going to have to say it."

"Excuse me?" He set his glass down and leaned back in his chair.

"I want you to say the words to me. What exactly you want me to do. I need to hear you say it."

That was the most ridiculous thing he'd ever heard. Why in the world—? She must be some kind of sicko, he reasoned. But whatever. For all his inquiring, she was the best. And he needed the best, if this were to be done right. He grabbed the fresh glass of bourbon and drained it.

He wiped his mouth with his napkin, leaned in closer, and stared right into her ice-blue eyes. "I want you to kill the president of the United States of America."

PART 2: DIVIDED

CHAPTER 19

Chinese Territory

Keene felt the barrel of the SKS-56 pressing against the back of his skull. Boz was on the ground, seemingly unconscious. The guard in front stood with his weapon pointed at Boz. The words of the Prophet's note rang in his ears.

"It's imperative that you both make it back safely."

He quickly raced though his options. He had one guard down, one in front, and one in back. The one in back was really his only threat right now. The other guard had his focus on Boz. He could disarm the guard behind him, no problem. But the one in front, if Keene made any move, would certainly react. And he was on the other side of the door. That didn't make for too difficult a task, but it would probably require making more noise than he wanted to right now. Though they were at the top of an overpass, and it was night, there were still people around. That little convenience store was only a quarter mile away. He could see it down the road. If those other guards were still there, they would possibly hear the gunfire and immediately come.

The other guard stepped forward, closer to the door, obviously satisfied that Boz was unconscious. Keene saw his opportunity and moved swiftly.

He gently leaned back, just enough to nudge the guard behind him backward. When he did, he kicked the driver's-side door forward, as hard as he could.

The door exploded forward and crashed into the front guard's nose, immediately knocking him off his feet, causing his rifle to fall to the ground. Keene could hear the cartilage crunch as the door smashed his face. At the same time that he kicked the door, he swept his left arm up behind him and turned his body left, into the sweep. The gun barrel clanked hard against the door frame and fell loose from the guard's hand.

Continuing with his body moving left, he brought a crushing straight right hand, in a chopping motion, across the rear guard's windpipe. The guard immediately reached for his throat and began to spasm, trying desperately to breathe.

Keene was on top of him quickly. He delivered a flat palm to the man's solar plexus, and then punched him as hard as he could in the left side of his head. The guard slumped to the ground as his eyes rolled back into his head. All of it in less than five seconds.

As he turned back around, the front guard was beginning to regain his balance and his bearings. The guard had already retrieved his SKS-56 and was bringing it up to level, pointed at Keene's head. Keene kicked the door again and was rewarded with the same result. This time, the man screamed in agony as the door connected with his already-broken nose. The man fell to his knees, dropping his gun.

Keene raced around the door and got behind the guard, cupping his mouth to muffle the man's wailing. He placed his forearm under the man's chin and began to squeeze. Within a few seconds, the man went limp as Keene choked him out.

With all three guards down now, Keene turned his attention to Boz, who was lying facedown on the pavement. Suddenly, Keene heard the engine of another vehicle coming down from the other side of the overpass. Then he saw the headlights playing on the trees. Whoever it was, was about to happen upon them right in the middle of this little soiree. He needed to make sure Boz was okay. But first, he needed to deal with whoever this was.

Seconds later the headlights and engine noise gave way to a small pickup truck. The pickup rolled out from the tree line and onto the overpass. As it got closer, it began to slow down. Keene had already taken his post, with one of the guards' SKS rifles at the rear of the military truck.

The pickup came to a stop, just in front of where Keene was standing. The passenger's-side window lowered and a voice called out.

"Anybody there?"

Keene stayed still and quiet.

"Hey!" the voice called again. "If you're an American and need help. . ."

Keene knew he was taking a big risk here. But Boz was still lying on the pavement. He needed any chance he could get right now. He raised his hands above his head, still holding the SKS—in case this went south quickly—and began walking out from behind the military truck toward the pickup. "I'm an American. Don't shoot!"

The driver's-side door to the pickup opened up and an older man—probably in his late fifties—with long wisps of white hair sticking out from under a ball cap stepped out. He looked fit for his age but carried himself with a slight limp. Keene knew at once that if this did go badly he could take the old man out quickly and quietly.

"Easy there, son." The older man was also holding his hands up for Keene to see he was unarmed. "I just want to help. What's going on here?"

Keene decided right away he wasn't going to tell this man the truth. "Me and my friend were just taking a walk and these guards stopped and jumped us. Guess they just wanted to beat up on some Americans. But my friend got popped in the back of the head with a rifle. He's hurt. I need to go look at him."

The older man looked at Keene, then to the front of the military truck, then back to Keene. "You say they jumped you?"

"Yeah."

"What for? What were y'all doing out walking after curfew?"

The last thing Keene wanted right now was to get into a debate with a stranger. "What are you doing out driving after curfew?"

The older man crinkled his nose. "Good point." Then, "Where's your friend?"

Keene lowered his arms, and the SKS, and started walking back toward the front of the military truck. "This way."

Boz was right where Keene had left him a few moments ago. Still facedown. Still unconscious. He rolled him over and checked to make sure Boz was still breathing. He was, and that was good, but Keene knew he needed to get Boz out of there. And quick. Someone else could come by at any second and then this party was going to get out of hand. He looked over his shoulder to the older man. "Can you help me? Get his feet. I'll get his arms."

The older man just looked at him. "And what do you suppose we do with him?"

Again, Keene ran through his options. One, he could take the military truck and leave the guards. There wasn't any place to hide their bodies, so he'd just have to leave them in the road. And that was going to have to be the case, regardless of whatever else he did. Two, he could knock the older man out and take his truck. But that wasn't really something he wanted to do. The older man had stopped and offered to help. Three, he could ask his new friend to take him and Boz somewhere, till he could get Boz awake and ready to move. He hated to involve this poor guy, but it looked like he didn't have a choice at the moment.

The older man walked around the front of the door and examined the guards' bodies. "You do this?"

Keene was still checking Boz for other broken bones or fractures from falling hard to the pavement. "Yes, sir. I guess I did."

"Hmmm. . . Who did you say you were, again?"

Keene didn't make eye contact with the man. "I didn't."

The older man leaned down to where Keene was. He took off his jacket and undid the button on his shirtsleeve. He rolled it up, just past the elbow and showed it to Keene.

Keene smiled at the older man's tattoo. A sudden wave of relief swept over him.

The old man looked at him. "Now, I've seen work like that before." He pointed at the three downed guards. "But not in a long time. Not since I was back in BUDS." He stuck his hand out to Keene. "Name's Lynch. Gary."

Keene took the man's hand. "Nice to meet you, Ranger." Referring to Lynch's tattoo.

"Tell you what," Lynch said. "My place is about a mile and a half back that way." He pointed back up the overpass. "Your friend here is going to need a bed and that head cleaned up. I'll take you back to my place. Let's go."

"What about them?" Keene pointed to the guards.

"Agh, let 'em be. This neighborhood? They get jumped all the time around here. The main station will send around some more patrols. But that's about it. There's still a bunch of us here who haven't quite given in to their ways yet."

Keene picked Boz up from his arms, while Lynch grabbed his legs.

"We'll put him in the bed. You can ride back there with him," Lynch said. "Like I said, I just live about a mile and a half back up the road."

"Thank, you, Mr. Lynch."

Lynch nodded and got back into the cab of the truck. Keene rapped his knuckles on the top of the cab when he was all set in the back. Lynch did a quick U-turn and headed back up the hill.

Lynch was true to his promise. A couple of minutes later the truck was pulling into a short drive of a one-story, brick ranch-style home. It had a small porch with two rocking chairs on it, and a chain-link fence that started out from the side of the house and continued around back. Keene could hear the barking of the dog as they pulled in the drive.

Lynch opened the door to the house and came back around and helped Keene get Boz out of the truck and inside. Lynch led as they carried Boz down the hall to a spare bedroom. He told Keene to put Boz in bed while he went down the hall for medical supplies. He returned a few minutes later with some sterile gauze, antiseptic ointment, and some bandages. Keene removed the lampshade on the bedside lamp and held the bare lamp over Boz's head in order to get a better look at the wound.

"How is it?" Lynch asked.

"I've seen worse," Keene said. "Heck, I've had worse!" He and Lynch both laughed. "He'll be all right. Gonna have one mother of a headache, but he'll be all right."

Keene stood up and offered his hand to Lynch. "Thank you, Mr. Lynch. For everything. If it's all right with you, I'd like to let him rest. When he gets up, we'll get out of your hair. I don't want to cause you any trouble."

Lynch showed Keene back out into the living room. "You two stay long as you need. No one here but me. And I don't get many visitors. My son's gone across the mountains. My daughter already lived in Virginia. And my wife died two years ago, next month."

"I'm sorry to hear that, sir."

"Oh, it's okay. Took me awhile to adjust, but I'm getting on just fine now." Lynch pointed to one of the recliner chairs. "Take a seat, son. You hungry?"

Keene realized right then that he still hadn't eaten anything. By all accounts, he should be so weak that he shouldn't be able to stand on his own two feet. Let alone take out a small band of armed guards on an overpass. He closed his eyes and said quietly, "Thank You, Lord."

"How's that?" Lynch asked.

Keene opened his eyes. "Oh. . .nothing. Yes, sir. To be honest, I'm starving. Anything would be fine."

"You like chili?"

"Love chili, sir."

"Well, I happen to make the worst chili you'll probably ever eat. But I got a whole pot of it left over from yesterday. You want some?"

Keene laughed. "Yes, sir. That'd be fine."

Lynch fixed Keene a big bowl of chili, topped with cheddar cheese and complete with a sleeve of saltines. Keene dove in as soon as Lynch set it down. And Lynch was right—it was probably the worst chili Keene had ever eaten. But he was starving and he downed the whole bowl.

When he was finished, he placed the bowl in the sink and refilled his water. He realized that, while he and Lynch had been carrying on for over an hour now, he had never told Lynch his name. And Lynch hadn't asked. *Strange,* he thought. But okay. He came back into the living room where Lynch was sitting in one of the recliners. He sat down in the other one.

Keene shifted in his chair to look at Lynch. "I never told you my name."

"I know who you are."

Keene hesitated. Did he tell Lynch a fake name back at the overpass? He couldn't remember; everything had happened so quickly. "You do?"

"Yep."

"How's that?"

Lynch tipped his ball cap back and looked up at Keene. "Son, everyone who's ever worn a uniform knows who you are. And most everyone who hasn't. Especially after what you did up in Massena."

Keene was speechless. He'd been out of circulation for so long now, he realized he really didn't know what was going on around the country, aside from what little the Prophet had told him. He realized that he had put Mr. Lynch in a precarious position and that he needed to get himself and Boz out of there as quickly as he could.

"Mr. Lynch, I'm sorry. I didn't mean for you to get involved in this. We'll be gone soon as my friend wakes up."

Lynch frowned and waved him off. "Sit down, son. Rest while you can. You haven't put me in the middle of anything. You didn't force me to do anything I didn't want to do. Besides, it was kind of exciting. I don't get much excitement these days."

Keene sat down as he was told. "I don't get it."

"Get what?"

"You said your kids are both across the mountains. Safe. Why aren't you there with them? You're a former ranger. It's not like you couldn't have found a way to get back. Why would you stay here? I mean, living like this? Their rules and everything."

Lynch seemed to think about that for a few seconds. Finally he said, "Well, it's not because I've lost my patriotism. I love this country. Always have. It's why I became a ranger. My kids and I don't really see eye to eye, since their mom died. They think I betrayed her."

"How's that?"

"Helen—that's my wife—got real sick. Doctors said by the time we found out, she only had a couple months to live. Helen didn't want to spend those couple months in the hospital, hooked up to machines and doped up on medication. She wanted to be home."

"And you did what she asked."

Lynch nodded. "And they think I just let her die. Didn't try to save her." Then, "You believe in God, Mr. Keene?"

Keene laughed to himself. "I've recently reconsidered my position on Him."

"You asked me why I'm still here."

Keene nodded.

"Because this might be where I live, but it ain't my home. Doesn't make much difference to me, either way, who says they're in charge."

"I'm not sure I understand."

Lynch reached across the chair to the end table. He opened the drawer and pulled out a worn, leather-bound Bible. "I gave my life to Christ ten years ago. Helen is responsible for that. She started going to church. Next thing I knew, I was getting dragged alongside her. Didn't take long after that, I found myself talking with one of the pastors there, asking all sorts of questions I *thought* I knew the answers to. Long story short, God got ahold of me. I gave my life to Christ and haven't looked back since. I stay here because Helen is buried a few blocks from here. I like to go there and sit and pray. My home is with God. And whenever He decides to call me back there, I'm ready to go. Until then, I'm going to stay right here."

Keene nodded again. "I understand. I lost a wife, too."

"And if we don't get out of here, we may both be seeing her again soon."

Both Keene and Lynch turned around to see Boz standing in the hall. Keene shot up out of the chair and went to his friend. "Hey, man. You okay? How you feeling?"

"Like I got hit in the back of the head with an SKS-56," Boz said. "Where are we?"

Keene introduced Boz to Mr. Lynch and caught him up on the last couple of hours. Boz thanked Lynch for all his help and offered to return the favor however he could.

"You two just get to where you need to go safely," Lynch said. "And just keep those of us who are still here in your prayers."

"That I can do," Boz said.

"You okay to move?" Keene asked.

"I'll be fine. Some Advil or something would be great."

Lynch went to the kitchen and returned with a bottle of ibuprofen and water. He tossed them to Boz and said, "You can keep these. Got another bottle in there." Then he tossed a set of keys to Keene. "Those are for the truck. Take it. You two don't need to be on foot."

"I've got a car waiting for us on Briley Parkway," Boz said. "Besides, if we got stopped, they'd run the tags and it would come back to you. Really, I'm fine. We can walk it."

Keene tossed the keys back to Lynch. "He's right. We can't ask you to do any more."

Lynch nodded. "You two be careful. I'll make sure I say a prayer for you tonight."

"We'd appreciate that," Boz said.

Keene and Boz headed back out into the night. They had already lost almost three hours. They couldn't afford to lose any more if they had any shot at getting back to the mountain range by morning. Lynch had drawn them a crude map of the neighborhood where they were and a shortcut to get back to where Boz had stashed the car. If they moved quickly, they could be there in twenty minutes.

Sticking to Lynch's map, the rest of the trip was quiet and easy. The walk was short, but it consisted of a lot of up and down hills, in and out of cul-de-sacs, and skirting property fences. Finally, they came through a small row of trees. Briley Parkway stood in front of them. On the other side of the road, International Plaza. And on the other side of that, the Nashville Airport. A short way down that road, Boz said, was a business park. That's where the car was.

Keene frowned at him. "You parked next to the airport? That place is going to be crawling with guards."

"Belly of the beast, kid. They'd never expect it."

By this time of night, traffic on Briley was almost nonexistent. But they waited by the tree line for a few minutes anyway, trying to listen for cars coming from either direction. It seemed quiet in both directions. Finally, they agreed to move. Keene was the first over the guardrail. Boz followed shortly behind. In just a few seconds, they were across the road and out of sight, behind the first office building of the business park.

"How much farther?" Keene asked.

"Back behind that building." Boz pointed to one of the tallest structures in the park.

They made their way through the parking lots of the buildings until Boz grabbed Keene's arm to hold him up. "Around there," he said.

Keene was in the lead and moving quickly when he stopped short all of a sudden. Boz literally ran into the back of him. "What's up? Why the stop?"

Keene didn't speak but held up a balled fist—the universal *hold* command. He backed away from the corner of the building and motioned for Boz to follow.

They retreated back to the front of the building before Boz spoke. "What's up?"

"Company." Keene pointed back over his shoulder.

"CG?"

"What? Who?"

"CG," Boz said. "Chinese guards."

Keene nodded the affirmative.

"At this time of night?"

Keene pulled up short. "I don't know. You tell me. You leave anything in that car that would point to you or me?"

Boz just looked at him. "Really?"

Keene realized it was a stupid question. Boz was a spook. Or had been. Either way, not even an amateur would make that mistake. "Right. Sorry."

Boz moved around Keene to take the front. "Let me look when we get to the other side."

They finished making their way around to the south side of the building this time. Boz gently eased his head around the corner to take a peek. He pulled his head back and motioned for Keene to follow.

"That's not our car," Boz said when they were back around front.

"What do you mean?"

"Just what I said. That's not our car." Boz gave a frustrated look. "The one behind it, two rows back, is ours."

"Then what gives?"

"Did I get here before you?" Boz said. "I don't know. Let's go take another look."

Keene grabbed Boz by the arm to stop him. He had a different idea.

"How's your head?" He gave Boz a mischievous look.

"It hurts," Boz said dryly.

"Good. That'll make it believable."

"What are you thinking?"

"I only saw two. And they're in a regular patrol car, not a military truck. There's a good cover of trees along the side of that lot. You straggle out there, like you're hurt, and distract them. I'll do the rest."

"Are you *trying* to leave a trail of bodies in our wake?"

"I didn't say I was going to kill them. Just incapacitate them. Besides, you said so yourself. We need to move. We can't be waiting them out. We don't even know what they're doing back there. Or if more are coming."

Boz gave a short sigh and nodded. "Okay. I'll give you two minutes to get in place. Then I'm going out."

"Roger that." Keene set his backpack down on the sidewalk. "We'll come back for it."

Boz nodded and set his down, too. Keene started counting off the seconds in his head as he made a long sweeping arc around the front parking lot to the small tree line that separated the back parking lot from the next business over. He had just gotten in place when he saw Boz come around the corner, stumbling and holding his head.

Boz was good, Keene had to admit. For a moment, even he forgot that Boz was only a distraction. The man really looked like he was badly injured. He thought about Boz's head and realized he probably wasn't acting.

It only took a couple of seconds before Boz had the guards' attention. They turned almost immediately when Boz appeared from the corner of the building. Both were shouting something to Boz and both had their hands out, motioning for him to stop. But Boz just kept limping toward them.

Both guards left the side of the car now. That was the opening Keene was waiting for. With their backs to him, he darted out from behind the trees and covered the twenty-yard span in a matter of seconds. The guards didn't even hear him coming up behind.

He and Boz got to the guards at the same time. Boz, who had been limping and holding his head, suddenly switched gears and lunged out at the guard to Keene's left. Keene realized that Boz was covered, so he focused on the guard on his right. Each man dispatched his guard in a matter of seconds, having made hardly a sound. They picked up the fallen guards and dragged them back to the car they had been standing by. Keene reached into his back pocket and produced a roll of duct tape—something he had borrowed from the bed of Lynch's truck. He taped the guards' mouths and wrists and then pushed them under the car. They would wake up in a few hours with a few aches and bruises, but nothing worse.

Boz pulled the car around front and picked up Keene, who had gone back to retrieve the backpacks. Keene jumped in as Boz hit the gas.

"Well, that was fun."

"Yeah, well, I've had about all the fun I care to for the rest of this trip," Boz said. "Let's pray we don't get stopped the rest of the way."

"Roger that," Keene said.

CHAPTER 20

Raleigh, North Carolina

I said, who *are* you? And what are you doing in my house?"

The man was dressed in finely tailored slacks and a blue blazer. His hair was silver and parted over to one side. He had a strong jawline and bushy eyebrows that were narrowed into a menacing scowl.

Megan loosed her Glock from her grip and let it dangle from her finger as she held her hands up in surrender. Eli did the same.

"My name's Megan Taylor, Mr. Hayes. I'm with the FBI."

"What are you doing in my house? And how did you get in here?"

"That's a complicated story." Eli chuckled.

"Please put the gun down, Mr. Hayes. We only came here to talk to you," Megan said.

Hayes motioned them away from the desk with the gun. "Both of you, over here. Away from the desk."

Megan and Eli did as they were instructed.

"Now, I'm only going to ask this one more time. What are you doing in my house?"

Megan began to lower her arms. "Mr. Hayes, I'm going to holster my weapon and show you my ID, okay?"

Hayes nodded. "Do it slowly, young lady."

She did as she was told and eased the Glock back into its holster. Next she used her right arm to open her jacket and reached her left arm inside to grab her ID. She pulled the flip-fold wallet out and handed it to him. Hayes took it but never let his eyes drift from her or Eli. He held it up so that he could look at it out of his peripheral vision.

"See?" Megan said apprehensively. "Megan Taylor. FBI."

"And who are you?" Hayes shifted his gaze to Eli.

"Eli Craig, sir."

"He's with me."

Hayes's demeanor was calm and cool, Megan noted. If he was shaken in any way by her identification, he didn't show it. "We came to ask you a few questions, sir. We let ourselves in the back, because we didn't want to make a big scene with the guard out front."

"And why is that?" Hayes asked.

"Um." Megan cleared her throat.

Eli jumped in. "With everything that's happened in the last few months, we felt it wouldn't look favorably for you—the Chief Justice—having a couple feds show up at this hour unannounced. I mean, should the media catch wind of it."

Hayes gave a short *hmph*. He turned his attention back to Megan. "What kind of questions?"

"Just some questions about someone you might know, sir. That's all. But like my partner, here, said, we didn't want to make a scene. So we just let ourselves in."

"About that. . ." Hayes looked quizzically at them. "Am I to assume you somehow bypassed my security system?"

"No." It was Eli, and he was smiling. "You don't need to *assume* anything. I bypassed it."

Megan almost reached over and punched him right in the jaw. Hayes was standing three feet away with a hand cannon pointed at them and Eli was cracking jokes. She was about to apologize when Eli continued.

"Before we leave, though, I'll put it back. And then I'll show you how I did it. That way you can call your security company in the morning and tell them. I'm sure they'll want to know."

Hayes gave another *hmph*. He looked at both of them for another few seconds. Finally, he lowered the revolver. "Follow me."

He led them back out into the kitchen. As he entered the archway, he said, "Lights up." Immediately, the interior lights in the kitchen came to life. He motioned for them to take a seat at the small table next to the french doors. "Now, what is it you want to know?"

Megan cleared her throat. "Mr. Hayes, I'm sure you know these past couple months have been tough for our country."

Hayes nodded.

"And I'm sure you're aware that President Walker is in a tough position right now." She waited for some kind of acknowledgment. Nothing. "I mean, there are many who want to just move on with life, reexamine our policies, and move toward restructuring our government to adhere to more of what the founders intended—"

"And what makes you an expert on what our forefathers intended, young lady? I'm a state supreme court justice, and I have trouble, at times, discerning what our forefathers intended. And that's my job."

"I meant no disrespect, Your Honor. I'm merely saying that. . .there seem to be two camps—if you will—of people right now. One is just trying to rebuild and move on. The other believes that we should fight to take our country back."

"And which do you subscribe to?" Hayes asked.

"That's not important, sir." She noticed Hayes's frown. "What is important is, regardless of what one believes, we have to abide by the rule of law. Surely you can appreciate that."

Again Hayes dismissed her. "Why don't you skip to the part where you tell me what you want?"

Megan shifted in her seat. "We came here to ask if you could help us."

"Help you?" There was genuine surprise in Hayes's eyes.

"Yes. We understand you may know a man named Gavin Pemberton?"

It was subtle, and many people might have missed it. But Megan saw the corner of Hayes's mouth twitch. She wondered if Eli caught it, too.

"Gavin Pemberton?" Hayes asked, seemingly searching his mind to recollect. "That name sounds familiar, but. . .no, I'm sorry. I can't say I know him. Who is he?"

"Really?" It was Eli. "Because we heard that the two of you might actually be close friends."

Hayes gave a nervous, dismissive laugh. "Young man, I just told you that I might've heard his name. I think that if he and I were old chums, my answer to your previous question would be starkly different. Don't you think?"

Megan decided to jump in and try and catch him off guard. "Where did you say you know him from, again?"

Hayes didn't bite. "I didn't. I merely said that I might've heard his name." He crinkled his nose. "Wait a minute. . . . Pemberton. . .yes, you know, I am familiar with that name. Isn't he that tobacco farmer? Billionaire, I think."

"That's the guy," Megan said. "Likes to dabble in politics."

Hayes waved her off. "I'm sure I don't know anything about that."

"And you're sure you've never had any run-ins with him? No business dealings or anything?"

"You know. . ." Hayes looked like someone turned the light on inside his brain. "I remember now. I did have some dealings with Mr. Pemberton. About thirty years ago." He shook his finger and smiled, as if he were proud of himself for remembering. "Seems a young family brought a lawsuit against the big tobacco companies. Mr. Pemberton was one of the named defendants. Big case. It was all over the news. Made it to the state supreme court."

"And how did that play out?" Eli asked.

Hayes gave another *hmph*. "That was thirty or so years ago, son. I can't remember every decision handed down from the court. I wasn't even a judge then. I think I worked for the law firm that was representing all the defendants. I was a junior partner at the time. I remember, because myself and my other two junior partners spent three months straight without any sleep, preparing files and depositions. But as far as Mr. Pemberton goes, I don't think we ever met."

Megan looked to Eli and nodded. She started to stand up.

"What did you say you were looking for Mr. Pemberton for?" Hayes asked, raising his eyebrows.

"It's probably nothing," Megan said. "Thank you for your time. Again, sorry about. . .you know. . .just letting ourselves in."

"Glad I could help," Hayes said. Then, "You can go out through the front door. I'll ring the guard and let him know you're coming through."

"Thank you," they both said.

"Oh, and next time you need to speak to me, Ms. Taylor—which I assume will be never—go ahead and check in with the guard. I'm a big boy. I can take care of myself when it comes to what's left of the media around here."

Megan smiled and nodded as they exited the house. She waited for the door to close behind them before speaking.

"You see his lip twitch when I said Pemberton's name?"

"Yep. You see him act all innocent and proud of himself that he *recalled* having worked for the firm that defended Pemberton?"

"Yep."

"So what do you think?"

"I think we need to keep an eye on Mr. Hayes."

"My thoughts exactly," Eli said. He winked at the guard as they passed through the front gate.

Hayes closed the door behind the FBI agent and her partner. How in the world did they end up at his house? And why were they asking about Gavin? Surely no one could know what he and Gavin had been doing. There was no way. They'd been too careful. And everyone they *had* talked to. . .well, he and Gavin had enough dirt on all of them to put them away for a lifetime.

Suddenly, he began to feel faint. He walked back into the kitchen and poured himself a glass of water. He drank it down in two long gulps.

That was better.

They can't know anything. This was just a fishing expedition, he told himself.

He reached inside his blazer pocket and retrieved the handkerchief tucked away inside. He wiped the bead of sweat from his forehead that was now trickling down his nose.

He tried to convince himself he had nothing to worry about. He was sure of it. His and Gavin's friendship was something neither of them advertised. Ever since they'd known each other. It just wasn't good for their social circles. He was from an elite family of law and business. Gavin's family were a bunch of rich, redneck tobacco farmers. And though they shared much of the same political ideology, their families saw each other's social status as different as the Hatfields and McCoys. Not that their families actually knew each other. Just that neither family would have ever accepted the friendship of the other. It would have been bad for their image.

So he and Gavin had always kept their friendship quiet. As well as their business dealings. No, he decided. No one would ever suspect his involvement with Gavin on a ten-dollar business deal. Let alone what they had been working toward. Well, unless someone came across the fact that there actually *was* somewhat of a history there. Hayes had cross-examined Gavin on the stand in that tobacco case. He had discreetly informed the senior partner that he and Gavin were friends, and that he could paint Gavin in a favorable light. The senior partner had agreed. Hayes had made the Pembertons look like a family of choirboys. *Yeah,* he admitted. That might raise some eyebrows. And, of course, what if someone were to dig a little further, and discover he and Gavin had been lacrosse teammates at Yale? At least for the first week anyway, until Gavin had cross-checked him in practice, dislocated his shoulder, and torn his rotator cuff. Gavin had offered to drive him to the hospital himself. Hayes's lacrosse career had come to an abrupt end, but a friendship—more than thirty years old now—had been born.

Suddenly, he felt a little light headed again. He wiped another bead of sweat and reached for the phone. He dialed the number and waited for a series of clicks and beeps. He was reminded again of the aggravation of dealing with these landlines. Finally the other end was picked up. "It's your dime."

Hayes said, "Why can't you just ever answer the phone like a normal person?"

" 'Cause I know it bothers you," Pemberton snapped. "What do you want?"

Hayes wiped the sweat from his brow again. "We have a problem."

CHAPTER 21

Alex Smith sat in the car across from the Super 8 Motel on Capital Boulevard. She was supposed to already be back with Farid, so she called their room from the pay phone at the Quick Mart next door to the Super 8. She wanted to be there with him. She wanted them to go out to a nice dinner and then maybe hit a couple late-night spots in town. But something else was currently demanding her attention.

She had noticed him the moment she walked in to meet Pemberton. He was sitting alone, at a table by himself. It wasn't that he had done anything peculiar. All he had done was to look her over as she walked by. Not an uncommon occurrence. *I am, after all, very attractive.*

The problem was once she sat down to talk with Pemberton, she had casually glanced around the room, as was her custom. That's when she noticed. He had been staring at her—or Pemberton—or both. Regardless, as soon as she had looked in his direction, the man shifted his gaze away quickly. Too quickly. She made a mental note of it and continued on with Pemberton.

As she left, she noticed the man was purposely avoiding looking at her. She left the restaurant and walked across the street to where her car was parked. She took her time, so as to give the man a chance to leave and follow her—she had assumed that would happen next.

She slowly pulled away from the curb and watched the rear view. She hadn't even completely merged into traffic when the man exited the restaurant, jumped in a car parked almost right in front of the door, and pulled out, three cars behind.

Normally, she would lead a tail like this somewhere deserted, where she'd give him the slip and then double back on him. And then she would kill him. But given what she'd heard about Pemberton, she figured this

108

guy was probably tasked with following her. And since she already had other plans, she decided just to lose him. She quickly found a shopping mall and parked in the garage. She got out of the car and hurried into the entrance, making sure the man was close behind. As soon as she was inside, she ducked into the first store. It had a glass front and gave a view of the entrance where she'd just come through to the parking garage.

His car pulled into the parking garage and slowly approached her car, but the man never got out. Instead, he stopped directly behind her car for a couple seconds then pulled away. If she had to guess, the man had just written down her plate number. No matter, it wouldn't give up any information. The car was a rental. Under a fake name. She told herself to just wait for him to leave, and then go meet Farid. But the pull was too strong. She couldn't let it go. As soon as the man was out of sight, she quickly exited the garage and got back in her car.

Outside the garage, it only took her a couple of seconds to spot the vehicle again. He was making a left at the light. Fortunately, the light was red. There were three cars in front of her, which gave her the perfect position to follow him. The green arrow appeared and the man made his turn. However, the three others behind him seemed to have nowhere to go in a hurry. They slowly puttered through the intersection, causing her to almost miss the light. She got as close as she could to the car in front and followed it through as the light flashed red again. An oncoming car blew his horn at her, but she ignored it and continued on.

Now she was sitting here, outside Super 8 Motel, deciding what to do. The man had been inside for almost a half hour. And the lights in his room had just gone off. Given his age, she figured he was probably turning in for the night. She could just let it go for now, go have dinner with Farid, and then later that night, come back.

On the other hand, if she did let it go for now, there was a small possibility the man could leave again, and she might never find him. Also, it would ruin her night with Farid. She would be consumed with thinking about it. And she had already promised herself—since she couldn't remember the last time she had a *real* date—nothing was going to ruin this night. Then she thought of something else. If she did go in there right now, rough the guy up a bit, find out who he was and why he was tailing her, and then just kill him, it would put her senses into hyperdrive. She would feel that coursing through her veins for the rest of the night. And that could only heighten the evening she had planned with Farid.

She gave it five more minutes and then turned the car off, got out, and started walking toward the motel.

At seventy-six years old, Nolan Peterson was still in great shape. He could still run five miles—and did, three times a week. He ate healthy. Didn't smoke. Didn't drink—except for the occasional social dark beer. Typically, he got up at six o'clock and went to bed at eleven. Seven hours sleep, that's all he ever needed. But not today. Today, he was tired.

He wasn't sure if it was because his age was starting to catch up with him, or if it was because he'd been running himself ragged these past few days. Ever since his friend had called him a couple of days ago, his interest had been piqued, and he'd been up late every night since, doing some good ol' fashioned spy work. Then, when Jennings had called, it pretty much set him on course. It aggravated him that Jennings would send those other two agents to take him out of play. Jennings thought he'd lost a step. But he was still sharp as ever. And he'd proved it tonight. He'd given those two agents the slip. Sent them off chasing after that judge. He hadn't lied to them. He really had learned that the judge was some kind of friend of Pemberton's. He just chose to omit the fact that he knew where Pemberton was. So he'd decided to follow Pemberton himself. And then the blond showed up.

From the moment she'd walked into the restaurant, he knew something was off about her. He just couldn't put his finger on it. The way she sauntered into the place, he figured she was some kind of call girl or something. But then she intentionally made an effort to check out the room again, once she was seated. Call girls, as far as he knew, didn't make an effort to make sure they weren't being watched. This girl did. Then she left, almost as quickly as she showed up. And Pemberton made no effort to leave.

He decided—on a whim—to follow the girl. But it turned out to be a bust—at least for now. She'd led him to a shopping mall. But at least he got the plate number from her car. He had a friend back home who could run the plate. He'd call him tomorrow. Right now, the excitement of the day had left him exhausted. He spent ten minutes getting ready for bed, brushing his teeth, changing into some flannel pants and a T-shirt, and washing his face.

He wasn't much of a TV guy, so he just crawled in bed and grabbed his book from the bedside table. He figured he'd read for a few minutes until his eyes started to feel as tired as the rest of his body. It only took another ten minutes before he was spent. He reached across the bed and killed the light.

He had almost completely drifted off when he heard the soft knocking on the door. Who in the world could it be? He certainly wasn't expecting someone. No one he knew, knew where he was. Then it hit him. It must be the two agents. He didn't know how they tracked him down, but they *were* cut from the same cloth as he was. He supposed, if he were them, he could've found himself by now. He got out of the bed and walked to the door. He decided that, if they were going to roust him out of bed, he was going to at least give them some grief. He opened the door and turned back into the room without even looking at them. "Took you long enough," he said, walking back to the bed. "I could have found me three hours ago."

He was caught off guard when he felt the hand push him, face-first, down into the bed. He rolled over to say something but stopped short. The words got caught in his throat as he stared up into the face of the blond woman from the restaurant, who was holding a Walther PK380, and pointing it right at his head.

"Who are you?" Peterson asked.

"Funny," she said. "I was going to ask you the same thing."

CHAPTER 22

Chinese–US Border

It was just after six o'clock, and the sun was trying to lift itself up over the mountain range. Boz had been driving for the last couple of hours while Keene slept. Keene hadn't realized it until after the episode in the parking lot on Briley Parkway, but the two altercations with the Chinese guards had left him completely drained. It had been quite awhile since he had had to expel that kind of energy. Those weeks in the Chinese prison camp had taken a toll on him.

He knew Boz was injured and needed rest, too, so tired as he was, he'd insisted Boz take the first shift sleeping. He promised to stick to the route Boz had mapped out and assured his friend he would wake him before any trouble arose. Boz had reluctantly agreed to let Keene drive. Within ten minutes of being on the road, Boz was out.

Keene had let him sleep for the next three hours while he maneuvered the route, which consisted of small stretches on Interstate 40 mixed with two-lane county roads. Finally, when they'd gone almost as far as Johnson City, Keene couldn't hold out any longer. He woke Boz and changed places with him.

Keene was completely out when he felt Boz nudging his arm. Everything in him wanted to ignore it. He could've slept for the next two days. But the tone that accompanied the nudge made him sit up straight.

"Jon, wake up. Now."

He blinked and rubbed his eyes as he tried to focus. "What's up? Trouble?"

"Not yet, but probably."

Keene stared ahead and finally saw what Boz was talking about. They were nearing the border.

"I was hoping we'd get here sooner," Boz said. "Would have made this a little easier. Sun's going to be up soon."

"How's your head?"

"It's all right. Still tender. About an hour ago, I forgot about it and let my head fall back against the headrest. I'm surprised you didn't wake up when I yelped."

Keene laughed a short laugh. "Bro, I was out! Would've taken a lot more than you crying like a girl to wake me up."

Boz shot him a sideways glance.

"So what's the plan?" Keene said.

Boz shrugged. "Well, the plan *was* to park a half mile out, walk the rest of the way, quietly avoid the guards, and sneak through. The same way I got here. But now that the sun is coming up. . ."

"Sounds like a good plan. What's the problem?"

Boz looked at him like he hadn't heard a word Boz had just said.

"Well, for starters, there are five CG back in Nashville who, by now, have probably run it up the chain that you and I were the ones who gave them their makeovers. Seeing as how this is the closest place for us to try and cross, I'm guessing there's probably going to be about triple the number of guards that were there last night."

Keene thought about that. "You're probably right. Still doesn't change the fact that we need to get across."

Boz nodded. "So what do you want to do?"

"Hey, this is your mission. I'm just the asset. You tell me."

"Asset?" Boz rolled his eyes. "Whatever."

Keene decided it was time to get serious. "Okay. Give me the recon. What do we know?"

"The first thing is we need to get off this road. In about another two miles, we're going to be sitting ducks with nowhere to go. I've got some topography maps in my bag. We'll use those to see what's the best way to approach the gate. After that, we'll have about a five-mile hike. I have a car stashed. Let's just hope it's still there."

"Hope?"

"Well, the CG aren't supposed to cross the border for anything. The mountain range is ours. Part of the cease-fire agreement with Chin. But those woods are dense and thick and have nothing in them but wildlife for miles sometimes. The Chinese like American deer. So it's not uncommon to hear about them leaving their posts and going hunting. And there are only so many roads that you can travel on in there. So if one of them happened upon the right road between yesterday and today. . ."

"Then we're going to have longer than a five-mile hike."

Boz didn't reply but turned the car off the road onto a dirt road. Keene didn't know if his friend knew where he was going, or if the road just looked like a good place to get off. Either way, their time in a car was over. At least for now. He hoped.

The pale blue hovering over the mountaintops was beginning to give way to a thin line of pink. In another half hour, it would be fully daylight. And then they would be fully exposed.

Boz stayed on the narrow dirt road for another three-quarters of a mile and then pulled over to the side. Nothing but trees and thick forest lined them on either side.

Keene got out and looked around. "You know where we are?"

"Nope. But I'm about to find out."

Boz grabbed his bag from the backseat, retrieved some loose papers, and laid them out on the hood. He clicked on his flashlight and studied the maps for a second.

"Here." He pointed with his finger. "We're here. And the CG post is there." He moved his finger across the page. "We need to cross here." He looked up to the sky and then to his watch. "And we've got about a half hour to do it."

Keene looked down at the map to where Boz had pointed. "That's almost two miles. With gear. And don't forget the guards that are probably waiting for us—me."

"Hey, it's not my fault you're such a big deal." Boz smiled. "Maybe if you'd been more careful a few months ago, we wouldn't be in this situation."

Keene slung his pack over his shoulder. "Let's move it, Chappy. Double time."

"Roger that."

The two took off through the trees, headed straight east. They tried to move as silently as they could, but with the pace they needed to keep—in order to try and beat the sun—they weren't. Fortunately, no CG were anywhere to be found as they approached the border. However, that wouldn't be the case for much longer.

As they approached the clearing Boz had pointed out on the map, they could see the barricades set up less than a thousand yards ahead. The border crossing was situated in the middle of what used to be I-40 as it entered the man-made canyon that had been cut years ago for the interstate to pass through the mountains. On either side of the barricades a chain-link fence topped with razor wire ran as far as the eye could see north and south. On the other side of the razor wire stood jagged cliffs and nearly impenetrable, thick forest, filled with sudden drop-offs and chasms. Mother nature's own barricade, which made this border crossing the only viable option for at least twenty miles in either direction.

The sun was coming up fast now. They didn't have much more time. Keene looked at Boz, who had hung his head and was shaking it back and forth.

"What's wrong?"

"I was afraid of this."

"What?"

"When I crossed here last night, there weren't even one-third as many guards." He pointed to the large military trucks and sandbag barricade stations that were set up every fifty feet or so. "And those weren't here at all."

"They know we're coming."

"Looks that way."

Keene shrugged. "Well, I'm flattered they think you and I need this much resistance."

"Yeah. . . ," Boz said slowly.

Keene could almost see the wheels spinning in Boz's head. "What?"

"They have no idea that it's just you and me. Far as they know, there's an entire team here to extract you. And they're prepared for it."

"And what better way to get by them," Keene said, "than to give them what they're expecting?"

"Exactly."

"That's great. But where are you going to get six more guys to go rush that barricade?"

"Good point."

Keene thought for a moment. "I've got an idea."

He quickly relayed his plan. They would separate and try to draw a few guards into the woods where they were. They would disarm the guards and take them captive. From there, it was up to Boz to make the rest of the plan work.

They skirted the tree line of the clearing until it brought them to within twenty yards of the post on the far north side. The scenario couldn't have played out any more perfectly. Four guards stood post. Two were leaning against the chain-link fence, talking with each other. The other two were sitting down behind one of the sandbag barriers, checking their weapons. The closest guards from these four were more than a hundred yards farther to the south.

Boz nodded to Keene, who had climbed up one of the bigger trees and was perched atop a long, thick overhanging branch. "Okay, here goes nothing."

Boz cupped his hands and pointed his head toward the four guards. "Hey!"

Immediately, the four guards snapped to. One started barking orders to the other three, who immediately pulled their weapons up into firing position and started toward the tree line. The fourth guard, however, stayed put. And then he reached for his radio.

"Someone didn't tell that guy the plan," Keene said nervously.

Boz, who had taken up a position behind an adjacent tree, whispered back, "Remind me to dock his pay."

The three CG entered the tree line, sweeping their weapons back and forth, moving slowly. Keene had a good vantage from up in the tree, but Boz was completely blind. The good news was they were about to pass right under Keene. Keene had to time this perfectly, or else Boz would be left exposed.

As the three guards short-stepped their way under the tree, Keene let out a low whistle. At the same time, he dropped from his perch. As he fell, he came down between two of the guards and scissor-kicked them. The blow knocked the guards in either direction; both lost their weapons.

As Keene jumped from the branch, Boz darted out from behind the tree. The third guard was completely caught by the surprise of Keene falling from the sky. He had turned to look, just as his two comrades got knocked aside. That gave Boz the second he needed. He quickly moved behind the third guard, grabbed him under the chin from behind, placed his knee in the middle of the guard's back, and snapped. From there, he moved to the second guard and took him out, as Keene lunged for the first guard and finished him off. All three guards lay motionless in the fallen leaves.

"They dead?" Keene said, looking at the two guards Boz had dispatched.

"Nope." Boz pointed at them one at a time. "Sprained back, and choke hold. Yours?"

"No. But he's going to need a lot of physical therapy. When he wakes up. For the next twenty years."

"What now?"

Suddenly sirens began ringing up and down the barricade.

"Well, I'd say the plan just went out the window."

"I knew I should have let you take all three of these guys and go after that fourth guy."

"Wouldn't have mattered," Keene said. "Soon as you gave the call, he was on the radio." He looked around at the guards. "Quick. Grab their weapons."

The two of them quickly took the guards' NP-42 pistols and their SKS-56 rifles, along with the ammo they were carrying. They needed to move. In moments the entire area would be swarming with guards.

"Follow me."

Keene took off running to the fence, where the three guards had come from. The fourth guard was fumbling to get his pistol out of his holster as soon as he saw Keene. Keene raised the NP-42 he'd taken from one of the guards and fired two short bursts, catching the guard right in the leg. The guard dropped instantly, screaming in pain. As Keene caught up to him, he swung a hard left hook at the guard's head, knocking him out.

A large military truck was stationed only yards away from the guards' post. He hoped—no, prayed—the keys were in it.

"This is crazy," Boz called from behind.

"Got a better idea?"

"Nope. Just saying."

They reached the truck. Keene jumped into the passenger side. "You drive. I'm a better shot."

Boz didn't argue.

The keys were in the truck. Boz fired it up, pushed the clutch, and slammed the truck in gear. "There's two ways to get on the other side of that barricade. Stop, shoot all the guards, and walk through; or drive right at it, shoot all the guards, and ram through with the truck."

Keene looked ahead at the scene unfolding before them. The sun had finally begun to crest over the mountain. "Well, seeing as how they're all running this way, I'd say let's stay in the truck and ram it."

"My thoughts exactly."

"Oh, and one more thing." Keene looked up to the sky. "Please, God, help us get through this."

Boz pushed the clutch and shifted gears. "Amen!"

The twenty or so guards who had been racing toward them all stopped and took a knee. At once they leveled their SKSs and opened fire. Bullets pelted the front of the truck as Boz barreled on toward the gate. Keene checked the magazine from the SKS he'd taken from the guard, slammed it home, and leaned out the window. He sprayed a wide arc of gunfire across the field in front of him. Most of the guards who had been shooting dove for cover. Others continued to fire.

This time, Keene took aim through the red-dot sight and began to pick off the guards. And now that Boz had gotten the truck up to speed, and didn't have to shift, he had his Kimber out the driver's-side door, firing as well.

They were coming up on the main gate, but the problem was they were coming at it from the side. No chance to ram it from this angle. Boz jerked the wheel and almost threw Keene out of the truck. Keene caught his balance and continued firing. "A little heads-up next time, huh?"

"Sorry."

The truck was moving away from the barricade now, heading west, on the main road. Keene climbed back inside the truck. Behind them, guards were piling into the other four trucks. Within seconds, the guards were following behind.

Keene moved the canvas separating the cab and the back of the truck and began to climb in the back. He wanted to start shooting from the rear. "Lord, could use some help here." He'd no sooner moved the canvas when he realized his prayers had been answered. Lying in the back of the truck was a .50 caliber BMG, complete with nine-inch tripod.

"Hey, Boz. . ."

"Yeah?"

"I need you to buy us thirty seconds. And then turn this junk heap around and head straight for that gate."

"Why?"

"You'll see."

Keene jumped in the back and grabbed the machine gun. He grabbed the chain of ammo and fed it into the gun. Next—in between trying to catch his balance from the truck rocking back and forth as Boz weaved to try to evade the guards' bullets flying at them—he turned around, grabbed his knife from its sheath, and began to cut the canvas top covering the bed of the truck. Once that was done, he reached back, grabbed the .50 cal., and heaved it on top of the cab of the truck. "Okay, turn it around."

"Hold on to what you got." Boz slammed on the brakes and turned the wheel. The truck skidded as the rear end swung around. They were facing the guards head-on.

Keene didn't wait. He opened fire on the guards coming right at them. The machine gun ripped through the oncoming trucks. One by one, they lost control and either ran off the road or flipped over as their drivers had pulled too hard on the wheels trying to evade the deadly machine-gun rounds. Finally, all four guards' trucks were out of commission. The only thing in their way now was the main gate, which still had a good number of guards.

Boz was headed straight for the gate. Unlike the fence that ran from either side of it, it was made of eighteen-foot-tall chain-link fence with metal straps crisscrossing the chain-link for extra reinforcement. On either side of the gate itself stood two round, makeshift concrete towers—probably fifteen feet in diameter—that rose another ten feet above the gate and fence. Keene took aim right at the base of the left tower.

Shards of concrete began to fly in all directions as Keene blasted the tower's foundation. Every guard who had been kneeling or standing in front of the tower was getting peppered by the debris. They all began to scatter and take cover.

The better news for Keene and Boz was the fact that the tower wasn't that stable to begin with. So as Keene continued firing, the tower began to crumble and slide down off its foundation. In a matter of seconds, the whole thing was going to come crashing down. The bad news was it was going to do so right in front of the gate.

Keene pounded on the cab of the truck. "You better punch it, Boz."

"Roger that!"

Keene held on as Boz shifted the truck again. The truck lurched forward even faster. Keene changed his aim and began laying down a wide arc of gunfire again, on both sides of the gate. They were almost there.

The tower continued to slide. The truck was less than twenty feet from the gate. If they didn't reach it in the next couple of seconds, the tower would come crashing down right on top of them.

Boz swerved to the right and missed a huge chunk of concrete as it fell. The nose of the truck slammed into the gate and sent it flying. But just as they hit the gate, the rest of the tower gave way and fell, slamming into the rear of the truck. The truck bounced hard, once, then shot to the right. The rear end of the truck pounded into the tower on the right, which sent the truck shooting back to the left.

Keene tried to hold on, but the impact was too much for him. His left side crashed into the steel sides of the bed. As the truck bucked from the collision, he was thrown from the back. He flew a good twenty feet before landing on the hard pavement of the road on the other side of the gate.

He knew immediately that he had at least two broken ribs. His arms looked like they'd just gone through a cheese grater, and he could feel his left ankle already beginning to swell inside his boot. As he looked back, he saw the truck crushed under the rest of the fallen tower.

Boz was still inside.

CHAPTER 23

Raleigh, North Carolina

Megan woke up as the first rays of sunlight slipped through the blinds. She and Eli had returned to the hotel after their failed trip to Hayes's house. She was still mad over the fact that neither she nor Eli had done a better job watching for Hayes. She'd spent the better part of the evening fuming over how they'd been caught off guard by a defense attorney.

Eli's room was next to hers, connected by an in-room connecting door. She got out of bed and pounded on it three times.

"Hey! You up? Hey! Eli? You awa—"

The divider door swung open. Eli was there, wrapped in his blanket. He looked like he was still sleeping. "Well, aren't you just a bright ray of sunshine."

"Actually, I hate mornings. Always have. But if I've got to be up this early, then I'm not going to sit around hungry. Let's go. Get dressed."

"Just go back to sleep," Eli said from under the covers. He had already fallen back on the bed.

"Let's go, Eli. You've got twenty minutes. Then I'm leaving you."

Eli poked his head out from under the blanket. "Like you can get ready in twenty minutes."

Megan smiled. "Yeah? Ask your uncle Boz about that." She closed the divider door and headed to the bathroom on her own side.

Twenty minutes later, she knocked on the divider door again. Eli opened the door, fully dressed and ready to go. He looked at her with raised eyebrows. "I'm impressed."

"Let's go."

They left the hotel and drove down the street where they had seen another diner the night before. The front desk clerk told them it would be a good place for breakfast, and he was right. The service was fast, the eggs were soft, the bacon crisp, and the pancakes golden brown.

The waitress came by and asked if they would like another round of coffee as they finished. They said yes and asked for their check. She cleared their plates and left again. They were discussing what their next move was when Megan felt the vibration of the sat-phone in her pocket. She told Eli to grab the check and stepped outside the restaurant so as not to draw attention. With cell signal still nonoperable, someone using a sat-phone would draw unnecessary attention.

"This is Taylor."

"It's Jennings."

"Is everything all right?" Jennings's tone sounded nervous.

There was a pause on the other end.

"Sir?"

Megan felt her chest tighten. Boz and Jon should've returned this morning. She'd been waiting to hear that they'd made it back safely. Now, she had a sudden sickening feeling.

"Sir, is it Jon and Boz? What's happened? Are they okay?"

"What? Ah. . .no. I mean, no. It's not Jon and Boz. I haven't heard anything from them yet."

A wave of relief swept over her. "What is it, then?"

"I need you and Eli to check something out for me."

"Sure, anything."

"I got a call this morning from someone I know. An informant of sorts. Said there's something I needed to look into."

"Does it have anything to do with Pemberton or Hayes?"

"Don't know. He just said that there's someone there I would be interested in. He's at the Super 8 Motel on Capital. Room 119."

"Okay. We're going to go follow Hayes today. We can swing over there in a little bit."

"No, go now. We can't take the chance of whoever it is leaving."

"Okay. We're on our way."

"Call me when you get there. Let me know what's going on."

"Will do."

Megan closed the phone.

"Who was that?" Eli had come up behind her.

"Jennings. Let's go. We need to go check something out."

"Something to do with Pemberton?"

"Probably. But I don't know."

"Any word from Uncle Boz?"

"Not yet."

They jumped in the car, Megan driving. "Look at that map and find Capital Road, or Boulevard, or whatever."

"What are we looking for?"

"Super 8. Room 119."

Capital *Boulevard*, as Eli informed her, was only a short drive from where they were. Megan turned the car and headed that direction. Once on Capital, they stopped to ask which direction the Super 8 was. Ten minutes later, they pulled in the parking lot.

Megan checked her weapon and got out of the car. Eli did the same and followed. They approached the room slowly and quietly, looking around for anything suspicious. Nothing seemed out of the ordinary. And at this hour of the morning, not even the housekeeping service was working.

As they got near, Megan motioned for Eli to take the other side of the door. With her back against the wall next to the door, she reached her arm out and knocked on the door.

"Hello?"

Nothing.

"Hello? Anyone home?"

Still nothing.

Eli pulled out his lock-picking kit and showed it to her.

"Yeah," she said. "But make it quick. I'll keep a lookout." She moved away from the wall and in front of the door to shield Eli from any unwanted eyes. It only took him a few seconds before he'd finished.

"Okay," he whispered, standing up. "You ready?"

She nodded and signaled she would go in low. She used her fingers to count to three and pushed in the door.

They went in quick and quiet. It only took a second to realize they were too late. The body was lying on the bed with a pillow covering the face. A single bullet hole showed through the pillow.

Megan reached for the pillow and pulled it away from the face. Immediately she felt her heart sink.

"Peterson." It was Eli.

Megan threw the pillow against the wall. "Why couldn't he just do what he was told? Why didn't he just—" She kicked the small end table.

Eli reached out and grabbed her arm. "Hey, this isn't our fault."

Megan pulled a chair out from the table along the wall and sat down. "I know. It just hacks me off, is all. I mean, we told him. 'Stay out of it,' we said."

They both remained silent for a few minutes. Finally Megan spoke up. "So, if he's dead. . .and we were with Hayes last night. . .how do you suppose he ended up this way?"

Eli shrugged. "If I had to guess, I'd say Peterson sent us after Hayes on purpose."

"You saying Hayes was just a ruse? That he's not involved?"

"Didn't say that. What I mean is if Peterson sent us after Hayes, it was because he had a lead on something better."

"Pemberton." Megan smacked her hand on the table.

"Probably."

"Got to call this in. Jennings is not going to be happy."

She retrieved the sat-phone from her pocket and dialed the number.

"This is Director Jennings."

"It's Taylor, sir. We're here."

"And?"

"And. . .looks like Peterson didn't do like we asked him to. He's dead, sir. Single gunshot to the head."

Jennings was quiet for a few seconds. "I was afraid of that."

"So you knew?"

"No. . .I didn't know. I figured. The guy that called me works the night shift there. Company guys have used that motel for years. He's always been a kind of Johnny-on-the-spot for us. He knows just about every operative that's been there for the last thirty years. Guess he either saw or heard it. Then he called me. . .I called you. . .and. . ."

"Yeah."

"Yeah."

"So what do you want us to do now?"

"Call the locals. Then put the scene back the way you found it and get out of there."

"You don't want us to wait?"

"You want to be there for the next nine hours answering questions?"

"Not exactly."

"Good. Then I want you to go see the front desk manager and tell him you want to talk to Fred Vargas. He's the night guy I told you about. Go find out what he saw. Or heard."

"Got it. Any word yet from Jon?"

"None. Go find Vargas. I want to know what got Peterson killed."

CHAPTER 24

Chinese—US Border

Keene pushed himself up onto his knees and looked back at the gate. The entire thing had crumbled into a pile of twisted chain-link fence and rubble. Dust and smoke were quickly filling the air from the wreckage.

Keene knew that they had successfully taken out most of the guards. The .50 caliber machine gun had wreaked havoc on the Chinese barricade and its men. But there were still a few stragglers. And reinforcements would be there soon, if they weren't already pulling in. He had to act quickly. The cab of the truck was exposed and Boz was a pinned target—if he wasn't already dead. He began to say a prayer as he pushed himself the rest of the way up onto his feet and began running to Boz.

Boz was slumped forward, lying on the steering column. His face was awash with blood, leaking from what looked like a fresh wound to his forehead—probably from slamming headfirst into the steering wheel.

Keene grabbed the door handle and pulled. Nothing. The door was jammed. On the other side of the rubble, he could hear what was left of the CG barking orders to one another. *It will only be a matter of seconds before they come over that pile,* he thought. He raised his leg and placed his foot on the rear fender beside the driver's-side door for leverage. Then with every ounce of strength he could muster, he pulled on the door. The door began to creak and grind as it protested but finally gave way. Keene threw it open and reached inside to grab his friend, who was coming around.

He'd just gotten Boz out of the cab when he heard the first of the guards coming after them. He slung the SKS rifle he had draped over his shoulder around, holding Boz with one arm and the rifle with the other. Without looking, he took off, dragging Boz and firing the SKS blindly behind him. Though they were in the middle of the road, the tree line for the mountains was on either side of them. If he could just get to cover, he was sure he could get them both out of there.

Suddenly, a loud whooshing sound came from around the bend in the road. Then an explosion of massive gunfire. Keene had just reached the tree line when he saw the source of the attack. A wave of relief washed over him as he watched a Black Hawk helicopter come from out of nowhere and open fire on the Chinese barricade. Quickly, he picked up his friend again.

"Let's go! Our ride is here."

Keene threw Boz's arm around his own shoulder and began running to the Black Hawk, which had landed in the middle of the road. Four men had jumped from the helicopter and were laying down cover fire. Keene pushed Boz up and into the waiting chopper and then jumped in after him. The four men, now that their assets were secure, retreated back into the Black Hawk just as it was lifting off again. In moments, the bird was in the air and headed east.

Keene smiled a huge smile as he recognized his rescuers. The men he'd spent an entire night with, carrying out a mission to stop Chin from launching a nuclear device on Washington, were sitting before him.

"Took you long enough, Ramirez!" Keene shouted over the wash of the rotors.

"Foust couldn't find his good luck teddy bear!" Ramirez laughed.

Foust, who was reaching out to shake Keene's hand, gave Ramirez a *hardy-har-har* sarcastic laugh. Then to Keene, "Good to see you, sir."

"You, too," Keene said. "Thanks for the ride."

Foust, Ramirez, Kirkpatrick, and Jenkins were four special ops guys that Keene had handpicked for the mission in Massena. The four of them had successfully managed to stop what could have been the complete annihilation of the United States during the Chinese attack. It was there that Keene had left his men and followed after Chin.

Keene introduced the men to Boz, who had fully come around, while Jenkins looked over Boz's injuries.

"You're going to feel it for a few days, but you'll live," Jenkins said.

Boz nodded and thanked him.

"Does Jennings know you guys are here?" Keene asked. " 'Cause Chin is going to be livid!"

"Who do you think sent us?" Kirkpatrick said.

"Isn't he worried that Chin will retaliate?"

"Guess it was a risk he was willing to take," Ramirez answered.

"What's our ETA to Washington?" Keene asked.

"About two hours," Ramirez said. He threw Keene a small bag wrapped in plastic. "We figured you two would be hungry."

Keene unwrapped the plastic to find two cheeseburgers from his favorite fast-food place. He handed one to Boz and looked back at Ramirez. "You have no idea!"

CHAPTER 25

Megan and Eli were parked outside the residence of Fred Vargas. They'd gotten the address from the day manager, after Megan reluctantly showed him her ID. They then told him the local police would be showing up—there had been an accident in one of the rooms—and he was to keep staff out of the room until the locals got there. Megan wondered how long that directive actually lasted—since she and Eli had bolted before he could ask any more questions.

Vargas's house was a ranch-style. Probably constructed in the early 1980s. She could tell from the design—the pinkish-brown brick, the turn-around drive connected to the covered breezeway that led to the two-car garage, and the fact that the house showed several years of weathering. A single, older-model Toyota sat parked outside the garage.

"Well, this is it," Megan said, putting the shifter in PARK. "Let's go."

They got out of the car and went to the door. They knocked. Nothing.

"Probably asleep," Eli said. "Guy worked all night."

This time, Megan balled her fist and pounded heavily on the door. After a few seconds, she could hear someone moving around inside. Finally, the door opened up, revealing an older Latino gentleman. He shielded his eyes from the bright sunlight spilling in at him.

Megan stepped forward. "Mr. Vargas?"

"Yeah. Who are you?"

"I'm Megan Taylor. This is Eli Craig. Kevin Jennings sent us to talk to you. May we come in?"

Vargas stuck his head out the door and looked around. "You alone?"

"Yes, sir."

He motioned them inside and closed the door behind them. "Sorry the place is a mess. Maid comes next week."

Both she and Eli smiled at the old joke. "Sorry to bother you, Mr. Vargas. We won't be long."

Vargas motioned for them to sit. "So I guess the guy in room 119 *was* one of yours?"

Megan nodded. "His name was Peterson."

Vargas hung his head and pinched the bridge of his nose. "Aw, man. . . What was Peterson doing down here? I haven't seen him in like. . .twenty years."

Megan didn't try to hide her surprise. "You know him?"

"Yeah. . .I know pretty much all you spooks who used that place. Peterson was a nice guy. Shame."

"Why didn't you tell Jennings it was him when you called?"

Vargas shrugged. "Didn't know. I went into the room, saw the body lying on the bed—with the pillow and the blood—and I just got out of there. Didn't touch anything."

Megan was confused now. "I'm sorry, Mr. Vargas, I guess I missed something. Why would you call Jennings? Why not the locals? What made you think it was a Company guy?"

Vargas nodded. "Because I've seen hits like that before." Vargas cleared his throat, which spun into a coughing fit. "Sorry," he said again. "Can I get you guys something to drink?" He stood up and walked into the kitchen.

"We're fine."

Vargas returned with a giant orange plastic cup and sat down. He held the cup up for them to see. "My wife—God rest her soul—used to get onto me about these cups. Said they were an eyesore. Always used to ask me, 'Why can't you just use a glass glass like everyone else?' But I've had this here cup for almost fifteen years. It's my favorite—"

"Mr. Vargas. . .you were saying. . .about Peterson?"

Vargas snapped his fingers and pointed at her. "Peterson. Right!" He shifted in his seat, took a big gulp of whatever it was he was drinking, and set it down on the little table beside his recliner. "So last night, the front desk calls me in my office. Says someone's complaining about their heat. Won't come on." Vargas shrugged his shoulders. "I'm thinking, it's not even cold. It's nice outside for this time of year. Why do you need to turn your heat on?"

Megan squinted and looked at Eli who just shrugged.

"Sorry. . .rambling again. Anyway, I grab my tools and head out. And that's when I noticed the car sitting across the parking lot at the Quick Mart."

"What car?" Eli asked.

"Same car that was there had been sitting there for nearly an hour. Had someone in the driver's side. Couldn't see who, though."

"What's the car got anything to do with anything?" Megan asked.

Vargas looked at her like a father about to scold his daughter. "Ms. Taylor, you spend enough time around your kind and you learn to notice things. Things like a rental car with someone in it, just sitting in a parking lot and watching a motel."

"How do you know it was a rental?"

"Had one of those company license plates on the front. Avis, or Enterprise. . .couldn't make it out. Too dark. But that car was sitting there when I went up to fix a light fixture in 229 earlier. And then, when I went to go fix that heat unit, it was still there. That job took me about twenty minutes. When I left the car was still there, but the driver wasn't."

"What kind of car?"

"Typical rental. Silver, base-model sedan."

"Did you see who was in it?"

"Not then. I went back to my office to put my stuff away. Then I got a craving for a candy bar. So I went back out to the vending machine—which sits back in that little cove by the front office. That's the only thing bad about a *motel* versus a *hotel*. Everything's outside. I had just taken my shoes off and gotten comfortable when it hit me that I wanted that candy bar—"

"Mr. Vargas, please. . ."

Vargas smiled at her. "Sorry. Rambling again. . . Anyway, I went to the machine. And wouldn't you know it, the thing ate my money. Now, those things are managed by a third party, so I can't get in to them. But I really wanted that candy bar, so I decided to go over to the Quick Mart."

Megan was beginning to think she and Eli were wasting their time. "Mr. Vargas, I'm not sure I understand how any of this is important to Peterson."

Vargas held up a finger. "I'm getting to that." He took another drink from his cup. "Now, if there's one thing I've learned over the years from hanging out with you spooks, it's to be suspicious of random cars that stake out motel rooms and then just leave. So, after the car was out of sight, I walked down that side of the rooms and just looked around."

Megan was sitting up in her chair again. "And?"

"And that's when I saw the door to 119 cracked open. So I knocked. No one answered, so I knocked a little harder this time. When I did, the door pushed open a little more. And that's when I saw it—Peterson, I mean."

Eli tilted his head and scrunched his brow. "But when we got there this morning, the door was shut."

Vargas drew in his mouth. "Yeah. . .I might've closed the door behind me when I left." Then, hurriedly, "But only to make sure that no one else would go in! Then I went back to my office to call Jennings. But I couldn't get ahold of him until right before I left to come home."

Megan thought about everything Vargas had said—which was pretty much a whole lot of nothing. She would have to call Jennings and tell him that Vargas was a bust. She nodded to Eli, who took her cue and stood with her. "Thanks for all your help, Mr. Vargas."

Vargas stood with them and led them back to the door. "Listen, I know it's not much, but you guys need to check out that car. Whoever that lady was, she's the one who killed Peterson."

Megan stopped dead in her tracks. She slowly turned back to Vargas. "I'm sorry. What did you just say?"

Vargas's eyes went wide and he slapped himself in the forehead. "Oh, yeah! The lady. I almost forgot."

"What lady?" Megan said.

"The lady from the car."

"You said you couldn't see who was in the car," Eli said.

Vargas nodded. "I couldn't. Earlier. But when I went to get my candy bar—as I was leaving the Quick Mart—I saw a woman getting into that car. A woman. Which is crazy, right? Because, I mean, how many women assassins can there be? Right?"

There were a million thoughts going through Megan's mind right then. Everything from a prostitute to a bad dope deal. But Peterson was seventy-six years old. She doubted either of those would prove right. Suddenly she had a sickening feeling in her stomach, as Vargas's words hit home. *How many women assassins can there be?* "Mr. Vargas, what did she look like?"

Vargas smiled. "Well, I only saw her for a couple seconds, when she turned around to get in the car. But there's no way I'd forget that face. She was beautiful." His eyes trailed off, as if he were savoring the memory.

"Mr. Vargas, please!" Megan said.

"Oh, right. Yeah. She was tall and thin. She was wearing a long coat.

She had very strong features. I'd say probably Eastern European. . . ."

Megan could feel her chest constricting. *No way. . .it can't be. Absolutely impossible. . .*

". . . She had longish, blond hair. . . ."

Megan cut him off. "Her eyes. Did you see her eyes?"

Vargas nodded quickly. "Yeah. Right before she got in the car, as I was walking past her, she stopped and looked right at me. We were right under the streetlamp. I saw them. They were deep blue. Like ice."

Megan felt a chill run down her spine. Her head began to spin and her mouth went dry. She caught Eli out of the corner of her eye.

"Megan, you okay? You look like you just saw a ghost."

Megan shook her head. "No, I'm not okay. And I didn't see a ghost." She pointed at Vargas. "But I think he did." She dialed the sat-phone and waited for Jennings to pick up.

"This is Taylor. I think we have a serious problem."

CHAPTER 26

The first thing Jennings did when Boz and Keene returned was send them to Bethesda for a complete medical evaluation. It only took looking at the two of them to see that they had been lucky to get out of Chinese territory alive. He was immediately glad that he had sent Ramirez and his team to wait for them at the border. He'd known that decision was going to come with some blowback. And right now, he was dealing with it. President Walker had stormed into his office the moment he'd heard.

"I can't believe you would do something this stupid, Kevin!" Walker yelled. "You know how sensitive our situation is right now. We have half this country wanting us to go back to war with the Chinese already. You just threw a truckload of fuel on that fire. . . ."

Jennings let him rant. There wasn't much more he could do. It *was* stupid. If he were Walker, he'd probably fire himself. Effective immediately. But he had to do it nonetheless. And Walker was going to have to accept that.

". . . and what's more. . .Chin has already threatened retaliation! How am I supposed to lead this country back from the brink of destruction if every time I turn around you're off playing cowboy? I thought we were on the same page."

Jennings just looked at him.

"Say something! Anything!"

Jennings sat up in his chair. "Mr. President, I understand the risk I took. And I understand what's at stake here. But you need to know that under no circumstances was I about to let the two men responsible for saving what's left of this country die on that border. I gave my men explicit orders. *Do not engage unless absolutely necessary.* They were only there to pick them up once they crossed. They had no choice. Keene blew

133

up the entire checkpoint with a military truck and a fifty-caliber machine gun. And they were both injured in the escape. They would've been killed. I couldn't let that happen."

Walker's face turned red again as he pointed at him. "It wasn't your decision to make!"

Jennings matched his tone. "You're right! It wasn't. I didn't make that decision."

Walker looked at him confused.

"The Prophet told me to make sure that Jon and Boz got home. I was following orders. Period!"

That seemed to get Walker's attention. "I don't understand. What's going on?"

Jennings drew in a long breath. He'd been dreading having this conversation, ever since the situation presented itself. But he'd known, sooner or later, he'd have to bring the president in. It was, after all, a matter of national security. Especially with the news he'd just gotten from Megan and Eli. "Mr. President, I believe we have bigger problems than the Chinese right now."

Walker hung his head. "What now?"

"As I told you before, the Prophet contacted us, told us he had Jon, and that we needed to come get him. What I didn't tell you—and not because I have any hidden agenda, but because I wanted to investigate a little to know exactly what we're dealing with—is the Prophet has given us a new warning."

Walker's face got red again. "And you didn't tell me?"

Jennings held up a hand to hold him off. "Like I said, I wanted to dig a little before I brought it to you. You have enough going on trying to get the country back to some sense of normalcy without having to worry about something we know nothing about yet."

Walker ran his hand over his face. "So what *do* you know?"

"First of all, I know any threat you get from Chin is going to go away. He might blow a little hot air over all this, but that's all it's going to be. Hot air."

"How do you know that?"

"Because, think about it. They have what they came for. They knew we wouldn't launch an attack on American soil. And we didn't. And we've agreed to not advance back on them and he knows we won't. But if they push us—now that we've got our bearings, even as disjointed as they seem—it would be ugly for him. Getting Jon back is just one of those things that people like Chin and I—well, let's just say Chin *gets* it.

"Secondly, I know because the Prophet said Chin is not our problem. We're our problem. Or, at least, some of us are the problem."

Walker stared blankly at him. "I don't understand."

Jennings spent the next ten minutes getting Walker up to speed with what information he had. He started with his initial conversation with the Prophet and finished with the news about Peterson. When he finished, he folded his hands and waited for the president to respond. Walker, however, just sat there with a grimace on his face. Finally, Jennings broke the tension. "Do you have any history with this Pemberton guy?"

Walker looked at him as if he'd accused him of murder. "What's *that* supposed to mean?"

Jennings held up his hands. "Whoa, easy, Mr. President. That wasn't an indictment. It was a question. Apparently this guy's heavy into politics. I just thought. . .with your family's rich political history, maybe you've crossed paths. Been to a dinner together. Something."

"Never heard of him."

"See, and there's my problem. Apparently, not too many people have. There's no record of him ever being involved in anything. But if you ask the right people—and trust me, Peterson knew the right people—they'll tell you that Pemberton is a heavyweight."

"How's that possible?"

"You tell me. I've come across some people before that have some gaps in their records. But I'm the director of the CIA. If I want them found, they get found. Not this guy. This Pemberton guy's squeaky clean. He doesn't even *have* a file."

"How is that possible?" Walker asked again.

"It's not," Jennings quipped. "That's my point. This guy has gone to incredible lengths to see to it his name isn't attached to anything other than the family tobacco company."

Walker gave a dismissive flick of his hand. "Maybe he's not involved."

Jennings narrowed his eyes and leaned forward. "Then why do I have a dead former agent in Raleigh who was perfectly alive before he started asking about Pemberton?"

"Good point."

"Yeah."

"So what exactly is this Pemberton fella supposed to be doing?"

ROBBIE CHEUVRONT AND ERIK REED

"I'll let you know, soon as I know. In the meantime, you need to continue to try and bring the nation together. There's still a lot of divided opinions of what we should be doing. It's imperative that you persuade the people that Quinn—the Prophet—isn't some quack. That God did, indeed, bring this upon us, and we need to accept what we've been given moving forward."

"I'm doing my best, Kevin."

"I know you are, sir. Just keep up what you're doing. Leave the spy work to me and my people. Soon as I know what's going on, I'll let you know."

Walker stood to leave.

"There's one other thing." Jennings stood with the president. "President Grant woke up."

Walker stared blankly at him for a moment. Then, "So what do we do? I mean, does he know everything that's happened? Does he remember anything? Is he all right?"

Jennings shook his head. "I don't know any more than he woke up. I'm going to go find out more this afternoon. I thought I'd go pick Jon and Boz up myself and check in on what's happening."

Walker began to pace back and forth. "You let me know the moment you find out. I mean, this changes everything. If he's all right. . .I mean. . . technically, he's still the president. I'll need to turn everything back over to him."

Jennings gave an assuring nod. "Let's not get ahead of ourselves. We don't know what's going on with him just yet. You've done a good job leading this country. The people are looking to you right now. You're their president."

"If President Grant is awake, the American people need to know."

Jennings narrowed his eyes. "We have no idea how President Grant is right now. The doctors say they need to run tests. They'll probably be doing that for the better part of a week. We have no way of knowing whether or not he's even capable of resuming office any time soon. What the American people need is a president with his faculties fully functioning. If even a hint of President Grant's status gets out, there could be more chaos than we can deal with right now. I have given explicit instructions to everyone even remotely associated with President Grant's situation to lock it down. I suggest you do the same." He sighed and pinched the bridge of his nose. "Please trust me. We don't need that kind of attention right now.

You're the president. Let's just move forward."

Walker seemed to weigh all of what Jennings had just said. Finally, he nodded. "You're right. We'll keep this under the radar. For now."

Jennings relaxed a bit. "Mr. President, you're fully capable of doing this job. You're a good man. And the people need that right now. So go do what you need to do."

Walker nodded. "Thank you, Kevin. I appreciate your encouragement." He turned to leave but stopped short. "I had planned to give a radio address tomorrow. Just to reassure the people that we are headed in the right direction. I've been thinking about making a proposal to Congress to amend the Constitution. I want to include language that defines this country as a nation centered on Christian principles. And I'm going to suggest we begin making quite a few policy changes. Starting with this upcoming Christmas season. After our conversation here, I think I'm going to propose it during that address. You know, put it out there to the people. I think it's about time we drew some lines in the sand."

Jennings smiled. "Well, I'm certainly not the Prophet, but if I had to guess, I'd say that's exactly what God would want you to do."

CHAPTER 27

Raleigh, North Carolina

Pemberton had been ignoring the phone all morning. It had rung, it seemed, at least fifty times in the last four hours. But he didn't care. He knew it was either Hayes or the governor. And he didn't need to talk to either of them right now. Right now, he was in strategic planning mode.

He had it all laid out on several pieces of paper, strewn about the table in front of him: who was supposed to do what and when. As long as everyone did what they were supposed to do, Walker and the rest of those idiots in Washington should either be out of the way—or better yet, dead—by the end of next week.

He looked it all over once more. Ran it all through his head again. Try as he did, he couldn't find a hole anywhere in the whole thing. Satisfied, he reached inside his shirt pocket and pulled out a Louixs. He clipped the end, stuck it in his mouth, and rolled it around his tongue a couple of times. Then he lit the tip and took three long drags, to stoke the ember. Once the cigar was burning successfully, he pushed back from his chair and stood up. He grabbed the old phone off the side table in the hall and stretched it outside onto the porch. The wind was picking up again, so he had to pull his collar up. He hated the thought of the cold finally settling in. He'd hoped to make it to Christmas with this sixty-degree weather. He picked up the receiver and punched the numbers in. Hayes answered on the first ring.

"Where have you been? I've been trying to get you for over five hours."

Pemberton spit a piece of loose tobacco over the rail. "Busy."

"Busy! Do you have any idea what happened to me last night?"

Pemberton rolled his eyes. "No, but I bet you're going to tell me."

"I got home from dinner and two federal agents were in my house. In my private study!"

Hayes had his attention now. He sat up in the chair and gripped the phone tighter. "Who were they and what did they want? And how the heck did they get in your house? What kind of place you running over there, Milton?"

"They bypassed my security."

"No kidding."

Hayes ignored the jab. "They wanted to know about you."

Something akin to an acidic taste filled his mouth. He'd spent his whole life staying away from the feds. He'd spent a lot of money and had to quiet a lot of mouths over his business dealings. This did not sit well with him. At all. "*What* about me?"

"They wanted to know if I knew you. Asked me if you and I have had any business dealings." Then, "Gavin, I think we've got problems."

Pemberton agreed. But he wasn't about to show any sort of weakness. Especially to Hayes. Hayes was already wishy-washy enough. He didn't need the man going into full-on panic mode. "And of course, you told them that you and I are old buddies."

"I did no such thing!"

Pemberton imagined Hayes hyperventilating on the other end. "Calm down. I'm just jerking your chain." He let a couple of seconds of quiet pass by. Then, "Listen, Milton, we've talked with a lot of people over the last few months about this. Can't be done without people getting involved. Not everyone is as tight to the vest as you and I are." He said that knowing full well that Hayes could be as loose lipped as a drunken sailor at times. But he needed to reassure his partner that everything was fine. At least for now.

"But if they're asking about you, then don't you think they already know something? I mean, we're supposed to meet with everyone when we go to Washington in a few days. How do we know that hasn't been compromised?"

Hayes had a point. He'd have to do some digging. "We don't. We'll just have to be extra careful. And take steps to make sure we're not." Then, "Who did you say those agents were, again?"

"That's what's weird. They said they were FBI. One was a lady, said her name was Taylor. The other was a Brit. . .Craig or something."

Neither name rang any bells with him, but that didn't matter. If they were asking about him, they needed to be dealt with. And he had just the idea for them. "I'll take care of them. You just make sure you're at the Shed at seven thirty sharp."

"I'll be there. Is everyone else confirmed?"

"Everyone, plus one."

Hayes was quiet for a moment. Then, "I don't understand. Someone else will be there? I thought it was going to be just the four of us."

"Yeah, I'm bringing a date. You're going to like her."

Pemberton placed the receiver back in the cradle and began to think about the two agents that had come to visit Hayes. He'd known his old friend since their days at Yale. They'd been through quite a lot together. But nothing as important as this. It bothered him that Hayes had so easily become a target for the feds to get at him. As bad as it troubled him, he began to wonder whether or not his old friend had finally outlived his usefulness.

CHAPTER 28

Megan and Eli spent the rest of the morning and afternoon waiting. Waiting on what, they had no idea. They were currently sitting in the car, parked a half block down the street from Hayes's address. They barely had a view of the drive—just enough to see any car coming or going. And so far, none had done either.

After leaving Vargas, Megan had spent twenty minutes on the phone with Jennings. He told her that Jon and Boz were safely back. That he had them over at Bethesda getting a full medical evaluation. She relayed the message to Eli, interrupting Jennings. Both she and Eli celebrated while Jennings was left hanging on the line. It was the best news she'd heard in months.

"Don't you let Jon tell them he's fine," she said. "Make him listen to them."

Jennings assured her that he was in charge. Not Jon.

They spent the rest of the conversation talking about the possibility of the woman Vargas saw being Alex Sokolov, a.k.a. Alex Smith. Jennings said it wouldn't surprise him.

"Kevin, I watched the woman die!" she said. "I *physically* watched her take her last breath."

"How long did you stick around after?" Jennings asked.

"I didn't. Are you kidding? I was in Dubai in the middle of the start of World War III. And. . .I had just called in a bomb threat to the airport, caused a massive wreck on the road leading into the airport, and then got into a gunfight with a trained Russian assassin. I wasn't looking to put down roots."

"My point exactly."

Megan knew he was right. She'd heard of people being brought back to life by doctors ten minutes, twenty minutes, sometimes an hour after death. She had no idea what had happened to Alex Smith. And now, she feared, the woman was back. "I swear, I think that woman is the spawn of Satan."

Jennings half laughed. "You might actually be right."

She'd meant it as an attempt at levity, but given the last few months, it wouldn't surprise her. "Let's hope not."

"Amen to that," Jennings said.

"So what now? Where do we go from here?"

"I want you two to sit on Hayes. I want to know where he goes, who he talks to, or who comes to him."

"What about Alex? If she's here, something big is going down. We need to stop her."

"*If* it is her, and she *is* there, then you need to stay as low to the ground as you can get. She's obviously not in Raleigh to take in the sights."

Megan got it. "Peterson."

"Yeah, and the last thing I need is you running into her. We've got enough going on without trying to explain why half the city of Raleigh got blown up by two of my agents and a supposedly dead assassin. So stick to Hayes. If he doesn't lead you to Pemberton in the next day, we'll switch gears. But my gut says those two are closer than they'd like anyone to know. And like I said before, if there's one thing Peterson was good at, it was intel. If he said Hayes and Pemberton are in cahoots with one another, I buy it."

Megan had given Jennings her word that she would follow his orders and not go looking for Vargas's woman from the parking lot. Which led them to sitting here in the car for the last—she checked her watch—six hours. And not even a delivery truck had appeared anywhere near Hayes's place. It was getting on close to dinnertime now and the sun was starting to set. Megan looked over to Eli, who had been napping. She nudged his shoulder. "Hey, get up."

Eli sat up in the seat and rubbed his eyes. "Getting dark."

"Yeah. And I'm hungry. So sit up and pay attention while I get that bag from the trunk."

Before taking up their position, they had stopped at a convenience store. They had no idea how long they would be sitting there.

She pulled the lever on her seat so it would lay down. Then she turned around and removed the seat cushion from the back of the rear seat, allowing her to reach into the trunk. She retrieved the bag and set her seat back up. She dug inside and pulled out two premade sub sandwiches wrapped in plastic wrap, a couple of bags of chips, and a zip-up cooler large enough for two soft drinks. She handed Eli his. She hadn't realized how hungry she was until she took the first bite of her turkey.

Eli thanked her and took a bite of his roast beef. "You know, I'm kind of impressed that we've been here all this time, and not once have you mentioned having to go to the loo."

Megan wiped some mustard from her chin. "The *loo?*"

"You know, the water closet, washroom. . ."

Megan nodded. "You mean the bathroom."

"Yes, the bathroom."

"Well, neither have you."

"Yes, but I'm a trained spy. I've learned how to. . .how do you say. . . *hold it.*"

She took another giant bite of turkey. "And I'm a girl. We can last all day, sometimes, without going."

"How is that possible?"

Megan thought about it for a second. "I don't know. I guess we just. . . don't think about it. It's like when you forget to eat."

Eli just looked at her like she was crazy.

"Trust me. It's just a girl thing."

"I had a girlfriend tell me that once. Back at university—whoa!" He stopped short and caught the half-eaten sandwich Megan had just tossed him.

"Heads up, chief," she said. "We're moving."

An old pickup truck was waiting to pull out as the gates to Hayes's driveway began to slowly creep open.

Eli quickly stowed the sandwiches and drinks while Megan turned the engine on and got ready to drive.

She waited for the truck to completely pull out onto the road and take off before easing out onto the road behind him. She stayed as close as she could without risking being made.

"How do you know that's him?" Eli asked. "The man has two Mercedes and a Range Rover in the garage and a Porsche sitting out front. I never saw an old pickup truck."

"I don't know. Maybe he keeps it around the side in a shed or something. But it's him. There's a picture of him standing outside that truck in his office. He was duck hunting or something. Had some camouflage overalls on and a shotgun, posing with some hunting dogs."

"Probably drives that thing when he doesn't want to be recognized."

"Exactly."

"Lucky for us you like to look at other people's pictures."

Megan nodded and let off the gas as the truck's brake lights lit up. "Hey, grab the map. There's not much traffic out here and I don't want to get spotted. I'd like to know, as he turns, how far ahead I can leave him before we run the risk of losing him to a random turn."

"No problem." Eli reached behind him and pulled the map up front.

The first ten minutes or so were sketchy. Light traffic in the residential area made it harder to stay back and remain unnoticed. But once they got into town, it became easier. With more cars on the road, Megan was able to shorten the distance between them and even change lanes a couple of times, without drawing any attention. Once they got through town, however, it was a different story altogether.

They found themselves on Durant Road, a two-lane running parallel to the I-540 bypass. The road was long, winding, and there weren't many cars out. It was after dark now. Megan was having a hard time keeping the truck in view. A couple of times, she had hung back, only to make the bend in the road and not see the truck's taillights. Cautiously, she would speed up a little, easing around a bend, only to see the truck rounding the next curve.

After ten minutes of this, she came around a big sweeping bend that opened up into a long stretch of road. Even in the dark, she could tell there was at least a mile of straightaway ahead of her. And no pickup. She hit the gas, hoping to see the faint red glow of the truck's rear lights ahead. She pushed the car hard to gain some ground, but even after the next bend, which gave way to another long straightaway, the pickup was nowhere to be found.

Hayes had vanished.

CHAPTER 29

Washington, DC

It was just after dark when Jennings arrived to pick Keene and Boz up from Bethesda. Keene was none too happy with his boss, either. He launched into Jennings the moment he came into the room.

"A full workup, Kevin? Seriously? I've been here for over six hours now, getting poked and prodded like some kind of guinea pig. Who knows what they've been doing to Boz. They took him out of here a few minutes ago. For the fourth time."

His boss just smiled at him. "Good to have you back, Jon."

Keene shook his head, jumped off the bed, and tugged at the medical gown he was wearing. "And where are my clothes? I've been wearing this stupid thing all day."

"Calm down, Jon. They're only doing what I told them to do."

"That's my point!"

Just then the door reopened and Boz walked in. Fully dressed. "What are you doing still wearing that thing? It's time to go. Get dressed."

"Oh, I'd love to," Keene said sarcastically. "Just as soon as they bring me my stuff," he yelled, leaning out the door into the hallway.

Both Jennings and Boz laughed.

"I'm glad you two think this is funny."

Jennings held his hands up in surrender. "Hey, I'm just trying to make sure you're good. I mean you *have* been gone for a while now. We just needed to make sure Chin didn't implant any devices in you, and that you're completely healthy."

"I'm fine," Keene said. "Now can we please go?"

Jennings nodded. "Yes. I checked with the doctors on my way in to make sure everything was good. A nurse is on her way to bring you your things."

" 'Bout time."

Just then one of the nurses that had been in and out of his room all day appeared, carrying a stack of clothes. She handed them to him. "Here you are, Mr. Keene. Thank you for cooperating with us today. You're free to go."

Jennings shot a look at Keene. And then back to the nurse. "Did you say he was cooperative?"

"Yes, Director. Mr. Keene was a good patient."

The nurse turned and left. Jennings looked back to Keene who just shrugged. "What?"

"I know what the tests say, but are you sure you're all right?"

Keene just sighed. "Jennings, I've been in a Chinese prison camp for five months. I knew five minutes after I walked in here what you had planned for me. I figured I'd just deal with it."

Jennings smiled and looked at Boz. Boz laughed and said, "I think our little boy is *all grown up*."

Keene elbowed Boz out of the way and pushed past Jennings. "Ha-ha. Now let's go."

Outside, Jennings had a car waiting for them. Keene jumped in first and leaned over the seat to the driver. "Hey, I don't know where Jennings told you to take us, but I don't care. We're going somewhere to eat."

"That's exactly where I told him we were going," Jennings said, piling into the vehicle.

"And you're buying," Keene said. "Especially after everything you just put me through in there."

Jennings just shook his head and told the driver where to take them. Fifteen minutes later, the three of them were sitting at a quiet table in one of the city's favorite local restaurants.

Keene hadn't had the time or opportunity to tell Boz—much less Jennings—all that had happened to him from the time of his capture to the Chinese barricade early that morning. The three of them spent the entire dinner with Keene filling them in.

When they left the restaurant, Jennings instructed the driver to take them back to his office. Keene really only wanted to get back to his house and lie down in his own bed. But he knew it would have to wait. Megan and Eli Craig were in Raleigh, Jennings had told him, trying to get a lead on what the Prophet had warned them about. And they had things to talk about.

Jennings waited until they were all settled in his office before he finally started. He told Keene about what the Prophet had told him concerning the threat. He then filled him in on how he had made some calls, which led him to Peterson, which caused him to send Megan and Eli south.

When it was Keene's turn, he told them about how the Prophet had confirmed pretty much the same thing to him, but that he really didn't have any details. Except that the Prophet had told him that he was going to be the one to stop it.

"I have no idea what that means," Keene admitted. He looked to Boz. "What do you think, Chappy?"

Boz shrugged. "I'm not sure, Jon. I don't know if that means that you're physically supposed to stop it, or if you have information that will help us, collectively, stop it. . .or. . .I don't know."

Keene rolled his head around. His neck was getting stiff and he was getting tired. He was about to suggest they call it a night when Jennings spoke.

"I'm not sure if this has anything to do with it or not, but there's one other thing I found out this morning."

Keene turned to his boss. Jennings had a concerned look about him. And that concerned Keene.

"Megan and Eli found Nolan Peterson dead this morning."

Keene listened as Jennings told them how the call from Vargas had led them to the body.

Halfway through the story, Keene could feel the hair on the back of his neck standing up. His senses were tingling even before Kevin finished. He knew whatever was coming next was not going to be good.

"So did Vargas ever get a look at who was inside the car?" Keene asked.

"I'm getting to that," Jennings said. "Vargas said that as he was looking out into the parking lot, he saw a woman getting back into the car."

There it was. Alarms started going off inside Keene's head. The kind that said, *Whatever you're about to hear next, Jon, you're not going to like one bit.*

"Vargas said when she turned into the streetlight, he saw her face," Jennings said.

"Who was it?" Keene asked.

Jennings pinched the bridge of his nose. "I think it was the Russian."

CHAPTER 30

Raleigh, North Carolina

Alex Smith stood outside the old farmhouse with Pemberton as they waited for the last two guests to arrive. She still had the events of last night racing through her mind. It was one of the best nights she could remember. It had started when Pemberton spilled who it was he wanted eliminated. The president. What were the chances? Twice in one lifetime? Then, as if it couldn't get better, the unexpected run-in with that poor old man. The sheer ecstasy that coursed through her veins, as she waited outside the motel, deciding how to dispose of him. In the end, she decided to just make it quick. A single shot to the head. Quick and clean. Instantly she had been flooded with the satisfaction of being back in the game. It had set the tone for the rest of her night with Farid.

The wind began to kick up, so she pulled her collar up over her face as they waited for the final two guests to arrive. The governor, as Pemberton introduced him, was already there. That only left Irving and Hayes.

She saw the beams of a pair of low-riding headlights punch through the trees at the front of the drive. Even in the dark, she could tell it was an old pickup truck. The dimness of the headlights gave it away. A few seconds later, Hayes pulled into the gravel next to Pemberton's pickup. She checked her watch: 7:28 p.m.

"Well, lookie-there. Right on time. There's a first time for everything."

Hayes ignored Pemberton's barb. Instead, he walked over to the governor. "Joe, good to see you." He and the governor shook hands. Then he pointed to her. "And who might you be, young la—"

Pemberton cut him off. "Let's save introductions for when everyone's here."

Hayes huffed at him and stuck his hands in his coat.

Within minutes, another set of headlights pierced the trees. They

148

all watched as the headlights bounced back and forth along the winding dirt road, until finally an Infiniti FX-hybrid came to rest beside the other vehicles. A very distinguished-looking man stepped out and walked over to everyone.

"Pemberton, you need to fix that stinking drive. I think I just knocked my oil pan out."

"It's a farm, Irving. If you ain't got enough sense to drive your pickup, then I don't feel sorry for you." Pemberton turned around and started walking toward a shed that sat just a few yards away. He stepped inside briefly and then returned.

She heard a *click-phsst* as the concrete slab beside her began to move. Pemberton motioned for everyone to follow as he descended a set of concrete steps. She fell in line and started down the stairs. After a few seconds, the slab moved back into place.

Inside, Pemberton showed everyone to a sitting area complete with a nice wooden round table and a few chairs. One in particular stood out to her. "Nice chair."

Pemberton extended his hand. "Be my guest."

"I use to have two of them at my old place," she said.

Pemberton shot her a look that said he was impressed. She sat down, remembering how comfortable the Aresline could be.

The others all took a seat while Pemberton went to the bar and fixed some drinks. When he came back, he passed them out. "A toast."

Everyone raised a glass.

"To new partnerships. And a better future."

Everyone nodded and drank as Pemberton sat down with his guests.

"Thank you all for coming," he started. "Everyone here knows why we're here." He pointed to Alex. "I'd like to introduce you all to my acquaintance. This is Alex Smith. And she is going to be very helpful in our endeavor."

Everyone took turns nodding to her and mumbling hello. She politely reciprocated.

Pemberton continued, "What's the deal, Irving? You get to Sykes, or what?"

Irving set his glass down on the table. "I'm afraid it's not good news. I drove up there to meet him. We talked for about two hours."

"What did you tell him?" It was Hayes.

"I didn't *tell* him anything, Milton. You want him to go straight to

Walker and blow this whole thing up before it gets started?"

Instantly, the two men began arguing. Alex sat back and watched. It was amusing. For the level of seriousness this conversation held, they were at each other like schoolboys.

Finally, Pemberton slammed his hand on the table. "That's enough!" Then to Alex, "I apologize, Ms. Smith. Everyone's just a little on edge these days."

She gave a curt nod. If these men had known she was largely responsible for the fact that they were in this situation to begin with, they'd probably try to kill her right there. "I understand."

"Now," Pemberton said, turning back to the men, "let's start again."

Irving gave Hayes a sneer and continued, "As I was saying, Sykes isn't going to budge. When I asked him what he thought about everything going on, he said he wouldn't do anything differently. Said that Walker, for all the negative press, is doing exactly what this country needs."

"Then how do you suppose we move forward?" the governor asked.

"We can't do anything without Sykes," Hayes said. "He controls the military. Even with Walker out of the way."

"Wrong," Irving said.

"Wrong?" Pemberton said.

"Sykes might be in charge of the military. But he's a soldier, just like the rest of them. He's an order taker. And right now, Walker doesn't sneeze without Jennings giving him the okay."

"So we get rid of him," Pemberton said.

"What do you mean, get rid of him?" Hayes asked.

Pemberton looked to her. "What do you think, Alex?"

"It can be done."

"What can be done?" Hayes asked.

"If the situation is right, I could do them both at the same time," Alex said.

Hayes looked at Pemberton. "What is she talking about?"

"What do you think she's talking about? Killing them, of course."

Hayes shot up out of his chair. "Now, hold on just a minute. No one said anything about killing anyone."

"How did you think this was going to go, Milton?" Pemberton asked. "You think we were just going to go in there and drag Walker out and tell him Joe was the new president? You're naive, man! Walker has to go. And I mean *go*. And if Sykes won't side with us, Jennings has to go, too. You heard Irving. Sykes follows orders. If Walker isn't giving them, Jennings is. This is war."

"It's *going* to be a war, if you start killing off the president and his CIA director!" Hayes said.

"Don't be an idiot! We've always known that it was going to come to this."

"Not me. Maybe you. I told you that we could do this through the law. Walker is abdicating his responsibility to protect this nation. All we need is enough of Congress to—"

"Wake up, man! Listen to yourself. There is no law! We're half a country. And that half is divided. You want change? Then we're going to have to take it!"

This is fun, Alex thought, *watching these guys fight between themselves.* But she had no intentions of being here all night while these idiots tried to figure out how to get the job done. And possibly change their mind about her. It was time for her to step in. "Excuse me, gentlemen."

Everyone got quiet.

"Mr. Hayes, I'm sure somewhere in your mind you envisioned a scenario in which bloodshed could be avoided. However, I'm just going to be honest with you. Even if the governor can accomplish what you've proposed, that's not going to happen. At a minimum, Jennings will need to be removed. He won't sit by and watch the governor steal the presidency. And if the governor *can* accomplish what you've suggested, Walker will still be a problem."

"Who are you, anyway?" Hayes snapped at her.

Alex allowed her peaceful demeanor to shift. She narrowed her eyes and cocked her jaw. "I'm the one person in this room who can give you what you want. I've removed world leaders, dictators, and heads of state— all so men like you could do what you want to do—restructure a nation. So if you're done acting like the sanctimonious defense lawyer that you are, why don't you sit down and shut up."

Hayes looked at her with a stunned expression and sat back down.

"I like her, Gavin." Irving laughed.

"Now," she said, taking her seat again, "if you'll allow me, I'd like to offer you a solution to your problem."

"Please, go ahead," Pemberton said.

"Mr. Irving, you're the former secretary of the navy, are you not?"

"I am."

"And governor, you are the intended successor to President Walker, yes?" The governor nodded.

"And it would not be far fetched to assume that, as president, you would have the power to call the former secretary back to duty, should something happen to Secretary Sykes. Right?"

"I would suppose it wouldn't be far fetched at all. Especially given our relationship."

Alex was lost. She had no idea what the man was talking about. However, Irving took care of that.

"Joe is my son-in-law."

Alex smiled. "Even better!" She clapped her hands together. "See? Problem solved. With Jennings out of the way, the governor can remove Sykes and call Mr. Irving back to duty, who can then instruct the military to do whatever you wish."

"So then." Pemberton rapped his knuckles on the table. "The only thing left to decide is when."

Alex looked at him. "How soon are you ready to take over the White House?"

Pemberton rubbed his chin. "Well, Joe is a pretty popular guy around here. But I don't know how much the rest of the country knows him. It's going to take a week or two to stir some dust up."

"And I know just how to start," Irving said. "Sykes said Walker is going to give some sort of big speech tomorrow. He's gonna try and rally the country behind him over this idea of turning back to our godly principles. Sykes said Walker has something big he wants to announce. I say Joe goes up there and makes a scene."

Pemberton snapped his fingers. "Yeah, that's good. Soon as Walker announces whatever it is he's going to announce, Joe can come out and immediately counter it."

"I can do better than that," the governor said. "I'll stand in the audience. And when he starts in, I'll make him debate me right there. In front of his God and everyone."

"Good," Alex said. "It's settled. However, there is still the little matter of protocol." She winked at Pemberton. "Did you have something to ask me?"

Pemberton rolled his eyes and sighed. "Ms. Smith. . .we would like you to kill Kevin Jennings."

Alex smiled and nodded. "I'll begin making preparations to take

Jennings out. And in a week or two, once the governor has the American public stirred to the point of utter contempt, if need be. . .I'll pay Walker a visit and tip the scales in your favor."

Pemberton smiled. "And with Joe and Jake leading the charge, we'll kick the Chinese back where they came from."

CHAPTER 31

Megan slammed her fist on the steering wheel. "Shoot!"

"I don't get it," Eli said. "This map doesn't show any turnoffs after that huge bend back there for another two miles."

"There's no way he could've gotten that far ahead."

"Not the way we were following him," Eli agreed.

"Well, he must've turned in somewhere. Did you see anything? I didn't."

Eli shook his head. "No, I was looking at the map. But that doesn't mean it's not there."

Megan hit the brakes and swerved the car around. "Hold on."

Eli quickly reached up to grab the handle on the top of the door frame as his body weight was pushed against the door. "What are you doing?"

"Turning around. We missed a turn somewhere."

"Yeah, but we can't just go creeping down the road looking for it. You might as well hang a big flashing sign on the roof saying, 'Hey where'd you go?' "

Megan knew he was right. If there was an unmarked turnoff, and it was some sort of driveway, driving by slowly could give anyone who was watching a heads-up that someone was there. "Okay. Then we'll just have to go steady and not miss it."

Eli looked over to her with a serious face. "You know we've got one, maybe two shots at this before we'd be advertising ourselves again. Right?"

"Let's not miss it, then."

"Right. You take your side, I'll take mine. We'll go back to the big curve and come back through. If we don't see it by then, we'll have to just. . ."

"What? Have to just what?"

154

Eli shrugged. "I don't know. We'll think of something."

The speed limit on the old two-lane was forty-five mph. Megan set the cruise control on thirty-eight mph and started off. She tried to scan every inch of what was passing by her, hoping to catch some narrow dirt road they might've missed. Unfortunately, she didn't. And neither did Eli. They had returned to the spot in the road prior to the big sweeping curve. She turned the cruise off and turned the car around again.

"See anything?" she asked Eli.

"Nothing. You?"

"Nope. Nothing but trees." She reset the cruise and started back. "Okay, I'll take this side. You got that one."

Eli nodded. And rolled down the window. "Gives me a better look."

Megan nodded and rolled hers down as well.

They were halfway down the straightaway when Eli sat upright. "I think I just saw it."

Megan was about to hit the brakes when a pair of headlights appeared in the rearview mirror. Instead, she turned off the cruise and accelerated to the speed limit. "Company behind us."

Eli turned in his seat to see the approaching car. It wasn't gaining on them, but it was the third time, now, that they'd passed by this stretch of road. Couldn't be too careful. "Just keep it steady and see if they come up on us. If they do, just keep driving until we reach a turnoff. Then take it. See what happens."

Megan did as Eli instructed, while Eli kept his head turned just enough to see behind them. Suddenly, Eli tapped her shoulder. "That was it. That was the road."

Megan looked in her rearview again to see that the headlights had disappeared. Whoever it was behind them had turned off Durant Road. "That must be where Hayes went."

Eli turned back around. "Okay. So, here's the deal. We can't just leave this car sitting out on the side of the road. But we can't go back and turn in there, either. We have no idea how long of a drive—if it even is a drive—or road that is. Or what it leads to."

"Can't be another road. That was just pine straw and an opening," Megan said. "Has to be a drive of some sort. But you're right. There's no telling how far back it goes or where to."

"Right. We need to ditch the car and go on foot. How far from that entrance do you think it was back to the big bend?"

Megan thought about it for a second. "I don't know. Quarter mile?"

"That sounds about right." Eli reached for the map again. "Keep driving and pull over where we turned around before."

Megan did as Eli said and continued on around the small bend until the obscure turnoff was out of sight. She went a little farther, just for good measure, and then pulled a U-turn and then moved over to the side of the road.

Eli, not bothering with the small penlight he'd been using, turned on the dome light. He traced his fingers along the map and then pointed. "There."

"What?"

"That's about where they turned off. Look here."

Megan looked with Eli as he pointed out the large bend in the road.

"We can park at the start of that bend and cut through the trees," Eli said. "Even if that drive, or whatever, goes straight north, as long as we walk due west from here,"—he pointed—"we ought to run right into whatever's there."

"Sounds like a plan to me." She put the car in Drive and took off.

It only took a few minutes to drive back to the start of the huge bend. Instead of U-turning the car this time, Megan just pulled over to the side of the road. She wanted to be facing the way they needed to leave. Just in case. They got out of the car and checked their weapons. Both satisfied, they hurried across the road and into the trees.

Eli had been spot on. They had only walked a couple hundred yards before they cleared the trees and came upon a narrow dirt road. Looking back down the way, they could now see why it had been so hard to even see it in the first place. A long row of trees lining the main road only had enough of a break in them for the road to exist. The two giant trees' branches on either side of the entrance had grown into each other and hung low over the entrance. There was just enough of a clearing for a vehicle to pass through.

Looking the other direction—to where the drive was headed—they could see the outline of a small farmhouse, with a few lights on, about five hundred yards away. They were currently just off the dirt drive in what was opening up to be a large field that ran along the dirt drive all the way to the house. The field, it appeared, had been left unkempt intentionally. The weeds and grass were waist high. They decided this was to their advantage. They could skirt the dirt road via the field and take cover quickly, should another car come through that opening in the trees. They gave themselves about a twenty-yard berth from the road and began moving toward the house.

"What do you want to do when we get there?" Eli whispered.

"How 'bout go knock on the door and see what they're doing?"

"Works for me."

Megan rolled her eyes. *Typical guy,* she thought. "We're going to do what Jennings said. We're going to stay back and watch."

"I guess that works, too," Eli said, sounding disappointed. Then, "Unless someone shoots at me. Then it's game on!"

Megan had to laugh at Eli's candor. "Okay there, James Bond."

Eli pulled up beside her. "You do realize that I, technically, *am* the real James Bond?"

Megan rolled her eyes again. "Yeah, and Boz is, *technically*, the real Jack Ryan, and Jon is, *technically*, the real Jason Bourne."

They continued on in silence as they approached the house. When they were fifty yards out, Megan stopped.

Eli moved over to her. "What is it?"

"How many cars you see?"

"Five. Two pickups, an SUV, a crossover, and some sort of sedan behind that. Can't make it out, though."

Megan nodded. "That's what I see, too." She let her gaze drift toward the house. Several windows stood opened on the ground floor—not unusual, given the unseasonably warm weather. She lowered her head and strained to listen. "You hear that?"

Eli stood motionless for a second. "No. I don't hear anything."

"Me either. That seem strange to you?"

"Maybe. That house has to be close to a hundred years old. Well built. Probably pretty good soundproofing."

"I see at least four windows open on the ground floor. We should be able to hear someone talking inside."

"We should get closer."

Megan shook her head. "No way. Jennings said to stay back. What if they're down in the basement or something? They could come up any second."

Eli pointed to the vented siding on the foundation of the house. "You see that? That's a crawl space. That house doesn't have a basement."

They sat there, crouched in the tall grass, for another minute in silence before Eli finally said, "The real Jason Bourne, huh?"

Megan laughed to herself. They were back to that now? "He probably thinks so."

"Hmm. I think I'm going to like him." Then, "Sit tight. I'm going for a closer look."

Before Megan could reach out and grab him, Eli was gone.

She had to admit, though, he was swift and quiet. If she hadn't watched him leave, she wouldn't have even known he was in the grass in front of her. She was trying to spot him when she suddenly saw a flicker of movement next to one of the pickup trucks. Eli had somehow completely crossed sides of the field and popped up next to the cars on the other side of the dirt road. She tried to keep him in sight as he moved but lost him again.

She was starting to get a little worried. He'd been gone for nearly five minutes and she hadn't seen or heard anything. She was about to make her own way toward the house when a hand touched her shoulder from behind. She whirled around with a backhanded fist, which Eli caught in midswing.

"It's completely empty," Eli said. "No one's home."

"What? That can't be. We saw at least two of these cars come back here."

"I know what we saw. But I'm telling you there's no one here. I walked around the whole place."

Megan started to stand up. "Well, they've got to be somewhere. Let's go."

Eli nodded and said he'd lead her the same way he had just gone. Megan followed close behind. In just a few moments they were standing beside the house. They stood still for a few seconds, making sure it was still quiet. Satisfied, they began to move behind the house, around to the other side, where the automobiles were parked.

"Hey, check out the old toolshed. You think it's anything worth looking into?"

Eli turned to her. "I don't know, but take a look at that."

They were now in view of the parked cars. Two pickups, an SUV, the crossover, and the sedan that they couldn't fully see from the field. Eli was pointing at the sedan.

Megan felt her pulse quicken. She hurried over to the car to get a better look. It was a silver, base-model Toyota Celica and had an Enterprise rental license plate on the front bumper. She was about to open the door and check the inside of the car when the stillness of the night was interrupted by a loud *click!*

Both she and Eli picked their heads up and turned in the direction of the old toolshed. Megan put a finger to her lips, drew her gun, and started in that direction. She looked over her shoulder to make sure Eli was following.

Within seconds she was standing in front of the old shed, waiting, listening for whatever it was that she'd heard. She moved to step inside and immediately withdrew. The concrete floor inside the shed was opening up, and voices could be heard ascending from below.

CHAPTER 32

Washington, DC

Keene unlocked the door to his house and grabbed the knob. He was expecting to find a dark, cold house, full of cobwebs, several inches of dust, and probably some varmints camped inside. He'd been gone for five months now.

After dinner, Jennings had two other cars meet them at the restaurant to take him and Boz home. Jennings had told them to go get a good night's rest. They would start tracking down this new threat in the morning. And as much as he wanted to start right then, he knew Jennings was right. It had been an exhausting twenty-four hours. His body needed to sleep. And he didn't want anything more right now than to take a long hot shower in his own bathroom and then sleep in his own bed.

Suddenly, another thought occurred to him. What if varmints weren't what he had to worry about? Five months of the house sitting empty, there could be squatters. Or worse, crackheads. He pulled his gun and pushed the door open. What he saw surprised him.

The house had been completely cleaned. Even better than before he'd initially left to go track the Prophet in Texas. Clothes that had been left on the couch were gone. The dishes in the sink had been washed and put away. All the wood in the house looked to be freshly dusted. Even the coffee cup rings on his end table were gone, replaced by a note.

> *Jon, I hope you're not mad at me. But when Jennings told me*
> *he heard from Quinn and you were coming home, I stopped by and*
> *let myself in before I headed to Raleigh. I tried to clean up for you.*
> *There's even some food in the fridge.*
> *I want you to know that I've prayed every day since you've been*
> *gone that God would keep you safe, and bring you back to us. I hope*

you know it's only because of His grace and mercy that you're home. Can't wait to see you. Welcome back.

—Megan

Keene read the note again and felt his hand trembling. He sat down on the couch beside the table and put his head in his hands. Suddenly, everything he'd been through for the last several months came back to him like a flood. He felt the sudden urge to get on his knees. He pushed the table away with his foot and scooted his big frame out of the couch and slumped to the floor. He turned around and laid his head on the couch.

"God. . .I don't even know where to start. . .but I just want to tell You how grateful I am. I know that You could've left me there with Chin to die. Heck, I even asked You to. And I know Quinn says I'm supposed to stop whatever is happening now, but God, I just don't know what to do or where to start. So please help me. Lead me where You want me to go. Help me make the right decisions. And one other thing—will You please watch out for Megan?" Then, "And I'm not even sure how to end this whole praying thing. So, I guess. . .thank You, Jesus. Amen."

Exhaustion had completely taken over him. As bad as he wanted to get up, walk upstairs and take a shower, and then go jump in his bed, all he could think about right now was closing his eyes. He had just started to doze off when he felt the vibration of the sat-phone Jennings had given him inside his pocket.

"This is Jon."

"Jon, this is Quinn."

Keene picked his head up off the couch. Something was wrong.

"Go ahead."

"I know you're tired. And I know you just got home. But Megan and Eli are in trouble. You need to get Boz and go to Raleigh."

Immediately, Keene felt a surge of adrenaline course through his body. However tired he was when he walked in, he was wide awake now. "Where are they?"

"Raleigh is all I know. Jennings can give you details."

"I'm on my way."

He clicked the button to end the call and immediately dialed Boz.

"Hey, this is Jon. Quinn just called."

"What's up?"

"I'm picking you up in thirty minutes. We're headed to Raleigh."

CHAPTER 33

Megan heard the voices coming up from the hole beneath the old toolshed and froze. She looked around for someplace to take cover, but she and Eli were completely exposed. She looked at Eli, who waved her to follow him.

The field, he mouthed to her.

They both took off at a dead run. They only had twenty yards to get to adequate cover, but the voices were getting louder every second. She pushed as hard as she could to reach the tall grass. Eli was five yards ahead of her. When she was only a few feet away, she launched herself into the tangled weeds. She landed hard on her shoulder and rolled into the thick cover. She sat up from the grass, crouching next to Eli, as the first of several heads appeared out of the hole.

"That was close," she whispered.

Eli winked at her. "Fun, huh?"

She shook her head and watched as those who had been underground gathered together topside. They appeared to be finishing up their conversation. Some handshakes were exchanged, but one man stood off to the side. Alone. It was Hayes. Megan couldn't see his face too well in the dim light of the house, but she could sense by the way the man was standing apart from the others that something was wrong. Just then, another of the guests moved out from behind one of the others. Megan felt a chill run down her spine. The wash from one of the lights in the house had revealed the very thing Megan had feared since this morning. Alex Smith was alive.

Almost as soon as she thought it, Smith seemed to turn her attention from the other men. She stepped away as though she had heard something. She began walking toward the field where Megan and Eli were hiding. Megan reached behind her and placed her hand on the butt

162

of her weapon. She noticed out of the corner of her eye that Eli already had his in hand. Smith had advanced almost to the edge of the grass. She stopped and swept her gaze over the field.

"Ms. Smith, can I see you for a moment?"

It was one of the men from the group. Alex Smith turned and walked back to where she had come from.

"That chick gives me the creeps," Eli whispered when she was gone.

"We need to move. Now."

Megan stayed in a low crouch and began to retreat back the way they had come. Eli followed quietly behind. When they were a good halfway back, they both stood and took off at a dead run.

"We need to get back to the car and get it off the road before they leave," Megan said in between breaths. "Smith already sensed that something was wrong a minute ago. If she pulls out of here and sees that car on the side of the road, she'll know. And then instead of us hunting them, she'll be hunting us."

"There's no better sport than a good hunt," Eli said with a chuckle.

"Yeah, well, I prefer that we're the ones doing the hunting."

They came out on the other side of the trees. The car was across the road and waiting where they'd left if. They jumped in and Megan started the engine.

"We need to head back down the road to that gas station we saw a mile or so back," Eli said.

"For what?"

"It'll give us a good view as they pass us. We can pull out behind and follow."

"If they even come this way," she said. "And who are we going to follow? There's five of them."

"I say we follow Smith."

"Are you crazy? Eli, I've already had one run-in with that lunatic. She almost killed me. She'll spot us before we even pull out of the gas station. What about the guy wearing the sport coat?"

"We don't need to follow him," Eli said in a cold, flat tone. "I know who he is."

Megan was stunned. "You do? How? Who is he?"

"Former secretary of the navy, Jake Irving."

Megan's jaw dropped. "No way."

"Why would Irving—how could he even be involved in any of this?"

"I'm not entirely sure, but I believe that other chap that was standing beside him was his son-in-law."

Megan was completely dumbfounded. She was an American. A federal agent. If anyone should have a clue as to who those men were, it should be her. Instead, she was getting a civics lesson from an Englishman. "How do you know—"

"Hello. . .James Bond, remember?" He laughed. "Just kidding. I've had some dealings with Irving. Back when I served His Majesty's Royal Navy. I only know about his son-in-law because I attended the wedding."

Megan just looked at him.

"It was a diplomatic gesture." Then, "There. There's the gas station. Look, there are several cars there. Pull in facing the road, like you're getting fuel, and stop."

Megan did as Eli instructed. She put the lever in PARK.

"Now, get out and change spots with me," Eli said. "I'm driving."

"What? Why?"

"Because, I've been doing this a lot longer than you. And we're following Smith."

"You don't even know if she's going to come through this way."

Eli opened the door and got out. "Then we better hurry. So we're not sitting here arguing when she does."

"Fine."

She got out and went around to the other side. Eli got in the driver's side and adjusted the seat and mirrors. She reached into the inside pocket of her jacket. She had some gum in there, and her mouth was dry after running through the field. As soon as she stuck her hand in the pocket her heart sank and a feeling of dread settled in.

"Eli, we have to go back."

CHAPTER 34

Hayes couldn't believe his friends had turned on him so quickly. He had spent hours upon hours writing out the documents needed—complete with constitutional cross-references. Everything they needed to remove Walker from power was right there. Walker still hadn't appointed a new vice president. And with most of Congress already on his and Pemberton's side, they could've forced Walker to name Joe the next VP. They could've used that leverage to make Walker resign. Sure, it would be messy. A vice presidential nomination would normally have to go through a mandatory investigation and vetting process, followed by a congressional hearing, and then a confirmation. The plan was to forgo all of that and just anoint Joe as the new vice president. And the American people might question the legality of it, but he had it covered. Any open-minded judge could see it plainly. And the US Supreme Court was stacked with liberals. Walker would've had no choice. The country needed a tough president, and Walker definitely wasn't that man. With support of more than half of Congress—and Joe leading the charge for wanting to take over—it would've been a spectacular sight. One that the history books would've written about. And children for years to come would study how it all had happened. And he would've been known as the architect of it all.

"Well, gentlemen, if there's nothing else. . . ," Pemberton was saying to the others.

"Milton, you going to be okay with this?" It was the governor.

Hayes sat there with his arms crossed for a few seconds, not answering. Finally, he unfolded his arms and leaned into the table. "I guess I'll have to be, won't I?"

"Then it's settled." Pemberton smacked his palm down on the table. "Let's get out of here."

The five of them made their way topside. Joe, Gavin, and Irving all stood around, shooting the breeze, talking about meaningless, stupid things. The woman leaned against her car—which was currently blocked in—acting as though she couldn't care less about anything the men were talking about. He didn't blame her. He didn't even want to be near them right now. He turned and walked away in the other direction.

He had just walked past the corner of the Shed when he noticed something on the ground, lying just beside the tin siding, but almost obscured by a clump of tall weeds. Had he not happened to look in that direction, he might have never seen it. He bent over and picked it up. A leather wallet of some sort. He opened it and looked inside. Immediately, his breathing became labored. He felt like he was going to pass out. He had to bend over and put his hand on his knee and catch his breath. This couldn't be. How in the—? He looked again, just to make sure his mind wasn't playing tricks on him. There it was: FBI, MEGAN TAYLOR.

He quickly folded the wallet and placed it in his inside coat pocket. He couldn't let anyone else know he had been followed. He had to think. He had to get out of there.

He walked back over to the others, trying to remain calm—though his hands were trembling uncontrollably inside his coat pockets. "Fellas, I believe I will retire for the evening. Thank you all for coming to meet with me and Gavin tonight. I know I got a little excited down there, but I think you're right. This is the way we need to proceed."

Pemberton winked and slapped him on the shoulder. "Atta boy, Milton."

Irving and the governor nodded. "Tough times require tough decisions," Irving said.

Hayes began to feel nauseous. Right now, he just wanted to get away. He ran a hand through his hair. "I guess you're right, Jake. We'll do whatever it takes." He jumped in his pickup truck and started the engine. He noticed that the woman had left her car and was staring out into the field. She looked as though she was searching the field for something. Again his chest started to tighten. Was Taylor out there, watching them right now? He couldn't take it anymore.

He whipped the truck around in the drive and punched the gas.

Alex was leaning against her rental car, trying to ignore the random, generic conversation the other men were having. All she wanted right now was to get back to the Marriott. She and Farid had another spectacular night planned. She still couldn't leave yet. Irving had her blocked in. She stepped out from behind Irving just to get some space.

When she did, she caught a faint whiff of something as the wind blew into her face. It was subtle, but she was sure she caught it. It smelled like. . . she couldn't place her finger on it. But she'd smelled it before. She walked toward the field to see if she could smell it again. It had come and gone so quickly, she wasn't even sure if it had come from the field.

She stood there for a moment, sensing something was amiss. Normally, when she felt like this, she would go into full-on operation mode. But maybe she was being paranoid. Besides, she was out in the middle of a field in North Carolina in the dark. And as far as the world was concerned, she was dead. No, she finally reasoned, she was just sensing the anticipation of being back in the game. Living in that weird tension between—

The sound of Hayes's pickup brought her back. She turned to see the man speeding down the dirt drive.

"Ms. Smith, can I see you for a moment?"

It was Pemberton. She turned around and walked back to the men. He spoke to her with his back to the others and asked her to stay for a minute. She nodded and stepped away, as the others said their good-byes and loaded into their vehicles.

She sensed something behind her. She turned to see that Pemberton was less than a foot away. She was a little unnerved at the fact that she hadn't heard him coming up behind her. The old man was sneaky. She would have to remember that.

"Alex—may I call you Alex?"

"Sure. Alex is fine."

"Good. I wanted to speak with you privately about—" He looked at her questioningly. "Is everything all right?"

She relaxed a little. "Yes, everything is fine. What did you need?"

Pemberton's dark eyes shifted back and forth. "I'm afraid we might have a problem."

"With?"

"Milton."

"How so?"

Pemberton let out a long sigh. "This morning—well, this afternoon, actually—I spoke with Milton on the phone. He was very distraught. Seems last night, when he got home, two federal agents were in his house."

"Go on."

"Milton and I have been friends for a long time. We went to Yale together. It's a long story. And I won't bother you with the details, but let's just say that we've both gone to great lengths to keep the fact that we're associates from people. Milton is a Supreme Court judge. I'm a cutthroat businessman. We're kind of like oil and water—we just don't mix well in social situations. You get what I'm saying?"

She nodded. "I think so."

"The bottom line is, Milton is one of those big social activists. He loves this country, but he's just a nut about some things."

"What's your point, Mr. Pemberton?"

"The point is Milton has a hard time keeping his mouth shut about things sometimes. And I'm afraid he's going to be a liability. I've known Milton for over thirty years. When he left here a few minutes ago, he wasn't acting right. What if those agents got to him?"

It definitely was a possibility. She'd seen better men crumble under less pressure.

Pemberton swept his arm through the air. "And I can't have that. I'm sorry. I just can't. Milton and I are friends, but this is too important."

A tingle started to develop at the base of her neck. She could sense what was coming. "So what do you want to do?"

He looked at her for a long while. His face seemed to twist and turn. She could tell it was eating him from the inside out. She loved this part—the part where they wrestled with making the decision. They hemmed and hawed about it, usually. Just like Pemberton was doing now. But they always came around in the end. "Mr. Pemberton, what would you like me to do?"

"I think you know what I want you to do," he barked. "Do I have to spell it out for you?"

She smiled to herself. "Sorry, Mr. Pemberton. I already told you my rule. You have to say it."

CHAPTER 35

President Walker sat in his private study pouring over the speech he was going to give the next afternoon. He had torn up three drafts already and was on his fourth. He just couldn't get the wording right. The speechwriters had insisted he let them craft the speech, but he had shut them down. This was going to be one of the most important speeches that any president in American history would give. It had to be perfect. And it had to come from him. Not a team of writers.

His plan was twofold. One side was to call the nation to unity and continued repentance, continuing to ask God for direction and committing to following His lead, no matter what that looked like. The second side was to introduce the proposal of the constitutional amendment. This would be an amendment in which the country would take some hard-line stances on some issues, many of which were major social issues the government had evaded or abdicated its responsibility for by continuing to implement policies that pleased the special interests, not the people. And most certainly did not serve God.

He had spent the last fifteen minutes praying about what this draft should say. He felt like he was ready to start writing. He grabbed his pen and a piece of paper, just as the phone on his desk rang. He grabbed the receiver. "Hello?"

"Mr. President, this is Dr. Simmons."

The president's personal physician.

"Yes, Dr. Simmons. What can I do for you?"

"Sorry to bother you, sir. But I'm afraid it is urgent."

"Go on."

"President Grant is awake, sir."

"Yes, I heard earlier, from Kevin Jennings. That's wonderful news,

Doctor. How is he?"

Simmons gave a short laugh. "He's astonishingly well, sir! He wants to see you."

A myriad of emotions began to take hold of him. Thankfulness, joy, relief—and fear—all seemed to flood him at the same time. "What, now?"

"Yes, sir. He said—"

Suddenly, Walker heard the phone pull away on the other end, as if the doctor were holding it away. He could hear some discussion on the other end, but it was muffled. Then, the phone started clattering again. He held his own receiver out and looked at it. "Hello. . .Doctor, are you there?"

Finally, the rattling stopped and he could hear the phone being picked up, along with a faint "Give me that thing!" Walker smiled. He knew the voice.

"Hello? Gray, are you there?"

Walker smiled. His friend sounded like he hadn't missed a beat. "I'm here, Calvin. You giving Dr. Simmons a hard time?"

"I'm going to give him something, all right."

Walker heard his friend pull the phone away again. "I'm still your boss, Dr. Simmons. Don't you give me any lip!"

This time Walker was laughing. "Good grief, Calvin! Give the man a break. You've been in a coma for four months. I mean, you got shot in the head—which, by the way, only proves what I used to tell you. That you are the most hardheaded man I've ever met."

Now Grant was laughing on the other end.

The two continued on for a moment before Walker finally brought them back. "I'm glad you're awake, Calvin. I've been praying for you."

"So I've heard," Grant said. "Listen, Gray, I want you to come down here and see me tonight."

"I'd love to, Calvin. But I'm going to be giving a speech tomorrow—one that I think you would be proud of, actually. And I don't have even the welcome written yet. I need to stay here and finish."

"Actually, Gray, that's exactly why I want to see you."

"I don't understand."

"Tess and I have spent quite a lot of time this afternoon, talking. She's caught me up on everything that's happened since. . .you know."

"Did she tell you that she gave me your Bible that night?"

"She did."

"I don't know if I'd be the man I am right now if it hadn't been for your notes and highlights, Calvin. I owe you a lot."

"You don't owe me anything. You just chalk that one up to God." Then, "But if you really do think you owe me, then bring your rear end down here and see me tonight." Grant followed that with a throaty laugh. Then, "Oh, oh. . .I gotta stop laughing like that. Makes my head hurt." He started laughing again.

Walker heard the phone pull away again. "No, my head's not really hurting! It's an expression." Then, back on the line, "Gray, listen. Simmons is about to make me get off. Needs me to go pee in a cup or something. Please, I know you're writing your speech. And I know a million things have to be running through your head right now—the least of which is whether or not I'm going to kick you out of that chair in a couple days. Well, I'm going to tell you right now, I'm not. That's your chair now. And you've done a good job with it. I just want to be there to help you however I can. And one thing I can do better than anyone in Washington is write a speech. Please, come see me. I would love nothing more than to help you put together what you're about to go say to our country."

Walker started to get choked up as Grant finished talking. He and Grant had been friends for a long time, though they had butted heads frequently in the past over political issues. He remembered when he'd first met Grant, how the man had inspired him. He'd always thought Grant had the type of character to aspire to. Deep down, he'd always wanted to be like Grant. He had just never allowed himself to be. At least until his back was against the wall. And in that moment, Calvin's Bible—the highlighted passages and notes that Calvin had written in the margins—had been used to bring him to the place where he was willing to allow God to shape him into who he needed to be—who he was now. And he could think of no better person to spend an evening with, writing possibly one of the most important speeches in American history.

"Go pee in your cup, Calvin. I'm on my way."

CHAPTER 36

We have to go back, Eli. Right now."

"And do what? Knock on the door and say, 'Excuse me. I think I lost my ID in your backyard while I was snooping around your property. May I have it back?' "

Megan slammed her palm into the dashboard. "If they find it, they'll know we were there. They could go completely underground—no pun intended. And we have no idea what they're planning."

"And that's why we're going to follow Sokolov. Whatever they're doing, she's going to be at the tip of it. Besides, you think finding your ID is going to stop them from whatever it is they're planning?"

Megan had to relent. Eli was right. Hayes already knew they were looking into him. It just meant they'd have to be more careful going forward. "You're right."

They sat there for another few minutes with only a few cars passing by on the road. Finally, they saw a silver Toyota pass by.

"That's her," Eli said. He put the car in gear and eased out onto the road to follow.

"How do you plan on not getting made?" Megan asked. "This woman is a pro. If she turns more than twice, she'll know something's up the moment we follow her."

Eli looked at her and smiled. He reached inside his pocket and pulled out a small device. "Ever seen one of these?"

Megan took the little box. It was no bigger than a cell phone and had a small screen on it with a blinking red dot. It looked like a GPS of some sort. "What is it?"

"That"—he said, pointing—"is an old-school tracking device. Works off radio signal. I just happened to slip it under the fender right

172

before that bunker opened up."

Megan had heard of them before but had never seen one. The technology was at least sixty years old. The way it worked was, the dot would blink faster or slower, depending on whether you got closer or farther from the transmitter. It wouldn't give you exact coordinates, but it at least let the tracker know if he were getting hot or cold.

Eli stayed back at least a half mile while they were on the two-lane. At one point, a couple of other cars even pulled out onto the road in front of him. While it wasn't ideal for following Sokolov, it helped them to remain unsuspicious. They continued following the Toyota all the way back into the city.

"Now it gets interesting," Eli said.

"Why's that?"

The Toyota was several car lengths ahead when they came to the first red light, as they entered downtown. Sokolov was in the center lane. That meant she had no intention, at least for now, of turning anywhere. Eli moved over into the right turning lane.

"What are you doing?" Megan asked. "She's going straight."

"You just watch the dot. I'm going to go one street over and run parallel with her. If that dot starts blinking slower, you let me know."

Eli made the turn and went one block up. He turned left again to put them going the same direction they had been a moment ago. Megan looked at the tracker. The dot was still blinking rapidly.

As they came to the next light, Eli pulled over to the side of the road. Before going through the light, he told Megan he wanted to make sure the transmitter didn't change pace. If it did, that meant Sokolov had turned. If she turned, the dot would either get faster, meaning she was headed right for them, or slower, meaning she turned the opposite direction. The light changed and the dot remained blinking at the same pace. Eli pulled back out onto the road and continued straight.

They did this for another eight blocks when, suddenly, everything went awry. They had been traveling west on New Bern Street, running parallel with Edenton—where Sokolov was—when the street took a small turn to the left. They followed the bend in the road as it came back around and straightened out. But as it did, they came face-to-face with a wall of city vehicles and orange cones. Apparently, a water main—or something— had burst. The entire street in front of them had been dug up and water was bubbling up from the hole, spilling out onto the street around them.

The road in front was shut down. A man in an orange vest, holding a pair of orange flags, was waving them to turn south on South Blount Street. With nowhere else to go, Eli turned the wheel and headed south.

"How far is the range on this thing?" Megan asked.

"Not far. If she makes one turn and gets more than a couple blocks away from us, we'll lose her."

Megan pinched the bridge of her nose. This night was getting worse by the second. She took turns looking back and forth from the tracker to the road. Eli had gunned the car after turning away from Sokolov. They were looking for the quickest right turn they could find. Unfortunately, the water main must've been a massive rupture. The next four right turns were all blocked as well. Megan looked down at the tracker, which was no longer flashing. She was staring at a solid red dot. She slammed her fist into the dashboard again.

"You've *got* to be kidding me!"

Eli pulled the car over to the side of the road. "Well, it was worth a shot."

Megan turned in her seat. "What is it with this woman? I mean, four months ago we had her in our grasp in DC and lost her. I track her halfway around the world to Dubai—with Marianne Levy—and kill her. And then she shows back up here, and I lose her again!"

Eli shrugged. "I guess she's like your personal nemesis."

"This isn't funny, Eli! That woman is single-handedly responsible for President Grant's assassination attempt. She worked with Chin and Levy to allow the Chinese to come across the border. And she almost killed Jon!"

"Megan, calm down. I wasn't trying to make light of the woman's résumé. I'm just saying that you can't control everything."

Eli was right again. "I'm sorry. I didn't mean to take it out on you. Heck, if it weren't for your little tracker, we wouldn't have even gotten this far." Suddenly she had a thought. "Hey, what if she's staying downtown in a hotel?"

"Makes sense. She'd be staying at a four-star hotel or better."

She pulled out the map again and opened it up. "Why?"

"Because, bigger, nicer hotels have lots of floors, lots of rooms, and lots of hallways leading to lots of escape routes. She'd want to make sure she had at least three ways out if she got cornered. I know I would."

"Okay. So let's get started."

The plan seemed to be a solid one. But after checking with the four biggest hotels in downtown, they had still come up empty. One of the desk clerks said he had seen someone that might fit the description, but that woman had been with a wealthy-looking Middle Eastern man. They looked like they were a couple.

Back in the car, Megan was frustrated. They were getting nowhere. It was getting late and they hadn't eaten. "Let's go grab a burger. We'll figure out what we want to do from there." She pulled away from the curb and took off.

They found a late-night drive-through and ate in the car, mostly in silence. When they were finished, Megan threw her bag and wrapper in the backseat and pulled the car out of the parking lot.

"Where are we going?" Eli asked.

"We're going to talk with Milton Hayes again. I want to know what he knows." She turned the wheel and hit the gas. "I don't care if I have to take him into custody and all the way back to DC. He's going to tell us what was going on at that farmhouse."

Eli nodded. "Fine with me."

Alex Smith walked arm in arm with Farid through the lobby of the Marriott Hotel in downtown Raleigh. While she had been at the farmhouse meeting, Farid had set them up with reservations at a nice restaurant. Afterward, they would visit a few more nightspots. But first, she had something to take care of. As they walked outside, she asked the doorman to hail a cab.

"What do we need a cab for?" Farid asked. "What's wrong with the car?"

"Nothing's wrong with the car," she answered. "But I have an. . .*errand* to run first."

"Seriously? Now?"

He wasn't mad. More like intrigued. The fact that he was reacting like this made her breath catch. This was crazy. Could she and Farid really have a life together? "You go on ahead, and I'll meet you there. You can have a couple drinks at the bar while you wait. I shouldn't be more than thirty minutes or so."

Farid looked at her curiously. "What if I wanted to come with you?"

She thought about that for a moment. It might be fun to take him along. Let him see her in action. But that was way too risky. Something maybe a rookie would do. No, she decided. It had to be this way. "I'm sorry Farid. I can't take you." She leaned in and kissed his cheek. "But I promise, I'll only be thirty minutes. And then we'll have the rest of the night to ourselves." She thought about Pemberton's plan and the timeline. "Actually, we'll have the next week or so to ourselves."

That seemed to make Farid happy. "Good. Perhaps tomorrow we can go somewhere secluded for a few days."

She kissed him again and put him in the cab. When he was gone, she gave the valet her ticket. Her car was brought around a minute later.

She'd thought about waiting to do this until tomorrow, or the next day. But after killing Peterson, her date with Farid had turned out to be *electric*. She figured why not go two-for-two?

She was a little distracted, though. Ever since she had left the farmhouse. Something was niggling at the back of her mind. She just couldn't place what it was. And it was bothering her. She reached over to the dash and turned the heat up a notch. When she did, the automatic fan kicked on, blowing a fresh scent through the vent, carrying the warm air up to her nostrils. Suddenly, it hit her. She realized what had been bothering her.

That scent. The one she had caught a whiff of, at the farmhouse. She'd smelled it before. In Dubai. She could remember lying there, on the sand bleeding out, as the FBI agent stood over her. She could smell her perfume—or lotion or whatever it was. But it was a distinct smell. The same one she had caught at the farmhouse.

She gripped the wheel tighter. What had Pemberton said?

"*Seems last night when Hayes got home, two federal agents were in his house.*"

No way. That would be the most monumental coincidence in the history of the world. The same agent who had tried to kill her in Dubai all of a sudden shows up in Raleigh, follows Hayes to a secret meeting, and hides out in the field while she stood right there? No way.

The hair on the back of her neck began to stand up. She didn't like that. When it happened, it meant whatever she was trying to convince herself of wasn't working. The logical side of her brain was trying to win out. And right now, it was winning.

How could Hayes be so stupid? Surely he had to know they would be following him. Even an idiot would take some precautions not to be followed. And what was *she* thinking? She was smack-dab in the middle of another plot to destroy America. Of course Jon Keene and his team would be involved. She should've expected it.

She pounded the steering wheel in frustration. She had let her guard down. All of this running around with Farid like some infatuated schoolgirl had clouded her judgment.

She gripped the wheel tighter and punched the gas. She would take care of Milton Hayes. And then she would deal with this mistake between her and Farid.

CHAPTER 37

Megan pulled the car off to the side of the road in front of Hayes's house. The guard shack was visible from where they were, but she couldn't see the guard anywhere inside.

"Where do you think he is?" she asked.

"Probably went to the loo." Eli laughed.

"Well, he better hurry up," Megan said. "I'm in no mood to be waiting around."

"We could just go over the wall again."

"Uh-uh. We're going in through the front door. And Hayes is coming out with us."

Eli held up his hands. "Hey, like I told you. I'm just along for the ride."

She recalled his taking off from her at the farmhouse. "Yeah, right."

She started to cross the street toward the gate when Eli called to her.

"Hey, wait a second." He stepped to the rear door and opened it.

"What are you doing?"

"Just grabbing a couple extra magazines. If Hayes decides to point that hand cannon at me again, I don't want to run out of ammo."

"Fine. Hurry up." She stood by and waited for him to catch up with her.

Suddenly Eli scrambled out from the backseat. "Megan! Get over here. Now!"

She had no idea what was going on, but his tone was anything but subtle. He had crouched down beside the car, as if he were taking cover. Out of instinct, she drew her weapon and started looking around as she hurried back to where he was.

"What is it?"

"This."

The tracking device from earlier was in his hand. And the little red dot was blinking furiously. Her eyes went wide. "She's here?"

"Her car is, anyway."

She leaned back against the car. "Okay, we have to think this through. If she's in there, it means one of two things. Either they're having a private meeting. . ."

Eli finished her thought for her. "Or she's here to make sure Hayes isn't coming with us."

Megan nodded.

"So how do you want to play this?"

She thought about it for a moment. She was too small to get over the wall on her own. "Can you scale the wall around back without me?"

"Yeah, I think so."

"Okay, then you go around back. I'll wait two minutes, and then I'll come through the front."

"What about the guard?"

She peeked her head up over the car. The guard was still nowhere to be seen. "Got a bad feeling about him. Not sure he's going to be an issue."

"Okay. Give me two minutes." He started to move.

Megan reached out and grabbed his arm. "Hey. Keep your head down and your eyes open."

Eli smiled at her. "No worries. I'm the real James Bond, remember?"

"That's what worries me." She pulled her sleeve up and started watching the second hand on her watch as Eli took off.

At one minute and fifty seconds, she darted out from behind the car and crossed the street. She stayed close to the wall as she approached the guard shack. When she got there, she popped her head around the corner and then right back. Nothing.

She stayed low and hugged the wall as it turned into the drive. The guard shack was only twenty feet away. She crept up to the side door and turned the knob. The door opened without any resistance. Inside, lying on the floor in a pool of blood, was the guard. He had been shot twice through the forehead.

A door on the opposite side of the guard shack led to the property on the other side of the gate. She opened the door slowly, her gun pointed ahead of her. The path leading to the house was empty. And she could see now that the lights in the house were all off, except for one upstairs, and another down.

She hurried across the circular drive, stopping once in front of the huge water fountain sitting in the grassy center of the circular drive. She tried to strain her ears to hear anything. But she couldn't hear a sound. She popped her head around once more to make sure the coast was clear. Then she took off at a dead run for the door.

She half expected to feel bullets whizzing by her head as she made her way to the door. But nothing came. She was beginning to wonder if maybe Hayes *was* having a private meeting with Sokolov. She went to turn the knob on the door but noticed that the door was already ajar. *So much for the private meeting theory.*

By this time, she was sure that Eli had made his way over the wall. She wondered if he had bothered to stop and disarm the alarm this time. She didn't know if it really mattered or not, but if it did, she hoped he had. The last thing they needed was to alert Sokolov they were there. Especially if Hayes was still alive. She wanted Hayes for herself.

She quietly pushed the door open and stepped inside, sweeping her weapon as she moved. Hayes's office was just off to the right, down a short hall. She decided to clear that area first.

She had just made it to the office when everything went wrong. She heard thumping coming from upstairs. Then shots. At least five. Then someone screaming. A man. But not Eli. No, the voice was too high pitched. It had to be Hayes.

She turned around and began moving quickly back down the hall. More shots. She made it back out to the foyer. More shots. And glass breaking. Then, more shots. Suddenly, a loud crashing sound came from above her. The banister from the catwalk above came crashing down into the living area. And with it, a body.

Megan screamed in horror as she realized what had just happened. "Eli—no!" She ran out into the room, firing her weapon blindly up at the catwalk. Eli lay with his leg twisted behind him and two bullet wounds through his chest.

She had just gotten to him when more shots began to ring out from above. She raised her weapon and began firing as fast as she could at the catwalk as she ran into the kitchen. "Lights up!" she yelled. Slowly the lights began to come up. She dove for the marble-covered island that stood in the middle of the room. She had just gotten behind it when more shots rang over her head and into the cabinets behind her.

"Nice to see you again, Ms. Taylor. It's been awhile."

The voice was evil, and it sent chills up Megan's spine.

"I thought I killed you," she yelled over the island.

"Yeah. Me, too. Guess not, though."

More shots.

"But you can bet on one thing," Sokolov shouted.

"Oh yeah? What's that?" Another four rounds hit the cabinets behind her.

"I'm the one walking out of here today."

Megan decided to take a chance and stick her arm around the side to fire. She braced herself and whipped her arm around the corner and let off a barrage of fire, almost emptying her magazine. "We'll see about that," she yelled.

Nothing.

She waited another few seconds. "Hey, Sokolov—you alive?"

She was answered by another round of shots above her head. *I guess so,* she said to herself. Then, "Hey! Why won't you just die? It would make my life a whole lot easier."

Another round of fire. This time, though, they were aimed right at the island. She heard the rounds splinter the wood inside. Another couple of rounds like that, and this island wasn't going to be much for cover anymore. She needed to move. But there was nowhere to go. The closest line of escape was a hallway that led to a set of bedrooms and the formal dining room. But it was fifteen feet away. And she would have to move out into the open to get there.

"Tell you what," Sokolov yelled. "Why don't you just come out here? I promise, I'll kill you quick. I won't just leave you here to die. . .like you did me."

Another round of gunfire came at her. This time, Sokolov hit her mark. Two of the rounds had come through the island. Megan was knocked back against the sink behind her as one round hit her in the shoulder. The other in the leg.

She began to panic a little. She had never been shot before. But she'd heard about it. All the rumors were true. You felt the impact, but not the pain. At least initially. It was the body's reaction to a violent injury. Shock. But it wouldn't last for long, she knew. Within minutes, she was going to feel both of those rounds. And it wasn't going to be pleasant. She had to move. Now.

She raised the gun over her head, above the island, and fired until she had emptied the magazine. She quickly ejected it and slammed a fresh one home. She stood up and started firing as she ran for the hallway. She made it halfway there when something like a freight train slammed into her chest. It knocked her down to the floor. She couldn't breathe. What was happening? Her vision was beginning to blur.

She tilted her head in the direction of Sokolov. She saw the assassin step out from behind the half wall that separated the kitchen from the living area and begin walking toward her. She had a twisted, noxious smile painted on her face. She raised the gun and pointed it at her head.

"Well, Ms. Taylor. It looks like I win this round."

Suddenly, Megan caught movement right behind Sokolov, as someone slammed into her from behind. Sokolov's gun pitched forward and slid across the tile floor of the kitchen. Sokolov scrambled to her feet and turned to see her attacker. Eli was there, on his knees with his Glock pointed at her. He let off a string of shots as Sokolov dove for cover. Megan heard her shriek. Eli must've hit her. He kept firing until his magazine was empty. Then he fell back to the floor in front of her.

Megan heard a door slam, then the sound of a car's engine. Then tires squealing. Sokolov was gone.

Megan forced herself up off the floor and tried to drag herself over to where Eli lay. She had felt for her sat-phone in her pocket but remembered she had tossed it in the console when she and Eli had started checking out hotels, trying to find Sokolov. Her breathing was becoming labored now. She felt weak. She only had a few more feet to go. If she could get there, maybe Eli had his sat-phone in his pocket. She almost got there before her arms gave out. She slammed back to the floor. She was so tired.

Maybe she would just close her eyes for a second.

CHAPTER 38

The steps to the G-5 lowered as Keene and Boz stood by the door ready to move the moment the stairs hit the ground. Keene had been trying to reach Megan on the sat-phones Jennings had given her and Eli for almost two hours now with no luck.

Keene had called Jennings on the way to pick Boz up and told him that they needed a plane. And they needed it now. He filled Jennings in on the call from the Prophet. Jennings made a few calls and told him that a G-5 would be waiting for them.

The flight was quick—they were only in the air thirty minutes. And Jennings had a car waiting for them when they arrived. Jennings had also caught Keene up to speed on what Megan and Eli had been doing for the last two days. When Keene heard they had been tailing Judge Hayes, he decided Hayes's place was where they would start.

The steps finally finished extending. Keene took them two at a time. He threw his bag into the back of the big Suburban and waited for Boz to jump in. Boz, once inside, opened a map and began barking out directions to him.

"I'm really worried, Boz. It's been two hours."

Boz kept his head on the map. "Everything's going to be fine, Jon. We'll be there in less than twenty minutes."

Raleigh International Airport was only about fifteen miles from Hayes's house in Cary. But that didn't make Keene feel any better. He remembered what the Prophet had said. *"Megan's in trouble."* He punched the gas and ran a light that was turning red.

At this time of night, there was almost no traffic. The fifteen-mile trip took right at twenty minutes. As Keene drove down the street to Hayes's address, he tried Megan's sat-phone once more. "It's still going to voice mail!"

"Jon, let's just get to Hayes's and see what's going on. We'll ask him the last time he saw them and go from there."

Keene slowed down as they approached the address. He immediately saw the car parked on the street. "They're here!"

Boz looked up. "Yeah, that looks like a fed car to me."

Keene screeched the tires as he whipped the big SUV into Hayes's drive. He slammed on the brakes when he realized he was about to run over the gate. It had been apparently crashed and was now barely hanging from its hinges.

Keene didn't even wait for Boz. He jumped out of the truck with his weapon up, sweeping the grounds. He started toward the house and watched as Boz came around the back of the truck and checked on the guard shack.

"Guard is down, Jon. Go! Go! Go!"

Keene took off at a dead run down the rest of the short drive. He took the small set of stairs leading to the front door in one leap. He kicked the door in on his way through. And immediately began yelling. "Megan! Eli!"

He looked to his left up a wide sweeping staircase that led to a catwalk. In front of him, the foyer opened up into a large living area. He saw the wood from the balcony lying on the couch in the middle of the floor. It still had part of the railing and spindles attached to it. Quickly he ran into the room and looked around. There, fifteen feet to his left, as the living area gave way to the kitchen, two bodies lying next to each other on the floor. "Boz! Get in here! *Now!*"

Keene ran over to where Megan and Eli lay. He quickly felt for a pulse on both of them. He had no idea how long they had been lying there, but the acrid smell of gunpowder still hung in the room. Fifteen, twenty minutes maybe? There was nothing on Eli. He couldn't find one on Megan either at first. But then he felt a faint blip, as he moved his fingers around her neck. He quickly ripped Megan's shirt open. "Thank You, God!" She was wearing a vest. He saw a hole just above her collarbone and one in her left shoulder. He reached around her back and felt the exit wounds for both. But there wasn't much blood, so there had to be something else. He lifted her left arm above her head. That's when he saw it. Just on the inside of her chest wall, underneath her arm, another hole. He felt around on her lower back for another exit wound. There was none. The bullet was still inside. He needed to get her to a doctor.

By this time, Boz was beside him, working on Eli. He had Eli's shirt off and was performing CPR.

"Boz, anything?"

"There's a pulse, but it's faint."

"Megan's got a hole with no exit wound. She needs to get to a doctor fast."

Boz looked at him. "Eli, too. Two wounds to the upper chest. I don't think it hit anything major, but he's losing a lot of blood. Neither one of them are going to make it if we don't get them help. And I mean like now."

Keene knew Boz was right. They couldn't stay here and wait for an ambulance. He pointed at Eli. "You get him. I've got her."

Together, they grabbed their friends and carried them back out to the Suburban. Keene pulled out the sat-phone and jumped in the front as Boz jumped in the back with the two patients, where he grabbed the first-aid pack from under the backseat.

"Lights and sirens the whole way, Jon."

"Roger that." Keene punched the speed dial for Jennings and slammed the gas on the big SUV, which fishtailed as he backed out into the street.

"This is Jennings."

"Megan and Eli have been shot. They're both critical. I need a medic at the tarmac in fifteen."

"I'll have him there."

Keene punched the button and threw the phone in the seat beside him. "What's going on back there, Chappy?"

"I'm working on it. Just punch it and go."

Keene already had the pedal pretty much to the floor. The only time he'd let off so far was when they had to take a curve. The sat-phone began buzzing in the seat. Keene picked it up. "Yeah?"

It was Jennings. "RDU has trauma EMTs on staff. They'll meet you at the hangar. You need to stay out of their way and let them work when you get there, Jon. You hear me?"

"Got it."

"You'll be landing at Andrews. I'll meet you there. They'll take them to Malcolm Grow until they can get them stable. Then I'll have them moved to Bethesda."

"I'm two minutes from the tarmac. We'll see you in thirty minutes."

Again he clicked off the phone and threw it in the seat. "How are they, Boz?"

"Just get us there."

Keene mashed the gas pedal as hard as he could.

When he pulled up to the plane, an ambulance was sitting outside. The steps were already down and a group of EMTs came running out to meet them. They threw open the doors to the Suburban and pulled Megan and Eli out, placing them on gurneys, then folded the gurney wheels under and hustled up the steps. Keene and Boz followed. Less than a minute later, the plane was in the air.

The EMTs had Megan and Eli in the back of the plane, where the galley opened up into a kitchen area. They were working feverishly on both of them. Keene couldn't tell who was doing what to whom. He and Boz just stood in the front of the plane, watching the chaos happening before them. Finally, Boz turned to him.

"Jon, we should pray."

Boz's voice jarred him back. "Wh–what?"

"Pray, Jon. We should pray for them."

"Ah, yeah. Sure."

Keene had been so caught up in what was happening, he hadn't even thought that praying was something he should be doing. He looked over to his friend who was already on his knees with his elbows in the chair in front of him. Keene knelt down beside him. "I'm still new at this, Boz. I don't know what to say or how to really do this." He hung his head as he felt Boz's arm come around him.

"You just talk to God, is all. That's it. Tell you what, you just pray silently. Just say whatever's on your heart. And I'll pray out loud for both of us. Okay?"

"Okay."

Keene folded his hands and let his forehead rest against his knuckles. He was about to start when he heard an EMT yelling. His heart plummeted into his stomach.

"We're losing her! We're losing her! Quick—get those paddles charged. I need to hit her right away!"

PART 3: STAND

CHAPTER 39

Washington, DC

President Walker strode through the hallway of the White House with an air of confidence. He had spent almost four hours with President Grant last night. Together the two of them had written what, he thought, was the best speech either of them had ever given. He couldn't wait till this afternoon to address the American people.

It was good seeing Calvin last night, he thought. The man was as alert and full of energy as he'd ever been. They spent almost the entire first hour of their meeting just catching up on the events of the last four months. The next three, though, were all business. Walker had shared with Grant what he intended the speech to be. Grant had patted him on the shoulder and said he couldn't think of anything more important that this country needed right now. Three hours later, the speech was finished.

Initially, Walker was going to give the speech as a radio address. But after spending time with Grant, he had decided to alert the television media. Though there were still some challenges with broadcasting, most of the cable outlets had worked tirelessly to get their stations back on line. Most coverage was news related anyway, except for reruns of previously recorded shows whose film hadn't been destroyed. Since satellite providers had been the least affected, cable companies and satellite providers had struck a temporary deal—for the good of the nation, if you asked them, but mostly because Walker had signed an executive order demanding it— and were sharing technology, in order that news could be viewed across what was left of the country. Walker had let it be known that he wished to have airtime on every station at five o'clock sharp. And that he was going to give the speech on the steps of the Capitol. The same place where the attempt had been made on President Grant.

He walked into the Oval Office and found the first party of his first

189

meeting of the day waiting for him—Secretary of the Navy Bob Sykes. Since the invasion, he, Sykes, and Jennings had kept a biweekly meeting. With the governmental structure all but in shambles, the three of them had been pretty much running the country.

"Bob. . ."

"Mr. President."

"What's going on today?"

"Continuing on with current operations, sir. Admiral Benbrough—with the Royal Navy—and I have been trying to lay the foundation for how they're going to move back to the United Kingdom. I think we've both agreed that a UK presence here for a while would not only be appreciated, but necessary. At least until we get our infrastructure back up to par."

"I agree. Make sure Benbrough knows how much we appreciate all his efforts. And I will make sure I call Prime Minister Bungard and young William and thank them for their public support." Walker looked around the room. "Where's Jennings?"

Sykes grimaced and gestured to his chair, behind the desk. "Why don't we sit down for a moment, sir."

Walker took his seat and waited for the secretary to continue.

"Mr. President, last night, Jon Keene and Boz Hamilton took a G-5 to Raleigh. You know already that Jennings had Megan Taylor and Eli Craig looking into this rumor about someone stirring up trouble with the Chinese. I know Jennings has briefed you a little bit."

Walker nodded.

"Last night, when Keene and Boz got there, they found Taylor and Craig at Judge Milton Hayes's home. Apparently, gunfire had been exchanged and Taylor and Craig caught the bad end of it."

Walker sat up in his chair. "Are they all right?"

"Last I heard, they were both in critical condition. But they're alive. Jennings is there now. Soon as either of them wakes up, we'll know what went down. All we know right now is they were shot. Judge Hayes was found upstairs in his room. Two shots to the head."

"So we don't know anything yet."

"Not much. But I think it's important that we all be on extra alert right now. Whatever Taylor and Craig uncovered got Hayes killed."

Walker sat back in his chair again. He folded his hands together and rested them under his chin. "This speech I'm giving today. . .it's going to stir a hornet's nest. I know the majority of the people are in agreement with me. But I have my opponents, too. They're not going to be a big fan of what I'm proposing."

"I spoke with Jennings earlier. He's in touch with the head of Secret Service and your detail. He's making sure we don't have a repeat of what happened with President Grant." Then, "Mr. President, are you sure you want to do this? I mean, at the Capitol?"

"Absolutely. I want this thing out in full public. The rest of the country needs to see people there, supporting what I'm talking about. And I'd like you and Jennings there beside me."

"Yes, sir. I think that would be good."

Walker stood up. "Thanks, Bob. I'll see you in a couple hours."

CHAPTER 40

Keene grabbed the doctor's arm as he exited Megan's room. "Any change, Doc?"

"I'm sorry, Mr. Keene. Not yet."

Keene had stood outside Megan's door since they'd arrived from Andrews Air Force Base. He hadn't slept. Hadn't showered. Hadn't even eaten since getting back. All he could think about was everything he wanted to say to her. And that he might not ever get the chance.

Boz had tried to get him to come away and sit in the lobby or go get something to eat. But Keene was having none of it. He felt as though it was his fault she was even lying in there, fighting for her life. He should've left for Raleigh the minute he and Boz got back to Washington.

He'd thought about her every day while he was gone. If he had to be honest, he couldn't *stop* thinking about her. It was one of the only things that kept him going. And that was something he hadn't dealt with since he'd met his wife. His wife had completely destroyed any attempt he'd made at trying to be cool. No matter how deadly an operative he'd become, no matter how hard he tried to appear suave and debonair to those around him, she could see right through him. When she died, he thought he'd never look at another woman that way. And then he met Megan. He remembered the first time he met her. She had marched into President Grant's office and stuck her hand out to shake his. He had underestimated her grip. Before he knew it, his knuckles were crunching against themselves. He remembered thinking, *This woman is going to be a pain in my—*

"Jon."

He looked up to see Boz coming back down the hall at him. "Yeah? What's up?"

"Any change?"

"None yet. Eli?"

"Same."

They both stood there for a second in silence. Finally Boz said, "We need to go. Walker is going to give a speech on the steps of the Capitol in about an hour. Jennings wants us there."

"Yeah, I heard. I guess he's not worried about what happened with President Grant."

"Guess not. Anyway, I think it'll be fine. Jennings has Secret Service and every fed he can find stationed every three feet for six square blocks."

Keene halfheartedly laughed. "You know what they say about assumptions."

Boz shrugged. "Yeah, well, that's why we're going."

Keene turned and grabbed the knob on Megan's door. "Give me a second. I'll meet you in the lobby."

Boz said okay and left again.

Keene entered the room and sat in a small chair beside Megan's bed. She had tubes and wires protruding from her body. She had a breathing mask on, which led to a ventilator next to the bed. The little plunger rose and fell every couple of seconds inside the tube, helping her breathe. He reached out and held her hand and rested his head on the bed rail.

"Megan, I'm so sorry this has happened to you. I should've been there. I should've come to Raleigh the second we got back. I shouldn't have let Jennings keep me here." He reached up and brushed a strand of hair from her face. "I promise you, though, Boz and I are going to finish this. Sokolov will pay for everything she's done. You just stay here and get better, you hear?" He let go of her hand and stood up. "I have to go now. But I'll be back. I promise."

He looked at her for a few more seconds then turned to leave. The door to her room opened up and her doctor came in.

"Mr. Keene, you can't be in here. I'm sorry."

"I was just leaving." He brushed past the doctor as he moved toward the door. He turned and grabbed the doctor's arm. "Hey, don't you let her die."

"We're doing everything we can, Mr. Keene. I promise."

"You just make sure that you do. Because if you don't"—he drilled the doctor with a hard stare—"you'll have me to deal with."

Boz was waiting for him in the lobby. They got in the car and headed south toward the Capitol. The speech was scheduled to start in forty minutes.

They badged their way through the checkpoints and the guards all the way to Capitol Hill. One of the Secret Service agents directed them to pull their car behind the Capitol building.

"It's like déjà vu," Keene said.

"Yeah, let's just hope this one turns out differently than the last one."

"Roger that."

Making the turn, another guard motioned them along and pointed for them to park in the grass up next to an entrance. Jennings was waiting for them as they got out of the car.

"All right, guys. Walker is in the rotunda. We've swept the perimeter at least a hundred times. I've got agents from every department you can think of covering about five and a half square blocks."

Keene shook his head. "I don't care, Kevin. This is still a stupid idea."

Jennings shrugged. "Doesn't matter. Walker wasn't taking no for an answer. So I want the two of you within ten feet of him at all times. Got it?"

They both nodded.

"Good. Then let's go."

Governor Joe Nolan moved through the crowd, shaking hands and making pleasantries with the other senators and congressmen who were in attendance for the president's speech. He had made the trip earlier this morning, ready to launch the initial phase of what Pemberton had dubbed *The Uprising.*

Even with all the communication woes the country was still facing, word had leaked about the content of Walker's speech, and the press was frothing at the mouth out on the steps. *They have no idea the story they will have to run with tonight,* Nolan thought.

The CIA director, Jennings, who he had seen standing next to Walker all this time, shouted above the noise that had risen in the rotunda and asked for everyone's attention.

"All right, everyone. Here's how this is going to work. All of you"—he pointed to the crowd—"are going to go through that door over there. When you get outside, please take a seat on either side of the podium. Remember, there are people on the steps. The press is here, and so are some citizens. President Walker has invited them to be his guests. So watch your mouths, unless you want to be quoted saying something you're going to regret tomorrow. Let's move."

The governor laughed to himself. *Regret?* He wasn't going to regret anything he was about to say. He was *counting* on being quoted!

He did, however, have a different idea about where he wanted to be for all of this. The fact that there were citizens on the steps gave him the idea. What better way to stand in opposition of the president than to stand with the people of this nation—among them, representing them. He stuck his hands in his coat pockets and followed the line outside.

Keene stood next to Boz and Jennings alongside the president, as the line of congressmen and senators passed by. He really didn't like any of them for a threat, but after what they'd been through, he didn't want to take anything for granted, either. But something did catch his eye, about halfway through the procession. He leaned over to Boz.

"Hey, you know who that is?"

"Who?" Boz scanned the line back and forth.

"There, standing beside Nora Redding, the senator from North Carolina."

"I don't know, her husband?"

"No," Keene said hesitantly. "That's Governor Nolan. Also of North Carolina."

Boz's eyes shifted toward him. "First of all, how do you know who the governor of North Carolina is? And secondly, why do I all of a sudden not like that?"

Keene's eyes narrowed as he watched the senator and governor from North Carolina pass by them. "I'm a history buff. I just know stupid random things like. . .who the governors of states are. And. . .you don't like it, because I don't like it, either. Too much of a coincidence that Megan and Eli are in a bed fighting for their lives because of what they were investigating in *his* state."

"And I told you before," Boz said, "I don't believe in coincidences."

Keene watched as the governor disappeared through the doorway. "Yeah. Me either. Let's go talk to him." He started to move when Jennings caught his arm.

"No, let's don't."

Keene shot him a look. "And why not?"

"Because you two are supposed to be focused on Walker. That's where I want you. Now, let's move. The president is ready to go."

Jennings turned back to the president. Keene leaned into Boz. "Soon as we get out there, you find where he's sitting. If I see first, I'll give you a heads-up. Either way, I want to know where that man is at all times."

"Roger that."

CHAPTER 41

President Walker tried to gather his thoughts one last time before heading out onto the steps. The line of senators and congressmen had almost disappeared out the door now. They would be moving any minute. He turned to see that Jennings had stepped away for a second, talking to Keene and Boz. Jennings patted Keene on the shoulder as Keene and Boz began to move toward the doorway. Jennings turned back to him.

"Sorry about that, sir. Just some last-minute clarifications. You ready?"

Walker was ready, but there was something he wanted to do first. "Ah, Mr. Hamilton. . .may I see you for a moment. Before you take your post?" Then to Jennings, "You and Keene go ahead. I'll come out with Boz."

Jennings gave a quick nod and turned to join Keene as Boz came near. "Yes, Mr. President?"

"I wanted to share something with you that I thought you'd appreciate."

"Yes, sir."

"I spent the evening with Calvin last night. He's doing remarkably well."

"Yes, sir. I saw him today at Bethesda—while I was visiting Eli and Megan."

Walker silently chastised himself. "Oh, that's right. I'm very sorry to hear about what happened with them. Any word?"

Boz shook his head. "No, sir. Not yet."

Walker reached his hand out to Boz's shoulder. "I know I don't have to tell you this, but God has it under control. I will continue to pray for them." He gave Boz's shoulder a final squeeze and let go. "Well, if you spoke with Calvin, you are aware of what I'm about to go out there and say."

"Yes, sir. I am. I think it's something that has been a long time coming."

Walker looked at his watch. "Then we better not keep them waiting any longer." He extended his hand. "After you."

Walker followed Boz through the door and outside onto the steps. A podium was fixed in the center of the steps. Members of Congress sat on either side, while hundreds of reporters and civilians lined the steps below. Walker stepped up to the bank of microphones and waited for the crowd to settle.

"Ladies and gentlemen. . .members of Congress. . .good evening. I want to thank you all for coming. Typically, I would be addressing all of you via my biweekly radio address. However, I felt I would like to make this a little more public. Besides, God has favored us with unseasonably beautiful weather for this time of year. I would hate to waste it!" Small bits of laughter and applause spread through the crowd. "I'm going to get right to the point. So please forgive me for not following typical political protocol and wasting your time." Again the laughter rose above the crowd. Once it settled, he continued.

"These past weeks and months have left our country in a new place. We are not used to being in a position of vulnerability. And yet this is where we find ourselves. America has always been the trailblazer. We've always helped to dictate what comes next. Both here at home and abroad. And while the incredible people of this country continue to try and put the pieces back together and find a way to move on, many of us are still wondering, where do we go from here?

"I'd like to encourage everyone here today. All of you are aware of the man who calls himself the Prophet." He paused as the mention of Quinn Harrington brought murmurs throughout the crowd. He held his hands. "The Prophet has been in contact with us recently."

Immediately an uneasiness settled over the crowd. The last time a president addressed the public and the Prophet had been mentioned, the Chinese had become their new neighbors.

"Ladies and gentlemen. . .please. . .as I said before. I bring encouragement today." That seemed to help quiet the crowd. "The Prophet has assured me—us—that God has decided to allow the United States to remain."

Immediately, a smattering of applause and cheers rose up from the crowd. Some even started chanting, "U–S–A! U–S–A!" Again Walker held his hands up to quiet the crowd.

"This is truly good news, friends. We should be grateful and humbled. And we should celebrate." Again, a small applause. "But we should also beware. God has given us an opportunity to do as He has instructed us to do—repent, as a nation. Now, I know that many of you have individually experienced major changes within your lives and your families' lives. And that is a wonderful thing! I'm encouraged, each and every day, as I hear stories from many of you about how this event has brought you closer to God, or has caused you to see God for the first time. And I look forward to many, many more.

"However, I believe there is so much more to do. Yes, I believe God's intentions were for us as people to reevaluate our own situations and come to grips with where we are spiritually. But I also hear the words of the Prophet's warning to us—to call the *nation* to repentance. And so, today, on the eve of the most wonderful season of the year, the Christmas season, I am calling for Congress to propose a new amendment to our Constitution."

Immediately, a cacophony of noise erupted throughout the crowd. Cameras from the news reporters began flashing as they shouted questions at him. Some of the crowd began to shout with dissent, while others began to raise the chant of "U–S–A! U–S–A!" again. Walker held up his hands to quiet the crowd. "Ladies and gentlemen. . .please. . . ladies and gentlemen. . .

"Thank you. What I am proposing is an amendment that will once and for all identify America as a nation founded on Christian principles. This amendment, in no way, would stand in contradiction to the First Amendment. Individually, the American people will have the same freedom you've always enjoyed. Nor am I talking about a state-sanctioned church. What I *am* speaking about is an amendment with language that says this country will be a country that makes policy based on Christian principles. And that means that there are many policies currently in place that will need to be abolished."

At this, the crowd erupted into a frenzy. He had expected this on some level, but the crowd was now beginning to turn on themselves. Verbal jousting began to give way to pushing and pointing and shouting at one another. He looked to his side and noted the look of concern on Jon Keene's face. A moment later, Keene was at his side.

"Mr. President, I think we might need to take you out of here."

"Absolutely not!" Walker said. "I'm not going anywhere."

Suddenly, someone began shouting over the noise from the people. Walker turned his attention away from Keene. The man was standing on the steps, among the reporters, and was, somehow, getting the attention of the people. A few seconds later, he had successfully quieted the ruckus. The man turned and began walking up the stairs toward the platform.

Keene began to feel a sense of uneasiness as the president continued to plow through his speech. Walker was only five minutes into it, and already he had generated laughter, panic—at the mention of the Prophet—and cheers in support of God's decree to spare the nation.

He had spoken with Boz briefly on the ride there. Boz told him he didn't know exactly how it was going to play out, but that the president and President Grant had spent the better part of last night crafting this speech. And it centered around proposing a constitutional amendment— one in which the United States would declare itself a Christian nation. And though Keene hadn't seen a copy of the speech, he knew that Walker had just let the cat out of the bag.

He kept his body positioned forward, scanning the crowd for possible threats. So far, he hadn't seen anything that caused his internal alarm to go off, but there was just a general sense of uneasiness. And he couldn't put his finger on it. And then his gaze fell to the middle of the crowd of reporters.

It made no sense. Why would Governor Nolan be standing in the middle of a crowd of reporters, and not on the platform with members of Congress? A current of tension began to undergird the crowd. He brought his attention back to the speech.

". . . And that means that there are many policies currently in place that will need to be abolished."

The crowd erupted. He began to see skirmishes breaking out, as the people seemed to be taking sides. Pushing and shoving. People were yelling at one another. He looked to the side and noticed that even the members of Congress were beginning to argue among themselves. He looked to Walker, who had locked eyes with him. This needed to stop now. He moved from his position to where Walker was standing.

"Mr. President, I think we might need to take you out of here."

Walker looked at him defiantly. "Absolutely not! I'm not going anywhere."

He was about to insist—by way of grabbing the man and dragging him out, if necessary, when someone on the steps below began to shout above the crowd. Surprisingly, the crowd began to quiet and give him their attention. Before Keene could even look, he knew who it was. Now he had a pretty good idea why the man had situated himself among the reporters. He finally turned to see Governor Joe Nolan holding his hands up and commanding the crowd.

"Ladies and gentlemen. . .please. . .please. . .calm down for a moment. If you'll give me a chance, perhaps I can help bring some clarity to this mess."

When the crowd finally settled, Nolan turned and started up the stairs toward the platform. As Keene moved to put himself between the governor and the president, he noticed that Boz and three Secret Service agents had already moved to intercept. When Nolan got within five feet, Boz put his hand out on the governor's chest to stop him.

"Excuse me," Nolan said and tried to move Boz's arm to the side. But Boz didn't budge. Keene winked at his friend and gave him a smile. Boz still had it.

"My name is Governor Nolan," he yelled over his shoulder for the crowd to hear. "From the great state of North Carolina."

A small pocket of applause and cheers came from the crowd.

"We know who you are, Governor," Keene said. "What do you want?"

The governor ignored Keene. Instead, he looked to Walker with his arms held out. Walker nodded to Boz. Boz removed his hand and allowed the governor to continue up the steps.

"What can I do for you, Governor?" Walker asked.

Keene didn't like where this was headed. He leaned into the president's ear. "Sir, I don't think this is the time or the place for this. Please, let us take you out of here. If you'd like, we can bring Nolan along. You two can talk in private."

Walker kept his attention forward, on the approaching statesman. "Thank you, Mr. Keene. But I think we'll be fine here." Then to Nolan, "What's this about, Joe?"

Keene did not like this at all. He looked to Boz, whose face said he shared Keene's concern. Boz came around behind the president and Nolan to Keene. Keene leaned in to whisper to him. "If this gets out of hand, I'm yanking him out of here." He pointed to Walker.

"Roger that. I'll be right behind you."

Nolan stepped over to the side so that he was sharing the podium now with Walker and turned into the bank of microphones. "Mr. President. As I walked up here, you asked me what can you do for me. Well, sir, I will tell you. You can start acting like a president and protect the people of this country."

CHAPTER 42

Alex Smith woke to find herself in the bed of her hotel. Alone. The drapes were open, so she could see that the sun was beginning to set. But she had no idea what time it was. What was more, she had no idea what day it was, or how long she'd been there in the bed. Her shoulder and her leg were throbbing. She looked down to see the bandages covering her arm and leg.

The trip to Hayes's house was a complete disaster. Everything went wrong. She should've taken more precaution. Pemberton had just told her that Hayes had been visited by those agents; she should've suspected they'd be back. She just didn't figure on them coming back that night. Yet another careless mistake.

Taking out the guard at the gate was child's play. The kid barely even looked up at her when she got out of the car and approached the window. He had his nose stuck in some comic book. She didn't even wait for him to get the little window all the way open before she stuck the nose of the PK380 in and placed two rounds in his forehead.

From there, she had simply knocked on the door. Hayes seemed startled to see her but let her in without question. Once inside, she merely showed him the weapon and led him upstairs to his bedroom. She made him sit on the edge of the bed, where she asked him a series of questions. Hayes swore that he had not talked to anyone, especially the agents who had visited him. He pleaded for his life, crying like a child. She actually believed him, which made the fact that she was about to kill him all the more pathetic. She raised the weapon and pointed it at his head. That's when she heard the creaking of the floorboard behind her. She turned her head just in time to see a man pointing a Glock 9mm at her. Without even a second's pause, she whirled around and started firing.

She knew she had hit the man with her first shot, but she couldn't be

202

sure about the second. He dove to the side, back out into the hall, just as she pulled the trigger. She turned back around and shot the judge—who had lunged for his *Judge* revolver on the bedside table—then ran out into the hall to finish off the agent.

As soon as she got into the hall, she saw the man on his knees, trying to get back on his feet. She took two steps toward him and kicked him just as he started to stand. She fired again as he crashed into the banister. Another shot landed directly in his upper chest as the banister shattered and carried him over the edge. She was about to shoot again when she heard a woman scream. Then a hailstorm of bullets came at her from below. She dropped to the floor of the catwalk and peeked her head through the opening where the banister used to be. She saw the woman, who had rushed over to her partner. Rage filled her as she recognized Megan Taylor, the FBI agent that had left her to die on the side of the road in Dubai. She stretched her arm out over the opening in the railing and emptied her magazine. She picked her head up just in time to see Taylor running into the kitchen.

It was only a matter of seconds before she had Taylor pinned behind the kitchen island. Then she had decided to toy with her. She was going to enjoy every last second of killing her. Taylor finally sprung from behind the island. But she was ready for it. As soon as Taylor showed herself, she pointed the PK380 and began to fire. Taylor only made it four feet before she fell to the floor. Alex smiled as she walked toward her, taunting her—telling her how she was going to be the one walking out of here this time.

Suddenly, everything changed. Taylor's partner had managed to get to his feet and hit her from behind. She watched as her PK380 flew from her hand across the tile floor in front of her. She tried to get to it, but Taylor's partner had fired off a bunch of rounds at her. She didn't even remember how many. What she did remember was the hot, searing pain that had ripped through her thigh and her left shoulder blade, as Taylor's partner hit pay dirt with two of his rounds. In that moment, she only had one choice. Get out. She saw the door that led outside from behind the little eat-in kitchen table. She sprang to her feet and darted outside. She'd made it to the car, half expecting Taylor's partner to come rushing outside, firing after her. But it never happened.

By this time, she was getting dizzy. She knew she was losing blood. She had to get help. She did the only thing she could think of. She thumbed through her little black book, which held all the numbers of people she had for emergency contacts. She stopped at the first gas station she came to, and used the pay phone to call the number of someone who gave her the name and number of someone she could contact in Raleigh. After that, she called the restaurant where Farid was supposed to meet her and got him on the phone. When he picked up, she breathed a sigh of relief. "Farid, I've had an accident." She gave him the number of the contact in Raleigh, told him to get supplies and meet her back at the room.

She made it back to the hotel and somehow sneaked her way past the front desk. She got to the elevator and hit the button for the fourteenth floor. She felt like she was going to pass out at any second. When she got to the room, she collapsed on the couch. Fortunately, Farid showed up only a few minutes later. He barreled through the door carrying a brown paper sack and ran to her where she lay on the couch. He ripped the hem of her cocktail dress and tore the sleeve on her right side to expose her thigh and shoulder, and then immediately went to work.

"This isn't bad," he said. "You'll be fine. But it's going to hurt when I take the bullets out."

"Just do it. I can handle it."

He pulled his belt from his trousers and gave it to her. "Here. Bite down on this."

He took a bottle of alcohol from the brown paper sack, undid the cap, and poured it over her thigh and shoulder. Next he took a small scalpel and held it in his hand like a pen. He used his fingers to spread the skin around her shoulder and then stuck the knife inside the wound. The pain shot through her arm and down her side. She felt nauseous for a moment, and then her eyes began to flutter. She remembered taking a breath. And then she had blacked out.

As she looked around the room now, she noticed that Farid's jacket was hanging on the chair of the little table by the door. She remembered thinking that she had made a mistake. That being with Farid was stupid— that it was going to cost her. That she was going to have to get rid of him. But he had saved her life. Twice now. And sitting here thinking about him. . .mistake or not, she decided she liked having him around.

The door to the room opened and Farid walked in. He had a smile on his face as he saw her sitting up in the bed. "How are you feeling?"

"Better. Thank you."

He leaned down and kissed her. "You gave me quite a scare last night."

Okay, so there was one question answered. She had been out for almost a whole day. She gave him a flirtatious grin. "Am I going to die, Doc?"

He winked back. "Not from this. The bullet in your shoulder wasn't deep. It'll be sore for a couple days, but it'll be fine. The one on your side was just a graze. It took a chunk of skin and muscle, but never got inside to do any damage. You'll probably feel like you have a cracked rib, but again, nothing serious. We probably need to stay here another day or so to let you rest." Then, "What happened?"

She recounted everything that happened from the time he left her in the cab until he found her back at the hotel. When she finished, he sat there staring at her.

"What?" she said.

"Nothing. Just that this is the second time that woman has caused you harm. I would like to see her dead."

She laughed a short laugh, which sent a pain down her side. "Yeah, well, don't worry. As soon as we get out of here, I'm going to grant your wish."

CHAPTER 43

Washington, DC

Nolan felt his blood surge as he turned toward the bank of microphones. "Well, sir, you can start acting like a president and protect the people of this country."

The crowd exploded. Those who had seemed to support President Walker were now cheering for Nolan. He held his hands up to quiet them.

"Ladies and gentlemen, for those of you who might not know who I am, my name is Joseph Nolan and I'm governor of the great state of North Carolina. I came here on behalf of my state and on behalf of the other twelve states that we now call this country." He turned to face Walker.

"Mr. President, for four months now, you have abdicated your responsibility and your sworn oath to our Constitution. We have seen a foreign enemy land on our shores, destroy our West Coast with nuclear weapons, occupy sovereign territory, and force American citizens to either run for their lives to this side of the Appalachian Mountains, or denounce their allegiance to this country and adopt the Chinese way of life. And what is your excuse for allowing this to happen? Some man who claims to be a prophet of God!"

Again, the crowd rallied.

"I say if the American people want to believe in some antiquated religious practice, fine. They are guaranteed that freedom under our First Amendment. But honestly, Mr. President, haven't we, as a nation, gotten past such ideological fantasies? To suggest that a sitting president would base his national security policies on the ramblings of a religious zealot—a lunatic—why, I submit to you that it's borderline treason!" He pumped his fist at the crowd.

Walker had gone completely red faced. Nolan believed if the TV cameras weren't there, Walker would punch him in the nose. Some agents from the Secret Service started to move in—*probably to usher either me or Walker out of here,* he thought. But Walker had held up a hand to call them off. Nolan shot a snide smile at Walker and turned back to the crowd.

"Ladies and gentlemen, we are the United States of America. Not some third-world country! We have sat by long enough while the Chinese steal our resources and persecute our citizens. We are the greatest nation in the world. It's time we showed them who they've messed with!"

At that, the crowd became unruly. People began to throw water bottles, paper, trash, anything they could find at the guards who were standing between them and the steps to the Capitol, as an energy began to permeate throughout the crowd. Walker pushed Nolan out of the way and tried to get the people's attention again. Again the agents began to move toward Walker, but he gave a swift slashing of his hand, telling them to stay back.

"Friends. . .ladies and gentlemen. . .please. . .calm down," Walker pleaded. "Hear what I have to say. This man is trying to bring dissension among us. This is what our enemy, the evil one, would have us do. We must not succumb to such naive ideals. Please, folks."

But it was too late. Nolan had already stirred the people to the point of near riot. And he was enjoying the effect he'd had. Finally, two Secret Service agents grabbed Walker by the arms and carried him back into the rotunda—apparently no longer caring if Walker objected or not—leaving Nolan alone on the steps in front of the crowd. He pumped his fist a couple more times to incite them again. It was all the guards could do to keep the people from plowing them over.

Finally, when he'd seen enough, and knew he had them where he wanted them, he held his hands up to quiet them down. After a few seconds, he had their attention again.

"Ladies and gentlemen, I am saddened by the state of our nation. Not too long ago, we were the most feared superpower on the planet. But then a few traitors and an administration that turned its back on this country's security brought this to pass on our nation. Not some god." A few cheers started rising up. But he quickly squelched them. "Now, listen. I don't hold anything against anyone for his personal beliefs. Personally, I have never seen any evidence that science can't refute to suggest there even is a God. So I'm sure not going to put the welfare of my country at stake just because some idiot crackpot comes on the scene and says that this God we can't even prove exists has brought judgment upon us. Who does he think he is? This is America! If there is a God, America is His gift to the world, not His enemy!" Again the crowd erupted.

"Friends, listen to me. President Walker is right. We have a long road ahead of us. It's going to take time to rebuild this nation to the state of greatness she once enjoyed. But you have to believe me. I and others believe that what President Walker would have us do—or not do, I should say—will ruin the very fabric of our country. Yes, we need to rebuild. Yes, we need to help our fellow citizens as they struggle through this crisis. And yes, we can be the great nation we once were. But we cannot get there by letting the Chinese occupy our lands. They must be dealt with.

"Now, listen. The infrastructure of this country is in shambles right now." He looked at the congressmen and congresswomen who sat and stood on either side of him. "And many of you are also responsible. Shame on you!"

This time, it took a full two minutes before he could quiet the crowd.

"The bottom line is this: President Walker would have you believe some higher power has, for whatever reason, taken out His frustration on our country. He would have you believe the only way to see this country flourish again is to remain in the state we are now. I disagree. I believe we have been shown we are—have been—vulnerable. That we have enemies, both foreign and domestic. And if we don't pull our heads out of our rear ends, we're never going to see greatness again.

"Folks, I want to see America returned to greatness. I want to be able to take my family on a vacation to Colorado to go skiing again. I want to take my family to the beaches of Gulf Shores again. I want to be able to cross that mountain range and not fear that I'm going to get shot by someone pretending to have ownership rights over the land my forefathers bled and died to secure! We can be that nation again. But we cannot be that nation under this administration.

"I have been the governor of North Carolina for going on seven years now. I have the executive knowledge it takes to run this country. And I know this is somewhat unprecedented, but I think we're a little past normalcy at this stage in the game. Therefore, in front of all of you. . ." He turned to face the cameras. "And to all of you watching or listening across these thirteen states that we now call a country. . .I want you all to hear what I'm about to say.

"Mr. President, the Constitution provides for you the opportunity to nominate a new vice president—yet another charge you have neglected. Given my experience as an executive and my desire to see this country back on the world stage—in its rightful place—I am officially demanding that you do so. And I submit to you that I am the right person for that position."

The crowd exploded with applause. It was as if he had been on the campaign trail for months and his opponent had been ousted for having an affair. The people were practically worshiping him. He didn't even bother to quiet them this time. He wanted them roused. He wanted the people watching on television to feel the energy in that place. He turned his head toward the rotunda entrance, as if Walker were still standing there listening.

"Look at these people, Mr. President. Listen to them as they applaud my courage to stand up to our enemies. Listen to them as they show their support for someone who desires to lead them!" Turning back to the cameras, he said, "Ladies and gentlemen, this is your country. You have the right to demand that President Walker listen to you. That he do as we ask him now and nominate me as vice president. And I make you this promise. As soon as he bows his ego and narcissism to the will of the people, I will see to it that he pays for his neglect of this country. My first order of business, as your new vice president, will be to oversee the process of having him removed from office and tried for crimes of treason against this nation! Then, by the power granted to me by the Constitution, I will assume the rank of your commander in chief. And unlike my counterpart, I promise to act like one! Thank you!"

With that, Nolan stepped back from the bank of microphones and raised his fists in the air. By tomorrow morning, the entire country would be calling for Walker's head on a plate. And he had just served it up.

CHAPTER 44

Raleigh, North Carolina

Gavin Pemberton didn't dance. He'd never liked it. Never thought it held any value. What was the point in bouncing around, jostling your insides, and looking like a fool in front of others. Even at his own weddings, he had to be forced to participate in the couple's first slow dance. It just wasn't something he did.

Until just now.

He sat on the edge of his seat, watching Joe give it to Walker. And, boy, did he! Joe had just taken the world's biggest sledgehammer and bashed Walker's skull with it—metaphorically, of course. Though he did enjoy, for a second, the thought of that actually happening. But Joe. . .good ol' Joe! He couldn't remember when he had ever been that proud of someone in his whole life. It took everything he had just to sit still and listen. Joe had him so fired up halfway through his speech, he couldn't sit still. And when he delivered that last line—the one about how Joe promised to *act* like a president—he was so excited, he shot up out of his chair and began to dance a jig. Right there, in the middle of the floor, smacking his palm against his leg and bouncing around the room, whooping and hollering. He was so excited, he almost forgot he had just had his best friend killed.

The thought jarred him and brought back the anger and bitterness he'd been dealing with all day. He sat back down in his chair, turned the television off, and threw the remote across the room. He was wrought up with contempt—how had Milton allowed himself to be found and manipulated by those agents?

Earlier the local news had reported that Hayes had been found dead in his home. The report said that they believed it was a home invasion. That gunfire had been exchanged and the home had been damaged, showing signs of a struggle.

Pemberton knew what the struggle was. Alex Smith was the struggle. Obviously, Milton had fought with the woman, trying to escape and save his life. He was disappointed that Smith hadn't been more tactful. But what did he know? He wasn't a professional assassin. Perhaps the struggle was staged to look like a home invasion. Perhaps that was how she worked. And obviously it did work. The police had said they were looking for more than one suspect, given the amount of damage and gunfire at the scene.

But as old and mean and set in his ways as he was, Pemberton still felt some sadness for his friend. In some respects, Milton had been closer to him than any of his wives. He and Milton had shared secrets he had told no one else.

In the end, he decided that Milton was a hero. The man died promoting the sovereignty of the country. He was just an unfortunate casualty of war. And it was better this way. Eventually, Milton would have become a liability. His flippancy about the social order and his extremely liberal ideals would have caused problems. Not to mention Milton was really a coward when push came to shove. Pemberton knew that eventually those agents or someone else would've gotten to him. And then who knows what kind of bad could've happened? No, it was better this way.

He walked over to the wet bar, poured himself a glass, and held it up. "Milton, my friend, may you rest in peace. I promise I won't let your death be in vain." He tipped the glass back and drained it.

He grabbed his car keys and his jacket. The weather was finally starting to turn cooler. He pulled the collar up over his neck and stepped outside. He had thought about calling, but he knew the old coot would be home. Besides, he didn't feel like messing with trying to get a landline call placed. It was still a crapshoot half the time. The idea had just come to him as he had watched Joe's speech. And he didn't want to explain over the phone.

He fired up the old pickup and pulled the lever in gear. He was going to see Jake Irving.

CHAPTER 45

Washington, DC

Keene woke up with a headache. He went to the bathroom, grabbed some ibuprofen, and chased it with a glass of water from the sink. He reached behind him and turned the shower on as hot as it would go and got undressed.

Last night had been the first night in almost a half a year that he had spent in his own bed. After the debacle at the Capitol, he and Boz had gotten President Walker out of there before a full-on riot could break out.

Walker had been furious and dumbfounded, all at the same time. He couldn't understand how this had happened—how what was supposed to be a defining point in the nation's history had turned into a series of attacks on his character, the nation's weakness, and the outright sovereignty of God. Keene, of course, didn't have any answers. They both had looked to Boz for his take.

"Guys, I don't know what to tell you," Boz had said. "All I know is that Quinn warned us this was happening. I guess we should've expected it."

"I expected *some* criticism," Walker had admitted. "But nothing like what I just saw. I mean, it was like getting picked off by a sniper. Who knows what the fallout of this will be!"

Keene had a pretty good idea. And he wasn't all that excited about it. But he wasn't going to debate it right then with the president in the car. He would wait until he, Jennings, and Boz could huddle up privately.

"Go home, Jon. Get some sleep," Jennings had said. "You need it." Then, "You, too, Boz. We'll meet up tomorrow morning."

As much as Keene had wanted to go back to the hospital and check on Megan and Eli, he knew Jennings was right. He desperately needed a good night's sleep. He hadn't caught more than four hours at any given time since he'd gotten back to Washington.

The sleep had been good; he had pretty much drifted off as soon as his head hit the pillow. He didn't even have time to enjoy—even for a couple of minutes—the fact that he was home and in his own bed. But when he woke the next morning, he just lay there, enjoying the feel of his mattress. Wrapped himself around his comforter, jostled the pillow around to get it just right. He'd almost, for a second, thought he was going to drift back off. But then his thoughts went to Megan. Last night. The Prophet. Chin and the Chinese. And the next thing he knew, his head was pounding with a headache.

He turned the water off and got out. Heading downstairs, he almost lost his footing and fell as he was startled to see Boz in his kitchen. His foot slipped and bounced to the next step, but he caught himself on the rail.

Boz turned around to see what the commotion was. "Hey, glad you're up. I'm making breakfast."

Keene continued down the steps and into the kitchen. "You're lucky I didn't shoot you." He stole a piece of toast from the plate sitting on the counter.

"How do you like your eggs?"

"From a chicken," Keene said.

Boz turned and gave him a sour face.

"Scrambled is fine." Then, "What are you doing here?"

"Couldn't sleep. Been up for about two hours. And since you and I are going to be spending the rest of the day together, I just came here. How'd you sleep?"

"Couldn't tell you. I was out before my head hit the pillow."

Boz brought plates filled with eggs, toast, and bacon to the table and set them down. Keene poured himself a cup of coffee and refilled Boz's. He sat down and looked at the food. "Thanks for this." He crammed a whole piece of bacon in his mouth. "I'm starving."

When they were finished, they headed straight for the car. Boz drove while Keene fished the sat-phone out of his pocket and waited for Jennings to answer.

"Where are you?" Jennings said.

"Well, good morning to you, too," Keene said. "We're on our way to Bethesda. Going to check in on Megan and Eli. See if there's been a change."

"Good. You see any coverage from the speech?"

"No. It was all I could do to keep my eyes open long enough to get inside my house."

"I'll fill you in when you get here."

"Roger that. We'll head that way soon as we check on Megan and Eli," Keene said as he heard the click on the other end of the line. He turned to Boz. "Jennings asked if I saw any of the reaction from the speech. You see anything?"

"Nope. Went straight to bed."

Keene decided to turn the radio on and see what the pundits were saying.

It didn't take long to find it. The first two stations were playing music; the next one was on commercial. The fourth, however, a local talk program, was right in the middle of it. The show's host was going on and on about how Walker had been made to look like an idiot. That Governor Nolan was the man of the hour. Nolan had in ten minutes gone from a virtually unknown politician—outside of North Carolina, anyway—to a rock star. It seemed that the majority of the country, so far, was calling for Nolan to be the next vice president. And in the next breath, that he do as he said and see that Walker was brought up on charges.

"Man, this isn't good." Keene reached over and turned the radio back off. "That guy is exactly what Quinn was talking about. And if I find out he had anything to do with Megan and Eli. . ." He let his thought trail off.

"Yeah," Boz said. "We definitely need to squash this as quickly as we can. I'm just not sure how."

Keene looked at him with narrowed eyes.

Boz shook his head. "And we can't just kill him. So stop thinking about it."

"What?" Keene shrugged.

"Don't *what* me." He laughed. "I know exactly what you were thinking."

"Would make it easier."

They rode in silence the rest of the way. When they got to Bethesda, the guard waved them through and they drove around the compound to the place they had parked before. They went inside and split up: Keene went to check on Megan while Boz went to see about Eli. Though they were in the same wing, their rooms were at opposite ends of the hall.

Keene found a nurse and asked if there had been any change. The nurse said that there hadn't, but she allowed him to go in and sit by Megan. He pulled the chair over to her bed and sat down. He reached up and took her hand.

"Hey, kiddo. How you doing? I know they're taking good care of you. I threatened them within an inch of their lives if they didn't." He smiled, though she couldn't see him. He watched as the plunger from the breathing tube rose and fell.

The door to the room opened and Boz came in. "Any change?"

Keene leaned back in the chair and let go of Megan's hand. "No. Not yet. Eli?"

"Doc said he woke up a couple of times, but that's about it. Didn't talk or anything. Just opened his eyes. Then he was out again." Boz pulled up a chair and sat next to the bed with Keene. "Jon, I want you to know something."

"Yeah?"

"I want you to know that God hasn't abandoned Megan. Or Eli. Just because they are lying in these beds like this doesn't mean He has lost control over this situation."

Keene bit his lip and turned his head away. He knew deep down that Boz was right. But he was still new at this whole *believing* thing. And he was having a hard time dealing with the fact that Megan was lying in the bed in front of him, and she had done nothing to deserve it. Himself, maybe. He had deserved a lot of things that had happened to him. He had fought against God for so long. . .well, he just understood things on his end. But Megan was different. He felt Boz's hand on his shoulder.

"Hey, look at me for a second."

Keene turned to face him.

"I know you're thinking, *Why her, God? What has she done to deserve this?* The answer is maybe she didn't do anything to deserve it. But we need to understand, Jon, bad things happen to good people sometimes. And it's not because God can't control it. It's because we live in a fallen and broken world. Remember what I told you before you went to Texas to look for Quinn?"

He remembered. "Yeah. This is how it's going to be until Christ comes back and restores all things."

"That's right. And we might not understand it fully, but we have to believe that God's plan is being worked out. The way He intended it."

"So if I were to go back across the border and kill Chin, you're saying God intended it?"

Boz let out a huge sigh and scratched his head. "Not exactly. . . maybe. . .but that's a theological discussion I don't think is necessary for us to have right now. Let's just say God is sovereign over all things, but we're responsible for the choices we make. And what matters is that we seek His guidance in all things."

Keene didn't fully understand it, but he mostly did. And really it didn't matter anyway because, ever since that night in his cell when he'd cried out to God, his whole paradigm of decision making had been changed anyway. It was as if, without thinking, he just automatically thought about what God would have him do. So he guessed that was a good enough explanation for now. "What are we supposed to do, then? Just sit and wait?"

"That, and we continue to pray for them." They sat there in silence for a minute. "And. . .we do what we're called to do. Right now, that's trying to figure out what's going on out there and putting a stop to it."

Keene thought about that for a moment. He agreed. But what were they supposed to do? They had no direction. They had nothing to go on except the Prophet's vague directive: stop the insurrection. And besides, right now all he really cared about was being here with Megan. He looked at Boz. "Every day, while I was in that cell, all I could think about was her." He looked back at Megan. "I mean, how ridiculous is that? I barely spent two weeks with her."

"Jon, sometimes it just happens that way. I can tell you she feels the same about you."

"How do you know that?"

"Every day that you were gone, she never stopped looking. Even when Jennings ordered her to let it go. She never did."

"And now I'm back. And she's here, in this bed." Keene sat back and ran his hand through his hair. He'd known for some time now that Megan had done a number on him. And the weird thing was, he was okay with it. But now, sitting here, looking at her fighting for her life, he felt something he hadn't felt in a long time. Fear. He was afraid that she wouldn't make it. That he would never have a chance to tell her how he felt about her. He looked back at Boz.

"When I lost my wife in that terrorist attack, it almost killed me. You told me you lost a wife, too."

Boz nodded. "That's right. I did. She got sick and they couldn't save her."

"So you know what I'm talking about."

"I do."

Keene looked back at Megan. "I don't think I can handle losing her, too." He felt Boz's hand on his shoulder again.

"You haven't lost her, Jon. She's right here. And by God's grace, she'll recover."

Keene felt the buzzing from the sat-phone in his pocket. "This is probably Jennings." He pulled it out and answered. "Hello?"

"Jon, this is Quinn."

Keene cupped the phone and mouthed, *Quinn!* Boz sat up and leaned in to listen.

"Hello? Are you there?"

Keene pulled his hand away. "Yeah, sorry. I'm here. Boz is here, too."

"Good." There was a hesitation. "I've been told to tell you it has begun."

"Yeah, we kind of gathered that last night."

"Yes, well, you need to know it's going to get worse."

"Quinn, I have no idea what you—He—wants us to do."

"You have two problems right now. The first one is immediate. The Russian woman is headed to Washington. She is working for Gavin Pemberton. That's who Megan and Eli were investigating. She's the one who shot them."

Keene gripped the phone tighter. Jennings told him he'd assumed it was Sokolov. Hearing it confirmed caused an anger unlike anything he'd ever felt to rise up inside him.

"I do not know why she is coming to Washington," Quinn was saying. "But you know what she does. So if I were you, I would assume she's coming for a job. Stop her."

"Gladly," Keene said.

"Second, General Chin is aware of the events of last night."

"I figured he would be."

"He won't be the aggressor. But make no mistake, if he feels threatened, he will do whatever he feels he needs to do in order to protect his border. You must make sure Pemberton doesn't gain control of the White House."

"It seems to me that Governor Nolan is the problem."

"Nolan is a mouthpiece. The only reason he's even in the governor's chair is because of Pemberton. If you remove Nolan, Pemberton will have another one waiting to take his place. It will do you no good to go after Nolan. Find Pemberton. He's the one behind this."

"And how do we do that? From what I hear, the man is a ghost."

"The same way you found me. Look for him."

Keene pinched the bridge of his nose. "Can't He just once—just one time—just tell us? Like, 'Hey Jon, go to this address. Pemberton's waiting for you.'"

Quinn sighed. "You know that's not how this works, Jon. You have the information you need. Find Pemberton and stop him. And find the Russian woman before she does any more damage. Before the president loses control over the people."

The line went dead.

Keene looked at Boz. "We need to go see Jennings. Now."

CHAPTER 46

Jennings was on the phone when Keene and Boz came in. He motioned for them to take a seat. Keene couldn't tell who was on the phone, but it sounded like a heated discussion. Jennings finally said good-bye and forcefully hung up the phone.

"You two been over to see Megan and Eli?"

"Yeah," Keene said. "Who was that?"

"SECNAV. He's all riled up over last night. Says he's got half his commanding officers scared to death that we're going back to war with the Chinese. The other half is chomping at the bit to go."

"And where is *he* with all of this?"

"He's on our side. He knows as well as anyone there's no way we could sustain a ground war with the Chinese. They have over a million foot soldiers over there. It would be a slaughter. Not to mention all the physical damage and the lives of Americans caught in the crossfire." Then, "Any word on Megan and Eli?"

Boz shook his head. "None yet. But we've got more problems to think about than that right now."

Keene took over. "Quinn called a little while ago. He says Sokolov is headed to DC. He doesn't know why, but assumes—as we should—that she's not here for sightseeing."

"And we don't know who the target is?" Jennings said.

"It's a short list," Keene said. "My money's on Walker. Quinn said she's working for Pemberton."

Jennings pursed his lips and rubbed his chin. "I don't think so."

Keene was confused. "What do you mean?"

"Doesn't make sense. Why would Governor Nolan do all that grandstanding about nominating him as the vice president, if Sokolov is

219

just going to take Walker out. Talk about a screwed up mess, then. Nolan would have to try and move in and take the White House by force. Even Pemberton knows that would never happen. No, he needs Walker in that seat right now. It's the quickest way to the White House."

"Then who? You? Me? Boz? Who?"

"I doubt it. You're not a threat to him. At least not in his mind. Me, maybe. But I doubt it. He knows if I get whacked, there's probably six more just like me waiting to take my place. And if he has any clue about anything, he knows it'd probably be you. And that's even worse."

"Thanks for the encouragement," Keene said.

"There's more," Boz said. "Quinn said that if Chin feels threatened, he'll do whatever it takes to protect his border. So you need to tell SECNAV Sykes that he needs to keep those boys in check. No matter what."

Keene sat up in his chair. "That's it. I know why Sokolov is here."

Both Boz and Jennings looked at him questioningly.

Keene couldn't believe that neither of them had got it. "SECNAV. She's here for Sykes." Keene could feel the adrenaline begin to pump. "Think about it. Sykes is in full control over the military. Yeah, he answers to Walker, but what if—just what if—he decided not to. How many of those men and women do you think would go against him if he turned on Walker?"

"Not many," Boz said.

"Especially with half of them already wanting to go back to war," Jennings added.

Keene was rolling now. It was obvious. "And guess who Nolan's father-in-law is—"

Jennings smacked his hand on the table. "Jake Irving!"

"Irving?" Boz shook his head. "The former SECNAV is Nolan's father-in-law?"

"That's right," Keene said. "And who do you think would be standing right there, offering his services to Walker, should something happen to Sykes?"

"That's pretty slick," Boz said. "I mean, you've got to admit, that's a pretty solid plan."

Keene was fired up now. Not ten minutes ago, he'd felt completely lost and helpless to do anything. Now, though, everything was different. He wasn't lost, no way. The tables were about to turn. Advantage: Jon Keene! He turned to Jennings. "Where's SECNAV right now?"

"He's at his house. You just saw me on the phone with him," Jennings said.

Keene stood up and grabbed Boz by the arm.

"Where are you going?" Jennings asked.

"We're going to see an old friend. Call the SECNAV and ask him how he feels about fishing." He saw Jennings already shaking his head as he turned to leave.

"No. No way. You're not using the secretary of the navy as bait."

Keene stopped and turned back around. "Kevin, we've probably got one shot at this, at best. We know *who* she's coming for. And we know *why* she's coming for him." He turned back around and opened the door. "Either you call him, or I will. Besides, I'm not going to use him as bait. That's what Boz is for."

CHAPTER 47

Raleigh, North Carolina

Alex Smith was still lying next to Farid when her pager started buzzing beside the bed. A couple of years ago, she had found a young tech geek in Hungary who had wired this pager especially for her. It worked off a radio signal. Which, now, she realized, was one of the smartest things she had ever thought of. Initially, it was a security measure. By using radio frequency instead of cell signal, she could be reached anywhere in the world without being traced. Now with cell signal down all over the United States, she was glad she'd kept the little thing. She reached over and looked at the display. It was the same number Pemberton had called her from the last time. She threw the thing back on the table and got out of bed. She needed a shower.

Farid stirred beside her as she pushed back the covers. "Where are you going?"

"Shower. I can't stay in this bed any longer."

"You need to rest."

She'd slept well last night. And she already felt a ton better. "I'm fine. Just stiff. A hot shower, and I'll feel like a new woman."

"What time is it?"

She picked her watch up from the table by the bed. "Eight thirty. I'm hungry. Why don't you get up and go get us some breakfast?"

Farid got out of bed and began to get dressed. "There's a coffee shop on the next block. What do you feel like?"

She told him what sounded good and gave him some small bills from her wallet. "That should cover it."

He quickly checked her bandages and told her to be careful as she washed. "The hot water will be good. But it's probably going to sting pretty bad."

222

She smiled at him. "I'll be fine."

Farid left, and she went to the bathroom and turned on the water. She got undressed and stepped inside. Immediately she winced as the hot water began to run down her shoulder and over her side. But after a few seconds the pain started to subside and she began to feel reenergized.

Farid was back by the time she was done. He gave her injuries the once-over and redressed them. "Whoever worked on this must be a remarkable doctor."

"Yeah? Why's that?" She laughed.

"You can barely even tell you got shot."

She rolled her arm around. "Yeah, tell that to my shoulder."

They ate the croissants and cheese Farid had brought back and finished their coffee. After that, she shed the robe she was wearing and began to get dressed.

"What are you doing? Going somewhere?"

She picked the little pager up off the side table. "Pemberton called. I need to see what he wants."

Farid looked at her with concern. "You still need a day or two's rest. Whatever he needs can wait. Can't it?"

She shrugged at him. "Don't know. That's why I have to call him."

She finished getting dressed and grabbed a room key. "I'll be back in a few minutes. I'll just go to the lobby and call from the business office." Farid's face hadn't changed. "Don't worry. I'm not going anywhere. I'll be right back."

When they'd checked in a couple of days ago, she had taken a quick tour of the place. She chose this particular hotel for its layout, the same way she chose every hotel she stayed in. It had multiple exits on multiple floors. Some led outside to the street, some to different levels of the parking garage connected to the hotel, and some led through tunnels through the basement to the loading docks. And there were side entrances for employees.

Along with the multiple exits, it had resources. One of those resources was a business center. And though the computers inside were all but useless—given the problems still with the country's Internet service—it had several telephones. The phones, she knew, were connected through the hotel's mainframe phone system—meaning all calls went out from the central line. Should anyone be able to ever trace any call made from the hotel, it would only appear to have come from the front desk or one of the main offices, unlike calls made from the rooms of the hotel, which were always routed through a secondary circuitry that split the lines up individually by room.

The business center was empty—something else she expected. Though the people of this country were doing their best to put the pieces back together, business travel would probably be minimal for quite a while to come.

She used her room key to open the door to the suite. Inside, four small cubicle stations had been set up, separated by individual dividers. Each had a computer, with a piece of printer paper taped to the screen that said OUT OF ORDER. Next to the computers, a phone.

She sat down in one of the makeshift boxes and picked up the receiver, waited for the dial tone, and punched in the numbers. Pemberton answered on the first ring.

"Mr. Pemberton, this is Ms. Smith. You called?"

"I did. Can you talk?"

"Not here. But I can meet you, if you need."

"I think that would be a good idea. There have been some new developments."

She thought for a moment. She definitely couldn't defend herself in a closed, isolated space. She wouldn't be able to move like she needed with the injuries. So meeting Pemberton alone was out of the question. She had no idea what "new developments" meant, but in her experience, it usually wasn't something beneficial to her. If Pemberton wanted to meet, it would have to be in a public place.

"Tell you what," she said. "There's a fast-food place on the corner of East Davie and Fayetteville. I'll meet you there in, say, two hours."

The line was quiet for a few seconds. "I had hoped to meet somewhere a little more private."

I'm sure you did. "Yes, well, there were. . .complications with my last appointment. I think the fast-food place would be better for me."

The line was quiet again for a few seconds before Pemberton came back on. "Fine. Two hours."

She hung up the phone and left the room. In the elevator on the way back up, she thought about her situation with Farid. The smartest thing to do would be to take him out to the middle of nowhere and put a bullet in his head. That was what she *should* do. But that wasn't going to happen. She had already given in to that fact.

So, then, what to do?

The doors to the elevator opened up. As she stepped out into the hall, a crazy idea popped into her head. She argued with herself the entire length of the hall, as she walked to the room. *There's no way, Alex.*

Sure. It could work.

What are you thinking! Are you mad?

No, I'm not mad! But I'm not going to kill him, either.

This is crazy! You're going to get yourself—and him—killed!

Maybe so. But at least I'll be happy.

She opened the door to the room and smiled. "Hey."

Farid was sitting on the bed, leaning against the headboard. He had the television on and was sipping another cup of coffee. "Have you seen this?" he said, pointing to the screen.

"I caught a little bit of it last night. After you fell asleep."

"This governor. . .Joe Nolan. . .has been on every news program all day long. He has really caused quite a stink. Do you think he could actually do what he's talking about?"

She drew in a breath and let it out. She sat down on the bed between him and the television. She grabbed the remote and clicked it off. While she'd told him most of the details of why she was there and everything that had happened, she still hadn't given him the grand scope of everything. It was time to do that now. "There's something I want to talk to you about."

Farid sighed and turned his head away. "Alex. . .please. Don't do this."

She was confused. "Do what?"

"This. . .you know. Tell me that you have to leave. That we can't be together."

She started laughing. "Farid, that's not what this is."

"It—it isn't?"

"No!" She reached down and grabbed his hand. "Not at all. Actually, quite the opposite. Listen, I've been thinking. What I do is dangerous. Obviously." She pointed to her shoulder and her side. "If it weren't for you, I'd be dead. And that got me to thinking. What if I had a partner, such as yourself, with your skills?"

"Partner?"

"Yes, think about it! We could travel together. I could take assignments. You could help out when I needed it. And if anything should go wrong. . ." She smiled. "Well, you'd be there to take care of it. Just like you have been."

Farid let go of her hand. His eyes shifted away.

225

"Farid?"

"Why can't you just stop? I mean, why can't we just disappear? Go somewhere where no one would ever find us?"

"I thought about that, too. And here's what I've decided. After this job, we can go anywhere you want. For a while. But this is who I am. Eventually, someone will come calling for my services. And when they do, I can't promise that I won't take the job."

Farid seemed to think about it for a moment. "Would I have to, you know. . .kill anyone?"

"I would not ask you to do anything you don't want to do."

"But what if that's what you needed from me?"

"Then it would be up to you."

Farid sat there, silent for a few seconds.

"Okay. I'll do it. But you're going to have to teach me how to do what you do."

She leaned in and kissed him. "Don't worry. I'll teach you everything you need to know. Starting now. Get dressed."

"Why? Where are we going?"

"I have a meeting in a little while. You're going with me."

CHAPTER 48

Keene picked Boz up at his house at nine o'clock sharp. He'd already been up since five and had been to the hospital to sit with Megan. The doctors didn't have any answers for him. Megan was still unconscious, though her body seemed to be healing well.

After leaving Jennings's office yesterday, he and Boz had gone to see someone Keene thought could help them. But he hadn't been home. They'd waited around for an hour, but he still never showed up. Keene figured the guy was probably at some comic-book store or something, wasting his life away. That's the kind of guy he was. A complete geek. They decided to head back to Bethesda to check in on Megan and Eli and try Keene's friend again in the morning.

Keene honked the horn as he pulled in to Boz's drive. Boz came out a second later carrying a backpack and jumped in the truck.

"You ready?"

Boz threw his backpack in the back. "Yep. Let's roll."

"What's in there?"

Boz just smiled at him. "I got you a present."

"Nice! What is it?"

"I'll show you later. Let's go."

"Nope. No way. Give it up."

Boz reached back and grabbed the bag. He unzipped it and pulled out a two-tone, custom Covert II, Kimber 1911. Complete with night sights and Crimson Trace Lasergrips.

Keene took the pistol and turned it over in his hands. "Wow. I don't know what to say. It's beautiful."

"That was my brother's. He was killed in Afghanistan in 2009."

Keene swallowed hard and handed the gun back. "Boz, I can't take this."

"Something wrong with it?"

"No it's—it's perfect. It's beautiful. I just told you that. It's just—"

Boz pushed the pistol back to Keene. "Please, take it. I would be honored for you to have it. And if my brother had ever had a chance to know you, he would've wanted the same thing."

Keene reluctantly took the Kimber. "Thank you. I don't know what to say."

Boz patted him on the shoulder. "Welcome home, Jon."

Keene put the truck in Drive and took off.

Twenty minutes later, Keene pulled into the same alleyway they had visited yesterday. As he got out, he saw Boz checking his weapon and scanning the area around.

"You reminded me of Megan just then."

Boz turned toward him. "How's that?"

"She did the same thing when I brought her here."

Boz laughed a little. "See? I told you she was sharp."

Keene crossed the alleyway and began banging on the door of one of the buildings. "Artie, open up."

Nothing.

"You think he's still gone?" Boz asked.

Keene shook his head. "He's here." He pointed down the alleyway to a rusted out Honda Civic. "Unless he sold it to a neighbor, that's his jalopy there." He banged on the door again. "Artie! Open this door. Or I'm going to shoot the handle off with my brand new .45 and let myself in."

Keene heard the latches on the inside being turned. A moment later, the door opened up.

"Holy crap—Keene! Man, I thought you were dead."

Keene pushed the door open and stepped inside. "You couldn't get that lucky." He turned back around and motioned for Boz to follow. "Artie, this is Boz. Boz, Artie."

"What are you doing here, dude?"

Keene turned around and gave him a cold stare.

"I—I mean, I'm glad you're alive," Artie stammered. "But what are you doing *here?*"

Keene continued down the hall and into the living quarters. He sat down on the couch and said, "We need your help again."

That seemed to calm Artie down. "Whew! Okay. . .good. For a minute there I thought I was in trouble."

"Why?" Boz asked. "What have you been doing?"

Artie looked at Boz and then back to Keene. "Who is he again? And where's your other partner? You know—that hot FBI agent you came in here with last time."

Keene bit his lip. He knew Artie couldn't know what had happened to Megan. And his candor was. . .well, it was just Artie. "She's had an accident. She's in the hospital."

Artie's eyes went wide and he swallowed hard. "I–I'm sorry. I didn't mean anything."

"It's all right. But that's why we're here. We need your help to catch the person who put her in the hospital."

"Sure, man. Anything I can do. What do you need?"

Keene looked at Boz. "I don't know if I ever told you or not, but Artie here is the one who led us to that warehouse in Chicago."

Boz raised an eyebrow.

"Yeah," Keene said. "Artie's got a knack for gadgets and widgets." He turned to Artie. "So I need something to help with surveillance."

Artie looked confused. "You work for the CIA, man. You guys got the best toys money can buy. What do you need me for?"

"I need you because radio frequencies won't work where I'm going to be. I need line-of-sight, remote, wireless Internet and cell signal–operated relays."

Artie rolled his eyes and blew out a long breath. "You're not asking for much, are you?"

"C'mon, Artie. I know you've got something."

"Man, if the feds found out I had this stuff, you know how much trouble I could get into? I mean, Internet and cell signal is down all over the country. In case you haven't noticed."

"Artie, we *are* the feds. Do you know how much trouble you're going to be in if you *don't* give me what I need?"

"Okay, okay. Calm down. Let me see what I can do."

Artie disappeared for a few minutes and came back waggling a small box over his head, with four antenna rods under his arm.

"What's that?" Keene asked.

"This is what you're looking for."

"Explain."

Artie took a seat beside Keene and placed the box on the table. He powered it on. "This is one of my little inventions. It creates a network of its own. It's good for about a thousand-yard radius. Cell signal and wireless Internet."

"What do you mean, its own network?" Boz asked.

"You set this box up where you want your network. Then you can program phones, laptops, relays, remote detonators—whatever you want to accept this signal. After that, anything inside the range of these antennae operates on its network."

"And there's no dead zones or dropouts?"

"Nope. It's completely contained. As long as what you're trying to control is inside the perimeter of these antennae, you're golden."

Keene smiled and slapped Artie on the back. "See, Artie? I knew you could help me out. Now, show me how to program all this stuff."

They spent another thirty minutes learning how to set up the network. When they were done, they showed themselves out and headed for Virginia.

Secretary of the Navy Sykes was waiting on the porch of his home when Keene pulled into the drive. Sykes lived in an upscale neighborhood with few houses in one of the nicer suburbs of DC. The houses were big, and the neighbors were at least a hundred feet apart, giving the property owners some privacy while still having the benefits of living in a community. Sykes's house was one of the last houses in the neighborhood and sat at the end of a road, backed up to three acres of woods.

Keene got out of the SUV and walked up on the covered porch. He stuck his hand out to greet him. "Mr. Secretary."

Sykes took his hand. "Good to see you, Jon. How are you?"

"I'm good, sir. Thanks for seeing us."

Sykes gestured for them to go inside and raised his eyebrows. "Well, I'm not sure how good an idea this is, but. . .I guess whatever it takes."

"Don't worry, Mr. Secretary. Nothing's going to happen to you. I promise."

"Yeah? How's that?"

Keene began to unpack the bag Artie had put together for him. "Because you're not even going to be here." He looked up to see Sykes narrowing his eyes at him.

"And where exactly am I going to be?"

"Don't care, sir. Just not here."

Keene explained what he was thinking to Sykes. They needed to give the appearance of Sykes being home, while he was actually somewhere else—and safe. Boz would stay at Sykes's house instead. The two men were roughly the same size, build, and age. From a distance, with the right disguise, Boz could easily pass for Sykes. And Sokolov—when she showed up—would only be able to see from the outside. As long as they kept the sheers on the curtains drawn, she'd only be able to see shadows. She'd have to get inside to figure out she'd been set up. And Keene had no intention of ever letting her get that far.

"How do you know she'll come here?" Sykes asked.

"Because as long as she thinks you're holed up inside, she won't have a choice. Pemberton needs you dead. It's the only way he can get Irving back in charge of the military."

Sykes recounted his meeting the other day with Irving to Keene and Boz. "I thought it was kind of strange, his just popping in like that. Irving's not one for just random visits and conversation."

"Yeah, that just confirms it for me," Keene said. "She'll be here."

"Where am I going? And how do you propose to get me out of here unnoticed?"

"You'll need to leave tonight. We'll take you out and I'll bring Boz back. I doubt she's already here. Quinn said she's coming. Not here. So I'm hoping we still have some time. Boz and I are going to go outside and set up this gear. When we get back, you need to be ready to leave."

CHAPTER 49

Raleigh, North Carolina

Alex sat at a table in the fast-food chicken place and waited for Pemberton to show up. Farid was seated at a table a few feet away. He wasn't supposed to do anything other than just sit there and watch. But if for some reason Alex needed to leave, he was to follow close behind.

Pemberton showed up a few minutes later. He went through the line and got a sandwich and then came and sat with her.

"Figured it'd look better if I was actually eating," he said.

"So what's going on?" she asked.

Pemberton looked around to make sure that no one was paying them any attention. "I would really rather we go someplace else."

"I'm comfortable here, thank you."

He leaned in so he could whisper. "Change of plans. Did you see the president's speech?"

"Highlights. After the fact. I was sort of out of pocket." She casually pulled her sleeve down over her shoulder to show him the bandage. "Those agents your friend told you about showed up while I was there."

"But you took care of it?"

"I did."

"Good." He took another bite. "The governor was spectacular. I've always known the boy could command an audience. But that was incredible. At this rate, Walker will be forced to nominate him for the vice presidency before tomorrow."

"So how does that change anything?"

"It doesn't, in the grand scheme of things. I still want you to do what I asked. I just want to rearrange the timetable. Walker needs to pay for his neglect of this country. But after Joe's speech, I met with Irving. He and I figure we need to rearrange our priorities. Walker will *have* to nominate

232

Joe. The American people are already demanding it. And most of Congress are, too. If he doesn't, the whole country's going to riot."

Alex thought about that for a moment. It was a well-thought-out plan. She couldn't really find any holes in it. Except one. "I don't know much about President Walker. But if he's anything like his predecessor, he is stubborn. Throw Jennings into the mix and he's dangerous. I wouldn't just assume that just because the American people are clamoring for Joe, Walker is going to give in, or that Jennings is going to let him."

"Walker's gonna fight this thing, no doubt. But eventually he's going to have to give in. It's just the way things work. He can't hole himself up in there like a dictator. He serves at the will of the people. Eventually, he'll have to go. But I want to speed that timeline up. And that's why I want you to change focus."

"Really? To whom?"

"Secretary of the navy, Sykes."

She thought about that. "Okay. I can do that. But what about Jennings?"

"Jennings might have sway over Walker, but trust me, there's no love lost between him and Irving. If Sykes goes away, the entire military would be in shambles. All Irving will have to do is show up and those men will follow him. It won't matter what Jennings says or does."

She still thought Jennings was a bigger problem. But Pemberton was paying the tab. Besides, she didn't care what happened to this country anyway. She wasn't planning on being here for much longer. Soon as this gambit was over, she and Farid were going to her house in the south of Italy for a while. "Okay. . .you're the boss."

"Good. When can you leave?"

"I'm going to need a couple days to recover from my visit with the judge. I can be there by end of the week."

"Good," Pemberton said. "And then with Irving stepping back in, Walker will have so much pressure on him to put Joe in place he won't know what to do."

"And if he still won't?"

"Then you can shift your focus back."

CHAPTER 50

President Walker sat in his office, completely at a loss for where to go and what to do. For the last several days, the country had been up in arms over his speech and Joe Nolan's appearance. It was as if the entire country had been blinded from reality. Every channel he turned on, he saw another reporter standing outside a pub or coffee shop, interviewing citizens. And every time, it was the same thing.

"President Walker is a spineless coward. . .he absolutely should nominate Nolan for vice president. . .and then resign." Or, "How do we know this whole Prophet thing isn't just some concoction of the administration to cover up the fact that they didn't do their job and got duped by the Chinese?" And his favorite so far, "You know what? Maybe God did bring judgment on this country. But what's done is done. Doesn't Walker think it's time to get over our punishment and take our country back?"

No matter the scenario, it seemed the whole of America had turned its back on him. Sure, there were the occasional folks who took up for him in the interviews. They were the ones who got it. They understood. They were willing to accept that God had dealt America this hand and they were to humble themselves and just move on. But they were few and far between. And even though there might be more of them than the TV people were showing, the majority of the country was firmly in Nolan's camp.

He needed some advice. For everything he'd faced since taking over as president, he had always had a sense of what to do. How to proceed. But this was different. He felt like he was completely at a loss. And he could only think of one person who might be able to point him in the right direction.

234

He got up and opened the door to the office and called to the Secret Service agent standing guard a few feet away. "Please tell Agent Carnes that we'll be leaving in a few minutes." The agent nodded and left to find his boss.

Forty minutes later, Walker entered Calvin Grant's room. Grant was sitting up in bed, with his wife Tess beside him. He walked to the bed and shook his friend's hand. "Calvin, how are you today?"

Grant nodded and said, "Doing well, Gray. The doctors have all said that they think I'm okay to leave tomorrow."

"They've run all their tests?"

"They've prodded and poked me more than a herd of cattle."

Walker laughed. Grant had always had a true Southern wit about him. Grant continued, "But that's not why you're here. Is it?"

Walker pulled up a chair and sat down beside the bed. "Tess, can Calvin and I have a minute?"

"Sure," she said politely. Then to Grant, "Honey, I'm going to go get a snack and some coffee. Would you like anything?"

"Some coffee would be good. Gray, you want anything?"

"Coffee, please."

Tess leaned over and kissed her husband's forehead and said she'd be back in a little while. Walker thanked her again and waited for her to leave. "Have you seen the news?"

Grant shook his head. "Yes, and it disgusts me. I've never liked Joe Nolan. The man's a conniving, manipulative politician."

"And an atheist."

Grant pointed back at him. "And an atheist! What he needs is for God to hit him upside the head with the Gospel!"

"Amen. I couldn't agree more." Walker sighed. "But unfortunately for us, I don't think that's happening anytime soon. The Prophet said as much."

Grant sat up in his bed. "The Prophet? So he's been in touch?"

"He's been communicating through Jon Keene."

Grant nodded again. "This country owes Mr. Keene a huge debt of gratitude."

Walker agreed. "Yes, it does."

"So why are you here, Gray?"

Walker thought about it for a second. "I honestly don't know. I'm just at a loss. I have no idea what to say, what to do. Nolan is on every television station that's up and running. Every five minutes, there's another audio snippet or video clip of some new accusation he's bringing against me. It's like he's on the campaign trail."

"He is."

"I mean—what?"

"I said, he *is* on the campaign trail. Look at him. He's setting up speeches up and down the coast. He's making appearances like he already is the president. In the last few days, he's been in front of every news camera and radio station he can get to listen to him. And they're listening to him, man! You want to combat this, you've got to get out in front of it."

"How? How do I get out in front of this?"

"The first thing you need to do is get out of your office and start putting yourself out there. Get in front of the media. Tell the truth."

"The people don't want to hear the truth."

"Tell them anyway. Tell them Nolan is dangerous. Tell them—I don't care, tell them I'm the one who believed the Prophet in the first place. We both know this whole ordeal was brought on by God. There was nothing we could do to stop it."

Walker thought for a moment. "You know what? You're right."

"You're dang right, I'm right!"

"No, I mean, you're right. The American people love you, Calvin. You're the most beloved president since Lincoln. And none of them know that you've regained consciousness—that you're completely fine. Maybe it's time we showed them. Maybe it's time we bring you out. You could tell the American people, with me, that Nolan is going to lead this country into a war we won't come back from."

Grant lowered his head. "I can't do that. It's not my place."

"What do you mean? I don't understand. I mean, think about it. With you standing beside me, telling the nation the truth. . ."

"You remember when I gave my speech at the Capitol?"

Walker did. That was the day Grant was shot. "Yes."

"You remember I froze, right before I had a chance to tell the people that God had told me to call the nation to repentance? I just stepped away from the microphones and stared at them?"

"Yes, but what does that have anything to do with anything? Now's your chance."

"No." Grant lowered his eyes. "I didn't step away from the microphones because I was afraid to tell them. I was fully ready to tell them. I stepped away because God told me to."

"I don't understand."

Grant drew in a long breath and let it out again. "I never told you. I never told anyone—except Jon Keene, Megan Taylor, and Boz Hamilton— the morning I called them to my office. But the Prophet had been sending me warnings for months. I—I wanted to believe him. On some level I *did* believe him. But I rationalized it, saying to myself that I couldn't just call the nation to repentance. People would think I'd lost my mind. I decided I would use the power of office to *influence* people through policy. But the warnings kept coming. And I knew deep within my heart the Prophet was who he said he was. But I also felt the need to investigate him as well. I needed to be sure he wasn't just a terrorist trying to threaten our nation. By the time I had let all of that go and chose to believe that he actually was sent by God, it was too late. On the steps of the Capitol, when I pulled away, I did so because. . ." Grant covered his face with his hands and began to weep.

Walker reached over and placed his hand on Grant's arm. "Calvin, it's okay. It's not your fault."

Grant composed himself after a few seconds and continued, "I pulled away because I heard God say to me, '*I love you, Calvin, but you should've trusted Me. You will not call the people to repentance now. That time has passed.*' "

Walker felt the air go completely out of him. He'd had no idea. He realized that Calvin had probably been dealing with this burden from the moment he woke up from his coma. He felt a deep sorrow for his friend. He knew Calvin must be tormented by this. "Calvin, look at me."

Grant picked his head up and looked to him.

"You are one of the most godly men I've ever known. Before—when I was just pretending to be a believer, thinking that I had everything worked out—I used to look at you with disdain. Your walk with God was like a bitter poison in my mouth. Every time I saw you, it reminded me of what I wasn't. And I held you in contempt for it. But you need to know the only reason I'm here right now—where I am spiritually—is because of you. And if there's one thing I've learned over the last few months. . .it's that our God is a God of numerous second chances. So don't you beat yourself up because you think you failed God."

Grant looked at him and gave a half laugh. "You're right. You definitely aren't the same person you used to be. And my heart is full of joy for that.

Thank you for your encouragement. What you said is true. And I'm not beating myself up over it. I know very well that God does not hold that against me."

Walker was confused. "Then what?"

"It just saddens me that I missed the opportunity. I don't feel condemnation for what I did. I just regret the fact that I did it. And that's why I can't do what you're asking. God told me. The time for me to call the nation to repentance has passed. That charge falls to you now. I will pray for you. I *have* been praying for you. Both Tess and I have, nonstop. But you need to be the one to fight this fight. So go do it."

Walker sighed. He heard what Calvin was saying, but he still didn't buy it. He felt deep within his soul that Calvin was wrong about this. But he would respect his wishes. For now. Because something was beginning to stir in him. The birthing of an idea was beginning to take shape somewhere in the recesses of his mind.

Grant looked at him curiously. "Gray, are you all right?"

Grant's voice brought him back. "What? Yeah. I'm fine."

"So you're ready to face Nolan? To put him in his place?"

There it was again. That sudden fleeting thought. He needed some time to flesh this out. God was stirring something in his mind. "Not yet. But I'm working on it."

"Good," Grant said. "Go get him."

Walker shook Grant's hand and turned to leave. "Tell Tess sorry I couldn't stay for the coffee." Suddenly he felt something like a prompting. He knew in a moment that God had instructed him to say something else. He looked back at Grant. "Hey, Calvin."

"Yeah?"

"Promise me something."

"Yeah? What's that?"

"The next time God tells you to do something, don't wait."

Grant laughed halfheartedly. "Don't worry. I won't."

Walker turned around and walked out of the room. He smiled and said to himself, "I'm going to remember you said that."

CHAPTER 51

It had been three days since Keene and Boz had removed SECNAV from his home. Boz had stayed upstairs, in the house, the whole time, while Keene had set up camp in the basement. It was a finished basement, complete with a guest room and bath, so it was easy for Keene to be down there. But the reality of it was, if Sokolov was watching the place, trying to plan her move, it wasn't working. Keene had a pretty good idea why.

"We don't even know if she's here yet," Boz argued. "We don't need to change the plan yet. Just give it time."

"We're running out of time, Boz. Nolan's out there getting his face in front of every camera available. Walker's got his back to the wall. Congress is demanding he make Nolan the vice president. The whole country's coming apart at the seams."

Keene knew he was frustrating Boz. But he also knew he was right on this. As long as they stayed holed up in this house, Sokolov wasn't coming anywhere near. "Look, I've sat on houses for days before without moving. You know why?"

"Why?"

"Because it was too quiet. The routine wasn't right. I knew they were waiting for me."

"I don't know, man. Maybe." Boz threw his hands up. "So what do you want to do?"

"It's not what I *want* to do. But I don't think we have a choice."

"Okay. Let's hear it."

"SECNAV has a routine. Just like anyone else. Sokolov is going to know that he has to leave every morning and come home at night. And if he's not doing that, she'll get suspicious. And she won't come. But if she sees SECNAV coming and going, like normal, she'll watch that for a day

239

or two. And then, when she's comfortable with his movements, she'll come for him."

"Here?"

"Yes. I still think she'll come here. The only place he really goes is from here to the White House. It'd be too risky to try and take him somewhere in between. Too many variables. No, she'll want to do it here. But she won't come unless she's sure he's alone, and it'll more than likely be at night."

"What do you mean? More than likely?"

"Well, if it were me, my preference would be to be here waiting for him when he got home. But this neighborhood is too busy. I wouldn't risk showing up here during the day or evening. People in these kinds of neighborhoods are nosy. And they typically know each other's comings and goings. Sykes is pretty high profile. So someone just showing up at his house—not in a uniform, not in a government vehicle with armed security—is going to cause suspicion. I would wait and make sure he was home. Then I'd watch the place. And then at about three in the morning, I'd come."

Boz gave him a sour look. "I hate it when you're right."

Normally, Keene would reciprocate with a smart-aleck comment. But in this case, he agreed. "Me, too. At least this time, anyway."

"Okay, then, so how do you want to do this?"

"We can't use you as a decoy. Inside the house, you could pass for him. But if he has to be seen coming and going, I'm afraid it's going to have to be him."

"We'll still need someone inside the house," Boz said. "We can't just leave him in here alone."

"I agree. You could stay in the house, here in the basement. I can follow him to and from the house. Once he's inside, you can give me the okay. I'll take up watch at night."

"You can't cover the whole house by yourself. And that's going to make for a long night, you keeping watch by yourself all night."

"Won't be the first time. Besides, we have Artie's little perimeter monitor. If anyone comes within a hundred yards of that place, you'll know. We can keep these cell phones on an open line. If anything happens we'll already be on with each other."

Boz sighed. "It's not the prettiest idea I've ever heard, but it's solid."

"It's our best chance at getting her," Keene said.

Boz handed Keene a sat-phone. "I guess you better call Jennings."

Keene took the phone and dialed the number. Boz quickly reached back over and took it from him. He hit the SPEAKER button and then handed it back to Keene as it was ringing.

"What'd you do that for?"

Boz laughed. "I want to hear Jennings when you tell him what you want to do."

The phone rang a couple more times before Jennings finally answered.

"This is Jennings."

"It's Keene."

"Everything all right?"

"Not exactly."

"What do you mean, not exactly?"

"We're not getting any bites. I think we're going to have to change bait."

CHAPTER 52

Alex Smith was back in Washington. And for a place that she really disliked, it seemed she found herself here too often. *But then again,* she thought, *gotta go where the money is.* She parked the car while Farid went inside to pay for their room.

The Wardman Park Marriott was one of her favorite hotels in all of DC. It was a massive structure located in a quiet area of town. It had subway access within feet of the property. The shops and restaurants nearby were exceptional. And the most important thing: she had at least twelve different escape routes at any given time, depending on the situation and need.

She met Farid inside the lobby and waited for him to finish at the front desk. A few minutes later, they were headed to their room. They had only brought a small bag each, so getting to the room was easy.

Once inside the room, Alex set her bag on the small table and unzipped it. She pulled out her PK380 and a Glock 30, a subcompact .45 caliber. She lifted her pants leg and strapped the PK just above her ankle. Then she removed her carry holster from her bag and fitted it inside her pants, on her side. She checked the magazine for the Glock, saw that it was good, slammed it home, and slid the Glock inside her waistband.

"Okay," she said. "All set."

Farid sat on the bed. "So you want me to just sit here and wait for you?"

She thought about it for a moment. "No. Actually, I'd like you to come with me. It's easier to blend in as a couple."

"Where are we going?"

"We are going to go play follow the leader."

Farid looked at her curiously. "I don't think I understand."

"SECNAV, Bob Sykes."

"Sec—what?"

"Secretary of the navy. We are going to go follow him around. I need to see his routine. And unfortunately, I don't have a lot of time to figure it out. I might have to improvise."

"Improvise? Why?"

"Pemberton wants him gone. Like two days ago. The governor's making huge waves, and Walker is being pressured on all sides to nominate Nolan for VP. But even if Walker does give in, Sykes still runs the military. It doesn't matter if Nolan gets Walker out of the way. Sykes will never follow orders to strike against the Chinese as long as Jennings is around. But if Sykes is out of the picture, Pemberton says Irving can step back in and take over the military. Once that happens, Walker and Nolan are a moot point."

"And do you think that will work?"

"Honestly? No. I think Kevin Jennings is more of a threat. That man has more influence than Pemberton knows. I would guess that he could keep Irving from moving the military. But I'm not paying the bill. So Sykes it is." She checked her gear one more time. "Okay. Let's go see where the SECNAV lives."

Keene sat in the corner of the Oval Office while Jennings, Walker, and Sykes sat deep in conversation. He had left Boz at Sykes's house and told Jennings he'd meet them there. Jennings was none too happy at Keene's suggestion that they go ahead and let SECNAV move around like normal. But in the end, he, too, knew Keene was right. Now it was just a matter of telling the others. That's why they were here now. Jennings was laying out how they would move from this point on. Keene was thinking about Megan when he heard his name.

"Jon, what do you think?"

"I'm sorry. What do I think about what?"

Jennings motioned for him to come join them. "I was saying, I don't think it's smart for President Walker to be out on the street confronting the media right now."

Walker jumped in. "I told you already. I've spoken with Calvin. He agrees. This is what needs to be done. I need to get out there and start making some noise of my own. You said so yourself, Jon. Bob, here, is more than likely Sokolov's target. Not me."

Walker was putting him in a tough place. "Yes, sir. I do believe Sykes is the logical target. But Sokolov is an opportunist. If you make yourself a target, she could very well shift gears. I don't think it's smart for you to be just putting yourself out there."

Walker stood up. "This is not up for discussion, gentlemen. The decision has been made. I will be leaving the White House this afternoon. I've already called the major networks and offered myself to them for interviews."

Keene had a bad feeling about this. "At least let us send someone with you."

Walker looked at him like he were an idiot. "I will have my detail with me at all times."

Keene didn't care. He knew a lot of great Secret Service agents. But they weren't trained like he was. And there was only one of him. He couldn't be two places at one time.

"And I'm sure they're fine men," Jennings jumped in. "But I'd feel better if one of my men were with you. What about Boz?"

Keene shot his boss a cross look. "Uh-uh. I need Boz in SECNAV's house."

Jennings gave him the same look back. "And I need to keep the president alive!"

"He's right, Jon." It was Sykes. "President Walker is the priority."

Keene was fuming now. "Kevin, can I talk you for a second? Alone?"

Jennings stepped away with him outside the office. When the door closed behind them, Keene lit in. "You know as well as I do that Sokolov's coming after SECNAV. Pulling Boz out of that house is a mistake. We need him in there. He's the only one who can pass for Sykes inside that house. And she has to see him moving around in there."

"Maybe so, but that still doesn't change the fact that Walker's going to be exposed. If I didn't agree with you about Sykes, I would put *you* on Walker. But I *do* agree with you. So I'm allowing you to stay with him. But I'm not about to let the president go walking down Pennsylvania Avenue, out in the open, without someone I personally trust. End of discussion!" Jennings opened the door and walked back inside.

Keene was furious. Without Boz inside the house, the chances of protecting Sykes decreased significantly. He couldn't be inside the house because he needed to be outside, monitoring the perimeter. If Sokolov somehow made it into the house without tripping the sensors, it would be too late by the time he got inside.

Regardless, he was going to need to figure something out. Jennings wasn't going to budge. He knew that. He opened the door to the office and went back inside. When he did, he noticed that Jennings and Sykes were gathering their things to leave. Jennings was on the phone.

"That's right. Fox News," Jennings said into the phone. "Okay. Just get there as quickly as you can. The president has agreed not to leave for the next interview until you get there." Jennings hung up.

"Boz?" Keene asked.

"Yes," Jennings said. Then to Walker, "He'll meet you at the station."

Walker stepped in between them. "I'm still on your side here, Jon. But you know how stubborn your boss is."

Jennings ignored the jab from the president. "Let's go."

"Where are we going?"

"My place. Remember, Sykes has been with me for the last three days. He needs to get his stuff if he's going back to his house this evening."

Keene didn't say anything, but instead, violently jerked his jacket off the back of the chair it had been sitting on—making sure Jennings saw it. He turned and left the room.

CHAPTER 53

Before coming to DC, Alex Smith had made some calls. She had been out of commission for four months and had no idea what she was walking into. She still had some contacts in town. They were able to catch her up to speed on how things were operating in the capital city. She found out, among other things, that Walker had moved Jennings's and Sykes's offices into the White House. With the potential of the peace status turning on a dime, and communications still sketchy, Walker wanted his top advisers within an arm's reach.

Because of that, she and Farid sat parked on Seventeenth Street NW outside the White House perimeter. It was as close as they could get, what with the added security since the Chinese invasion. They had been here now for almost forty minutes and still hadn't seen anything yet.

"What are we looking for again?" Farid asked.

Alex pointed across the street. "Since the invasion, everyone who works inside the White House enters and leaves the grounds through that exit." Another bit of information she'd found out. "Secretaries, staffers, Sykes, Jennings, all of them."

"So we're waiting for Sykes to leave."

She pulled the binoculars back up to look. "Yes."

"And then we follow him home?"

"Yes."

"Won't he have security?"

"Maybe."

"And then what?"

She lowered the binoculars again. "And then nothing. Remember, I told you, we need to just watch his routine for a day or so." She pulled the binoculars back up. "Unless. . .an opportunity presents itself."

She continued to look for another twenty minutes before she saw a line of cars appear at the guard shack. Two limos, bookended by two blacked-out SUVs.

Farid leaned across her to get a better look. "Is that—"

"The president. Yes," she said. "And that means that Sykes will probably be along in just a few minutes."

They had been listening to the news on the radio and had learned that Walker was scheduled to appear on at least three news stations this evening. And that meant that business at the White House was done for the day.

The president's motorcade had barely left the guard station when another blacked-out SUV appeared at the guard station. Alex raised the glasses once more. A broad smile crossed her face at what she saw. She threw the binoculars into the backseat and put the car in DRIVE.

"Is that him?" Farid asked.

"Yes," she said. "And he's not alone."

"Who?"

"Jennings." She waited for the SUV to exit the guard station and pull out onto the street and get ahead of them. She was surprised, though, that even after a few seconds, no one else followed them.

"No security detail," Farid observed.

She smiled and thought to herself, *Opportunity?*

She waited for the SUV to go through the light and then pulled out behind them. She had been following marks for over a decade. She had pretty much mastered the art of tailing someone in a car. But the man driving the SUV in front of her *was* the master. If she didn't do this perfectly, Jennings would spot her. And then she would have a problem. A hundred different scenarios ran through her mind of how Jennings would turn the tables on them, should she be careless and allow that to happen. None of which she wanted to deal with.

Fortunately, traffic was heavy. It was easy for her to stay back and unnoticed. But after about thirty minutes, she became curious. Unless Sykes and Jennings were neighbors, they weren't headed to Sykes's house. She had been this way before. With Marianne Levy. Marianne had driven her out here once to show her where Jennings lived—just in case she should ever need to pay him a visit. After that, she had studied the area and found at least three different routes to and from Jennings's house.

Opportunity?

"Hang on," she said to Farid. At the next light, she turned.

"What are you doing? I thought we were following them."

"We are. But traffic is starting to lighten up. And I don't think they're headed to Sykes's place."

She explained how she'd been to Jennings's place before. And that, if she was right, they could take a different route and get there about the same time. "And we won't run the risk of Jennings spotting us," she finished.

"What if you're wrong?"

She felt a small tingle in her spine. "I'm not wrong."

Thirty minutes later, she turned onto the street where Jennings lived. She drove at a decent speed—not too fast for anyone paying attention to notice, but not too slow, either. She just wanted to make a pass and see if Jennings was already there. She used her peripheral to look as they passed. No SUV.

Opportunity.

Jennings, strangely enough, was apparently not too concerned with privacy. His house was an older ranch-style that sat back from the road on a corner lot, with a long drive that led up to a two-car garage. There was no fence. No protective line of trees. Nothing. The only thing separating his home from his neighbor's was a small row of hedges that lined the left side of the front yard. The right side bordered the cross streets in front. If she parked down the street, on the cross street, she could see Jennings's drive and still be several hundred yards away. She stopped at the next intersection and turned right, to make the block.

A few minutes later, she and Farid were parked fifty yards away, in a line of other parked cars along the street. And given the direction Jennings was headed when she departed from him, they should see him roll right up to the intersection up ahead and then turn left—away from them. From there, the driveway was another immediate left. She had the perfect view. She crouched down in the seat and waited.

Less than three minutes later, a blacked-out SUV rolled up to the stop sign and turned left. Then it turned again. Into Jennings's drive. Alex watched as the car pulled up to the garage and stopped.

First Jennings got out of the driver's side. She saw Sykes come around from the passenger side. Then the rear driver's side door opened.

She felt her breath catch as she watched the third man—whom she hadn't seen when they pulled out from the guard station—get out of the

SUV. He stopped and looked around the area. She reached behind her and put her hand on the Glock—fully expecting to see the man come rushing toward them. After a couple of seconds, he began walking slowly, continuing to look around the surrounding area. Finally, he followed Jennings and Sykes into the house.

She felt that tingle in her spine begin to fade away.

Hello, Jon Keene.

"What are you doing, Jon? Get in here."

Keene took another look around the area. Something was off.

"Jon!"

He swept his gaze around again but couldn't see anything suspicious. He walked up the drive and went inside.

"What are you doing out there?" Jennings asked.

"Nothing. Just looking around."

"Well, get in here. Help Bob get his things from the guest room. I'll fix some coffee."

"Forget the coffee," Sykes called from down the hall. "What's for dinner?"

Jennings looked at Keene. "He thinks this is a restaurant and I'm some kind of chef or something. Three days I've been dealing with this." Then, yelling back down the hall, "How 'bout I send you a bill for eating all my food, huh? What about that?"

Sykes came back into the room laughing. "Hey, it's not my fault you're a great cook."

Jennings walked into the kitchen. "How 'bout it, Jon? You hungry?"

Keene really wanted nothing else but to get Sykes home. Sokolov was in DC. He could feel it. And he wanted to catch her. "I'm good. Thanks."

"Well, I'm not," Sykes said. "I could eat the south end of a northbound skunk. So what are we having?"

Jennings rolled his eyes. "I'll see what I have." Then, "Jon, turn Fox News on and see what's going on with Walker."

Keene found the remote for the TV and turned it on. The interview was already over, but the pundits were all seated around a big glass table debating it.

". . . I don't know, Jeff. Walker makes a pretty good argument. And who's to say that God didn't send this Prophet to warn us? I mean, I'm a man of faith. Surely it's not out of the realm of possibility. I think Walker is right. Nolan is dangerous, stirring up a conflict between us and the Chinese right now. We have enough problems to worry about."

"Listen, Chris, I'm not saying that you're wrong. But Walker took an oath to protect this country at all costs. And he swore that oath on a Bible! Don't you think that God would honor that? . . ."

A few others jumped in and gave their opinions. The whole scene was one step below a circus. Jennings came around the counter and told him to change it to CNN. Walker was going there right after Fox. Keene did and saw that it was the same thing. Except they were all weighing in on what Walker had said over at Fox, while talking about all the things the people at Fox failed to ask. The lead guy at the table seemed to satisfy them, though, when he said, "Well, in about twenty minutes, Butch will be sitting down with the president. You can bet he's going to ask some hard questions."

Keene tossed the remote on the couch beside him and tuned out. Something still didn't feel right. He sensed it when they pulled in the drive. But he couldn't put his finger on it. Maybe it was just because he was so angry with Jennings over taking Boz out of Sykes's house. He was still trying to figure out how he was going to handle that problem after he got Sykes home.

The phone ringing in the kitchen brought him back. He turned to see his boss pick up the receiver. Jennings nodded a couple of times and said, "Uh-huh. . .yes. . .that's great news. Yes. . .someone will be over soon. Thank you very much." He hung up the phone and looked at Keene. "Good news, Jon. Megan's awake. She's asking for you."

Keene felt his heart skip. *Megan's awake!* He sighed a huge sigh of relief. He felt as if an enormous weight had been lifted.

The news anchor on the television was giving everyone a five-minute warning. Walker was about to go live. Jennings came out from the kitchen and stood by the couch. "Jon, why don't you go?"

Keene felt an immediate surge of anticipation. He wanted to. More than anything. But he wasn't about to leave Jennings and Sykes alone. "I can't. I need to be here."

Jennings looked at him. "You *need* to go see Megan. There's no telling how long she'll be awake. They said they have her pretty sedated. Bob and I will stay here, eat some food, and watch Walker do his interviews. We'll be right here when you get back."

Keene had a thought. He'd already been toying around with the idea on the drive here. "What if we call Ramirez and the boys? They could sit outside while I'm gone. Besides, I think I can use them at the house."

Jennings walked back to the phone in the kitchen. He picked up the receiver and dialed. "Yes, this is Director Jennings. I need to speak with General Markus."

Jennings spent the next two minutes on the phone. He informed the general that he wanted Ramirez's team to report to his home forthwith. He gave General Markus the address and thanked him. He hung up the phone. "Ramirez and his team will be here within the hour. Markus is sending them as we speak. Does that make you happy?"

Keene smiled a little. "I guess it'll have to do."

Jennings grabbed the keys to the SUV off the counter and tossed them to him. "Get out of here. Go tell Taylor I need her back in the office by Monday."

Keene caught the keys but stayed put. "Thanks, but I'll wait till Ramirez gets here."

Jennings shook his head. "No. Go now, you stubborn mule. Ramirez's team will be here within an hour. Megan might be asleep again by then. And I need to know if she has any information that might be pertinent to what we're dealing with."

Keene hadn't really thought about that. All he was concerned with was just seeing her. He had to get his head on straight. Thinking about her was becoming a distraction. And as much as he wanted to just sit and talk with her—to just catch up on the last five months they'd missed— he knew Jennings was right. Megan could have important information.

He stood up and walked to the door. "I'll call if she has anything. But you call me when Ramirez and his team get here."

Jennings said he would.

Keene got in the SUV and backed out of the drive.

Alex watched as Jon Keene exited Jennings's house, got in the SUV, and left. And in a big hurry, at that. She didn't know what to make of it. Obviously, Jennings and Sykes weren't planning on going anywhere. Had Keene left for the night? Was Sykes staying at Jennings's house?

She smiled to herself. *You're pretty smart there, Jennings.*

She knew there was a possibility that Jennings knew she was alive—

especially since she didn't have the chance to make sure Agent Taylor was dead. That was something she still needed to rectify. And if Jennings knew she was alive, then he also knew it was more than probable that she would show up here in DC. She guessed he figured that keeping him and Sykes together was smarter than being isolated. Hence, Jon Keene being there with them.

But if that were the case. . .where was Keene going? And why would he leave them vulnerable like that? He must've been called away to something extremely important to leave Jennings and Sykes in such a hurry.

And then she realized. Keene *wouldn't* leave anyone vulnerable like that, let alone the director of the CIA and the secretary of the navy—the two most important people in the country, next to President Walker. Someone else must be on his way.

She felt the tingle in her spine return.

An idea quickly began to take shape in her mind. If Keene ran out of there like that, then whatever it was that caused him to leave wasn't planned. So neither would backup security be. And that meant whoever was coming, it would take them—she figured—at least twenty minutes, at best.

Opportunity!

She pulled her Glock out of the holster and checked to make sure she had a round in the chamber. She felt inside her jacket—just to make sure the extra magazines were there.

Farid looked at her. "What are you doing?"

She reached up and killed the dome light then opened the door. "Stay here and don't move. I'll be back in less than ten minutes."

Opportunity.

CHAPTER 54

Boz got to the news station just as Walker was finishing up. He had been listening on the radio the whole way.

Walker did a great job, he thought. He fielded every question thrown at him. And for someone who hadn't been a believer for very long, Boz was impressed with his knowledge of scripture and how he used it to respond to the interviewers' questions and comments.

The best part of the whole interview was when Walker asked them point-blank, "Do you honestly think this nation can handle another war with China right now? Look at us! Our military is stretched. Our resources are thin. They have over a million foot soldiers over there now. The only way to effectively win would be to completely destroy every square inch of land west of the mountains. And what good would that do us, Jeff? Sure, we might have defeated the Chinese, but at what cost? How many innocent lives are you willing to just throw away over there? How much of our land are you willing to obliterate?"

That had left them almost speechless. But Walker hadn't been finished. He kept on.

"Joe Nolan is a dangerous, power-hungry man. He has the audacity to stand in front of a news camera and accuse me of not fulfilling my sworn oath to our Constitution. Well, let me tell you something, Mr. Nolan. When I took that oath, I had my hand on a Bible, just like every president before me. And If I recall correctly, I said the same words that every one of my predecessors have uttered—'So help me, God.' Who, by the way, is the very God you deny even exists!

"Listen, fellas. I don't sit here and pretend to be perfect. I'm not saying I have all the answers. But one thing I've never been is a liar. I love this country with every ounce of my being. And I would *never* stand in front of the American people and ask them to buy into some half-cooked story about God sending a Prophet to help us get back to where we need to be if it weren't true."

After that, Walker had finished his interview with a plea. "Ladies and gentlemen"—Boz imagined Walker looking directly into the camera with a desperate look on his face—"Ladies and gentlemen, please, I beg you. Do not let Joe Nolan deceive you. There is no hope for our nation if we choose to go down the path that he is suggesting. The same Prophet who initially delivered God's warning to us before, now says that God has chosen to restore us. I can't tell you I know exactly what that looks like. However, I can tell you that God never fails to fulfill a promise. If you allow Joe Nolan to lead this country back into war with China—well, God help us all."

Boz flashed his ID to the man at the desk and was shown down the hall to where Walker was.

"You did a great job in there, Mr. President."

Walker shook his hand. "Thank you, Boz. It felt good—getting in front of that camera and getting a chance to expose Nolan. Let's just hope the American people were able to see it."

Boz was reminded of a passage of scripture just then. "Remember, sir. 'With man this is impossible, but with God all things are possible.' "

Walker smiled. "Matthew 19:26. It's become one of my favorite verses."

The head of Walker's detail came over. "Sir, we're ready to leave. CNN is waiting for us. Can I go ahead and tell them we're en route?"

"Yes, Agent Carnes. Thank you." As the agent turned away, Walker called him back. "Agent Carnes, you know Mr. Hamilton, yes?"

Carnes stuck out his hand to Boz. "Yes, sir. Good to see you. I guess you're with us?"

"Apparently so."

"Good to have you along. Jennings made it absolutely clear you're in charge. So you just holler at me if you need anything."

Boz thanked him and said he would.

Carnes called to the rest of the detail and they all headed for the motorcade. Boz opened the door to the limo and watched Walker climb in. He started to step in himself when Carnes called to him from the lead vehicle.

Boz stood back up. "Yeah, Zach. What's up?" He walked up to the lead SUV where Carnes was standing.

"Hey, Jennings didn't tell me much. Just that you were coming along. You want to tell me what's going on?"

Boz didn't want to alarm anyone unnecessarily. But Carnes was the head of Walker's detail. If Jennings hadn't filled Carnes in, then he probably expected Boz to. "I can't say that anything is going on for sure. You know the name Alexandra Sokolov?"

Carnes nodded. "Yeah. I know it."

"There's a good chance she's in DC. And with everything going on right now with Nolan and Walker, we just want to make sure everything's good. If you know who she is, then you know Jon Keene, Megan Taylor, and I have a history with her."

Carnes nodded again. "Yeah, I heard."

"Jennings just wants me along because I'm familiar with her."

Carnes bobbed his head one last time. "Good deal. That's all I need to know."

Boz started to turn back to the limo but stopped. "Hey, Zach."

"Yeah?"

"Honestly, I don't think we have anything to worry about. But let's keep an open channel on the radio. Just in case. No chatter unless it's absolutely necessary."

"Got it."

It was only a few blocks from Fox News on East Capitol Street over to First Street NE to the CNN offices. The motorcade pulled up to the front entrance and Walker's detail got out and did a quick check over the area. A few seconds later, Carnes gave the all clear. Boz and Walker exited the limo and stepped through the front doors.

Another reception was waiting for them as they walked inside. Walker and Boz were led to a green room while Carnes gave direction to the agents on where to take up posts within the building. Boz and Walker had just stepped into the green room when an attractive young lady appeared in the doorway.

"They're ready for you, Mr. President."

CHAPTER 55

Keene hurried through the hallway as he entered the hospital. Once he had gotten out of Jennings's neighborhood, it was lights and sirens the whole way.

When he approached Megan's door, a couple of doctors were standing outside, talking. Keene's heart immediately sank. He slowed his pace as he approached them.

"What's wrong? Is Megan all right?"

The doctor that he had spoken with before stepped forward to meet him. "Everything is fine, Mr. Keene. Megan is awake and doing well. We were just deciding on next steps."

Keene let out the breath he hadn't realized he was holding. "Oh, okay. Good. Thank you, Doctor. So, what *are* her next steps?"

"Rest. Lots of rest. As I told you before, the bullet under her arm punctured her lung. It also tore blood vessels. There was a lot of work done during surgery. It's mostly the reason why she's been unconscious—her body has just been in too much pain to wake up. She doesn't need to be doing anything even remotely exciting for another week or two. After that, we'll see. Maybe some physical therapy for the muscles in her shoulder and side. And we're going to have to keep a regular check on her lung. Make sure it's operating the way it should."

"Thank you, again, Doctor. We owe you a lot."

"Just doing what I'm paid to do." The doctor laughed. "And. . .I didn't want to get a visit from you in the middle of the night." He winked.

Keene felt a little convicted over that. "Yeah, I'm sorry about that. I was just really stressed and worried."

"It's all good, Mr. Keene. Now go see your friend."

Keene moved past them and opened the door. Megan was sitting up in bed. She had a small food tray in front of her that was almost completely empty. Only a cup of half-eaten Jell-O and some crumbs from what used to be a sandwich—or wrap or something of that nature—were left. Megan pushed the tray away as soon as she saw him enter.

"Jon!"

He walked over to the bed and sat down in the chair. "Hey, kiddo. How you feeling?"

"Like I got shot in the lung."

"Well, that's ironic. Because I think they told me you did get shot in the lung."

They both laughed a little and Megan began to cough. "Ohhhh. Don't make me laugh. It hurts."

Keene reached up and took her hand. "I'm sorry. I won't do it again."

He had done this every time he'd been here—hold her hand, that is. But it felt different with her awake. He liked how it felt. He even noticed that his heart had begun beating a little faster.

Megan began to cry. "I thought I'd lost you."

She squeezed his hand tighter. He squeezed hers back. "I thought I'd lost you, too."

She wiped her eyes with the other hand and the crying gave way to a light chuckle. "I guess maybe we're meant for each other, huh? We can't seem to get rid of each other."

Keene laughed and said, "I guess not."

They sat there for a few seconds in silence before Megan spoke again. "I never stopped looking for you. I just kept believing you were alive. That I was going to wake up one day and you were going to just show up." She started crying again. "But you never did, and I prayed and prayed. I—"

"I know. Boz told me."

He had thought about what he wanted to say to her the whole ride there. And now, here was his chance. But for the second time in as many days, he felt a tinge of fear. What if Boz was wrong? What if he told her and she just laughed at him? He took a deep breath and let it out again. He didn't care. He was going to say it. And whatever happened, happened.

"Megan, I want to tell you something. . .and I hope I'm not making an idiot out of myself."

Megan calmed herself again and wiped her cheek. "Okay."

"I had a lot of time to think when I was in that cell. I spent the first few weeks fighting back against Chin. I swore he wouldn't break me. But eventually. . . Well, you know what they say. Everyone breaks. And when I broke, I realized two things. One, that I had run from God for so long I couldn't even remember what I was running from. And one night, when I literally couldn't take it any longer, I prayed to God that He would just let me die." He looked up to see tears running down her face again. This time, he reached up and gently wiped them away. "But He didn't. Instead, I realized He had broken down all the walls I had built up, so I could see Him. So I could come back to Him."

"And have you?" she asked. "Come back to Him?"

"Yes, I have."

"I prayed for that. Every day."

"I needed it."

"What was the second thing?"

"What?"

"You said you realized two things."

"Oh, yeah. The second thing." He realized his palms were sweating. He wiped them on his pants and took her hand again. "I realized the biggest reason I had to get out of there. . .was to get back here to you."

Megan covered her mouth with her hand. Keene couldn't tell if she was trying not to laugh hysterically at him, or if she was completely freaked out and was trying not to show him.

"Megan. I—I'm sorry, I shouldn't have—"

She reached over and grabbed his shirt and pulled him up till they were face-to-face. "Yes, you should have." She pulled him in and kissed him softly.

CHAPTER 56

Chevy Chase, Maryland

Tony Ramirez turned his vintage 1998 Audi TT Coupe Roadster off Connecticut Avenue and headed for Jennings's place. He'd only been on the road for ten minutes, but General Markus had told him that it was imperative that he get there as quickly as humanly possible. Those were the magic words. The tarp came off, the top was put up—but only because the temperature had now dropped below sixty—and traffic laws became less of a mandate, more of a suggestion.

He had been cruising on Connecticut at about sixty-five mph, weaving in and out of the light traffic. But now that he was turning off the main thoroughfare and into a series of neighborhoods, he slowed it down. The last thing he needed was to hit some dog. Or worse, a child. He shuddered a little as he thought about why people would even let their kids play outside at night.

Jennings's house, according to the directions Markus gave him, was only another three or four blocks away. He slowed down a little more to make sure he didn't miss any street signs. He was beginning to think that he'd somehow passed his turn when he came around a bend and saw the Y in the road that Markus had told him about. *Good,* he thought. Jennings's place should be the next street up. He was already later than he wanted to be, seeing how he was the only one coming for now. The rest of the guys from the unit were all on their way, but they had been out on a training exercise when Markus called and had just gotten in. They had to check in and debrief first. Ramirez hadn't gone with them because he had been assigned to test out a new antiaircraft weapon earlier in the day, so he was free to leave as soon as the general called.

Finally, he said to himself as he came up on the four-way stop in front of Jennings's place. He stopped. Looked right. Looked left.

Wait. What was that?

He looked right again. Was his mind playing tricks on him, or did he just see someone sitting in a car parked on the street a little way down?

Immediately, he sensed something wasn't right. He turned the car right—away from Jennings's place—and started slowly down the street. As his headlights played along the cars parked on the side, he tried to recall what he'd just seen. How far down was it? Was it a car? Or was it an SUV? He had seen it so briefly, he wasn't sure.

The street was like any other street in any neighborhood. Some people parked in their driveways. Some people parked in their garage. And people who had multiple cars—pretty much everyone, nowadays—and packed their garage full of old furniture, basketball hoops, and boxes of useless stuff, parked on the street. So there were a handful of different vehicles on either side of the road. He was pretty sure, though, he'd seen it on the left side. He slowed down to look but didn't see anything. Maybe he imagined it. He'd already driven past the point he would've been able to see a person in a car—in the dark—from the stop sign. He went a little farther, just for good measure, and then turned around in a driveway and headed back.

Farid was getting nervous. Alex had told him to sit tight. She would be right back. But she had been gone now for going on twelve minutes. What was taking so long?

She had told him to get in the driver's seat. And if he saw a car coming, to just duck down out of the way. And if she wasn't back in fifteen minutes, then he was to drive away. She promised him she would meet him at the gas station on the corner of Connecticut and Knowles—the one they had passed on the way here.

He looked at his watch. Only one minute left. He began to argue with himself whether or not he should do as she instructed. He knew she could handle herself. But she had already been shot once in the last couple of days. He didn't know if she would be able to get out again if something happened. *No*, he decided. He wasn't going to leave. He would stay and make sure he got her out of there. He leaned over and reached inside the glove box and grabbed the .40 caliber Ruger she had put there. Alex had said not to use it unless he absolutely needed to. But he knew he would feel better if he had it in his hand.

Just as he was sitting back up, he saw a car pull up to the stop sign. He hesitated for a split second but then remembered what she had said. "*If you see a car, get down.*" He quickly pulled his knees up and slouched down under the steering wheel. His heart began to race. And then—headlights. He saw the lights playing against the inside of the roof of the car. And they were getting brighter. The car was coming toward him.

He pulled the slide back on the Ruger and readied himself.

He could tell the car was slowing down as it approached where he sat. The beam from the headlights moved slowly just above his head past the door, and then out the back window. The car passed him and he let out a quick breath. Then he heard it come to a stop. Only a few cars behind. His hands were beginning to shake now. He leveled the gun just above his head and was ready to pull the trigger. The car was turning around. And coming back toward him. He tried to steady himself, knowing that at any second, someone was going to rip his door open and find him there.

But it never happened. The car was going back the way it had come. He waited another couple of seconds and then slowly pulled himself up. Just enough to see over the dashboard.

Alex was in trouble.

CHAPTER 57

Boz stood just off to the side of the set, behind one of the cameras. Walker had been interviewing now for almost ten minutes. The first few were the perfunctory greetings and small talk. Boz knew the reporters would afford Walker the respect of his office—for a few minutes anyway. But after that, it would be open season. And Boz figured they had just about reached that point. Butch Larson, the interviewer and host of the program, finished fake-laughing at something Walker had said about his dog. Then he shifted in his seat. And his demeanor shifted with it. Boz knew it was time.

Here we go, Boz thought. He bowed his head and said a quick prayer for Walker. That God would give him the right things to say and not allow him to get tripped up or flustered. Larson cleared his throat.

"So, Mr. President, as you know, Governor Nolan of North Carolina has brought some pretty substantial charges against you. How do you want to respond?"

"Thank you, Butch." Walker folded his hands and set them on the table they were seated at. "Governor Nolan, I'm sure, loves this country. I do not question his patriotism. What I *do* question is his leadership and judgment in this situation."

"I'm not sure I follow you, sir."

"Butch, Governor Nolan is suggesting we take a military which is already stretched—let's don't forget that the previous three administrations did everything within their power to cut military spending, forcing us to decrease the size of all four branches significantly—and he wants to go punch the Chinese in the nose."

Larson laughed sarcastically. "Yeah, but who doesn't!"

Walker nodded. "I agree. I myself would like nothing better than to see the Chinese forced back to where they came from."

Larson thumped his hand down on the table. "Then why are we sitting here? You can't seriously think—even with a leaner military—that the men and women of this country who wear the uniform can't take our country back?"

Boz smiled because he knew what was coming. He and Walker had talked about this line of questioning on the way here.

"First of all, Butch, I would never suggest that our men and women couldn't accomplish anything. You know as well as I do that they are the best-trained soldiers in the world." Walker held up a finger. "But they are men and women who have children, families, mothers, and fathers who love them and want to see them safe. As president, I have assumed a responsibility that says I won't put their loved ones in harm's way unnecessarily or when the deck is stacked against them. The Chinese have an estimated one million soldiers on this continent. Have you done the math on that, Butch? They outnumber our men and women almost three to one now. It would be reckless to send—"

"Mr. President, we're talking about the sovereignty of our nation. You mean to tell me that men and women—of all walks of life—wouldn't take up arms, just as our forefathers did, to secure this nation?"

"Oh, now you want to demean the capabilities of our military men and women by suggesting the average citizen is capable of doing what they train months—years—to be able to do? All so you can suit your agenda? Sounds like someone else I've heard recently."

Larson's face turned red. He looked like a deer in headlights. Boz knew Walker had just landed a brutal roundhouse punch. And Walker didn't wait for a reply.

"Let me tell you something, Butch. This nation has walked around for years believing that we were invincible. We've been proud, arrogant, and foolish. Not because we aren't one of the greatest nations on earth. We were—no, still are—a great nation. The problem is we lost our way spiritually. Our own forefathers—the ones you so readily want to speak for—did a pretty good job of speaking for themselves. And with every chance they had to give us wisdom, they did so through the teachings of Christ and the Bible. They warned us, time and time again, to trust in the sovereignty of God. To turn to His ways when troubles sat at our doorstep. And what have we done? We've taken prayer out of school. We've taught our children it's more important to make sure we don't offend anyone, rather than stand up for God's truths. We manipulate and circumvent our

Constitution when it suits us. What we've become is a nation of fools. And five months ago, God decided to remind us of that."

Larson seemed to have regained his composure. "About that, Mr. President. Let's talk about this Prophet. Who is he? Where did he come from? Why haven't any of us seen him? There are many who believe that the whole Prophet thing is a hoax."

"Butch, I can assure you the Prophet is real. When we first learned about him, we sent a team of our best people to investigate who he was. President Grant's own personal spiritual adviser—a man who, by the way, has served our country as a Navy SEAL—was on that team. Everything the Prophet told us would happen, happened. Just like he said it would." Walker took a breath and let it out again. "I'll tell you another thing, too. He not only warned us, but he worked actively with us to help us secure the border we now share with China. If it weren't for him, we might all be raising the Chinese flag."

"Still, Mr. President. You have to admit. For the American people to just accept that God would send someone to do all of this is pretty fantastic. Wouldn't you agree?"

Walker nodded. "In a day and time such as this, where our faith has become so weak, I do agree. But it doesn't make it any less real. Just because you don't want it to be true doesn't make it so. Jesus said, 'Blessed are those who have not seen and yet have believed.' "

Larson gave a derisive snicker. "With all due respect, Mr. President, you're not Jesus Christ."

Walker nodded again. "True, but I know Him. Can you say that, Butch? That you know Him? Because if you did, I doubt we'd even be having this conversation."

Boz's eyes went wide. *BOOOM!* First a roundhouse, now a straight dropkick to the solar plexus. *Way to go, Mr. President!*

Larson's face went red again. But this time, it looked like embarrassment. "I hardly think my spiritual preference is the issue here, Mr. President."

Boz knew Walker wasn't going to let that just go. And Walker didn't disappoint.

"It's exactly what's at issue here, Butch. Your faith, my faith, the faith of the entire nation is the issue. It's the exact reason we're in this mess to begin with. This is what the Prophet was speaking of."

Larson jumped back in. "Again you bring up this Prophet. Mr. President—Jesus' words aside—how can you truly expect a broken nation to just trust a man who says he's sent by God when he won't even show himself? I may not be the most religious person in the world, but even I know Jesus was talking about Himself in that scripture you referenced. Not some Prophet who would claim to be sent by Him two thousand years later. If you want the American people to believe this Prophet is who you say he is, then how about you bring him in? Why don't we let *him* tell us? All of us. Not just you and a few select people in your administration."

Boz started to worry a little. He and Walker had talked about the possibility of Larson challenging Walker this way. And really, they had no answer for him. Quinn Harrington didn't just live down the street. They couldn't just go knock on his door and bring him in.

"He doesn't work that way," Walker said. "He contacts us when God leads him to."

Larson seemed to love that. He sat back in his chair with an accusatory look on his face. He folded his arms across his chest and cocked his head. "Of course he does," he said. "How convenient."

Boz let out a frustrated sigh. This is exactly what he knew was going to happen. And there was nothing they could do. Who were they to put God on the spot like that? At this point, all Walker could do was continue to plead with the people, and trust that God would work through that.

Suddenly, Boz saw a man run out from the control room toward the set. He came from the other side of the room. Carnes and the other agents already had their weapons drawn, pointed, and moving, but Boz got there first. He tackled the man in midair. The studio turned into chaos in a split second.

"Get off me!" the man shouted.

Boz had him pinned to the floor. "Who are you? Why were you charging at the president?"

"I wasn't charging at the president, you idiot! Get off me!"

Larson was out of his chair and coming over to Boz. "Hey! Wait! Don't hurt him."

"You know him?" Boz asked, still holding the man down.

"Yes! That's Martin Lloyd. He's our producer."

Boz took his knee out of the man's back. He grabbed him under the arm and hoisted him to his feet. As he did, he noticed that he was standing a good three feet into the set. All the cameras were trained on him, holding on to Lloyd. Everything that had just happened had been live on television. He felt a tinge of embarrassment.

"I apologize, Mr. Lloyd. I was just doing my job."

Lloyd jerked his arm away from Boz testily. "Whatever."

Larson said, "What are you doing, Martin?"

"I was trying to get out here and let you know there's a phone call for you."

Larson looked at Lloyd as if he were an idiot. "I'm in the middle of an interview!"

"Oh, you're going to want to take this call. Trust me. And on the air, too!"

"Why? Who is it?"

"He said he's the Prophet."

Boz couldn't believe what he'd just heard. Surely this was someone trying to make a mockery of President Walker—and of the interview. But Larson had already scrambled back to the table, where one of the studio hands had stretched out a phone and set it on the table.

Larson sat back down and pushed a button on the handset. "This is Butch Larson. Caller, are you there?"

"I'm here."

Boz's eyes went wide. He recognized the voice. It was, indeed, Quinn Harrington.

"Thank you for calling in, Mr.—"

"You can call me Quinn."

"Okay, Quinn. And you say you're this mysterious Prophet that President Walker has been telling the American people he's in contact with. Is that correct?"

"That is correct."

Larson looked to Walker. "Mr. President? Is this the man you recognize as the Prophet?"

Walker leaned in to the speaker. "Hello, Quinn. Good to hear your voice."

"Hello, Mr. President."

Larson's eyes went wide. "Quinn, it seems you've caused quite a reaction from many people. What do you say—"

Quinn cut Larson off. "Mr. Larson, please be quiet."

Larson sat back with a look of shock and disbelief. He'd probably never had anyone talk to him that way before. Boz smiled. *Get him, Quinn!*

"I have sat and listened to you and your colleagues for the last two days now," Quinn continued. "I've listened to you berate your—our—

president, a man that God has ordained to be in this position, with disdain and disrespect. Do you not know that God's Word says to honor your leaders? That every man who sits in a position of authority does so at the will of God?"

"Mr. Quinn, I hardly think—"

"That's the problem, Mr. Larson. You hardly think. Do you not know that the Bible says, 'You shall not put the Lord your God to the test'? And yet this is exactly what you, Governor Nolan, and the rest of your counterparts have been doing. God does not answer to men, Mr. Larson. He commands them."

Larson just sat there.

"However," Quinn continued, "because God is a God of mercy and compassion, and because it is His desire to see our nation turn from its ways and back to Him, He has permitted me to address you all.

"In three days, I will stand in the chamber of the House of Representatives and give an *early* State of the Union speech. I will speak God's decree upon this nation. He has instructed that I do this. He has been patient long enough."

CHAPTER 58

Keene stood there, motionless. Megan had just kissed him. He had hoped—no, prayed—the whole way here that when he told her his feelings for her, she would say she felt the same way. But he *definitely* did not expect this. Finally, he realized he was staring at her.

"Um. . .okay." He sat back down.

Megan laughed a little. "Okay? That's *it*? Just okay?"

Keene blinked a few times. He had to clear his head. Right now it was swimming.

"No. I mean, yes. I mean no, that's not *it*. There's more. At least I thought there was." He started laughing again. "I completely forget what I was going to say." He threw his hands up. "See there? You ruined it!"

Megan began laughing harder, which gave way to a small coughing fit. "Ouch. . .I can't laugh. . .it hurts," she said in between coughs.

"Megan, I know we only spent a short time together. . .you know, before I. . .before Chin took me. And I know that relationships built on the premise of stressful situations—and let's be honest, I can't think of a more stressful situation than what we went through—I know they usually don't work out. But I haven't felt like this since. . ."

"Since you met your wife?"

He lowered his head. "Yes. I know that's probably not the right thing to say. . . ."

"It's okay. I know how much you must have loved her."

"Please don't think that I'm comparing you to her. It's different."

"Jon, it's all right. You don't have to explain. The important thing is, I feel the same way. And as far as *stress* goes, we haven't seen each other for months. If the way I feel about you was going to change, there was plenty enough time for it to happen. But it didn't. I only missed you more. So

I think we're safe to pursue a relationship."

"Okay then."

"Okay then."

Keene wanted more than anything right now to just enjoy this moment. But he couldn't. "I need you to tell me what happened in Raleigh."

She recounted everything from finding Peterson to coming face-to-face with Sokolov in Hayes's house. Keene could feel his anger rising up. With every word she said, he wanted to stop Sokolov.

He was about to ask her more about the underground room at Pemberton's when he felt the sat-phone buzz in his pocket. He pulled it out and looked at the number. "This is Jennings. He probably wants to know what you told me."

He hit the button. "I'm in the middle of asking her right now, Kevin."

"Jon, it's Ramirez."

Keene knew that tone. Immediately, the blood drained from his face. "What happened?"

"It's bad, Jon. You need to get back here. Now."

"I'm on my way."

"What's happened?" Megan asked.

"I have to go. But I'll be back. I'll let you know as soon as I can."

He ran out the door and down the hall. On the way, he saw two marines. He stopped midrun and grabbed one by the arm. "Do you know who I am, Marine?"

The marine looked at him. "You look familiar, sir."

"Jon Keene. You know me now?"

Both marines snapped to attention. "Yes, sir! General Keene, sir!"

Sykes had field commissioned him a general five months ago, during the attack. And every time he'd heard someone call him that he'd hated it. But right now he needed it. "Room 131. I want you two on it, armed and at attention. You don't leave until you hear from me personally. Anyone other than the doctor tries to go in that room, you shoot him dead. That's a direct order. You got it?"

"Room 131. Yes, sir."

"Move it, marines! Now!"

The two marines took off at a dead run. Keene did the same.

Farid watched as the car rolled through the stop sign. It went past Jennings's house. He breathed a sigh of relief. But it was short lived. After a few driveways, the car pulled over to the side of the road. A man got out and began walking back toward Jennings's house. As he approached the drive, Farid saw the man was holding a gun.

Alex was in trouble.

He rolled his window down to try and strain to hear. Suddenly, he saw flashes of light inside Jennings's window, accompanied by a series of pops.

Gunshots.

He quickly started the engine. He didn't know if he should run, or if he should drive straight into Jennings's yard and crash the house. Suddenly, he saw someone running out the back.

Alex!

She ran out from behind the house and jumped a small row of hedges lining the neighbor's yard. She whipped her arm behind her as she ran and fired three shots. Farid saw the man from a moment ago run out after her and begin returning fire. He had to do something.

He pulled the gear lever and mashed the accelerator. He punched the button on the door to lower the passenger window. He swerved into the other lane and took a wide arc as he turned left, blowing through the stop sign. Alex was about twenty yards ahead of him. The man was gaining on her. Farid hit the gas again as he cleared the turn. As he passed the man chasing Alex, he pulled the Ruger up and fired out the passenger's-side window. The man dove into the grass. Farid saw Alex turn around and start firing at the man, just as he caught up to her. He slammed on the brakes and she dove in the open window. "GO! GO! GO!"

She didn't have to tell him twice. The tires squealed as he jammed on the pedal.

CHAPTER 59

Chevy Chase, Maryland

As Keene passed through the Y in the road, he could see the strobe of emergency vehicle lights bouncing off the trees ahead. When he got to the stop sign, he saw the ambulance in the drive. Ramirez was outside with four other men, the rest of Ramirez's team. He barely got the SUV in park before he was out the door and running through the lawn.

"What happened? Where's Jennings?"

Ramirez turned and had his hands up to cut him off. "Whoa, Jon. Stop. Jennings is alive. He's inside."

"Sykes?"

Ramirez shook his head.

"What happened?"

Ramirez started to explain, but Keene pushed past him and started into the house. Ramirez grabbed him by the arm. "Jon, don't go in there. It's a mess. And they're looking at Jennings."

Keene stopped. "I thought you said Jennings was okay."

"I said he's alive. But he was shot."

Keene pushed past him and went in.

As he stepped in, he saw glass all over the floor. Lamps had been shattered. The TV was shot out. The two windows in the living room were gone. And the back door leading from the kitchen was standing open. Sykes's body lay in the middle of the floor in a pool of blood. His throat had been slashed. And in the hall, leading to the master bedroom, two EMTs were putting Jennings on a gurney.

"Hey," Keene said. "Is he okay?"

"He's stable, but we need to get him to the hospital."

"Where are you taking him?"

"Bethesda."

Keene stepped out of the way as the EMTs rolled Jennings toward him. As they passed, Jennings reached out and grabbed Keene's arm. The EMTs stopped as Jennings pulled the breathing mask off his face.

He looked up at Keene. "Ramirez saved my life. Don't blame this on him. She was already here."

One of the EMTs reached for Jennings's mask and put it back on. "We have to go." They wheeled him out and into the ambulance.

Keene followed them outside and watched as they loaded Jennings into the back of the emergency van and took off. He felt his blood boil as he heard Jennings's words in his head again.

"*She was already here.*"

He had sensed something wrong when they first arrived here a few hours ago. He knew he should've checked it out further. But Jennings was yelling at him to come inside. And he didn't know if he could trust his gut, after being gone so long. He would never make that mistake again. He promised himself right then and there. He turned to Ramirez.

"What happened?"

"She must've already been here, man. I got here like fifteen minutes after Jennings called."

"What happened!" Keene said again.

"When I pulled up, I thought I saw someone sitting in a car down there." He pointed. "So I drove up that way. I went slow and looked inside every car I passed. But I didn't see anything. I turned around to come back. But it still didn't feel right. I went past the house and parked down the street—so I wouldn't make any noise coming in. When I got out of the car. . .man, I just knew. I pulled my weapon and approached the house. I decided to check the perimeter. And that's when I saw the back door open. I stepped up next to the doorway. Sokolov was standing there in the kitchen. She had a knife to SECNAV's throat. Jennings was in the hall, coming back into the kitchen. He had a gun pointed at her. And she was turned, using Sykes as a shield. I didn't have a clean shot. Neither did Jennings. She didn't know I was there, but Jennings saw me. As soon as she saw Jennings look in my direction, she slashed SECNAV's throat, pulled up a gun, and started firing. Jennings started firing back, but she hit Jennings and dropped him. I came through the door and started firing. She turned, shot out the window in the living room, and jumped out. I ran to check on Jennings. SECNAV was already gone. Jennings yelled at me to go after her. I left him and followed her out the window and chased after her. I got about a half a block when a silver car came out of nowhere and began firing at me. I dove for cover. By the time I looked up, Sokolov had jumped in the passenger side. They were gone."

"Did you hit her?" Keene asked.

"I don't know. I don't think so."

Keene sat down on the steps to the front patio. He pressed his palms into the sides of his forehead. Why had he not checked it out earlier? He knew. He knew!

"The DoD is sending a coroner to collect Sykes's body," Ramirez said.

"This is my fault, Tony. I knew something wasn't right earlier when we got here. I should've checked it out. But I listened to Jennings. I didn't trust my gut. It's my fault."

"Man, this ain't nobody's fault but Sokolov's. Just shut up with that mess. You know how this works, Keene. We act on what we see. Not what we think. The only reason I'm still standing here without a bullet hole in me is because I saw someone in a car up the street. Otherwise, I probably would've marched right up into that house and got my head blown off the second I stepped in that door. How could you have known?"

But he did know. And right now Sykes was dead, and Jennings and Megan and Eli were in the hospital, all because he hadn't trusted his gut.

He stood up. "This is going to end. Right now. I want Sokolov. Dead or alive."

All five of them nodded. "Roger that."

CHAPTER 60

Raleigh, North Carolina

Gavin Pemberton was about to lose his mind. He had been trying to get ahold of Alex Smith for three hours now. Had she not seen the interviews Walker had done on Fox and CNN? Did she not know that the whole plan he had been working toward was falling apart before his very eyes? He was so mad he could feel a vein in his neck pulsating.

He couldn't believe what he'd just witnessed during that interview. He'd kick the TV and break it, if he hadn't shot it with a twelve-gauge twenty minutes ago. Everything Joe had accomplished over the last two days. . .the support of the people, Congress calling for Walker to bring Joe in, the news media calling for Walker's head on a platter. . .it was all going so perfectly. And then those idiots at Fox and CNN decided to give Walker airtime. He had *personally* spoken with both CEOs of those networks. They had assured him they wanted Walker out, too. That they weren't planning on doing anything but trashing Walker and making Joe the hero.

That gave him a thought. He reached for the phone again and grabbed his little address book. He thumbed through the pages until he found the number he wanted and dialed. Jonas Shillings was about to get an earful.

"Hello?"

"Shillings, what are you people doing up there? I ask you to do one simple thing and you give me this?"

"Now, hold on a minute, Gavin. I haven't done anything. How dare you call me at home and disturb my family like this?"

"How dare I? How *dare* I? Shillings, have you forgotten about the pictures that I have in my possession? Have you forgotten about the taped phone conversations I have with you and a certain underage young lady? I bet your boy Larson would love to get ahold of those. Maybe he could find someone other than the PRESIDENT OF THE UNITED STATES TO INTERVIEW!"

"Gavin, you need to calm down. Right now. You need to understand that when the president of the United States calls you personally and says he's coming to your network to do an interview—not asks, tells you he's coming—there's not much you can do about it. Larson is the toughest, most indignant, disrespectful journalist on the planet. I would think that you would be thanking me for not letting someone like Janice Winters do the interview."

Shillings had a point there. Winters was the complete and total opposite of Larson. She would have probably tried to help Walker make his case.

"I can't help it," Shillings continued, "if this man who calls himself the Prophet decided to call in and turn everything upside down."

"Maybe he wouldn't have felt the need to call in if your man had better sense than to demand that Walker present him to the American people."

Shillings was quiet after that.

"Tell you what, Jonas, I'm going to do you a favor."

"What's that?"

"I'm going to give you the opportunity to have Joe on tomorrow to start bad-mouthing this Prophet. And you better make him look good."

Shillings clicked his tongue. "I've already spoken with him. He'll be here tomorrow at five o'clock."

Pemberton hung up the phone. He was still furious. And why hadn't Smith called him back? This was ridiculous! He decided to go pack a bag. He was going to Washington.

He was in the bedroom when the phone rang. He hurried back out into the living room and snatched up the receiver. "This is Pemberton."

"It's Alex Smith."

He had to control himself. He wanted to scream into the phone like he had with Shillings. But Alex Smith was not someone he figured he needed to make angry. "Yes, Ms. Smith. I've been trying to reach you all day. Is everything all right?"

"Everything is fine. I was actually calling to tell you some good news."

He could use some right about now. "Really? What's that?"

"Your order came in today. And actually, I was able to get you a buy-one-get-one-free promotion."

His order? Buy one, get one free? What the heck was she talking about? Then it clicked. She was talking in code. And that meant that Sykes was dead. And so was someone else. But who? Not Walker. He knew that. "Can you elaborate?"

"On the free item, you mean?"

"Yes."

"Sure. It's a *company* promotion."

Company? He thought for a minute. Suddenly, he knew. Jennings! "Really? A *Company* promotion, huh?"

"Yes, sir."

Pemberton was so excited, he almost forgot about Walker and this whole business with the Prophet. But then it came back to him. And now he had another idea. "Listen, Ms. Smith, I'm going to be traveling to where you are located. I'll be arriving tomorrow morning. I'd actually like to sit down and place another order with you. Can we meet?"

"Let me know when you get into town. I'm sure we can arrange something."

"Good. Then I'll look forward to seeing you tomorrow."

The line went dead.

Sykes was dead. And so was Jennings. He didn't know whether to laugh for his good fortune or cry because of Shillings's stupidity. It didn't matter. Either way, he needed a drink.

He walked to the bar against the wall and poured three fingers of twenty-year-old scotch. He sat back down in his chair and looked at the shot-out TV. He laughed out loud. His third wife had bought that TV. He hated it then. It was too big. Seventy-inch plasma screen. . .bah! Who needed something that big?

For a second he was frustrated that he was going to have to go buy a new one. Joe was going to be on CNN tomorrow. But then he remembered. He had just decided to go to Washington. He didn't need a new TV. He was going to be there in person. And he was going to be there when the Prophet gave his little speech, too. He wanted to make sure he had a front-row seat when Alex Smith put a bullet in the Prophet's head.

CHAPTER 61

Boz came as soon as he heard about Jennings and Sykes. He and President Walker had just returned from the news station to the White House when Chief of Staff Hardy met them at the entrance to the West Wing. He told them about Sykes, and that Jennings had been taken to Bethesda. Walker had insisted that he go to the hospital with Boz, but Boz wouldn't listen.

"Mr. President, the woman is one of the most highly trained assassins the CIA has ever seen. She's already caused a lot of damage tonight. Please. . .the safest place for you to be is here in the White House."

Walker finally agreed to stay behind. But only if Boz promised to call him with an update the moment he had any information. Boz had given his word.

When he got to the hospital, the entire place was on lockdown. He was glad to see that. He spoke with the marine at the guard station that had been set up at the front entrance and told him who he was. The guard called it in on the radio. The radio crackled back, announcing that Boz was clear to enter. Keene met him halfway down the hall.

"I guess you've heard."

Boz nodded. "Hardy told us when we got back to the residence. How is he?"

"He's going to be fine. He took one in the upper chest, just above his collarbone. It was through and through. The bullet missed everything. But one inch in any other direction. . ."

"That's good to hear. Where is he?"

"They just brought him to a room. They want to keep him overnight just to make sure nothing else is wrong. But they said he could leave tomorrow if everything checks out."

"And Sykes is dead?"

"He was dead when he hit the floor. She cut his throat."

"What happened, Jon?"

Boz spent the next ten minutes listening to Keene catch him up to speed. When Keene finished, Boz asked him what the plan was.

"I don't have a plan, Boz. Every time we've tried to get out in front of her, she's already one step ahead. I mean, we knew she was here in Washington. And we were betting she'd come after Sykes."

"And you were right about that. She did."

Keene shook his head. "Yeah, but we were wrong about where. I mean, how did she even know that Sykes was staying at Jennings's?"

"I don't know. But this isn't your fault."

"That's what everyone keeps saying."

Boz knew Keene was beating himself up over it. But if they were going to get through this, Keene needed to be on top of his game. Not doubting himself. "I'm only going to say this once. So pay attention."

Keene just looked at him.

"Jon, you're the best operative I've ever seen. I mean it. I've never met anyone with your level of skill. I've never met anyone with your intuition. Your instincts are impeccable. I'd be scared to death to ever get into an actual fistfight with you, for fear you'd literally rip my head off. You're quite possibly the best soldier the US military has ever seen. You're definitely the best CIA agent who's ever lived."

"So?" Keene rolled his eyes.

"So get your head out of your rear end and start acting like it. You know as well as anyone that you can't control everything. You just have to roll with it. And trust that God's plan is being worked out."

Keene looked at him and started laughing.

"What?" Boz said.

Keene shook his head. "That's about the worst motivational speech I've ever heard."

"Yeah, well. . ."

Keene turned and started walking down the hall. "Let's go, Tony Robbins."

Boz hurried to catch up. "Where are we going?"

Keene put his arm around him. "I forgot to tell you. There is *some* good news tonight. Your boy Eli woke up a little while ago. They just told me on the way out here to meet you."

Boz felt a huge sense of joy and gratitude well up inside him. "Thank

You, Lord. Thank you." He pulled out his sat-phone to call the president, as he'd promised.

Keene waited outside the door while Boz went in. Boz had invited him to come in with him, but Keene knew that Boz and Eli were close. Eli was like a nephew to Boz. He wanted to give them a minute before he came in. But he wanted to come in, for sure. He'd actually wanted to shake the man's hand and thank him for what he'd done during the invasion. If it hadn't been for Eli hijacking the entire Royal Navy and coming to America's rescue, who knew what would've happened? But more personally, Eli had saved Megan's life. And so Keene wanted Eli to know that he would forever be in Eli's debt.

He heard Boz call from inside the room for him to come in. He opened the door and stepped inside. Eli was sitting up in bed with his shirt off. He smiled. "So you're the real Jason Bourne."

Keene gave a short laugh. "I don't know about that." He stuck his hand out. "I'm Jon Keene, Eli. It's an honor to finally meet you."

Eli took his hand. "The honor is mine, Jon. And by the way, that was Megan who said that. Not me."

Keene shook his head. "Um. . . How's that?"

"Jason Bourne. That was Megan." Eli started flipping his hand back and forth and looking up, like he was thinking out a math problem. "See, I told her I was the real 007. Then she told me that you were the real Jason Bourne. One of us said that Boz was the real Jack Ryan—except that Boz never became president, which left her being one of the girls from Charlie's Angels—I didn't mention that, by the way. I think she might've shot me. . . ."

At this point, both Keene and Boz were laughing.

"Anyway, we left the whole conversation at my wanting to finally meet you. And now here you are," Eli finished.

Keene reached down and took Eli's hand in a tight grasp. And then he clasped his left hand over top, holding. "I can't ever repay you for what you did for our country. You saved our lives."

Eli nodded. "Just doing my job, mate. Glad I could help."

Keene continued to hold on. "And what you did in Raleigh, saving Megan like that. . . I owe you more than—"

Eli cut him off. "Hey, that's what brothers do. And from what I'm told, you were the one who saved us."

Keene locked eyes with Eli and knew right then that a friendship had been forged that would never be shaken.

"Are you girls going to blow smoke up each other's skirts all night?"

They all turned around to see Kevin Jennings standing in the doorway. Keene couldn't believe his eyes. He was both angry and astonished. "What in the heck are you doing in here? Does your doctor know where you are?"

Jennings looked at him with the same chastising look he had seen a thousand times. "Jon, when are you going to learn? I'm the director of the Central Intelligence Agency. I do what I want. I'm fine. I got shot in the shoulder. I'll be out of here by tomorrow. Besides, I heard Eli was awake." He shifted his focus to Eli. "How you feeling, son?"

"I'm good. Thanks for having them take care of me."

"You bet," Jennings said. Then, "Jon, did you tell him?"

It hit Keene immediately what Jennings was asking. Eli was a former British naval officer. He had coordinated the Royal Navy's rescue of the United States with Bob Sykes. The two were probably friends. He shook his head no.

"Eli, I have some bad news," he said. "Bob Sykes was killed tonight."

Eli hung his head and took a deep breath and let it out again. "How?"

Keene clenched his teeth together. "The same woman who put you and Megan in here."

"And did you catch her?"

"No."

Eli shifted in the bed and turned his head away. "Right. Well, Bob was a great man." There was a catch in his voice. "The world will miss him."

Keene reached over and put his hand on Eli's shoulder. "We'll all miss him."

They were all silent for a moment.

It was Eli who broke the silence. "I'm sure, then, by now you're probably aware that Jake Irving is caught up in this."

"Yes," Jennings said. "The last few days since you've been out have been exciting."

"Did he have anything to do with Bob's death?"

"Probably," Keene said. "He might not have ordered it. But he knew it was coming."

"Then he shouldn't be too surprised when I come for him," Eli said. "Where are we on everything?"

Keene caught Eli up to speed on all that had happened over the last few days. When he finished, Eli shook his head in disbelief. "I can't understand how anyone could be so selfish and stupid and smart, all at the same time," he said, referring to Pemberton, Nolan, and Irving.

By this time, Jennings had pulled up a chair alongside Keene and Boz. The impromptu gathering had now turned into an ad hoc strategy meeting. Jennings looked over at Boz. "Hey, what happened over at CNN?"

Boz's hand went to his forehead. "Oh my goodness! I completely forgot."

Now it was Boz's turn to fill everyone in. He told them how Walker had jousted back and forth with Larson, and how Walker had all but put Larson in his place when Larson had brought the conversation back to the Prophet. He finished with the Prophet's announcement that he would address the nation in three days. When he finished, Keene, Jennings, and Eli all sat there with their mouths open.

"So what does that mean?" Keene asked. "Did he say anything else?"

"Nothing," Boz said. "He just said he was going to address the country."

"We need to talk with Quinn," Jennings said. "Jon, do you know how to reach him?"

"No. But if he's going to show up to give some speech, I would imagine he's going to contact us soon. Boz, did he give any inclination what he was going to say?"

"He just said that he was going to speak God's decree for the nation. That God has been patient enough."

"Wow," Eli said. "This is going to be epic."

"So what should we do?" Jennings asked.

"Pray," Boz said. "'Cause whatever he's going to say, it definitely doesn't sound like it's going to be good."

They all started talking back and forth about what they thought the Prophet would say. Everyone was speculating on everything from a stern warning to a full-on pronouncement of judgment.

Keene felt the vibration from the sat-phone in his pocket. He pulled it out and looked at the display. He had no idea who it was. "Hello?"

"Mr. Keene. . ."

It was the Prophet. Keene snapped his fingers to get everyone's attention. "Hello, Quinn. Good to hear your voice."

"We need to talk."

CHAPTER 62

When Alex Smith woke up the next morning, she felt more alive than she had since she woke up from her coma. She could feel her heart pumping, her shoulder and side felt like she had never been shot, and the adrenaline rush from last night at Jennings's place was still coursing through her veins. She turned the water off from the shower, wrapped a towel around her, and walked back out into the room. She lay down in the bed and looked at Farid, who was still asleep.

Just looking at him this morning was causing her heart to race faster. He had saved her, again. She reached out and touched his hand and felt the electricity course through her veins. She had never felt anything like this for anyone. Farid stirred and opened his eyes.

"Hey," she said softly.

"Good morning, Alex," he said as he yawned and arched his back to stretch. When he was done, he looked at her curiously. "What are you thinking about?"

"I'm thinking that I'd be dead at least three times by now if it weren't for you."

"So maybe you should keep me around, then."

She arched an eyebrow. "Maybe."

He laughed and pulled the sheet back and got out of bed. "I'm going to go take a shower. What time is it?"

"Ten thirty. We're supposed to meet Pemberton in about an hour, so hurry up. I need to stop and pick up a couple things."

She watched him as he shut the door to the bathroom. *Yeah. I think I'll keep you around for a while.*

She felt her heart flutter, and her palms began to sweat. She leaned back against the headboard.

Alexandra Sokolov, I think you're in love.

She smiled. She liked the way that sounded.

An hour later, she and Farid sat at a small corner table in the back of a coffee shop in Dupont Circle, watching as Pemberton came in. He stepped up to the counter and ordered. When he got to the other end of the counter, the clerk handed him a cup encased in a brown cardboard sleeve. He took the cup and made a face as if he were disgusted. He walked to the back of the room where she and Farid were sitting.

"Who's this?" he asked, pointing to Farid.

"That's none of your concern. He's with me."

Pemberton sat down and put the paper cup on the table. "I swear, ever since those hippies in Seattle got famous, you can't find just a regular cup of coffee. Everyone wants to put chocolate, or caramel, or whipped cream in it. Tell them you just want a plain black cup of joe and they look at you like you're some kind of freak."

"So what can I do for you, Mr. Pemberton?"

"You see Walker's interview on CNN last night?"

"I was. . .preoccupied."

"Oh, yeah."

"But I saw the highlights on the news."

"Good, then you know that this guy calling himself the Prophet is going to be giving some little speech day after tomorrow."

"I do."

Pemberton sipped his coffee. "I would like it if he never got the chance to finish that speech."

"Do you know where he is?"

Pemberton shook his head. "No one knows where he is. That guy stays disappeared better than me." He laughed at his own joke. "But we both know where he's going to be."

Alex thought about it for a minute. The Capitol was a large building. She had already successfully pulled off one hit there. So she knew the lay of the building. But the fact that she had been successful there already made her think that it would be next to impossible to do it again. Security would be tighter than it had ever been. "I'm not sure that it can be arranged on such short notice."

"I'll triple your fee."

That made her really consider it. With that kind of money she could take two, maybe three years off.

"Well?" Pemberton pressed her.

"All right. But you'll need to wire the money first. Same account. If it's there by midnight tonight, I'll take care of it."

Pemberton stood up and drained the last of his coffee and put the cup back down on the table. He leaned down and looked her in the eyes. "And Walker, too."

"I thought you said you wanted to wait."

"I changed my mind."

Pemberton turned and left. When he was gone, Farid looked at her. "This thing that he wants you to do—can you do it?"

"Can I *do* it?" She laughed playfully. "What kind of question is that? Have you not been paying attention?"

"That's not what I meant," Farid said. "I mean, how are you going to get inside?"

She looked at him for a few seconds. "Well, I'm going to need a little help. But like I said before, that's completely up to you."

Farid didn't hesitate. "I'm in."

CHAPTER 63

Keene had spent the night sitting in a chair by Megan's bed. After the impromptu meeting in Eli's room, he had decided to come back and check on Megan. She was barely awake when he came in the room. He brushed her hair out of her eyes and kissed her forehead as she fell back asleep.

He woke the next morning to the sound of a nurse in the room clanking around Megan's bed. He opened his eyes and saw the woman changing out the little bags that hung next to the bed, sending fluid through tubes into Megan's body.

"Hey, what is that stuff anyway?" he asked.

The nurse whispered, "Just some antibiotics."

Keene thanked her for her service as she left. He spent the next thirty minutes just watching Megan as she slept. Finally she opened her eyes.

"Have you been here all night?"

He sat up and rubbed the cramp out of his neck. "Yeah." He looked around. "This is as good a place as any."

She rolled her eyes. "I'm not going anywhere, Jon. You could've gone home and got some sleep."

"I slept," he said. "Just not very well."

Megan laughed and reached for his hand. "I'm glad you're here. So what's going on?"

Keene caught her up on everything from last night's meeting in Eli's room. She was elated that Eli had come around and was doing well.

"And then, as if right on cue, Quinn called," Keene finished.

"What did he say?"

"Not much. Just that he was coming to Washington. And that he'd let me know where and when to pick him up. He also said that we should make sure that Pemberton, Irving, and Nolan are in attendance for his little speech. I told him I couldn't imagine that they wouldn't be."

"Agreed."

"I just wish we had something we could pin on Pemberton and the others," he said. "If we had proof, we could take them into custody."

Megan's eyes lit up. "Hey! When Eli and I were in Raleigh, we followed Hayes to a farmhouse out in the country. He met Pemberton out there. Nolan, Sokolov, and Irving were all there. There was some kind of underground bunker they were all in. Maybe there's something there."

Keene thought about it for a moment. Megan was right. Forget about the American public right now. If they had concrete proof that Pemberton and the others were conspiring against the president, they could arrest them and stop this whole ordeal.

"Tell me everything," he said.

Twenty minutes later, he was on the road. He fished the sat-phone out of his pocket and called Jennings. "I need the G-5 ready to leave in a half hour."

"Where are you going?"

"Raleigh." He filled Jennings in on his conversation with Megan.

"I'll have it waiting for you," Jennings said.

Next he called Boz. "Hey, get your stuff and meet me at Andrews in thirty. We're going to Raleigh."

Keene had been there already for five minutes when Boz showed up. "What's all this about?"

"I'll fill you in once we're in the air. Let's go."

Boz grabbed his stuff from the truck and headed up the stairs into the plane. Keene followed behind and let the flight crew know that they were ready to leave.

Jennings had a vehicle waiting for them when they landed. Keene and Boz threw their gear into the back of the Suburban, checked the map, and headed out. Twenty minutes later, they had found the obscure dirt road that led to the old farmhouse.

They parked in the drive and got out of the SUV, weapons drawn. They had no idea what they were walking into, so they approached the house with caution. After a quick check of the property, though, it was clear they were alone.

"Megan said it was under a concrete slab in the backyard," Keene said, as they finished clearing the house.

He stepped out the back door into the yard. Not much to see except a gravel lot birthed out of the dirt drive that led from the front of the house, a large field that made up the surrounding property, and a small toolshed sitting back from the house, nestled up against the overgrown weeds of the field.

Keene looked around the property. The old toolshed seemed to beckon him closer. He walked over to it and stuck his head inside.

A few old woodworking tools hung from some rusty nails on the wall. A weathered and cracked wooden bench sat propped up against the back. A light switch was positioned just inside the door. When Keene turned it on, a single bulb hanging from the ceiling popped and buzzed then came to life. He spent another five minutes going over the shed without finding anything. He was getting frustrated and was about to walk out when he saw a small button hidden behind some electrical wires. He pushed them aside and placed his thumb on the button. Underneath his feet, he heard the sound of an air lock give way. And then the grinding of concrete against metal.

"Boz! It's moving."

Boz stepped inside where Keene was standing over the opening in the ground where the concrete slab had moved, revealing a set of steps. He looked at Boz. They both checked their weapons. Then he pointed for Boz to follow behind as he started down the stairs.

At the bottom, they came to what looked like a steel reinforced door. It had a keypad on it connected to a lever. Keene took one look at it and said, "I've had about enough of this junk."

He walked back up the stairs and went to the SUV and returned with a backpack that he had brought with him on the plane. He unzipped the pack and pulled out three sticks of C-4 plastic explosives. He placed them around the keypad and the handle and pushed the little electrodes into the clay.

"That's a little bit of overkill, don't you think?" Boz asked, laughing.

Keene just looked at him. "No, I don't. If there's anything on the other side of this door, I want to make sure it's neutralized when we go in."

Boz shrugged his shoulders. "I'm good with that."

Keene stretched out the line from the electrodes back up the stairs. Boz followed. When they were topside, Keene looked at Boz. "Fire in the hole."

Boz turned his head and covered his ears.

Keene pushed the plunger on the little detonator he held. The ground below them shook as a huge plume of smoke rose up from the stairwell.

They quickly cleared the bunker after they had gone in—though they both knew that if there were anyone on the other side of that blast, they would've been incapacitated by the concussion of the blast, if not worse. But after a quick walk-through, they found it was empty.

The bunker was a state-of-the-art facility. It had four rooms, separated by tunnel-like hallways. Each room had its own purpose. One was a bathroom, complete with a shower and bathtub. Another was a large bedroom with a queen-sized bed and a set of twin bunk beds beside it, allowing for up to four people to sleep comfortably. The next room was a kitchen, complete with appliances and a pantry stocked with MREs. Enough to last ten people nearly five years. From there, the bunker led into a surprisingly spacious living area. There was a table set up at one end with an expensive-looking office chair, setting up a sort of office space. Three other, more common chairs surrounded the table. Just a few feet from there, a couch and oversized leather chair sat in the middle of the room, facing a flat-screen LED television.

"Looks like Pemberton was serious about his bugout plan," Keene said.

"This place must've cost a small fortune," Boz said.

They went through the bunker room by room, trying to find anything that would help them nail Pemberton. They had been over just about every square inch of the place when Boz called out to him from the living area.

"Hey, Jon. I think I found something."

Keene hurried out from the bedroom area, where he'd been looking. Boz was standing next to the flat-screen looking at a small hole in the wall.

"I think this is a camera."

Keene stepped over and took a look. Boz was right. A small lens was recessed into the wall inside the built-in entertainment center next to the flat screen. It appeared to be facing the office area of the house. Keene took out his knife and began to dig the camera out from the wood. After a few seconds he had the lens free, but it was attached to a cable that was running behind the wall. Keene looked at Boz and said, "Stand back." Boz moved back as far as he could go in the space. Keene took his knife and swung hard at the drywall. The whole thing crumpled inward on itself, creating a huge craterlike hole in the wall. Keene used his hands and began tearing the Sheetrock away from the framing.

He traced the camera cable all the way into the kitchen, where he found a hidden DVD recorder in a cupboard next to the pantry. Keene pushed the EJECT button on the machine and a disc popped out.

"Hmm. Wonder what's on this?" Keene said.

Boz took the disc from him and walked back into the living area. "Let's find out."

Boz stuck the disc into the player. He found the power button for the television and turned it on.

The disc started to play. Within seconds, the screen showed a view of the office area off to the left. An older man sat in the expensive chair, as four other individuals sat around the table with him. Governor Nolan, Jake Irving, Milton Hayes, and Alexandra Sokolov all sat at the table facing the man. "That's got to be Pemberton," Keene said.

Boz agreed.

Keene reached over and turned the volume up on the television. They watched the entire twenty-five-minute meeting. In it, they heard Pemberton lay out his idea for taking the presidency, the military, killing Bob Sykes and President Walker, and eventually, attacking the Chinese.

When the disc was done playing, Keene ejected it and put it in his pocket. "I think we have everything we need."

They took another ten minutes going over the place to make sure they hadn't missed anything then made their way topside.

When they were there, Keene told Boz to go get him some more detonation wire from the truck.

"Why? What are you going to do?"

Keene looked back down into the stairwell. "Well, I've already blown up the security system. Figured I'd just finish off the place. Besides, Pemberton isn't going to need it where he's going."

Keene spent the next few minutes wiring the entire place. After he was done, he came back up to the top of the stairs. He motioned for Boz to get in the SUV.

Keene pulled the gear lever and drove out into the field. Once they were far enough away, he stopped, got out, and walked around to the passenger's side. Boz was already out and looking back at the small shed. Keene grabbed Boz by the arm and pulled him down behind the truck. "I might have used more than necessary," he said. "You're going to want to duck." He winked.

Boz nodded and pulled his arms up over his head. "Fire in the hole."

Keene smiled and then tucked his head and pushed the plunger.

The ground beneath them shook, as a giant rumbling sound echoed under the field. The rumble gave way to an enormous blast of dirt, debris, and fire that shot up into the air in a mushroom cloud where the bunker was.

"That about does it," Keene said. "Let's roll."

Boz stood and followed him back to the truck. "Roger that."

CHAPTER 64

Alex didn't know what had gone wrong. How did she even get here? Where was Farid? And why was she back in this hospital?

She pulled against the restraints but to no avail. She was trapped. And her vision was blurry. Why couldn't she see? She heard a voice. It was coming from outside the room. It was that doctor again, talking about disconnecting her life support. She had to get loose.

No, wait. This was all wrong. This wasn't real. It couldn't be.

Somewhere deep inside the recesses of her mind, she rationalized with herself. *This is a dream, Alex. You need to wake up.* She fought against the restraints and closed her eyes, willing herself to wake up. She opened her eyes.

She looked down to see that she had tangled herself up in the sheet. It had wrapped around her wrists, holding her hostage in her dream. She shook it loose and reached for her phone. Eleven thirty. She looked back to the other side. Farid was beginning to wake.

"What time is it?"

"Late," she said.

Farid had a boyish grin on his face. "That's what happens when you stay up all night."

She leaned over and kissed him on the nose. "Yes, but we have work to do. I hadn't planned on sleeping in this long. Come on. Get up. I'm going to go get in the shower. Why don't you find us some breakfast. I'm starved."

Farid pushed the sheet back and got out of bed. "I can do that. What are you in the mood for?"

Alex gave Farid some money from her stash and disappeared into the bathroom. She took a quick shower and then spent thirty minutes changing her appearance. She had learned this skill long ago and was fairly good at it. She had several prosthetic pieces such as noses, ears, chin, and jaw enhancements. She cut her shoulder-length blond hair and dyed it black. Now it was close cropped and parted over to one side. Very business professional.

When she walked out of the bathroom, Farid was sitting at the small table eating a sandwich. His eyes went wide. "Oh my—you don't even look like yourself."

"That's kind of the point, Farid."

"Yeah, but I mean. . .I wouldn't even recognize you if I walked into you on the street."

"Again. . .sort of the point."

"Well, you've made your point, then. Bravo!"

"Good. Let's go. We have to run by a drugstore and an electronics store."

"For what?"

She reached inside a bag sitting on the bed and pulled out a set of IDs. "Marianne gave me these before my last job. They're actual Homeland Security badges. They'll pass any inspection given them. Except for the fact that my picture is on both of them. Since I don't look like that anymore, I need a new picture. And I doubt anyone is going to believe that you're"—she flipped one around and looked at it—"Anita Freilly. So I need some superglue and a digital camera."

"Then what?"

She grabbed the other sandwich Farid had set on the little table. She took a bite, grabbed her bag, slung it over her shoulder, and started for the door. "Then we're going to the Capitol to plant some gear. There's no way we'd be able to get what we need in there, even with good IDs. But if it's already there waiting for us. . ."

Farid finished tying his shoe and grabbed his jacket. "Good. Let's go."

They spent the rest of the afternoon buying supplies and working on the IDs. Alex showed him how to cut around the old photo, so it wouldn't cause anyone to notice. Next she pinned the sheet from the bed against the wall and took his picture. She showed him how to upload that into her laptop. "Even without Internet, these little things can still be useful," she said, opening the software program loaded on her hard drive.

When she was done, she gave the camera to Farid and told him to take her picture, exactly like she had taken his. It took him a few tries to get it right. But eventually, he got the picture Alex needed. Again, she repeated the process with the computer. Twenty minutes later, she held both IDs up to the light.

"There's not an overworked security guard on the planet that wouldn't look at these once and wave us through."

"Let's just hope that's what we find—an overworked security guard."

Alex looked at him. "Trust me. If there's one thing I know, it's American bureaucracy."

It was getting on into the evening when they arrived at the Capitol. Alex had a small briefcase and a backpack that held the equipment she needed. Getting past the guard wasn't going to be a problem. Not at this hour. What she worried about was anyone passing through the House chamber while she was stowing the gear. She just didn't have a logical explanation for why she would be putting a Tech-9, some extra magazines, and a couple of spare smaller handguns under seats throughout the room. That's where Farid came in. She would use her ID to gain access to the room then station Farid outside the door to stand post. If anyone should approach, he was to make a scene until she could come to him and take care of it.

"Here goes," she said. "You sure about this?"

Farid nodded enthusiastically. "Yes. Let's do it."

They walked to the side door by the steps at the rear of the building, where all the senators, congressmen, and congresswomen entered the building. Just as she figured, an older, overweight man holding a greasy sandwich sat behind the guard desk.

"Can I help you?" the man said, completely uninterested.

She pulled her badge and flashed it to him. "Micah Stanton." She pointed to Farid. "This is Ahmad Freeland. We're here on orders from Director Jennings to secure the House chamber and sweep it for explosive residue."

The guard looked suspiciously at Farid. "Ahmad *Freeland?*"

Farid looked at the man with disdain. "My mother's Arabic."

"And your father?"

"Isn't."

Alex was impressed with how Farid had reacted to the guard. But this was taking too long. "Hey!" she said forcefully, getting the man's attention. "You want to talk about my partner's family heritage all night? Or do you want to let us through so we can do our job? Or"—she pulled out her sat-phone and faked like she was pushing numbers—"I can just call Jennings now and you can tell him why I'm out here talking with you instead of getting the chamber ready for tomorrow."

The guard looked at her with a contemptuous stare. "Go on. But next time, tell someone I need to get a heads-up call beforehand."

"You can call someone right now, if you'd like," she said. "I'm sure Jennings would love to hear from your boss at this hour."

The guard reached beneath the desk and pushed a buzzer. The red light on the steel turnstile door turned green and they went through. They headed straight for the House chamber and never turned back around.

CHAPTER 65

Keene and Boz were both back at Bethesda. Keene parked the SUV and they headed for the front entrance. They were supposed to meet Jennings here that morning to see if he had gathered any more information as to the whereabouts of Pemberton and Irving. But Jennings had called before they could meet and sent them chasing after several dead-end leads.

After the flight back to Washington last night, they had piled together again in Eli's room with Jennings. Jennings had been discharged earlier in the day but had come back to hear the debriefing on what Keene and Boz had found. Megan was also allowed to be up and moving around, so she joined them as well.

They had spent a couple of hours talking about the bunker and everything they had found. Jennings had a DVD player brought in, and they all had watched the disc together.

"Now all we have to do is find Pemberton and Irving and bring them in," Keene said. "We'll start looking first thing in the morning."

They stayed around for a few more minutes before a nurse had come in to let them know that Eli needed rest; they were all to leave. Eli had protested, saying he felt fine, but the nurse was having none of it. She shooed them out like a mother hen. Keene had offered to stay with Megan again, but she insisted he go home and get a good night's sleep in his own bed.

"Listen, you're going to be busy tomorrow tracking down Pemberton and Irving. And Quinn is coming in, too. You need to sleep. And not in an uncomfortable chair. Go home."

He reluctantly listened to her. But before he had left, he found those marines that he had stationed outside her door again, plus two more. He ordered them to take posts outside Megan's and Eli's doors.

Now Keene and Boz were back. And Keene was frustrated. They had spent all day looking for Pemberton and Irving. They had sent Ramirez and his team to Irving's house in Richmond. Ramirez reported back that Irving was nowhere to be found. And there wasn't any information left behind to suggest that he had gone anywhere in particular. Keene figured that Irving was on his way here to make a play for his old job. But where he was or when he'd show himself was still up in the air.

Governor Nolan, however, was an easier target. He had been on the campaign trail again all day. Jennings found out that Nolan had been up in Rhode Island and the surrounding areas since yesterday but was headed back to DC on a train. Jennings said Nolan was expected to be back by evening, which it now was.

Pemberton was another case altogether. There was no record of him anywhere. They couldn't track credit cards, not that many places were even able to take them right now—unless they still had one of those old carbon-copy machines so they could manually send in the receipts to the credit card companies. But Keene knew in his gut that Pemberton was here in DC. Finding him, however, was going to be another story.

Keene and Boz had just gotten through the security checkpoint at the front entrance and met up with Jennings and Megan when the sat-phone buzzed inside his coat. He pulled it out and answered.

"Jon, it's Quinn."

Keene snapped his fingers and shushed the others. "Yeah, Quinn. Are you here in DC?"

"I am. I'm at Union Station."

"Okay. Boz and I just got to Bethesda. I'll send someone for you."

"I would rather you and Boz come yourselves."

Keene could feel the stress building in his neck. "Listen, Quinn. Boz and I found some stuff at Pemberton's place in Raleigh yesterday. We have enough concrete evidence to arrest him and the others. We're trying to find them right now. I want them in custody before you speak at the Capitol tomorrow."

"I appreciate that, Jon. However, I don't think that will be necessary."

"Quinn, listen to me. We're going to have our hands full enough trying to make sure Sokolov isn't anywhere near that place. We can't take the chance that Nolan and the rest of them will show up and cause another big scene like he did with the president."

"Actually that's exactly what's going to happen."

Keene crinkled his nose and rubbed his temples. "Seriously? And *He* told you this?"

"Yes. They will be there."

"How can you be sure? Is God going to just zap them there? 'Cause we've been looking for them for two days and can't find a trace of any of them. Except Nolan. We were about to go pick him up."

"No, I'm going to invite them." Then, "Please come and get me and take me to the White House. I need to speak with President Walker."

Keene let out a frustrated sigh. "Okay. We'll be there in a half hour."

Keene pulled the SUV through the security station at the West Wing. The guard looked inside the window and saw Boz next to him, and then looked in the back.

"Who's this?"

Keene looked to Boz who shrugged. He looked back to the guard. "He's with us. He's—"

The back window rolled down. "My name is Quinn Harrington. President Walker is expecting me."

The guard looked back to Keene. "Is that right?" Then to Quinn. "You're the Pr–Prophet?" he stammered.

"You heard the man," Keene said.

The guard looked back at Quinn then back to Keene. "I guess if he's with you, it's okay."

Keene didn't wait for any more conversation. He stepped on the gas and drove up to the entrance to the West Wing. Chief of Staff Hardy met them at the door. "He's up in the residence. He's expecting you."

Hardy led them through the hall and to the private elevator that led to the third floor of the White House, the president's private residency. Keene remembered the last time he was here, President Grant was telling him about the Prophet for the first time. Funny, he thought, how everything had come full circle. Now he was back in the residency *with* the Prophet. And instead of trying to protect the president *from* the Prophet, he was bringing the Prophet *to* the president.

They stepped off the elevator and through the main doors. Walker greeted them as they entered. He stuck his hand out for Quinn. "Mr. Harrington, it is an honor to meet you."

"For me, too, Mr. President. Thank you."

"I understand you wanted to talk with us tonight. . .about your speech tomorrow?"

Quinn nodded. "Yes, thank you. Do you have somewhere we can talk in private?"

Keene shot Boz another look. This one said, *Ah. . .what's going on here?*

Again Boz shrugged like he had no idea, just as Quinn turned to them. "I will need to speak with President Walker alone. Please wait here for us."

Walker led the Prophet down the hall into his private study.

"How do you like that?" Keene said. "We drop everything we're doing to go get him and bring him here, and he doesn't even include us in what's going on."

"I guess whatever they're talking about, we don't need to know."

Keene looked at him. "And you're fine with that?"

Boz let out a short laugh. "Jon, God *literally* talks to that man. I'm fine with whatever he wants."

Boz had a good point. But that didn't make it any better for Keene. He was frustrated with everything right now.

Just then, the doors to the private study opened and Walker stepped out. Quinn followed behind.

"That was quick," Keene mumbled to Boz. Then to Quinn and Walker, "Everything okay in there?"

"Everything's good, Jon," Walker answered. "I'll see all of you tomorrow. At the Capitol." He turned and walked back down the hall.

"What was that about?" Keene asked.

Quinn reached over and pushed the button on the elevator. "I spoke with President Walker about all that was going to happen tomorrow. I needed him to take care of a couple things for me."

"What about us? You going to tell us what's going on?"

Quinn smiled. "Jon, all you need to know is tomorrow is going to be a day you'll never forget."

CHAPTER 66

Washington, DC

Walker left the Prophet and Keene and Boz and went back into his private study. He took a moment to steady himself. His breathing was shallow and his hands were shaking. He couldn't believe what Quinn had told him. Part of the anxiety he was feeling was excitement. The other was pure fear. What was it going to be like? How was it going to happen? Would it be like it was for Quinn? Or would it be something completely different? Either way, it would be spectacular, he knew. He closed his eyes and said, "Okay. I'm ready."

Just then, he felt the urge to get on his knees and bow his head to the floor. Maybe this was it. A second later, he had the urge to start praying. This had to be it. He felt a heavy weight pressing upon him, like a presence pushing him further into the floor. He let it direct him. Before he knew what was happening, he was lying prostrate on the floor.

And then it happened.

He spent the next five minutes afterward crying. But not tears of sorrow. They were tears of absolute joy. Never in his life could he imagine what he had just experienced.

God had spoken to him.

When he had calmed himself, he picked up the phone and dialed the number Quinn had given him. He was still reeling from what had just happened. But he had work to do. His instructions had been crystal clear. The phone rang twice and then was answered. "Hello?"

"Governor Nolan. This is President Walker."

"Hello, Mr. President. How did you get this number?"

"You'd be surprised what I have access to. I'm still the president. At least for now, anyway. I'm afraid after tomorrow, though, that will no longer be the case."

The line was silent for a few seconds. Finally Nolan said, "I'm not sure I—I honestly don't know how to respond to that, Gray. May I call you Gray?"

Walker sighed at Nolan's disrespect. "Sure, Joe. Whatever you'd like."

"So what are you saying, Gray? Are you telling me that you're stepping down? That you're going to nominate me for the VP position? What about this Prophet? Isn't he supposed to make some sort of big speech at the Capitol tomorrow?"

"Yes, he is. I just finished meeting with him."

"Care to give me the inside scoop?"

Walker smiled. This was going to be like fishing with dynamite. "Actually he asked that I personally invite you. And your father-in-law. And your friend Mr. Pemberton."

The line went quiet again. Walker knew that Nolan was racking his brain, trying to piece it all together.

"I'm not sure who you mean. Mr. Pemberton? Are you talking about the billionaire tobacco farmer?"

"Yes, Joe. I'm talking about the man who pulls your strings. Gavin Pemberton. And please don't insult me further by acting like you have no idea what I'm talking about. I know very well your relationship with Pemberton. I know he personally got you elected to the governorship."

Nolan let out a snort. "Fine. I know Gavin. But I don't know where he is, or what he's up to these days. I haven't seen him in a while."

Walker was tired. He still had another phone call to make. He wasn't about to sit here and pander to this egomaniac. "I'm going to cut to the chase and save both of us a lot of time. Tomorrow, the Prophet is going to give a decree about what God has decided for this country. Apparently, you and God share an opinion."

"Yeah? That would be a first."

"As a matter of fact, yes. After the Prophet's speech, I will be announcing my nomination for vice president. And I will be stepping down as the president. This country cannot operate as it has these last five months. There will be changes to come. I would very much like it if you and your friends were in attendance. Trust me. You don't want to miss it."

Walker could almost hear Nolan salivating on the other end of the phone. Everything was going just as Quinn said it would.

"By that," Nolan said, "I guess I can infer that you *will* be nominating me for the position?"

Walker smiled. "Now, Joe. You know that I cannot officially make that declaration on the phone with you here tonight. Just promise me you'll be in attendance for the Prophet's speech."

"Oh, I'll be there. You can bet on it. And I'll make sure that Jake and Gavin are with me. They're going to want to see this in person."

"You do that. I'll see you tomorrow."

Walker pushed the button with his finger and hung up the phone. He let off the button again and waited for a dial tone. When he got one, he started dialing again. A few clicks and buzzes later, the line began ringing. This time it was answered on the first ring.

"Hello?"

"Hey, Tess. It's Gray. May I speak with Calvin?"

"Sure, Gray. Just a second."

Walker heard her pull the phone away and call to her husband. Then she came back on. "He's in the bathroom. He'll be out in a second."

"I'll hang on for him," Walker said, laughing.

After a few seconds, Grant came on the line. "Hey, Gray, what's going on? Everything all right?"

"Everything's good, Calvin. They got you peeing in a cup again?"

"Funny," Grant quipped.

Walker cleared his throat. "Remember last time I was there, you made me a promise? About how you'd never wait again when God asked you to do something?"

"Yes, I do. What's going on?"

"I just got done meeting with the Prophet."

"Wow! I bet that was exciting. What was he like? Did he tell you what his speech is going to be about tomorrow?"

"As a matter of fact he did. That's what I'm calling about."

"Really? How so?"

Walker smiled to himself. "Don't make any plans for tomorrow night, Calvin. You have somewhere to be."

CHAPTER 67

Keene and Boz were back at the hospital again. This time with Quinn in tow. Keene had tried to get more information out of Quinn on the ride there, but Quinn was tight lipped. He just kept deflecting Keene's questions.

"We can discuss all of this when we get to the hospital, Jon. It's important that the others hear what I have to say."

Keene finally let it go.

Now they were in a waiting area that Jennings had turned into a conference room. He'd had a nurse clear out the space. He then had the four marines that Keene had posted at Megan and Eli's doors stand guard at the end of the hall. Everyone was present, except Eli, who was being pushed down the hall right then in a wheelchair.

"Good to see you out of that bed, Eli," Keene said.

"Had to," Eli said. "I was about to go nuts just sitting there."

"Tell me about it," Megan said.

"Hey, at least you can walk," Eli answered. "I'm going to be bumming around in this jalopy for another six weeks."

Finally Keene stood up and introduced Quinn to everyone. They all gave the Prophet their attention.

"I'm very glad to meet all of you," Quinn said. "I know it's been an incredible five months. I want to thank you for not trying to kill me."

That got a few laughs.

"Thank Boz," Keene said. "I *wanted* to kill you. He talked me out of it." He laughed.

Quinn looked to Boz. "Yes. . .thank you, Boz."

"So what's going on, Quinn?" Megan asked. "I mean, I have to be honest with you. We're all kind of scared. I mean, you just call into a news

302

station and tell the world that you're coming to announce God's decree. Should we be worried?"

Quinn had a pained look on his face. "Honestly, Megan, I don't know."

"What do you mean, you don't know?" Keene asked.

"Just what I said," Quinn answered. "I don't know. He hasn't told me yet."

Jennings sat up in his chair. "You mean, you're just going to go in there tomorrow and. . .what? Wait for God to tell you what to say?"

Quinn held his palms up. "I know that may sound crazy to you all. But yes. That's exactly what I'm going to do. That's exactly what He has told me to do."

"Then what was all that with President Walker a little while ago?" Keene said.

"Jon, I'm only doing what God tells me to do right now. He told me to have Walker call Nolan and make sure Nolan was going to be there. Sometimes He gives me a whole thought-out scenario. Sometimes, He just gives me one thing at a time. Right now, He's giving me one thing at a time. I have no idea what God's decree for this nation will be tomorrow night. But I do know this. He wants, more than anything, to see this nation repent and turn back to Him. I imagine whatever His decree is, it will be an ultimatum."

"Why would God tell you to invite Nolan? I don't get it," Megan asked.

"He didn't say. Maybe it's so you can take them into custody. I just don't know. What I do know is that President Walker will be making a big announcement."

"What announcement?" Keene said.

Quinn smiled. "I don't know."

Keene was getting frustrated. "You're killing me, Quinn."

"I promise you, Jon. I'm not trying to frustrate you or anyone else. I don't know what Walker's announcement will be. God has chosen to share that with Walker personally. I only know it involves President Grant."

Keene felt his blood pressure begin to rise. "President Grant is going to be there?"

"Yes. And that is why it is imperative that security is tight. Outside of the people in this room and President Walker, no one knows President Grant is even awake. I expect it'll be quite a scene."

CHAPTER 68

Washington, DC
The Capitol Building

The scene at the Capitol building was just short of chaos. Reporters lined the halls and the inside of the House chamber. Senators, representatives, and their staffers were all crammed inside the room jockeying for the best seats. Quinn had even opened the event to the public. He said God had said whoever wanted to be there could be there. So the entire gallery was packed, and even more people were trying to get in. Those who couldn't stood outside the doorway pushing and shoving, trying to get a look inside.

Keene felt like he had been dropped into the middle of a war zone. He had, along with Jennings, put every available agent he could find from every department he could think of on the grounds. And still, if something bad were to happen, they would be hugely outnumbered.

His earbud crackled and he heard someone say something, though he couldn't discern the words. He pushed a finger in the other ear to try and mute out the noise. He picked his wrist-mic up to his mouth. "This is Keene. I lost that last transmission. Say again." The earbud crackled again. "This is Boz. I've got eyes on Nolan. He just arrived."

Keene had been waiting for this for the last half hour. Quinn was set to speak in the next ten minutes and Nolan hadn't shown up yet. "Okay. Are Irving and Pemberton with him?"

"Roger that. All three present."

"All right. Bring them in."

Keene waved his arm at the five or six agents in sight and gave them the prearranged hand signal. The agents all moved into place and began pushing spectators back out of the aisleways, creating a lane for Boz to come through. Keene moved to the center of the chamber and started moving people out of the front row.

"Okay people, I already told you. This section of seats is reserved.

You'll need to move."

The people grumbled and shouted curses at him. He had no sooner gotten them to move when a beefy, older gentleman waddled over and sat down. "Excuse me, sir. I need you to move. This section of seats is being reserved."

The man looked up at him. "Young man, I am Congressman Cartwright, from the Commonwealth of Virginia. This is my seat and I'm not—"

Keene grabbed the large man by his collar and hauled him up. "I don't care who you are, or what state you're from. If there even *is* another session of Congress after this, you can sit wherever you like. But right now, I said *move!*"

The man looked as if Keene had threatened him with his gun. His face turned pale and his eyes started darting back and forth as Keene let go. The man promptly put his head down and scurried off.

Just then, Keene looked up to see Boz entering the chamber with Governor Nolan. He was followed by former SECNAV Irving and an older man whose intensity made him seem younger. Keene locked eyes with him immediately. He wanted to see the man who was responsible for everything that had transpired these past weeks. He got a cold chill down his spine as Pemberton never looked away. Pemberton even smiled when their eyes met.

Suddenly, the massive crowd inside the chamber took notice of the fact that Nolan had entered the room. A few people began to shout support and clap. In another few seconds, the entire room had erupted in applause. Nolan painted a big smile on his face and began the descent down the aisle, waving and pumping his fist. By the time he had made it to the front, he had all but incited a riot. The place was going crazy.

Keene tried to sweep his gaze around the room to look for anything troubling. But it was pretty much useless. There were too many people. And they were all standing and shouting and clapping. He started feeling uneasy. The whole thing felt like it was about to get completely out of control.

Alex Smith and Farid Naser waited until Nolan arrived to make their entrance. Alex knew that when the governor showed up, the place was going to go nuts. Just this morning she had watched an interview with

Nolan on one of the major news stations. He had informed the reporter that he had spoken with President Walker just last night. Walker had personally invited him to the event. He said Walker had informed him that he would be making a big announcement. Nolan was asked if that announcement was going to include his being nominated for VP. Nolan had winked at the reporter and said, "I guess we'll just have to wait and see, huh?" He followed it up with, "But if I were you, I wouldn't miss it."

Alex walked to the same entrance she and Farid had come through last night. The same guard was there. She didn't even bother with her fake ID this time. She just nodded and said, "Hey."

"Hey," the guard said back. And then he pushed the buzzer and waved them in.

When they had cleared the guard, Farid looked at her. "This is way too easy."

"Told you. Bureaucracy."

She and Farid had already scoped out the room and had their plan in place. She would sit in the gallery up above the chamber. Farid would stay on the ground level. At some point, when Alex gave him the signal, he would yell, "GUN!" The panic that was sure to ensue would give her the opportunity she needed to take her shot.

They stopped short of the stairs that led to the upstairs gallery.

"Okay," she said. "This is it. You sure you're okay?"

He smiled at her. "Yes. I'm fine. Let's go." He turned to walk into the chamber.

Alex grabbed him by the arm and pulled him back. She leaned in and kissed him. "I love you."

Farid's eyes got wide and his mouth was open. Finally he blinked a few times and then pulled her close and kissed her again. "I love you, too."

She pushed away from him and giggled. "I'll see you in a little bit. Remember what I said. When you yell, you take off with the crowd. I'll meet you at Union Station."

"I'll be there."

Inside the chamber, the crowd exploded as Nolan entered the room. She squeezed Farid's hand and turned to go up the stairs.

President Walker and Quinn Harrington were being held in the Senate chamber on the other side of the building. Megan and Eli were with them,

306

along with Jennings and a few guys that Keene had handpicked to watch over them, Ramirez and his team. They had been sitting there for almost thirty minutes. Keene had promised to come and get them just before it was time. And now he was walking down the hall and through the rotunda to do just that.

He had gotten halfway when he pulled up short. There were still a hundred people or so lining the hallway. And he'd had to push past almost all of them just to get back to the rotunda. But something wasn't right. Something had caught his eye. And this time he wasn't going to let it go. He hurried down the other side of the hall to the Senate chamber. He needed Ramirez and the boys. Now.

He all but kicked in the door to the chamber as he got there, which immediately caused Ramirez and the men to jump in front of the Prophet and the president and then drop into firing position.

"Hey, hey, hey!" Keene said, holding up his hands. "It's just me!"

"Keene, I almost shot you," Foust said.

"Sorry. Listen. I need you guys to come with me. Now."

"What's wrong?" Walker asked.

"It's Sokolov. I think she's here."

Ramirez and his team immediately started checking their weapons and gearing up to move. But Quinn stepped in front of them and held up his hands. "Everyone stop."

"Quinn, what are you doing?" Keene said. "She's here! I need them to come with me. Now."

Quinn turned around to face him. "It's okay. You don't need to worry about Alexandra Sokolov right now."

Keene couldn't believe what he was hearing. Had Quinn lost his mind? If Sokolov was here. . . He pulled Quinn off to the side.

"Hey," he said in an angry whisper, "you need to tell me right now what's going on. I'm not about to send Walker out there knowing she's in the building."

Quinn looked at him with a completely blank expression. "Jon, I can guarantee you that President Walker is in no danger. You don't need to worry about Sokolov. Everything will work out the way He has intended it."

"So you're saying you know what's going on now?"

Quinn closed his eyes and nodded. "Yes."

Suddenly a lump formed in Keene's throat. "That doesn't sound good."

"Jon, do you trust that God has brought you here to this place, right now, for a reason?"

Six months ago, if someone had asked him that, he would have laughed. But now, after everything he'd been through—even though he was still trying to hold on to control—he had to say that he did. "Yes. I do trust Him."

"Then trust *me*."

Keene suddenly felt a tinge of sadness. He didn't know if it was because of what Quinn was about to tell the world, or because something was about to happen that he knew he couldn't control. No matter how hard he tried.

He met Quinn's stare. "Okay. I trust you."

CHAPTER 69

Keene led the president and Quinn through the rotunda and to the door of the House chamber. The crowd had quieted from the racket they had been making. Now it was little more than just the normal ambient noise of a crowd of several hundred. Keene looked around for Boz but didn't see him. He started to worry. Where had Boz gone? He looked around the whole room and still couldn't find him. He couldn't wait any longer. The president was ready to go.

He gave the hand signal again to the agents, and once again, they pushed the crowd back. The noise began to settle as the people inside the chamber took notice. When the aisle was clear, Keene stepped into the chamber with the president, the Prophet, and the rest of their entourage. The room fell to a hiss of whispers, as people pointed to Quinn, seeing the man who called himself the Prophet for the first time.

Megan and Keene sat down in some seats that Keene had been saving for them in the front row. Ramirez wheeled Eli next to them at the end of the row. The president and the Prophet walked to the podium. The room fell completely silent.

Quinn stepped up to the microphone and cleared his throat.

"Mr. President, ladies and gentlemen of Congress, Governor Nolan, ladies and gentlemen. . . My name is Quinn Harrington. I am the man God has appointed as a messenger to bring His Word to you.

"A little over seven months ago, God instructed me to contact President Grant and to give him a message. That message was that God had grown tired of our country's idolatry. We have, for far too long, ignored God's law, His love, and His mercy. And for that reason, God promised to bring judgment upon this land, unless we were to repent and turn back to Him.

"As you now know, that never came to pass. And as a result, God

309

allowed wicked men and women to bring to pass the invasion of the Chinese upon our land. What we now experience is a result of that."

The room exploded. People began to stand and shout. The noise had risen even louder than when Nolan had entered the chamber. Quinn held his hands up and something like a tidal wave of warm air passed through the room. Instantly the room quieted. Keene looked to Megan, who had the same look of awe on her face that he knew he must have. "Did you just feel that?"

Megan nodded her head yes. Quinn continued.

"Since that time, President Walker has tried to speak these truths to you. And while many of you have opened your eyes and seen the truth, others of you have rebelled against it. Some have even gone as far as to conspire against this country, like the men and women who brought upon us God's first judgment." He looked down at the front row. "Governor Nolan. Would you and your friends please stand?"

Keene looked down the aisle at Nolan, Pemberton, and Irving. They were looking to each other trying to figure out what to do. Finally, Nolan straightened his jacket and tie and stood. Pemberton and Irving followed. Quinn continued.

"Sir, you have demanded that President Walker uphold his sworn oath to the Constitution and assert his privilege of nominating a vice president. Is that right?"

Nolan looked around the room. "Yes, that is correct."

Quinn nodded. "And at this time, he would like to do so." He turned to Walker. "Mr. President?"

Walker moved up to the lectern. "Governor Nolan. You have demanded that I nominate a vice president. And you have also called for my resignation as president. I would like to announce to you that I am happy to grant your wish."

Again the room erupted. This time it was to cheers and chants of Nolan's name. President Walker allowed the interruption for a few seconds and then quieted the room.

"Ladies and gentlemen. I am happy to announce to you this evening that I will be stepping down from my duties as president and resuming my responsibilities as vice president."

A collective gasp filled the room. Nolan's face twisted into anger. "What! What are you talking about? You can't do that!"

"I most certainly can, sir," Walker said to Nolan. "Ladies and gentlemen, it is my great honor to turn the office of president of the United States of America back over to its rightful owner, President Calvin Grant."

Keene could hardly believe what he was hearing. Did Walker just say President Grant?

Just then, the doors to the chamber opened and Boz came walking in. He had a huge grin on his face. And behind him was none other than President Grant.

Walker leaned in to the microphone. "Ladies and gentlemen, I present to you the President of the United States!"

Once again, the room burst into a frenzy. Everyone stood and began applauding. Shouts of "U–S–A!" began to fill the room. Keene was even on his feet cheering Grant on. He looked down the aisle to see Nolan's reaction. The man looked like he was going to throw up right there. Pemberton looked like someone had shot his dog, and Irving looked as though he was about to be lynched.

President Grant took the podium and stepped up to the lectern. "Please, everyone...thank you...thank you...please..." Finally the room fell silent. "Mr. Walker, I accept your resignation of the office of president of the United States of America and hereby mandate, by executive order, that you resume your responsibilities as vice president."

Again the room applauded. Grant raised his hands to quiet the room.

"Ladies and gentlemen, seven months ago, I was called by God to give you a message. I failed in my duties to do that. But I have been given a second chance. So I will take this opportunity now to do so. However, there is something that I need to do first. So that you may know that Mr. Harrington is indeed a prophet of God and that he has been sent to call our nation to turn back to the One who so graciously gave her to us in the first place, Mr. Harrington will address Governor Nolan and his conspirators."

Grant stepped back, and Quinn stepped back up to the microphone. "Governor, sirs...will you please stand again?"

Nolan folded his arms and crossed his legs. "I will not! I do not recognize your authority. I do not believe in your God!"

Quinn thrust his hand at Nolan and pointed directly at him. "In the name of Christ Jesus, who has been given authority over all of heaven and earth, I command you to stand and give an account for your actions!"

Immediately, Nolan, Pemberton, and Irving all shot up out of their chairs, as if someone had pulled them out. The entire room gasped. Quinn continued.

"Governor Nolan, are you familiar with the account of Ananias and Sapphira given in the book of Acts?"

Nolan just stared blankly.

"The story itself is not relevant here. The lesson we are to learn from it, however, is. And that is that God judges sin. And not only will He judge sin at the end of all things, He does also in real time. Ananias and Sapphira were judged for their sin. And the judgment that God passed on them was to strike them dead right where they stood."

Keene's heart began to race. Was this really about to happen? Was God going to actually do this right here, in front of everyone?

Quinn continued, "You, sirs, have blasphemed the name of God, you have been an instrument of Satan. You and your counterparts have been judged. I pray that if there is any to be had for you, that God would have mercy on your souls."

And with that, Nolan, Pemberton, and Irving all dropped to the ground.

CHAPTER 70

Alex Smith was enjoying this little dog and pony show. First the Prophet, standing and talking about sin and judgment. Then Walker's big announcement. She had to admit, even she didn't see that coming. But that's not what had captured her attention.

No, her attention was captured by the two that sat in the front row, holding hands, like a happily in love couple. She actually knew what that felt like, for the first time in her life. It was going to make what she was about to do all the more sweet.

Regardless of what Pemberton had paid her for, she had her own agenda. Yes, she would take out Walker. And seeing him come back from the dead, she wanted to kill Grant as well. That one was just going to be for pride. She couldn't say she actually assassinated the president if he were standing here, now, resuming his office. Now could she?

But her main focus was on Jon Keene and Megan Taylor. Those two had been the bane of her existence for too long. This ended tonight. Only one of them was going to walk out of here alive. She swore to that. And she fully intended it be her.

She reached up under the seat to feel the Tech-9 taped to the bottom of the seat. She reached inside her coat pocket and felt the Glock resting against her side. Finally, she bent over and ran her hand over her ankle, where the PK380 rested. Everything was set to go. Now all she had to do was give Farid the signal.

She was about to move when the Prophet took the podium again. He called for Nolan to stand, but Nolan refused. She was almost jarred out of her seat when the Prophet yelled back at Nolan. She eased up for a moment. Her curiosity had gotten the better of her. She wanted to see where this went.

Suddenly, the Prophet said something about some old guy from the Bible and Nolan, Pemberton, and Irving all dropped to the ground. She could tell right away. They were dead. Immediately, the entire place burst into a panic. This was the moment she had waited for. She caught Farid's attention and gave him the signal.

Keene couldn't believe what he'd just seen. He jumped up from his seat and checked Nolan's pulse. Nothing. He looked to Quinn who just nodded to him, as if to say, *What's done is done.*

Immediately, though, the room was stirred. People were gasping and pointing. Some cries were heard, as well as some shrieks and shouting. Just when Keene thought it couldn't get any more chaotic, he heard the very thing he'd been dreading—no, anticipating—since he got here tonight.

"GUN! GUN!"

Instantly, people began screaming and pushing one another to get out of the chamber. Ramirez and his team immediately ran to the podium and grabbed Grant and Quinn. Suddenly, Keene saw something out of the corner of his eye. Someone had thrown a rope over the side of the gallery. And sliding down it was a woman with short black hair. She had a long, pointed nose and a round face. And she was holding a Tech-9 submachine gun. It didn't look anything like her, but Keene knew it was Sokolov.

Suddenly the chamber was filled with the sound of automatic gunfire. Everyone screamed louder and began trampling over each other. Keene drew his weapon to fire back at Sokolov. But someone knocked into him the moment he was about to shoot. His gun went flying in the air as he was knocked down. He scrambled over to get it. And noticed that Megan had pulled Eli out of the wheelchair and was taking cover under the first row of seats.

"Stay down!" he yelled to her.

He retrieved his gun and stood up. By this time, Sokolov was on the ground walking toward him. And firing at will. He dove for cover again and got off three rounds. He had no idea if he'd hit his mark or not. He looked to the podium where Ramirez was trying to get Walker, Grant, and Quinn to safety. He was about to stand up again when he saw Ramirez go down. That left Walker exposed. He stood up to fire just as Sokolov unleashed another round of automatic fire right at the podium. Walker's chest exploded in crimson and he fell immediately. Keene jumped up from behind the seats and started firing. He saw Sokolov spin around and slam into a row of chairs. He'd scored a hit. But where and how bad he didn't know.

He started moving toward the spot she'd gone down when he saw her pop up a few rows to the side. She was headed right for Megan. Keene panicked. He jumped over the seats and began running at her just as she brought her Glock up to fire at Megan's head. He pulled his weapon up and let go. Sokolov's arm dropped as her head snapped back, and she fell to the ground.

The room fell silent. By this time only a few people were left in the chamber. Those who were still there were at the back trying to push their way out the door. Keene walked over to Sokolov's body and used his foot to turn her over onto her back, keeping his weapon pointed at her the whole time.

As he turned her over, her arm flopped lifelessly to the side, letting go of the Tech-9. He kicked the Glock out of the other hand. She had two bullet holes in her forehead. She had managed to come back from the dead once. But this time, there was no chance.

Once and for all, Alexandra Sokolov was dead.

Keene lowered his weapon and went to Megan. He picked her up off the ground and held her. "Are you okay?"

"I'm fine," she said. She had a few tears rolling down her cheek.

Keene reached up and wiped them away. "She's gone, Megan. For good this time."

Keene felt a tapping on his shoulder. He turned to see a Middle Eastern man standing before him with tears in his eyes.

"Sir," Keene said. "Are you okay? Can I get you some help?"

The man just shook his head and began sobbing. "I loved her. And you took her away from me!"

The man took his hands from his pocket and produced a Ruger 9mm. He put it into Keene's chest and fired three times.

Keene felt the searing hot pain as the three rounds ripped through his chest. He heard Megan scream, "NOOOO!" and then saw Boz, Ramirez, and the rest of Ramirez's team rush at him and empty their magazines into the man who had just shot him.

The man fell to the ground beside Sokolov. As he took his last breath, he reached out and grabbed Sokolov's hand.

Keene slumped to the ground with Megan holding him. She was crying uncontrollably, saying, "No, no, no, no!"

He felt his breathing start to become shallow. And then he tasted blood. His lungs were filling with it. He coughed, and blood spilled from his mouth out onto his chin. He started to feel cold. He could hear the alarm in the background: *Annnng, Annnng, Annnnng.*

He looked up to see Megan crying and shaking her head. "Please, Jon. Please don't leave me. Please don't leave me."

Annnnng. . . Annnnng. . . Annnnng. . .

Suddenly, everything went dim. He could still hear the ringing of the alarm, but everything else around him had been drowned out. And he couldn't see anything, either. Just blur, everywhere he turned. Megan was gone, Boz was gone, no one was around. What was going on? What was happening?

Annnnng. . . Annnnng. . . Annnnng. . .

Just then, he looked to his left to see a pair of feet walking toward him. Whoever it was stood next to him and bent down. Quinn.

He coughed some more blood up. He could feel his life leaving him. Where was Megan? He forgot to tell her he loved her. Where was Boz?

Annnnng. . . Annnnng. . . Annnnng. . .

Quinn sat down beside him and reached over and grabbed his head and propped it back up so that he was looking at him straight on. "Quinn. . . What's happening? Where is everyone?"

"Jon, it was always supposed to be this way."

Annnnng. . . Annnnng. . . Annnnng. . .

"I don't understand."

Quinn held his head in his hands. "You will, Jon. You will."

He closed his eyes. He wanted to go now. "Quinn. . .I. . .have to. . .go."

"I know. But I need to tell you something first."

Annnnng. . . Annnnng. . . Annnnng. . .

"What's that? I'm. . .so. . .cold. . . ."

Quinn smacked him in the face. He opened his eyes again.

"Jon, listen to me. You must remember everything you've been shown. Do you hear me? Everything, Jon! Everything! You must remember."

Annnnng. . . Annnnng. . . Annnnng. . .

"Remember. . .yeah, I got it. . . . Must remember."

Jon Keene closed his eyes and exhaled.

EPILOGUE

Annnnng. . . Annnnng. . . Annnnng. . .
  Annnnng. . . Annnnng. . . Annnnng. . .
  Annnnng. . . Annnnng. . . Annnnng. . .

Keene sucked in a breath and sat bolt upright in bed. He was covered from head to toe in sweat. Immediately he panicked. He felt around at his chest for the bullet wounds.

Nothing.

He felt for his collarbone, where Sokolov had shot him before, shattering the bone.

Nothing.

Annnnng. . . Annnnng. . . Annnnng. . .
  Annnnng. . . Annnnng. . . Annnnng. . .

He was panting as if he'd just run a marathon. He smacked himself in the face a couple of times, hard, just to make sure he was awake.

Annnnng. . . Annnnng. . . Annnnng. . .

Finally, he got his breathing under control and reached over to turn the alarm off.

Annnnng. . . Annn—

He picked up his cell phone that was lying on the desk next to the bed. What in the world was going on? He felt like he was in the middle of a nightmare. He was completely disoriented.

The phone's message light was blinking so he turned it on. Maybe Megan or Boz had left him a message telling him what the heck was going on right now. He slid his thumb across the screen and watched it unlock. He pushed the e-mail button where the message icon was blinking.

When it opened, a video was there. It had no sender's address and no subject. He pushed Play.

The video took about a minute to buffer, but then the screen came to life. Quinn Harrington sat in the middle of a room in front of a camera.

"Jon, right now, you must be completely confused. Perhaps disoriented. . .maybe even nauseous. You should know—that's okay. I've experienced the same thing.

"You're probably wondering what's going on. I know that this is going to be hard for you to understand, but you must believe me. What I am about to tell you is true. Every word. So please. . .trust me.

"Jon, today's date is June 20, 2025."

What? How could that be? No, it's December. . . .

"What you have just been through is something few men in our history have had the privilege of experiencing. Daniel. . .Isaiah. . .the apostle John. . .are just a few of the men whose company you now share. Jon, God has given you a revelation. A vision. Everything you think you've experienced over the last four months, though it feels as real as anything you've ever known. . .has all been but a shadow of a future that could come to pass. But make no mistake: what you saw—everything you experienced, even seeing things from your counterparts' perspectives—is still something that is very much a reality.

"God has chosen you as His instrument to bring this nation to repentance. You have been given every bit of information you need to succeed in doing this. Jon, you have been shown the future. *You* are the man chosen to be God's Prophet. Not me. I'm just his messenger to you. *You are the Prophet.*

"Today, President Grant will call you into his office where he will confront you about the warnings that have been sent to him. It is your job to convince him that those warnings are of God. You must do this, Jon. Because as you already know, you have an enemy waiting at your doorstep. And unless Grant calls the nation to repentance within fourteen days, I don't need to remind you what will take place. God bless you, Jon. You are truly a blessed man."

Keene ran to the bathroom and bent over the toilet. He emptied his stomach and fought to breathe. Could this be possible? Could it have all been a dream? It couldn't have been. No, it was real. If it were a dream—a vision—how then could he be chosen by God for this? Before all of this happened he didn't even have a relationship with God. What about the prison camp? The war? The. . .the. . . Everything!

He finished being sick and ran cold water over his face. He ran back to the bedroom and looked at the phone again. The message was gone. *What? How could that be?* He hadn't erased it. It was just there!

He used his thumb to move the screen over to the next screen where the calendar was. He felt his breathing become shallow again as the date stared back up at him: JUNE 20, 2025.

He fell to his knees and began to sob. He had no idea what to feel. His whole life for the last five months—or at least what he had thought to be the last five months—had been a dream. A vision. . .whatever. He didn't know what to call it.

He put his head in his hands and began to pray. *God, please. . .please help me make sense of this. I'm so lost right now. I don't know what's going on. I need You, Lord. I need You! Please, God. Speak to me. If this is real, if I'm the one who is to do all of this, then tell me You're there. Please God. Let me know You're there.*

He sat there for a minute listening for something. Anything. Finally, just before he was about to sit up, he felt something push him back to the ground. And then he heard a voice.

"I'm here, Jon."

"Hello?"

"Jon, where are you?" Kevin Jennings asked.

"I'm checking something out. Why?"

"I stopped by your place a little while ago. You were already gone."

"Yeah, I had something I needed to do."

"Well, finish it up. President Grant just called. Your presence is requested at 1600 Pennsylvania Avenue. As in, right now."

"Are Boz and Megan there yet?"

"What? Who?"

"Oh, yeah. Never mind." Then, "Okay. I'm on my way."

Keene hung up the phone and rolled the window down on his SUV. He drove out of the parking lot slowly. As he left, he watched Marianne Levy enter the Homeland Security building.

I'll be seeing you soon, Marianne.

ABOUT THE AUTHORS

ROBBIE CHEUVRONT is the worship pastor of Northpoint Church in Corona, California, and cofounder of C&R Ministries with Erik Reed. He is also a songwriter and formerly toured with BNA recording artists Lonestar. Robbie is married to Tiffany and has two children, Cason and Hadyn, and is currently pursuing a theology degree.

ERIK REED is the lead pastor and an elder of The Journey Church in Lebanon, Tennessee. He graduated from Western Kentucky University with a BA in religious studies. He also graduated with his MDiv from Southern Seminary. Erik is married to Katrina, with two children, Kaleb and Kaleigh.

SHAWN ALLEN is the lead pastor and an elder of The Journey Church in Hartsville, Tennessee. He graduated with a BS in business management from Bethel University in McKenzie, Tennessee. Before vocational ministry, Shawn was previously in management as a police officer in Nashville. Shawn is married to his lovely wife of eight years, Miranda Allen.